Books by Conor Corderoy

Heat

A Love to Kill For
The Deepest Cut

The Deepest Cut

ISBN # 978-1-78686-147-4

©Copyright Conor Corderoy 2017

Cover Art by Posh Gosh ©Copyright 2017

Interior text design by Claire Siemaszkiewicz

Totally Bound Publishing

Published in 2017 by Totally Bound Publishing, Think Tank, Ruston Way, Lincoln, LN6 7FL, United Kingdom.

Totally Bound Publishing is a subsidiary of Totally Entwined Group Limited.

Heat

THE DEEPEST CUT

CONOR CORDEROY

Dedication

This book is dedicated to Lolly Adamopoulos,
who is adorable, fills the world with sunlight,
and always made me happy.

Chapter One

The call came at four a.m.

I groped for my phone. "Murdoch."

The geothermal disturbance on the other end was Russian Pete. "Murdoch...is Peter."

"Pete. It's four a.m. What do you want?"

"I need speak with you."

"Now?"

"*Da.* Now..."

* * * *

It was raining. It was always raining these days — damp and warm. I sat in the darkened car, listening to the liquid drumming and thinking of Maria, lying warm and soft in our bed. It would be first light in just over an hour. She wouldn't be up for another two. I pushed open the door and stepped into the dark road. Wet light rippled on the tarmac. Holland Park was on my left. Across the road on my right a terrace of Georgian houses slept with blind eyes behind the amber streetlights.

I loped through the tepid rain toward the black bulk of the park gates. The momentary glow of a cigarette told me one of Pete's men was waiting there for me. When I drew level, he dropped the butt in a puddle where it hissed and died. I said, "Where's Pete? What's this about?"

He jerked his head toward the interior of the park, among the black shadows of the trees. "Better Pete tell you."

I followed him through the big iron gate, wondering how he came to have a key. Then he led the way into the shadows under the great horse chestnuts. Our feet made damp crunching noises on the gravel.

He said, in his Russian baritone, "Be gentle with Peter. He is weeping lot this morning."

"Weeping?"

He just nodded silently and we went deeper into the woodland, where the rain was just a drizzle on the leaves above our heads.

They were at the statue of Lord Holland, over the wooden bridge by the pond—a small huddle of them—Russian Pete and two of his henchmen, three big black silhouettes surrounded by the glimmer of the rain and the puddles. And there was something on the ground. It looked like a bundle of saturated rags. Pete turned to face me as I approached. Even in the darkness, I could see his eyes were swollen and his face was wet. It wasn't from the rain.

I pulled out my Camels and offered him one. He shook his head. I lit up and blew smoke into the spitting drizzle. The bundle of rags was a young woman, lying on her back in the mud, staring up into the trees. Her coat was rumpled and twisted. Her arms were laid symmetrically by her sides and her legs were straight. A red rose rested in her mouth. The black handle of a large kitchen knife protruded from her left breast and there was a gaping, bloody hole where her belly should have been. Whoever had killed her had taken the trouble to lay her out there with care. I stood smoking for a while.

Eventually, I flicked ash and said, "Who is she? She family?"

Nobody said anything for a long moment. The guys just stood looking at Pete with the rain on their faces.

Finally, Pete said what I had already guessed but didn't want to believe, "She is my daughter, Eva."

I nodded. I knew what this meant, why I was there, and I didn't like it. "Who did it? Do you know?"

He shook his head. I looked again at the body, the way it was laid out—the rose, the knife in her heart, the savage wound in the abdomen. "Someone trying to scare you, move in on your patch…?"

He shook his head again. "Nobody."

I dropped my butt into a puddle. It hissed and winked out. I crouched down by her side, pulled out my pen torch and played the beam over her face and neck. Under the raindrops, her skin was gray-blue. There were blotches of purple bruising on her throat, like she'd been choked, but her blouse was saturated with blood, so she hadn't been strangled to death, just enough to make her unconscious and pliant.

I moved the beam down to her belly. I've seen some pretty nasty things in my time. I've even done a few of them myself when the occasion called for it. But this was about as horrific as it got. Her entire abdomen had been torn out. There had been no surgical precision here, just raw, brutal animal ferocity. I heard Pete choke and sob behind me and I switched off the torch.

I stood and said, "Who found her?"

Pete had turned away, his face hidden in his hands.

The guy who'd met me at the gate piped up, "Park policeman on his rounds. Half pass three. He recognize her because she come to park in mornings for coffee and see the paintings exhibition. She like this park."

I said, "A cop? Why didn't he — ?"

He knew what I was going to ask and interrupted me, "Cops know Russian Pete, *da*? He pay their mortgages…" There was some stifled laughing. Pete turned to face me, wiping his face with the back of his sleeve. His voice was raw. "They know that anything of interest to me, they report to me. It is courtesy. Chief constable is good friend of mine. You know…"

I nodded. I knew. That explained the keys. Anyone who was anyone in this town was in Russian Pete's pocket.

I said, "So, where are the cops now?"

"On their way. We have twenty minutes."

I stared at him. "For what? What do you want from me?"

He held my eye a moment then jerked his head toward what was left of his daughter. "If police investigate, maybe it is years before killer is found. And when they find him, what?" He shrugged his huge shoulders and looked around at the dark woodlands. "Maybe he go to prison for twenty years, to secure wing with psychologists to help him." He shook his head and spat on the ground. "No…you find him. You are smart, Murdoch. You not limited like police. You have no rules. I give you any help, any money—no matter. I get you what you want. I want man who did this. You find him."

"And when I find him?"

"Better you don't know."

I nodded. "Okay, Pete. I'll do what I can. When the cops are done, I want the forensics report. And I don't want the cops to know I'm involved."

His face began to crumple again and he pointed helplessly at Eva, at the gaping hole in her belly. "What is this, Murdoch? Why? Why he did this to my baby…?" His voice was weird, twisted with pain.

They led him away through the woodlands into the darkness beneath the trees, and I made my way back through the paling, gray light and the drizzle, toward my car, thinking that most times, what really hurts is not understanding *why*. Pain never hurts so much as when it's meaningless.

I got deep like that sometimes.

* * * *

Maria was still in bed when I got back. I opened the door and looked in the room. The curtains were closed but the window was open and a cool, damp breeze made the drapes waft softly and brought in the splash and splatter of the rain. I stepped over and sat on the edge of the bed. Her hair was rumpled. Her face was pale with sleep and I could just make out the few freckles on her cheeks and nose. I stroked away a strand of hair from her forehead. Her eyelids fluttered and she opened her eyes. They were sleepy, but she smiled. I glanced at the clock. It was seven a.m. She stretched with her arms above her head and I had a sudden impulse to hold her and feel her body, small and supple, against mine.

She said, "Where were you?"

"Pete called. Four a.m. He had a problem."

"Pete? Russian Pete?"

I nodded.

She frowned. "Didn't you say you weren't going to do jobs for him anymore?"

I bent and touched her lips with mine. She held my face with her small hands and the gentle peck grew into a long, lingering kiss. I felt the heat stirring inside me. She pulled away just enough to rub the end of my nose in an Eskimo kiss.

Her eyes were huge and dark. "Don't change the subject, big guy. Didn't you?"

I gave her my best lopsided smile and said, "It's not that easy, Maria."

She held my gaze for a long moment, smiling. Her eyes were warm, lids half closed. She whispered, "You want to make love?"

My belly was on fire and I could feel my heart pounding. I said, "You know I do."

She patted my cheek with her hand. "Well, this is how easy it is, Liam. *No.* See? Easy." She pushed me back and swung her legs out of the bed. "I'm going to have a shower. You want to put the coffee on?"

I went to make coffee. And, in just a few minutes, she came into the kitchen barefoot with wet hair, wearing a purple Japanese kimono with a golden dragon on it. She sat at the pine table and I poured her coffee. Black, no sugar, the way I took it.

"Pete is a very bad man, but he's been a good friend to me."

She was buttering toast but glanced up then back down and kept on buttering. I sighed. I meant what I was saying, but I couldn't find a way for it not to sound lame.

"I can't walk away from my whole life overnight, Maria. It's going to take time."

She bit into her toast and chewed, watching me. "How much time?"

I shook my head. "I can't tell you that."

"You made me a promise, Liam. You going back on your promise?"

"No."

"So?"

I looked down into my coffee. It was real black. "His daughter was murdered last night. She was twenty-three. Eva. A nice kid."

She put down her toast. Careful, like it might have consequences if she set it down the wrong way. "I'm sorry."

I nodded. "Yeah. He'd taken care not to involve her in his life. She was a good student, just finishing a psychology degree at UCL. Like I said, a nice kid. Closest thing I ever had to a niece."

She was silent a while, staring at her plate. "Was it gang related?"

"No..." I rubbed my face with my hands. "I can't make much sense of it. It looked..." I shrugged, staring at the table but seeing Eva lying in the mud with her dead eyes staring at the trees above her, raindrops sitting on her pupils. "It looked ritualistic. He swears nobody is trying to move in on him. Nobody would be that crazy. He's too powerful and too dangerous. Even the cops stay clear. It doesn't make any sense. Unless..."

She was watching me carefully. She said, "Unless?"

"Unless whoever killed her didn't know she was Russian Pete's daughter."

She sat back in her chair. "But, then what would the motive be?"

I drained my coffee and pulled a Camel from the pack.

I tapped it three times on my Zippo and finally said, "No motive."

"You're talking about—"

"A serial killer."

"That would account for the ritualistic elements."

"Yeah..."

"Liam?"

I searched her eyes. I knew what she was going to say. "What does Pete want from you? Why did he call you this morning at four a.m.?"

"He wants me to find who did it."

Her face went rigid. She picked up her cup, stopped with it halfway to her mouth, then put it down again. "That's what the cops are there for. You *promised* me. You promised me that you were *not* going to get involved in this kind of thing anymore. It was a condition of our living together, Liam."

"I know."

"So? What are you saying to me?"

"Maria, will you please stop talking and listen to me for a moment?"

She was staring at me. Her eyes appeared black.

"I'm doing it, okay? I'm changing. Between you, you and Russell are dragging me onto the straight and narrow." I gave her my lopsided smile, but she just kept staring at me, waiting. I sighed. "I'm making it happen, baby. But you have to understand that you can't just walk away from a guy like Pete."

"So what are you saying? If I live with you, if I make a life together with you, I'm making a life with Russian Pete, too? Like some kind of mad Russian mother-in-law?"

"No..."

"That's the word, Liam. Only instead of saying it to me, you should be saying it to Pete."

"You don't want me to do that."

"Excuse me?"

"Stop provoking me, Maria, and simmer down. I'm going

to do this my way and I'm going to do it right. That way it stays done. If I do what you're asking me to do, all I get—all *we* get—is a lot of trouble and grief. I do it my way and it stays done and everybody's happy. And besides… *I* want the bastard who killed Eva."

She was silent for a moment. Then she said, "So what are you going to do?"

"I won't take payment for finding him. I'll tell him my payment is that he doesn't use me anymore."

She nodded. "But it has to be for real, Liam. I don't want to spend the rest of my life with gangsters breathing down my neck."

We didn't say anything for a long while, just watched each other.

Then, I said, "Everything I do is for real. You know that. Now take that damned kimono off."

* * * *

An hour later, I lay listening to the rain outside. It had slowed to a damp patter. Her head was on my shoulder and her breath gentle on my chest. Her breasts were cool on my skin, and where she had her leg over my thigh, I could feel the soft brush of her hair. I let my hand explore the curve of her back and her hip, but my mind was drifting. All I could see was Eva, staring with dead eyes into the rain.

My thoughts followed the beam of my pen torch. The red rose against the pale gray of her skin. The gray-purple of her parted lips and the stem of the rose with its cruel thorns inside her mouth. It was a strange echo of the kitchen knife plunged into her heart, the beautiful, rich red flower in her mouth. Maybe it symbolized the loving words the killer had never heard from a mouth that was full of thorns—sharp, cutting, cruel words.

And the knife. The big, cold-steel blade of a kitchen knife, plunged deeply into her heart. Again, that curious juxtaposition of symbols—the heart, the universal symbol of love. The kitchen, the hub of any loving family, the smell of baking, Mom's apple pie, Mom smiling in her apron, giving food, giving love. All brutally killed with a single plunge of that large blade.

But the knife and the rose were almost surgical in their precision, as though the rage and hatred behind them were somehow controlled by grief, by a secret, enduring hope for love, as though somehow he didn't really want to do what he was doing — as though he didn't want to kill her. He only wanted to silence her and change her heart.

Maria stirred in her sleep, squeezed me and pressed her belly close against my side. Her belly. I reached for my Camels, fished one out single-handed and lit up, blowing smoke at the ceiling. The belly was all wrong. It was almost like it had been done by somebody else. There was no symbolism here, no surgical precision, no grief or restraint. Her entire abdomen had simply been ripped out, torn away from her body. And there was no trace of her organs — no gore, no blood, no spatter.

So maybe she had been killed somewhere else and taken to the park. The forensics team would establish that. But even if she'd been killed elsewhere, that didn't explain the radical difference between the placing of the rose and the knife and the savage, bestial attack on her abdomen. I lay and smoked and wondered why it mattered.

I carefully removed Maria's head from my shoulder, slipped my arm out and swung my legs off the bed. Then I made my way to the kitchen and brewed some coffee. As I sat naked, smoking and drinking, I thought that it mattered because it showed two completely different motivations. One was tortured but craving redemption. The other was uninhibited, bestial and destructive.

Like two different people.

Chapter Two

In the late afternoon, I climbed into my TVR Daemon and headed down the Cromwell Road to the A316 then to the M3 highway out to Walton on Thames. That was where Russian Pete had his country house and where he had retreated to grieve Eva's death.

I pulled into his gravel drive at a quarter after six and killed the V12. The rain had paused, but the sky was watercolor wet, with heavy patches of gunmetal gray. It was muggy and damp and my shirt was sticking to my back as I crossed to the big oak door.

The house was thirties mock Tudor. Back then, it was probably considered in bad taste. Anyone who was anyone back in the thirties had a real Tudor manor. But now that it was almost a hundred years old, it had acquired a kind of legitimacy. Whether it was in bad taste or not, it was huge and expensive with its own pool and tennis court. I pressed a button in a brass disk and heard a bell chime far away. After long enough to show that they really didn't care if I stayed or left but not quite long enough to make me leave, the door was opened by a very sad man in a white jacket and white gloves. His skin was olive and sallow and his eyes had dark brown bags under them. He looked at me without speaking, as though it was the sight of me that was making him sad.

"I'm Liam Murdoch. Pete is expecting me."

He nodded then turned away. Under his breath, he said, "Pliss…" which I supposed meant he wanted me to follow him. He led me down a dogleg passage to a large walnut door. He tapped softly with his knuckles, waited for a beat then pushed the door open. There was some murmuring. He faced me and in a voice full of the deepest regret, he said, "Pliss…" then stood back to let me in.

Pete was wrecked. He was the kind of man who couldn't grieve sitting down. He couldn't grieve in silence and he couldn't grieve sober. He grieved on his feet, noisily and drunk. He was standing by the fireplace with his huge back to me, holding a glass of what I assumed was vodka. From where I stood at the doorway, I could hear him sobbing.

I said, "Are you up to this, Pete?"

He nodded without looking at me, waving me in and spilling some of his drink as he did it. There was a drinks trolley. I closed the door, chose an Old Bushmills and poured myself a generous measure. Then I sat and peeled a pack of Camels. He was standing with his left hand covering his face and his shoulders jerking.

I lit up and, as I put my Zippo away, I said, "You should be sedated, Pete. You need to rest. It's too raw."

He turned and leveled eyes on me that had lost all their humanity. All I could see there was pain beyond understanding and an insatiable hunger for cruel revenge.

"We don't waste time. We hunt while trail is hot. Ask me." His voice was slurred.

I sucked on my cigarette and watched him through the smoke. Finally, I sighed and said, "What was she doing in the park at that time?"

He shook his head. "I don't know…" He went to drink but his glass was empty, most of it spilled on the carpet. He lumbered to the trolley and refilled it. "She tell me she want go out. Is late. I tell her no. She go to her room, angry with bad Papa." His face twisted into an ugly mask and he howled at the ceiling, beating his chest with his left fist and spilling most of the vodka he'd just poured into his glass. It was going to be a long evening.

He slumped into a chair, wiping the tears from his face with his huge palms. "Last thing she remember of Papa is she hate him because he say 'No'! All I want is to protect her."

"You didn't know she was out?" He shook his head miserably. "So, she snuck out somehow. Any idea where she wanted to go?"

He scowled at me under his large eyebrows. "She had boyfriend from college. I think he is nice boy. Educated. Psychologist, like her." He pronounced the 'p' in psychologist, and a drop of spit fell from his big lower lip. "She is going with him for two months and I say 'Eva, I want meet boyfriend. Bring him for dinner,' and 'No, Papa, no!' Always she is making excuses. Then she tell me boyfriend is *black!*"

I sighed. "So, you stopped her seeing him because he was black?"

He stared at me a long time, swaying. Then, "Black boy!"

I took a pull and repeated, "Did you stop her seeing him because he was black?"

"*Da.*"

"So, you think maybe last night she snuck out to go see him?"

His glass dropped to the floor and he curled up and buried his face in his hands, sobbing convulsively.

I gave him a minute, then said, "Pete, you are no use to me like this. You need to go to bed. Get the doctor to give you a sedative and let me talk to somebody who can actually help me."

After a time, he raised his huge head. His face was wet and shiny. "All the time, I am thinking she will open door, come in… I will hear her voice…" He looked away at the cold fireplace. "All time, I am imagine what she was feeling when he was doing that to her."

"Pete…"

After a long moment, he said, "*Da.*"

He forced himself to his feet and trudged unsteadily to the door. He opened it and staggered out, leaving it open behind him. Then I heard him bellowing, "*Melanie! Melanie!*" There was some muttering and, after a moment, a young woman stood in the doorway looking at me. She was probably in her late twenties, but she had a sixty-year-old soul. She had on sensible brown shoes and a tweed skirt, a white blouse and a small silver cross around her neck. Dark blue eyes and soft blonde hair pulled back in a low bun made her almost pretty.

"Mr. Murdoch."

I said, "Melanie."

"Mr. Rusakov…"

"Pete thinks you can help me?"

She didn't answer. Instead, she walked into the room and sat in a large burgundy Chesterfield by the fireplace, keeping her knees together and her hands on her lap, the way well-brought-up girls used to do sixty years ago. She looked at me in a way that seemed to say, 'Well?'

I crushed out my cigarette and said, "How do you know Eva?"

"I'm the nanny to the two youngest children. Eva is… was, a lovely person. We became friends."

"Did she tell you where she was going last night?"

She drew breath and held it while she studied the backs of her fingers in her lap. Whatever else she was, she was going to be a bad liar.

Before she could answer, I asked, "What time did you get off work?"

She raised her eyes, feeling safer. "At eight o'clock."

"So, you smuggled Eva out and drove her to her boyfriend's?"

She flushed and went from being almost pretty to seriously attractive.

I smiled. "Don't sweat it. He doesn't need to know, but I do. Is that what happened?"

She stared down at the backs of her hands again. "It seemed harmless at the time. Mr. Rusakov is so unreasonable – and *racist*." She caught herself and looked at me – worried I might tell and worried about the consequences if I did?

I let the smile go up the side of my face. "Don't worry. I

know what he's like. And there was no way you could have known what would happen. But I do need to know where you took her."

She gave a small sigh. "Mr. Rusakov had recently discovered that her boyfriend Mark was black. He is a deeply prejudiced man and he immediately forbade her ever to see him again."

"When was this?"

"About a week ago. She had not gone out since then. She had been working hard, studying. Then last night…" There was a catch in her voice and she bit back a sob that sounded genuine. "Last night, she said she wanted to go out. Mr. Rusakov blew his top. He said he knew where she wanted to go, that he would not have her going out with—"

"I get the idea."

"Anyway, she went to her room and after a while I went in to see if she was all right. That was when she told me she was planning to sneak out while he was watching TV, having his nightly half-bottle of vodka, and she begged me to drive her to Mark's house."

"Where is that?"

She hesitated. "In Hammersmith, on the river. It was a fairly simple drive, down Kensington High Street from Knightsbridge."

She wouldn't meet my eyes. I fished another Camel out of the pack and lit it. I took my time inhaling then sipped my whiskey. I said, "What is it you're not telling me?"

She was quick to answer, "Nothing!"

"Tell me about Mark."

Again, she hesitated, shook her head, as though gathering her thoughts. "Um… He's a very nice young man. He's a year behind Eva on the psychology degree—very well-mannered, articulate…as you'd expect."

"He lives alone?"

She shook her head. "No. He's still at home. He lives with his mother."

Somewhere in my mind an alarm bell rang. I said, "No

dad?"

She shrugged. "There was a stepfather, I think. But he doesn't seem to be on the scene anymore."

I nodded. "I'm going to need a photograph of Eva, and I'll need Mark's address."

Her face went rigid. She said, "Of course." She stood then hesitated again. "Mr. Murdoch, I am absolutely certain that Mark was not responsible for—"

I cut across her. "Take it easy, Melanie. I'm not jumping to any conclusions. I just need to know her movements last night."

She was still hesitating. "It's just that whomever you bring before Peter as a suspect will be tried and sentenced without a jury or due process of law."

I watched her through the smoke. I said, "I know. That's why I'm going to make sure I get the right guy."

She nodded then left the room on quick, efficient feet.

* * * *

I phoned Mrs. Edwards, Mark's mother, from the car. I apologized that it was late and told her I had something urgent I needed to discuss with her about Eva Rusakov. She agreed to see me and said Mark would be there. From her voice, I figured she didn't know Eva was dead. I told her half nine. She said that was okay.

I hung up and sat in the closing dusk, tapping an unlit Camel on the steering wheel. I was wondering how Mark would react when I told him Eva had been murdered. My brain was telling me he was going to put on an act. My gut was telling me something else, but I didn't know what. I finished my smoke and made the short drive over.

Martha Edwards and Mark lived on Mall Close, a quiet, leafy cul-de-sac by the river. Dusk had turned to dark and I could see light spilling from their bow window into the small front garden. I rang and it was Mark who opened the door. He was tall and lean and athletic. He was very

19

dark, maybe Sudanese. He stood watching me with no expression on his face.

I asked, "Are you Mark?"

His English was perfect. "Who are you?"

"My name's Liam Murdoch. I'm a friend of Eva's."

"She never mentioned you."

He wasn't exactly hostile, but he wasn't exactly warm, either.

I said, "Can I come in? I need to talk to you. It's important."

He raised an eyebrow and almost smiled. "Important to whom, Mr. Murdoch? Are you a friend of Eva's or a friend of her father's?"

I studied his face, wondering where the hostility was coming from. "I'm a friend of the family, Mark. I'm not here to bring you a message from Pete, if that's what you're wondering. I need to tell you something, and I need to ask you some questions. This is important to you."

Something in my voice, in my face, or maybe in what I'd said, got through to him.

He frowned and, after a second, he stood back. "Come in."

The drawing room was at the rear of the house on the right of a short hallway that was carpeted in gray with cream walls and a couple of prints. Mrs. Edwards was sitting on a large, cream sofa with her hands clasped between her knees and her eyes fixed on her shoes. She was an attractive woman in her late forties. The furniture was comfortable, lived in and in good taste. She didn't greet me when I went in, but Mark gestured to one of the big chairs and said, "Please sit down, Mr. Murdoch." He sat opposite me, watching me and waiting for me to talk.

Before I could, Mrs. Edwards suddenly spoke up, raising her chin, turning her head toward me but looking away with her eyes, as though she were scared of what she was about to say. "Mr. Murdoch, if Mr. Rusakov has sent you—"

Before she could get any further, Mark held out a hand to her, as though he were stopping traffic. "Mum…please. Let

Mr. Murdoch tell us why he is here. Let's not jump to any conclusions."

I watched them both a moment, then said, "Whatever you may think I'm here for, I'm not. I'm not Pete's hired muscle and I'm not here to deliver a message for him. I know he didn't like Eva hanging out with you, Mark, and I know why, but frankly, I don't give a damn about that. All I need is to ask you a few questions."

Mark frowned while his mother resumed her study of her shoes.

He said, "Questions?"

I nodded. "Eva was here last night, right?"

"What of it?"

I knew what I wanted to ask—just one question—but I was going to stalk him for a while, to get the feel of him. I said, "What time did she get here?"

His eyes shifted to his left and up. He was remembering. "About half past eight."

"And what time did she leave?"

He thought about it. I watched his eyes. Top left again, remembering. Then his face contracted and his eyes dropped down and to his right. He was remembering how he'd felt when she'd left. He'd felt sad. He shook his head. He didn't like what he was remembering. He said, "About eleven."

"Did you leave with her?"

He frowned. "No..." Then, "Well, I..."

I interrupted him. Now I was going to ask him what I really wanted to know. "Did she come here to break up with you?"

He fixed me with his eyes. The look was intense. He was angry. Then his gaze wavered and shifted. He was about to lie but thought better of it and glanced down at the floor, rubbing his right hand with the fingers of his left. He said, "Yes."

"But you didn't want to let her go."

Anger flashed across his face. "She wasn't leaving me

because she wanted to! She was leaving me because her father — your employer! — demanded it because I'm *black!*"

I was going to tell him to take it easy, but suddenly his mother was speaking for him. It sounded like that was something she did a lot. "We have never played the race card, Mr. Murdoch. We have never done any special pleading for ourselves. We have never set ourselves aside or played the victim. My first husband was black, from Barbados, where I am from. But my second husband was white, an Englishman and a good, honorable person. That you should come here now, telling us Mark cannot see Eva anymore because he is *black!* Because he is *not good enough* for her! We may be black, Mr. Murdoch, and your employer may be a billionaire, but what we have, I have earned" — she held out her palms to me — "with these *black* hands. And with the sweat from this *black* brow!" She stared at me with wild eyes, paused, then went on, "It is not the product of crime, extortion and murder. It is not the product of a black *heart!*"

She had finished, but she kept eye contact with me. I shifted my eyes to Mark. He was staring at the floor between his feet, like a strange echo of his mother. I couldn't make out if his expression was one of embarrassment, shame or anger — maybe all three.

I looked back at her and said, "Take it easy, Mrs. Edwards. Let's get a couple of things straight so we can start understanding each other. First of all, Pete is *not* my employer. I don't work for him. I don't work for anybody. But, most important, he doesn't pay me. So, you can both quit calling him my employer.

"Second, I am not here to deliver a message from him about Eva. I don't give a rat's ass if she was Mark's girlfriend or not." I turned to face Mark, who was still staring at the floor. "Frankly, if you made each other happy, I think you'd be stupid to split up. But whether you split up or stayed together is nobody's business except yours." I waited for a reaction, but there wasn't any. Neither of them seemed to be very curious as to why I *was* there. Finally, I said, "I am here because Eva was murdered last night and I want to find who did it."

It was brutal. Maybe it was even cruel. But I needed to see Mark's reaction.

He seemed to turn a deep shade of yellow. He stared hard at the carpet then raised his gaze to look at me. His face screwed up and his lips moved on silent words until he said, "*What?*"

Meanwhile his mother was shaking her head and saying, "No! No! No, Mark, no—" and she was reaching out for him.

I ignored her and said, "I'm sorry. Her body was found early this morning. There is no doubt that she was murdered."

But Mrs. Edwards was standing, grabbing at her son, her face twisting into an ugly fist of pain. She seemed to claw him to his feet and, as he rose, she enfolded him in her arms and suddenly he was holding her, burying his face in her neck, sobbing like a small boy. I wanted to leave them to suffer in private, but I needed to know what had gone down between Eva and Mark—and his mother. So I sat and watched them clinging to each other and sobbing. Eventually, I pulled out my Camels, eased one out of the box and poked it in my mouth. Two got you twenty that social conditioning would make them stop crying long enough to tell me to put it out. I flipped the Zippo and leaned into the flame. By the time I'd exhaled, he was pulling back and wiping his eyes and she was turning to face me. Her face and her voice were resentful, like it was my smoking that had caused Eva to get killed.

She said, between sniffs, "Can you please not smoke in here?"

I gave her my sweetest smile and said, "Sure, where would you like me to put it?"

She left in search of an ashtray, wiping her cheeks with the palms of her hands.

I turned to Mark, who was lowering himself back into his chair, muttering, "It can't be… It can't—"

I cut across him and said, "So, she came here to break up with you."

He stared at me a while, like he didn't know what the hell I was doing there. Then he blinked, looked about the room and shook his head.

I said, "Is that why she came here?"

Finally, he nodded, then shrugged. "Not really… In a way… She was determined not to accept any help from her father." He wiped his eyes with the heels of his hands. His breathing was shaking. "She knew what he was and how he had made his fortune, and she wanted no part of it. She was good and decent. But if she moved out of his house now…then…that would mean accepting money from him to get an apartment. And if she did that, it would have to be on his terms. He would own her."

"Meaning you couldn't be a part of her life."

"Exactly." His lip began to curl and tremble, but he fought it. "She went so far as to say she was afraid for my safety. She wanted to take a break until she had graduated. Then we could move in together without owing him anything. But now…?"

He buried his face in his hands. Mrs. Edwards came in with a cup full of water. She took the cigarette from my fingers and dropped it in the water. Then she left the room with it, holding it at arm's length, like it was radioactive.

I ignored her and asked Mark, "How did you feel about that?"

He shrugged, raised his face and stared at the ceiling. His cheeks were wet. "I didn't like it, but it made sense, in a way. I told her to come and stay here with us…with me." He glanced at the door. Upstairs we heard a toilet flush. "But she wouldn't." He looked at the floor. "She said three would be a crowd."

"Were you mad?"

He shook his head. "No. You're barking up the wrong

tree, Mr. Murdoch. I saw her to the bus stop. I wanted to see her home, but she was insistent she would go alone." His voice went thick and he seemed to choke. His eyes flooded. "She got on the bus and that was it." Then his face crumpled and his voice went into a strange whine. "Oh, God...oh, God...if only I'd gone..."

I gave him a moment, then asked, "What bus?"

He took a while to answer, wiping his eyes over and again, until he had his voice under control. Then he said, "One of the Heritage buses, the N9 Special. It would have been about eleven-fifteen."

I figured he'd had about all he could take and I left. I killed an hour dunking olives in a couple of Martinis on King Street till eleven, then I strolled down to the N9 bus stop. It came along just before a quarter after eleven. It was called a Heritage bus because it was an old, red, hop-on-hop-off double-decker with an open platform at the back and a conductor who wandered around saying, "Any more fares, please?" It was a bit of the old London that the Londoners wanted to preserve for themselves, but that was preserved for tourists instead.

I got on and sat at the back, near where the conductor stood. He looked Mediterranean and, when he spoke, I knew he was Italian.

I handed him my money then, as he gave me my ticket, I said, "Listen, maybe you can help me." He asked me how with his face and I said, "I'm looking for my sister. She went missing yesterday."

It's a stereotype, but, like all stereotypes, they're based on some kind of truth. Mothers and sisters are every Italian's weak spot. I had him hooked straight away.

He frowned, shook his head and spread his hands all at the same time. "Your sister?" He made a long, hissing noise through his teeth. "'Ow can I 'elp?"

"I think maybe she took this bus last night. Maybe you saw her. She's pretty..." I smiled, full of brotherly pride, and pulled out the photo Melanie had given me and showed it to him.

He held it, nodding and shaking his head by turns. "*Porca miseria!* Yeah, yeah, I see her. Last night. Other times, also. She come on this bus. Nice..." He smiled at me, handing back the picture. "Nice girl. Polite. Always nice clothes. Elegant."

A couple got on, talking about a film they'd seen at the Odeon and he wandered off after them to get their fares. He came back a couple of minutes later, holding on to the overhead rail. "What 'appen? How she went missing?"

I shrugged and spread my hands. "Families, right? She had a row with our dad..." I shook my head. "Was she with anyone?"

He frowned, reassuring me, "Nah! She was alone..." Then he suddenly shrugged, dancing his head around and putting up his hands. He made a 'Tsk!' sound and said, "*Bene*... alone. She get on alone, but then her friend come and sit with her."

"Her friend?"

He pulled a face of total disgust that only Italians know how to do. "Yes, *porco, pezzo di merda*, small, many spot on his face, the big glasses like a *telescopio*." He began to laugh, holding his hands like binoculars in front of his eyes. "The cheap clothes, you know? Not like her, always elegant— Giorgio Armani, Gucci—" He kissed his fingertips.

I cut in before he started off again and asked, "So this guy got on and sat with her?"

"*Certo!* He one stop after her, and he stay talking with her until the Albert 'All. Then they get off together."

I thought for a moment. "Had you ever seen them together on this bus before?"

He nodded. "Yeah, yeah, couple of time."

I got off the bus and watched it pull away into the night. I stood with my back to the Albert Hall, stuck a Camel in my mouth then leaned into the flame of my Zippo. I blew smoke into the hot night air and looked across the road at the blackness of Hyde Park. Half an hour's walk back in the direction I'd come from was Holland Park. I glanced at my watch. It was half past eleven. She and her mystery friend would have climbed off the bus right here at this time last night.

What made her do that? And what did she do then?

Four hours later, she was lying under the trees with a kitchen knife in her heart and her guts ripped out.

What happened during those four hours?

Chapter Three

I watched the butter melt into my heavy rye toast and knew I wouldn't eat it. I stood and found a bottle of Jameson in the drawing room, brought it back to the kitchen and spilled some onto my black coffee. Maria watched me do it, chewing, but said nothing. I peeled a fresh pack of Camels, poked one in my mouth and lit it. We sat looking at each other. Her, chewing and drinking black coffee. Me, smoking and drinking coffee laced with whiskey.

After a moment, she sighed and dropped her napkin on the table. "Want to talk about it?"

"How do I crack those four hours?"

"Let the police do it. They have the resources to canvass the people who were at the Albert Hall bus stop that night… You haven't."

I told her again what she already knew. "I can't involve the police."

"They're already involved. They have the body. They're investigating."

"They don't know about Mark and they don't know about the guy on the bus. They don't even know she was on the bus, and they're not going to find out. You know that."

She stood and started collecting the plates. I sucked on my cigarette, took the smoke deep, held it, then let it out slow. She was at the sink with her back to me.

I said, "She was on the bus on her way home. This guy gets on one stop after she does. They know each other. He sits with her and they talk. Then she gets off with him at the Albert Hall."

She was washing plates and didn't answer.

I went on, "So that means one of two things. She'd already planned to get off at the Albert Hall, for some reason we don't know about, and he got off with her, or he persuaded her to get off with him."

She picked up a hand towel, turned and started drying her hands, leaning her ass against the sink and watching me. She shrugged. "Makes sense." She dropped the towel and crossed her arms. "So where do you go from there?"

I closed my eyes. I could smell the coffee and the cigarette smoke, and I could feel her gaze on me. I knew she was mad, but I had to ignore it and focus. I said, "Either they went somewhere together or they parted. He went his own way, and she went on somewhere else, to a meeting that she had already arranged."

I opened my eyes. She was still watching me with her arms crossed. She said, "How will you find out?"

I thought for a while. Finally, I said, "Like you pointed out, I can't do the kind of canvassing the cops can. But if she had arranged to meet someone, that someone is either a person she knows or a person who knows someone she knows."

She shrugged again. "Could be someone she met online."

"Eva? I don't think so, but I'll get Pete to have any computer or tablets she had examined."

Her face was going rigid. I knew she was getting madder and I wasn't sure why.

She said, "Don't forget that she would have had access to computers at UCL. You'd better have them looked at, too."

I nodded. "Yeah. But I'm pretty sure Eva wasn't hooking up with unknown people online. That wasn't her style. Besides, she had a boyfriend. But you're right about UCL. I'm curious about this guy on the bus. Where did she meet him? Where would she meet anyone? Her two points of contact with people were through her father and through the university."

"So?"

"I need to talk to her tutors and her classmates."

"But you can't just turn up and start asking questions. So?"

"So, I need to talk to Russell. He can arrange for me to meet her tutors."

She had a smile you could call humorless stuck on her face. Her arms were crossed so tight that she could have choked a python, and now she had crossed one leg over the other.

I said, "What's eating you, Maria?"

She raised her eyebrows high. "Me? Nothing at all."

I crushed out my cigarette and stood. I was going to call Russell. She was watching me.

As I reached the door she said, "So, what shall I do this weekend?"

I turned and frowned. "What do you mean?"

"We were going to Cornwall this weekend, remember? Today is Friday. I'm assuming the weekend is off. You're going to be busy. So, what do you suggest I should do?"

I sighed. She was right and I had forgotten. "His daughter was murdered, Maria. I have to help him."

She shook her head. "Of course. Please, don't worry. I understand your priorities perfectly."

"I told you. My condition for doing this is that—"

She cut across me. "Please, Liam, don't. If you're going to do it, just do it. You know what they say about actions." She pushed away from the sink and past me into the hall. Over her shoulder, she said, "They speak much louder than words!"

A few seconds later, I heard the bedroom door close. It didn't slam, but it wasn't far off.

* * * *

Russell was at his house in Fishbourne, just outside Chichester. I figured I'd drive down, talk to him and give Maria a chance to cool off and see things with a bit more clarity and perspective. Next weekend, I'd take her to Paris to make up for not going away to Cornwall. I took it slow, with the soft-top down, and enjoyed the breeze and the freedom. It was good to be out and moving. And, though I didn't like to acknowledge it, it was good to be alone. I wanted Maria in my life like I wanted the air I breathed, but adjusting to this new life wasn't always easy.

I pulled up in front of Russell's place about one in the afternoon. It was a hot one in late summer, and there were big thunderheads gathering over the Chichester Channel, but the sky was blue. A tall, red brick chimneypot rose above the thatch roof of his old, pre-Tudor manor house, and a blackbird sat watching me and singing a long, complicated tune into the molten sun.

I didn't bother hammering on the ancient oak door. Instead, I walked to the wooden gate that gave on to the garden at the back of the house. As I expected, he was sitting there. He was in baggy, cream-linen trousers, a shirt that seemed six sizes too big on his scrawny frame, huge black sunglasses and a straw hat. He looked luminous against the brilliant green of his lawn. He was sitting at a garden table under a blue and white parasol, reading a newspaper. The smell of honeysuckle and roses was strong on the warm air. I paused for a moment, leaning on the gate, waiting for the blackbird to draw breath.

When it did, I said, "Hello, Russell."

He had a trick of talking to me as though he were picking up a conversation we had momentarily paused a few seconds earlier, even though I hadn't seen him for weeks — or even months, as was the case now. He glanced up as he turned a page and said, "I see the Monopolies and Mergers Commission has allowed the HEAT Corporation's bid for the Llyn Celyn fusion reactor. That will bring problems."

I opened the gate and said, "I'm fine, thanks. How are you?"

He scanned the page in front of him. "Where's Maria? You haven't brought her? I like her. She's good for you."

"She's busy."

"Have some lemonade. It's in the fridge. Bring the jug, will you?"

I went into the kitchen, took two glasses and the jug of lemonade from the fridge, brought them out and put them on the white wrought-iron table under the parasol. I pulled up a chair and sat while he leafed through the paper. I filled the glasses and finally he folded the paper and laid it down.

He said, "The High Energy Atomic Technologies Corporation. HEAT. It pleases us, doesn't it, when an acronym amounts to an actual word. We are eternally in search of meaning..."

I knew when Russell started talking like this that he was leading up to something and taking his sweet time about it. Normally, I would sit and wait. Whatever Russell was rambling about, it was usually worth listening to, but this time I cut in. "I need your advice, Russell, maybe your help, too."

He gazed at me from behind his huge, black sunglasses and I realized he was waiting for me to go on.

I took out my cigarette pack and pulled one free. "Russian Pete's daughter was murdered the night before last."

He didn't react. He didn't even look surprised.

"He's asked me to find the killer."

"How can I help?"

I described the murder scene to him and my meeting with Mark and Mrs. Edwards. He listened without moving until I'd finished.

Then he said, "So you think it's a serial killer."

I shrugged. "It could be. It has some of the hallmarks, but then there are things that don't fit."

"So, you want me to introduce you to Eva's tutor."

"Can you?"

"Juliet Loss. Did you know she was a consultant profiler for the FBI?"

I watched him for a moment. He was completely expressionless.

I said, "No. How did you know she was Eva's tutor?"

His gaze wandered out toward the mill pond across the road from his house, where the bulrushes were swaying in the warm breeze. He sighed. "It's not always easy to keep track, you know... Sometimes I flag things, 'useful'... Has Hook been in touch?"

He turned to me, smiling as though he'd answered me and now we were moving on to a more interesting subject.

I said, "No. Can you introduce me?"

"Yes, yes, of course. I'll have a word. Odd choice, isn't it?"

"What do you mean?"

"Makes you wonder why the killer chose her, of all people."

I shrugged. "Typically, a serial killer selects his victim at random."

"And random results very rarely show any kind of meaning, beyond the fact of being random."

I shook my head. "I'm not following you."

He scratched the tip of his nose with a long, bony finger. "Two things stand out about this murder, Liam. The first one you noted yourself."

"The incongruence between the rose and the knife and the ripped-out abdomen?"

"Indeed. The other..." He took a deep breath and screwed up his face, as if he wasn't convinced himself about what he was going to say. "Well, if I wanted you, Liam Murdoch, to investigate a murder and to have that investigation facilitated, of all the people you know, whom would I kill?"

It sounded ridiculous, but I thought about it because I have learned over the years always to think about what Russell says. In the end, I shook my head. "Okay, I see what you mean. Pete would ask me to find the killer, and he would pull strings to allow me to do that. But why would anyone want me to investigate a murder?"

He nodded. "Yes, that *is* the question, isn't it?

I shook my head again, feeling oddly uncomfortable. "I don't see it, Russell. It's not a credible motive."

He sat back, apparently gazing at the blackbird that was

still sitting on his chimney. He sipped his lemonade and listened to it sing its long, convoluted song. "Perhaps not," he said. "Talk to Juliet. That is the obvious next step. See where it leads you."

I watched him and, after a moment, I said, "If you're right, that's what the killer would expect me to do."

He turned to look at me with his large, black glasses, but he didn't say anything.

We had a late luncheon and I headed back to London about five, feeling I was more confused than when I'd come down. What Russell had suggested was absurd, and coming from anybody else, I would have dismissed it without a second thought. But Russell was the smartest guy I had ever met, and it was second nature to me to listen to what he had to say. On the other hand, he was well into his eighties, and the bigger your brain, the more there is to go wrong... Either way, he'd fixed up a meeting for me with Professor Juliet Loss at UCL the next morning and I had a strong hunch that meeting would lead me in the right direction.

I got home around half seven. Maria wasn't there. For some reason that made me uneasy. I called her cell. It rang, but she didn't answer. She'd known I was coming back this evening and it was odd that she hadn't told me she was going out. After half an hour, I tried again. Still no answer. I sent her a Whatsapp saying "Hey, where are you?" and regretted it after I'd sent it. She'd see she had two missed calls and a Whatsapp. I felt that made me look needy and I was mad at myself for caring.

At half eight, I went down to Noddy's Diner for a sandwich and a couple of Martinis. I climbed onto a stool, feeling sour, and ordered a Scotch instead of Martini or Irish. Noddy gave me a weird look and I asked him for a steak sandwich, rare. Then I peeled a new pack of Camels. Technically, it was illegal to smoke in public places, but since the surprise landslide of the Independent Party and the Vaasa Accord of 2020, a lot of EU-based laws were not enforced, especially if you had the right friends in the right places—and Noddy had all the right friends in all the right places. I flipped my Zippo and lit up, blowing smoke at my whiskey. I glanced at my phone. There were no messages. I downed the whiskey and showed Noddy the empty glass. He refilled it then leaned his huge black forearms on the bar.

"'Sup?"

I eyed him. "What is that, an order to drink?"

"No, it's English for 'what's eatin' you, dude?'"

I turned my glass around a few times, looking at the deep amber inside it, like I might find some kind of answer in there. I said, "You ever been married, Noddy? Lived with a woman?"

He grunted. "Fuckin' heart problems." He blew through his teeth with genuine sympathy and shook his head. "You know what Freud said."

I regarded him curiously. "You read Freud?"

He raised an eyebrow. Usually Noddy spoke in a dense, impenetrable Cockney that only he understood.

"A vastly underrated philosopher of our time... He said, 'We are never so defenseless against suffering as when we love, never so helplessly unhappy as when we have lost our loved object or its love.' So, no, mate. I keep my *liaison dangerous* on a strictly shag-only basis—no strings, no emotional fahkin' involvement. Bit of the old how's yer father, bit of the old"—he gave me an elaborate wink—"*Blitzkrieg mit dem fleischgewehr* then it's good mornin', good day and catcha later."

So now, whether through pity or because the occasion had seemed to call for it, he'd slipped into plain English. I swirled my drink and took a pull. He was waiting for me to say something, but there was nothing I wanted to say, so he went on.

"I mean, look at you. You was always 'appy-go-lucky, no fahkin' worries, master of yer own fate." He shrugged. "Now look atcha! Let me guess. It's gotta be one of three fings. Either you've met another girl and you wanna shag her—"

I frowned and shook my head. "No way, Noddy!"

"Don't interrupt. Yer feelin' you is no longer master of your own fate."

I shrugged.

He continued, "Or, most likely, you are beginning to suspect she might be gettin' interested in somebody else."

I said, "That's ridiculous." But my lack of conviction was as obvious to him as it was to me.

He gave a huge sigh and made a lame attempt at wiping the bar. "It happens, me old mucker. What can I say? That's why I never get involved, right? They want your undivided attention, and, if you don't give it to them, they get bored and their eye starts rovin'. But if you *do* give it them, you ain't a bad boy anymore. You're needy. They get bored and their eye starts rovin'. Can't win. Women are bad news. I fought you knew that."

He wandered away to pull a beer. I didn't believe any of what he'd said. Not about Maria. I wasn't cut out for the whole domestic thing. Neither was she, but we were learning. We were putting it together so it would work. I looked at my phone. Nothing. It was nine o'clock.

The sandwich came after ten minutes. I ate it slowly, straining to ignore my phone. I had another couple of whiskeys then headed home at ten with still no message but a sick hole in my belly.

When I got in, the apartment was empty and dark. The heat was humid and oppressive. I stripped off my shirt and went to the fridge for a beer. I stood in the door and uncapped the bottle, feeling the cold air on my skin. I drained half then went and opened the window that overlooked Kensington Church Street. I sat on the windowsill, staring down at the black cabs, the red buses and the night traffic,

I was on my second beer when the Harley appeared around the corner. I knew it was a Harley by the sound. It was unmistakable. It had high handlebars and the guy driving it was wearing black leather and blue jeans. The girl on the back was petite. She had long black hair under her helmet and she was holding on tight.

I knew it was her before she dismounted and took the helmet off. I watched her hand it to him. They talked a moment. I saw him beckon to her with his hand. She smacked his arm away and I heard her laugh. He pointed his left finger at her like a pretend gun and revved the engine with his right hand. Her laugh was loud, almost a squeal.

He drove away and I saw her disappear into the building below me. It was ten past eleven. A couple of minutes passed and I heard the key in the lock. I kept staring at the street. I felt too sick to talk. She came in with quick steps, opened the door and stood looking at me. I didn't look back. I still felt sick.

After a moment, she said, "Hi," like she was greeting an acquaintance she was fond of.

I turned to face her. "Where were you?"

She put her hands in the pockets of her jeans and bit her lip. Her eyes seemed mad. She said, "I had nothing to do. I was bored, so I checked into evening classes at Birkbeck College."

I could feel my heart racing and I was struggling to keep a hold of my anger. "On a Saturday? Until eleven at night?"

She walked to a chair then dropped into it, with her hands still in her pockets. "Where were *you*?"

"I told you where I was. I went to see Russell. We talked, we had lunch and I came home. Alone. In my own vehicle."

She stared at me. She said, "What does that mean?"

I said, "Who is he?"

She turned away. Her expression was hard to read. She may have been mad, but she may have been biting back tears. Eventually, she said, "His name is Steve."

I watched her awhile but she wouldn't meet my eye. Finally, I asked her, "What's going on? Are you involved with him?"

Now she turned to face me and her eyes were bright with anger, but she didn't speak.

I felt sick and lightheaded. I pushed on. "How long has it been going on?"

Her cheeks flushed red. "Oh, for God's sake, Liam! I met him *today!*"

"And already he's bringing you home at eleven at night and flirting with you?"

"*What?*"

"Where were you, Maria? Where did you meet this guy and why did he drive you home on his bike?"

"I told you. I was *bored.* I went to Birkbeck College to check into evening courses!"

"Until eleven o'clock at night? How stupid do you think I am?"

She was on her feet, stabbing her finger at me. "Right now? *Very!* A group of us got to talking with one of the professors, then we stepped out for a drink at the local pub. Honestly, I was mad at you, so I was *not* in a hurry to come home. But I got up to leave before half ten. Then Steve said he was leaving, too, and he'd give me a lift. That is *it!* But, frankly, Liam, I do *not* owe you a damned explanation. I am *not* accountable to you."

We stared at each other in silence.

Finally, I said, "Really? Because if I came home at eleven o'clock at night without letting you know where I was and not answering the messages you sent me, there is one person in this world I would feel I owed an explanation to. There is one person in this world I would feel accountable to — you. We are not acquaintances. We are not even friends, Maria. We made a commitment to each other — or doesn't that mean anything anymore?"

She came and stood over me. Her anger was changing to sadness. "You tell me."

I stood and gripped her shoulders. The knot of fear in my belly was suddenly a hot hunger for her. "I am as committed to you as I was the first day I met you and when I pulled you from the flames at the Abbey of Thelema! I love you, baby, but I don't know what the hell has got into you."

She pushed at my hands, trying to free herself from them. "Then why am I stuck here day after day alone? Why are you always out with Pete or Russell or Noddy or whoever the *fuck* you hang out with?"

"Baby, I told you —"

"What do you think I *am*?" She thumped me in the chest as she said it. "What the hell did you think I was going to *become*?" She thumped me again. "Some good little *fucking wife* sitting at home while you're out drinking with your *fucking* criminal *fucking* friends?"

She thumped me one last time and stepped back. I could see her chest rising and falling. Her breathing was coming hard.

I started to say again, "Baby, I told you it would take a little time…"

She pointed at me and her eyes were bright with anger and tears. "*Your* time, Liam, not mine!"

She turned and walked away, into the bedroom, then slammed the door. I stood looking at it. There was a wild pounding in my chest that was probably panic and a burning in my belly that was making me feel sick to my stomach. I went over and pushed the door open. She was sitting on the edge of the bed with her hands between her knees. Her face was wet with tears. I kneeled in front of her and took her hands in mine.

"Maria, baby, we don't need to do this. We can talk. You know I'd do anything for you."

She said, "I tried talking to you, but you're so *obstinate*." But the anger had gone out of her.

I took her face in my hands and I kissed her. She seemed suddenly small and tender. Her lips trembled. Then she was holding my face, running her fingers through my hair and pulling me to her. A kind of madness welled up inside me, fogging my brain with heat. I pushed her onto the bed then stood. As I tore off my shirt, she scrambled backward, climbing to her knees, yanking her blouse from her jeans. Her eyes were wild.

I threw my pants across the room and stood looking into her eyes. I was as hot as a Carolina reaper on a bed of jalapeño peppers and as hard as Chinese declensions in the pluperfect subjunctive. I could feel my heart pounding hard and my breathing was shallow and trembling. I watched her take off her jeans and her lacy pants and we were both naked, staring at each other.

I whispered her name and she shuffled toward me, clumsily, almost falling on the quilt, smiling up at me. Then she had her left hand on the back of my neck and she was kissing me, long and slow and deep and her right hand, cool and small, was wrapped around me, gently stroking me, back and forth. Then the whole world was her skin under my hands as I caressed her back, feeling the curve of her waist, the fullness of her hips and ass and her small hand holding me, feeling me. I buried my face in her hair and found her delicate neck, bared for me. I bit, too hard, and she moaned and came to me, clawing my back, and pain and pleasure fused into a kind of weird ecstasy.

We fell and I was on top of her. Her legs opened and I lay between them, feeling the silk of her thighs against my hips. Her fragile smallness was making me crazy. I looked down on her face and knew she was the most beautiful thing I had ever seen. Her breasts, pale and smooth, lay spread beneath me and I was hungry for her. Then our skin was fused, and she was no longer cool and delicate, but warm and moist with perspiration.

I was biting her ear and, as I slid inside her, I could hear her whispering, "Baby, oh, baby…" and our voices became one.

Next, we were grappling each other, and I had her beautiful face in my hands, kissing her mouth, searching for her tongue. We were in a frenzy, like we were going to consume each other whole. Then we were coming, exploding, and I could feel her tightening around me in a crazy spasm, and we roared and screamed with one voice. Every time it seemed to finish, it started again, with another spasm, like electricity surging through us.

Even after we had collapsed in a tangle of arms and legs, it wasn't enough. The fear I had felt of losing her had turned into an insatiable hunger, and, as she lay limp with her eyes closed, moaning, sometimes crying out, I licked the sweat from her skin, bit deeply into her white flesh, then moved from her neck, down over the gentle swell of her breasts, over her flat belly to the moist silk between her legs. There I took great mouthfuls of her, owning and possessing her in a passion of madness as she squeezed me between her thighs—as though, if I went deep enough inside her, I would never lose her.

* * * *

It was dawn, and the birds were making a riot outside the window. We were still tangled, holding tightly like we never wanted to let each other go. I lay, staring at the shadows around the ceiling, watching them slowly turn to morning. After a while, I became aware that she was awake, too, with her head and her hand resting on my chest. I kissed her hair and sensed her smile.

She said, "I guess we were a bit stupid."

I smiled on one side of my face, though she couldn't see me. "I guess…" Then, as a lame joke, "But the make-up sex was worth it."

She gave a small laugh, but after a moment she shook her head. "No, it wasn't. Let's never do that again."

I nodded. "Agreed."

She shifted around so she could look up at my face. "So, what happens now?"

I kissed her and stroked her cheek. "You mean after scrambled eggs and coffee?"

She didn't answer, just kept watching me, waiting for a real answer.

Finally, I said, "Baby, you know I will do anything for you. You know I will make the changes in my life and leave these people behind. You know I will do it."

She raised an eyebrow, but she was smiling. She wasn't mad. "I sense a 'but' coming."

I shook my head. "No but. It isn't even a promise I'm making you. It's just a fact."

She frowned. "Okay... So...?"

"We can't hold each other to ransom, baby. We can't blackmail each other. We are who we are, and we have to hold one another with open hands or all of this means nothing."

She dropped her eyes and I stroked her cheek with my fingers.

"When I went for you at the Abbey of Thelema, I knew I would probably die. I knew we would both probably die that night. I would rather die making your life a little bit better than live, knowing you weren't part of mine. But I can't *make* you part of my life. It only makes any sense if you are here because you want to be."

Now she looked serious. "What are you saying?"

"I'm saying that the same applies to you. I will change my life because I want to, because I want to be a better man for you. But I wouldn't be a better man — I wouldn't be me — if I reneged on my promise to Pete, my promise to Pete and to Eva. She was a nice kid, Maria. She didn't deserve to die the way she did. I need to find who did it. I promised, and I'm going to keep my promise."

I used my elbows to lever myself into a sitting position. She sat up, with her legs crossed, close, facing me. I stroked her tangled hair from her face. Her cheeks were a little flushed and I suddenly wanted her again.

Instead, I said, "I'm going to ask you to support me in this, Maria — for us, to make it work. And, when it's over, I'll walk away from Pete and the whole scene, and I'll never look back. But, right now, I need you to be there for me. This is something I have to do. I can't force you, just like you can't force me not to do it. But I'm asking you…to stand by me."

She was thoughtful for a long time. Then she nodded and finally looked me in the eye. "I love you, Liam, and I guess I love you for who you are. So, I'll stick by you. But I need to know that when this is over, you'll be done with the Russian Petes and the gambling and all this kind of life."

"I'm done with it already, baby. But I owe this to Eva — and to her dad."

Chapter Four

Ten o'clock the next morning I pulled up in Russell Square, parked at a meter and put my 'doctor on call' sign on the windshield. Loss had an office on the fourth floor of one of those Georgian terraces that Birkbeck College had bought for itself. I stepped into a small reception hall that was dark, carpeted in dull green and had a slightly uneven floor. The receptionist had a navy-blue uniform, flaccid, perspiring skin and eyes untroubled by thought. I told him who I wanted to see and he said, "Fourth floor, room 4D, but it's the only room up there, so you can't miss it."

"Where's the elevator?"

"Ain't no elev...lift."

The stairs were a steep, unlit maze that seemed too long and winding to be contained in such a small building. They climbed, dropped, twisted then climbed again until I was completely lost and disorientated. After long minutes, I finally made it to the top floor and found room 4D. I knocked.

There was no response, but after thirty seconds the door opened and a short woman of anything between sixty and seventy-five stood looking up at me with intelligent, searching eyes. She was wearing a pale blue cardigan, a double string of what looked like real pearls and a pair of Armani jeans that might have cost as much as the pearls.

She smiled and said, "Mr. Murdoch?"

I told her I was, then asked, "Are you Dr. Juliet Loss?"

She left the door open but turned and walked away from me, speaking over her shoulder. "Do come in. Russell told me to expect you this morning. Can I offer you some tea?"

I don't drink tea, but she was like Miss Marple, and, when you visit Miss Marple, you just have to drink tea...out of bone china...and nibble at biscuits. I said that would be great.

She spoke into an ancient intercom on her desk and said, "Karla, be a darling and bring us a pot of tea, would you? And some nice biscuits."

The room was surprisingly large, with two sash windows overlooking the gardens in the square. The walls were cream and the furniture was eclectic. She gestured me to a huge, ancient chair with a throw over it, and she sat in a Swedish thing in white leather.

As we sat, she said, "The throw conceals all the bits where the stuffing is coming out." She laughed with her eyes and added, "I call it Freud's unconscious chair. All the broken bits are under the surface, and because you are not aware of them, you have the illusion of comfort."

I smiled. The chair was comfortable. I said, "Is that a psychologist's joke?"

"It's a psychoanalyst's joke. Not all psychologists believe in the unconscious. That was Freud's great discovery, and it belongs to his creation, psychoanalysis."

The door opened and a pretty, blonde European girl came in with a tray. On it was a bone china teapot, two cups and a saucer of biscuits. She set it down on a small table next to Dr. Loss. Then she left without saying anything. Dr. Loss began to pour.

She said, "You see? We weren't aware of her, but all the while she was out of our perceptive field, she was doing something for us. Then she emerged into our perception with the tea made. Almost like magic."

She popped two biscuits on my saucer and handed me the tea. When she'd finished pouring her own, she went on. "Our unconscious is like that. It is working all the time. At its most basic, it is making you breathe, making your heart beat. It will make you digest your tea and your biscuits, but it does a lot more than that, too. It makes you decide whether you like tea or biscuits or the old lady you are talking to, or if you want to fuck or rape the blonde girl who brought in the tray."

She had my attention. I was holding the cup halfway to my lips, staring at her. Her eyes sparkled as she sipped then set the cup and saucer down on the tray. She held my gaze with hers and said, "It is also responsible for making all the assumptions and generalizations that we make. Sweet little old ladies in cardigans don't say 'fuck' and talk about rape."

I sipped my tea. I said, "Okay, you surprised me."

She became more serious. "In psychoanalysis, Mr. Murdoch, we explore the darkest side of the human psyche. And, believe me, the human psyche can get very dark indeed. To be an analyst, you must first go through analysis yourself. Eventually, you give up all preconceptions and you lose the ability to be shocked."

I considered her a moment. Finally, I said, "I guess so, especially if you specialize in profiling serial killers."

She smiled, but it was strangely devoid of any expression. She said, "What did you want to ask me about Eva?"

"Who did she hang out with? Who were her friends?"

She held a biscuit and considered it from several angles, like she thought it might be an inappropriate biscuit. "Are you asking me to point the finger at someone?"

I shook my head. "She rode the bus from Hammersmith to the Albert Hall. Most of the way, she was talking to a guy. They got off together and, four hours later, she was dead in Holland Park. I need to know who that guy was."

"You think I might know?"

"I don't know. All I want is to get some idea of who she hung out with, who her friends were. One thing might lead to another."

She seemed to come to a decision about the cookie and bit it in half, then she met my eye. "There was Mark, of course. He was a year behind her on the degree course. Very bright young man. They became intimate. I don't believe her father approved."

"I've spoken to him."

She raised an eyebrow. "Is that why she was in Hammersmith? Visiting him?"

I nodded.

She looked sad for just a moment. "Pity. She told me she might go to see him. Her father was putting pressure on her. Then there was Stefan, an Indonesian student on an exchange from Holland. He's unremarkable. More interested in drinking and having fun than learning about psychology, I think." She sighed deeply. "Aside from those two, she kept pretty much to herself, Mr. Murdoch. She was always polite, always willing to stop and exchange a few words with everyone, whether it was a professor or the doorman. She was delightfully unaffected. You might say dedicatedly so, as though making a point to herself and the world that she was *not* her father's daughter."

It wasn't much to go on. I was reserving my judgment about Mark, and I'd pay a visit to Stefan in due course, but my gut was telling me it was a waste of time. I said, "She was laid out neatly. She had a rose in her mouth, with all the thorns on and a kitchen knife placed with surgical precision into her heart. Then her entire abdomen had been ripped out. To me it sounds"—I shook my head, searched for a more accurate word, but settled on—"*wrong*."

She glanced away, to the floor by her right foot. Her eyebrow twitched. "What is it exactly, about this murderer's method of killing his prey, that strikes you as wrong?"

I thought about it. I said, "It looks like the work of two different killers."

"Explain that to me."

I sighed and reached into my pocket for my Camels. I said, "Mind if I smoke?"

She smiled." All psychoanalysts are neurotic, Mr. Murdoch. I'll join you. I love Camels."

I handed her one, flipped the Zippo, lit her up then lit mine. I inhaled deeply and noticed that she was holding the smoke down. I exhaled through my nose and smiled at her. She smiled back as she let it out.

"A bad habit," she said.

I said, "The rose in the mouth, the careful positioning of the body, the surgical precision of the knife in the heart... It all suggests grief to me. The emotional pain of lost love. It feels like a careful, almost ritualistic attempt to elicit love." I shrugged and shook my head, aware that I was out of my depth. "Anyway, it's all very precise and careful, and it's about love—a stab in the heart."

She nodded. "That's excellent. Very well observed."

"But then there's the abdomen, ripped out as though by a rabid beast. It would take immense strength to do that, and you'd have to be in some kind of frenzy."

She nodded. "Which is completely at odds with the positioning, the rose and the knife."

I nodded then shrugged again. "Am I right? This isn't exactly my field."

She got up and went to her desk to get an ashtray. She tapped ash into it as she walked back slowly. She said, "Yes, very probably. I'd need the forensics report and a day or two, but I could build up a profile for you, if you want."

"Yeah, that would be good. Is there anything you can tell me now?"

She squinted at me through her cigarette smoke. It was a strange gesture in an elderly woman with a cardigan and a string of pearls. "The true serial killer is never a woman. A woman can be a multiple murderer, Mr. Murdoch, but never a serial killer. And they are very rarely black. It isn't unheard of, but it's extremely rare."

"What's the difference between a serial killer and a multiple murderer?"

She flicked ash and nodded. "A murderer typically goes through three stages. He or she will first establish a relationship with the victim—usually a relationship of love, but not always. In time, that relationship will provide a motive for murder. It might be betrayal, jealousy, money...

Those are the most common. And that motive will provide the *desire* to kill. And the murderer will then act on that desire."

She took a deep drag, tipped her head back and held the smoke down, like she was smoking a joint. She was obvious about it, like she was flaunting something, but I didn't get what. I gave her my best lopsided grin and said, "Where were you in the summer of '68?"

She narrowed her eyes at me without lowering her head, still holding the smoke. Then she blew it all out in one stream and said, "Mostly in bed with Rick Wright. It was a good year. Better than '69. And by '70, it was all over, bar the shouting. But we were talking about serial killers.

"With the serial killer, the process is totally reversed. First, he feels the desire to kill. It starts as a fantasy and he knows it's a fantasy, but it begins to build, very much the way sexual frustration builds over time into an imperative need to have sex. But, with a serial killer, that desire — that need — is stronger still than the need for sex."

She held my eye, as though challenging me to be shocked. I was struck again by how incongruous she was. I kept my face blank and she went on.

"This desire to kill provides the motive for killing. Exactly the reverse of a normal killer, you see? And this motive drives the serial killer to find a random person — anyone, it doesn't matter who, but someone who fits his profile for a victim. It's different with each killer. And when he has found his victim, he will begin to stalk them — sometimes for a short while, sometimes for days — and he will establish a relationship with them. Then his hunger to kill becomes so powerful that he can no longer distinguish between reality and fantasy. The flood of dopamine and serotonin into his brain drives him into psychosis — and now he will kill." She paused, watching me. Then said, "The normal process runs backward."

I stared at her. "Are you telling me that a serial killer is not psychotic?"

She gave a small laugh. "Only in the immediate build-up to the kill and during the kill. Think of yourself in the build-up to an orgasm, Mr. Murdoch. It's like a fever, isn't it? You lose all sense of proportion. Behavior you would normally consider unthinkable suddenly becomes not only possible, but urgent, imperative...needed. The limits of reality begin to blur and you become capable of things you would normally only fantasize about. Aren't you a little psychotic then?"

We sat for a while, just looking at each other and smoking. My mind went back to Maria and to the bestial, crazed animal she'd brought out in me.

Finally, I asked, "So, if they're not crazy, what makes them want to kill?"

She laughed. It was like the screech of a parrot—a harsh, hard laugh, with her beady eyes watching me. It shocked me.

"Do you know what the autonomic system is, Mr. Murdoch?"

I crushed out my cigarette and said, "Sure, it's part of the nervous system."

"It's the part that deals with what we might call involuntary behavior. It is at the heart of our unconscious. At its most basic, it makes our organs work—our hearts beat, our intestines—"

"I get it."

"Apart from that, it imbues us with five basic drives. Do you know what they are?"

I shrugged. She was a Freudian, so I said, "The sex drive... Go ahead. Tell me."

"In order of irresistible compulsion..." She held up her hand and counted them out on her fingers. "To breathe, to piss and shit, to drink and eat, to fuck...to kill."

I stared at her. "If you are trying to shock me, Doctor..."

"I am not trying to shock you. I am making you aware of what you are dealing with. There is nothing insane or unnatural in the desire to kill. In the last century or two, we have suppressed that drive in the name of civilized society, but look at human history, for heaven's sake. When we are not killing animals for food or sport, we are killing other people so that they won't get their hands on *our* food...or land or gold or..." She trailed off.

After a moment, I nodded. "So, the drive to kill is naturally there, but—"

"Not but... *And. And* his social indoctrination is not strong enough to suppress it. *And* other factors in his life, like violent or cruel parents or siblings can fuel that drive, so he follows it, goes with it...and any number of other factors can play a part." She shrugged and shook her head. "I need to see the police report. Then I can give you a more precise profile. In the meantime, typically you would be looking for someone who seems inadequate, with low self-esteem, awkward among women, who had a difficult relationship with his mother...but until I see the report..."

* * * *

I sat with my ass against the hood of my TVR. The sky was heavy with gray clouds and the heat was relentless and unforgiving. I speed-dialed Pete.

"*Da...*"

"Pete, I need the forensics report on Eva."

"I heff..."

"I need two copies. I need one biked to me and the other to Professor Juliet Loss at the University of London."

"Who is—?"

"Fuck you. Don't ask questions, Pete. I haven't got time now. Just have them sent."

He muttered something in obscene Russian then hung up.

I walked to the nearest Nero's Coffee Shop, bought a paper on the way, ordered a double espresso then sat outside, listening to snatches of Ella and Sinatra through the door as it opened and closed.

Brussels was complaining to the British government that

the HEAT Corporation was in breach of a treaty agreement, whereby an EU company should have been awarded the contract to develop the software to run the Llyn Celyn reactor. Instead, it had gone to NanoSoft, an American company in San Jose. British Prime Minister, Thea Ledder, had hit back, saying that Brussels still hadn't assimilated the fact that Britain was no longer one of its states and would make its own sovereign decision about what was best for the British people. America got the contract because Silicon Valley made the best software, and Britain wanted the best. I vaguely remembered Russell saying, *'That will cause problems.'*

On the science page, buried between a biochip-pacemaker and a robot that used AI to dance the samba, there was a paragraph about how the IPCC had underestimated the rate of melt on Greenland…again, with possible crop failures in the Ukraine and the Midwest US as a result.

There was nothing about the murder of Eva Rusakov. That didn't surprise me. Publicity wouldn't help anyone at this point, except the odd girl who might decide not to walk home alone at night, but who gave a damn about her? Not Pete, and not 'the authorities'.

I dumped the paper on the table and fished out a Camel. I flipped the Zippo, thumbed the flint and lit up. I watched the street. The glare and the heat were already intense. I looked into my coffee. It was real black and, when I drank it, it was bitter. Two or one? Two killers or one killer? Two working together? One seeking to silence his mother's cruel heart, the other seeking to brutalize her, each getting off on the other's work? I didn't know. I couldn't know. I needed the forensics report.

I walked back through the molten heat, climbed into the Daemon then headed back through the mid-morning traffic toward Church Street as heavy drops of rain began to fall.

When I got there, there was a Harley parked outside my block on the meter. I felt a slow burn of anger in my belly and told myself to take it easy. I rode the elevator, trying to think about Dr. Juliet Loss, but knowing what I was going to find when I opened the door.

I could hear her laughter from the landing as I stepped out of the elevator. He was clearly a funny guy. Maybe I should be ashamed that I unlocked the door and slipped in silently, but ashamed isn't something I do real easy. They didn't hear me step into the drawing room. She was leaning back on the sofa, laughing with her eyes screwed shut. Steve the biker was sitting too close to her on the sofa. For a moment, I thought I recognized him, but I dismissed the thought. His knee was touching her thigh and he was telling some gas of a story that had her in stitches, leaning forward with his hands up like claws, pulling a face.

"Und zis guy is coming to me like a *monster*, und saying, *Stefan! Stefan*…und he is going to grab me like *so!*'

He was about to grab her, and, maybe if I'd been smart, I would have waited to see what happened next, but I didn't want him to grab her and maybe I didn't want to know what would have happened next.

So, I cut across him and said, "Am I interrupting?"

He jumped, but she just turned, looked at me and smiled.

Then she was on her feet, coming around the sofa to me. "Hi, honey!" She gave me a peck on the mouth. Any other time it would have felt normal. Right then it felt cold. "This is Steve. He dropped in to say hello."

He was on his feet, doing a weird dance with his knees, like he was trying to adjust himself into his pants. He had those chiseled features people from the Pacific often have and dark brown eyes, with lots of hair swept back. Women probably found him gorgeous. I guessed he was twenty, seven years younger than Maria.

I said, "Hello, Steve."

He was still dancing. Now he shrugged a couple of times, too, and said, "Yuh, hi… So. Maybe I should go."

I tried to hold his eye, but he was scanning everywhere.

I said, "Don't let me scare you away."

He looked straight at Maria, who was smiling at him. "So,

I see you again, yuh?"

I said, "You not going to see me again, Stephan?"

He shrugged a couple more times and said, "Yuh, sure," and to Maria, "You see me out." It wasn't a question.

She said, "Sure."

And they walked into the hall. He closed the door behind him and I heard their voices drop to a mutter. I stepped over and put my hand on the handle. I heard him, low, almost urgent, "I see you again, yuh?"

And Maria, "Sure."

"Just you and me...wizout..."

I counted four seconds of silence. Four seconds can be a hell of a long time. Then the fire in my belly got too hot and I pulled open the door. They weren't kissing, but he was leaning close to her and he had his hand on her arm. They both stared at me in silence, like I was interrupting. I held Steve's eye till he turned away. Then I looked at Maria.

I said, "There's a real bad smell. You mind if we keep this door open?"

Steve said, "I go!" He opened the door and left.

I watched her but she wouldn't meet my eye. She went to the sofa and dropped back into the place she'd been before. I went to sit on the windowsill and pulled out a cigarette.

I said, "You want to tell me what that was about?"

She seemed exasperated and spread her hands, her eyes dancing up, left, right. "About? It wasn't 'about' anything. He just popped in for a visit."

I was turning the cigarette over in my fingers. I examined it. It wasn't lit yet. I spoke to the cigarette, not looking at her. "How stupid do you think I am, Maria?" I raised my eyes and saw that she was watching me. "When I walked in, he was about to pounce on you."

"Oh, for God's sake!"

"Is this going to be a problem? Because we talked this through yesterday and I thought we'd resolved it. Then I come home today and I find you on the sofa with a guy who is about to jump on you. So, you tell me now, Maria.

Have we got a problem?"

She stared at me awhile, chewing her lip. Then she said, "He was not about to jump on me."

"How do you know?"

She screwed up her face. "*What?*"

I lit the Camel and exhaled the smoke. "How do you know he wasn't going to jump on you?" I pointed at the sofa. "You were lying back and you had your eyes closed." She flushed and I saw the muscle in her jaw begin to dance. I went on. "I walked in and you were lying back, laughing, with your eyes closed, and he was leaning over you, with his hands like claws, and he was saying, 'Und zis guy is coming to me like a *monster*, und saying, *Stefan! Stefan*… und he is going to grab me like *so!*'"

I saw her suppressing a smile at my imitation of his accent, but I didn't feel like smiling back.

She shrugged. "He's very funny…"

I kept my voice level. "If I hadn't spoken up in that moment, he would have jumped on you."

She sighed and rolled her eyes.

I said, "If he had, what would you have done?"

Now her eyes flashed at me. It was hard to read her expression. She might have been mad or she might have been worried. She stared at me but she didn't answer.

I said, "You need to think about it?"

She said, "Liam, stop it!"

"You are telling *me* to stop it?"

She drew breath. The doorbell rang before she could speak. I held her eye and, after a moment, I went and opened the door. There was a messenger with a crash helmet and a large manila envelope.

He said, "Liam Murdoch?"

"Yeah,"

"Sign, please."

I signed and took the envelope inside. Maria was watching me. I opened it. It was the forensic report. I dropped it on the table and turned to her. I felt angry but, above all, I felt

55

sad and a desolation like I was losing her and there was nothing I could do to stop it.

Finally, I said, "There are two things that destroy a relationship, Maria. The first is jealousy. The second is stupidly making your partner jealous. You need to decide if you are serious about us or if you're just here to play games."

Her cheeks flushed. She said, "And you need to ask me that?"

"Apparently, I do."

After a moment, she got up and left. I heard the front door close. It didn't slam. It just clicked, but it sounded final.

Chapter Five

I watched from the window. A twist of anxiety knotted my gut. I had a feeling there was a wave of madness overtaking us and I knew I had to do something to stop it. I took my phone from my pocket and hit her speed-dial. I watched her stop on the sidewalk below and pull out her phone. She looked at the screen a moment. Then there was the imperceptible movement of her thumb and the ringing stopped. I felt sick and watched her walk away, down the hill toward High Street Ken, till she was eventually swallowed up by the crowd.

There was nothing I could do. I wanted to run after her, grab her, shake her, hold her and kiss her, but it would be pointless. If she came back—*when* she came back—it would be because she wanted to, not because I'd made her.

I dropped into a chair at the table and stared at the forensics report. I had to focus on it. Maria had to get this out of her system. She had to make her choices, and I had to give her space to do that—whatever the outcome. Right now, I had to focus on Eva and her killer.

I spilled the papers onto the table and began to read. At first, the abstract had no surprises. Death was by exsanguination. There were numerous injuries to the body, including severe bruising to the neck, consistent with strangulation, also to the thorax and arms, consistent with having been beaten and thrown about. However, none of these injuries had proved fatal.

The heart had been penetrated by a large, Sabatier kitchen knife, but this had not caused the exsanguination. This wound had been inflicted postmortem. There was no internal bleeding from the knife wound. According to the report, the body had already been completely drained of blood before the stabbing. This was also true of the rose. The cuts made by the thorns had caused no bleeding, either.

The exsanguination had been the result of violent ripping out of the organs, including the intestines, from the victim's abdomen. Rip and tear marks on the skin, ribs and vertebrae suggested this had been done in three separate stages.

I turned to the paragraph that dealt with the bruising to her neck. The killer had been wearing gloves, but the size of the bruises suggested a male of average-to-low height, with powerful hands. Pressure seemed to be more or less equal in both hands.

The knife had little to reveal. There were obviously no prints. The knife was razor-sharp and had been driven in with minor force.

In the paragraph about the abdominal wounds, the examiner was so shocked by what she had seen that she had been moved to comment. In thirty years of practice, she had never seen anything remotely similar. She estimated there had been three massive blows of enormous strength. First from right to left, suggesting the killer might be right-handed. This first blow had partially disemboweled the victim, but was of such force that it had fractured two of the vertebra in her lower spine. The next blow had been from left to right. By now, the victim was on her back, certainly unconscious but possibly dead. The third attack was not so much a blow as a process of ripping, by which the abdominal cavity had been stripped virtually bare of organs and entrails.

She could only speculate about how this process of disemboweling had been performed. It may have been with a particularly savage weapon, designed to imitate claws — though, if that were the case, the man wielding it would have to be of enormous strength. In her opinion, the attack was consistent with a large, predatory animal. The ripping and tearing were most consistent with the claws and jaws of a Komodo dragon.

I rubbed my face, poured myself a Bushmills and lit up a Camel. Two killers — an average-to-small guy with his pet Komodo dragon.

I took my drink, my cigarette and the report over to the sofa. I stretched out and started reading through it again, absorbing the minute details. As I had assumed, Eva had not been killed at the park. She had been killed somewhere else and had been taken there to be positioned and found. Whatever they say on TV crime dramas, it is impossible to tell time of death from body temperature or anything else, but I knew she had last been seen at about half past eleven. Allow a minimum of half an hour to get the body to where it had been found and another half for her to get where she had been killed. Time of death had been between twelve and three.

I picked up my cell and dialed Dr. Juliet Loss. It rang for fifteen seconds then went to voice mail. I hung up and tried again with the same result. I took another slug of whiskey. The room was warm and my eyes were getting heavy. I forced myself to focus on the report, trying to read over the dialogue that was going around and around in my head, where I was explaining to Maria that we had a good thing that was worth fighting for.

An examination of Eva's clothes showed massive saturation with blood, which all seemed to be her own. This was consistent with having been suddenly and violently disemboweled. Nothing else of interest had shown up except some fibers on the back of her coat, which might have become attached when she had been hurled to the floor. These were reddish-purple woolen fibers. The wool was Turkish in origin and the dye was Tyrian purple, a rare dye that was a mucous extracted from the hypobranchial gland of a medium-sized predatory sea snail found in the eastern Mediterranean. This suggested she had been thrown down onto a Persian rug, probably an expensive one.

The Albert Hall. Knightsbridge. It was nighttime and Eva was getting off the bus. Knightsbridge was expensive. There were a lot of expensive apartments there that might have Persian rugs. I could see Eva walking, the million lights – the headlights, the street, the shop-window lights, the blaze of lights from the Harrods superstore – doing nothing but accentuating the night. She was small and vulnerable, walking beside a guy who carried the darkness with him and inside him – a nervous guy, a guy with shifting eyes and anxious hands. A guy who was terrified of his own blackened lust.

But it wasn't Eva. It was Maria, and I was struggling, wading through the crowd, trying to reach her, and the lights, instead of illuminating a path toward her, blinded my eyes until all I could see were coats – big, woolen coats – blocking my path, obstructing my way, making it hard to breathe. I began to hit out, punch and kick. It was what I had always done. It was the only way I knew. I grabbed at the coats – pulled, yanked, pushed – battling my way, trying to find her, knowing that with every second, she was more completely lost in the darkness.

Then I broke through. She was there, lying on the tarmac. A circle of people stood around her, staring. Staring, not at her, but at me. She was wearing a coat. A Sabatier knife protruded from her breast. Her eyes were closed and a breeze softly moved her black hair across her brow. She looked beautiful. Peaceful. Dead.

A great black and bloody hole gaped where her belly should have been.

I said, "That was her womb."

Then I saw it. A crocodile, or a Komodo dragon, straddling her, chewing at her belly, but watching me – the crowd and the dragon watching me. I could hear it grunting and breathing as it chewed.

It was the breathing that woke me. It was a matter of a fraction of a second. At first, I thought it was the breeze on my face. The same breeze that was moving the hair across Maria's brow – gentle, peaceful. Then I realized it was rhythmic, and there was a soft blowing, a grunting to it. I opened my eyes. It was still night. A faint, luminous square was the window, open. Traffic outside. A large bulk obscured the square. A grunt, a snuffle, breath on my face.

A knot of hot fear twisted my gut. A powerful sense that the black bulk was close. Another low grunt and breath brushed my face.

It was smelling me.

I scrambled backward and fell off the sofa in a heap. I was yelling. I could hear a wild, thrashing movement. I stumbled to my feet, bellowing like a madman and saw the black shape move swiftly across the luminous square of the window. My hand was already on the switch. It snapped on and the room was filled with light. There was nothing there. I could hear my own breathing, ragged in the silence. I moved quickly to the window and looked out. It was dark — one made more obscure and confusing by the moving headlamps and the diffuse streetlights. I thought I saw a shadow move along the façade of the building, but it could have been my imagination. I turned back and stared at the room. Nothing was overturned, nothing broken. Everything was normal. A dream. A night terror.

How long had I been asleep? I looked at my watch. It was gone ten. I'd been asleep five or six hours. I rubbed my face and ran my hands through my hair. Then I heard the key in the lock.

I stood frozen against the window as I heard the door close. Four seconds pulsed then the drawing room door opened. Maria stood in the doorway, one hand on the handle, looking at me. Her eyes were sad, regretful, but there was a smile there. I struggled to remember what had happened.

Finally, I said, "Where were you?"

She closed the door behind her and took two steps toward me. "I went to see a friend. Liam. I…"

"What friend?"

She sighed and closed her eyes. "Not Steve. Not a man. A woman friend."

"Who?"

"Liam, please, listen. That isn't important now. Will you listen to me?"

I watched her. I didn't say anything.

After a moment, she went on. "I'm sorry. You have been driving me *nuts*…but that doesn't excuse me behaving like a silly adolescent bitch, trying to make you jealous. Will you forgive me?" She took another step forward, then faltered. "Liam?"

I was scanning her skin, her hair, her eyes. My heart was still pounding. I said, "How long have you been here?"

She frowned and gestured at the door. "I just came in. Liam, are you okay?"

I shook my head. "I don't know. I had a nightmare. It was vivid. I thought there was somebody here."

Her bottom lip curled in and her eyes flooded with tears. Next, she was rushing to me, wrapping her arms around me, burying her face in my chest, sobbing out her words. "Liam! What's happening to us? Hold me. Tell me we're going to be okay."

I put my arms around her, kissing her head and smelling her hair, knowing it was her, feeling my terror at losing her dissolve with her tears. I took her face in my hands, kissing her mouth and her cheeks and the salt tears from her eyes.

I kept telling her over and over, "It's going to be okay, baby. Everything is going to be okay."

We kissed for a long time. Eventually, she pulled away, looking up at me. I kissed her eyes gently, one after the other, and stroked her hair, wet from her tears, away from her face.

She said, "I went to see a friend. You don't know her, Liam, but she's somebody I met recently. She's really kind and sweet and wise. I told her what was happening." She glanced away, out of the window—not seeing the street but her own thoughts? "She made me see that I was lying to myself. You were right. It was stupid. I was using Steve to claim your attention." She looked up into my eyes, smiling, then giggled. "I don't even like him. I think he's a pain in the ass."

We both laughed with relief.

I kissed her again and she said, "Make us a drink, will you? I could really use one. I'm just going for a pee." She made a little knock-kneed dance. "I'll be right back," and she disappeared into the bedroom, to the en-suite bathroom.

I rubbed my face and shook my head to try to clear it. I could use a drink myself. I went to the drinks tray and mixed her a Martini, extra dry, and poured myself a stiff Bushmills. I heard the toilet flush and a moment later the bedroom door open. I turned, a drink in each hand and she was coming toward me, smiling. I handed her the Martini. We held each other's eyes as we toasted and sipped.

She licked her lips. "Perfect. You make the best Martini in the world — after Noddy."

I smiled. "Thanks."

She placed her palm on my chest. "And, Liam, thanks for the lovely rose. Such a sweet thought."

I frowned. "What?"

"The rose, on my pillow. It's beautiful, though you might have taken the thorns off!"

My heart was pounding and I was shaking my head.

She was still talking. "I'm joking. It was such a sweet thing to do."

I said, "No, Maria."

"Especially after I've been such a dork —"

"No, listen —"

"Reds are my favorite."

I took hold of her shoulders. "Maria, honey, listen to me." She stopped, staring at me curiously.

"Maria, I didn't put a rose on your pillow." I watched her face drain to a pallid white.

"What do you mean?"

"It wasn't me. Somebody was here."

Chapter Six

My phone was ringing. Maria was staring at me. I was struggling to keep a grip on reality. Too many memories were flashing back. I forced myself to snap out of it and grabbed my cell.

"Murdoch!"

"This is Detective Inspector Grant of Scotland Yard's West London Murder Investigation Team, Mr. Murdoch. Detective Chief Inspector Morgan has asked me to call you."

I frowned. "What about?"

There was a moment's silence, then a sigh, as if he really didn't like saying what he was going to say. "He has asked me to liaise with you."

I took the phone away from my ear and stared at it, like I might be able to see his face in it. I put it back to my ear and said, "*Liaise* with me? What are you talking about?"

"That was my reaction exactly, sir. There has been another murder, with the same MO as Eva Rusakov's. I understand this is a courtesy we are extending to Mr. Rusakov. I have sent a car to pick you up, Mr. Murdoch."

I was silent a moment, struggling to gather my thoughts into some kind of rational sequence. Finally, I said, "Have your driver pick me up at Noddy's Diner on Portobello Road. It's at the top, on the corner of Oxford Gardens."

There was a little pause. Then he said, like it meant more than just the words, "I know where it is, Mr. Murdoch."

I hung up then turned to Maria. She was still staring at me, chewing her lip. She drew breath but I cut across her.

"Get your toothbrush, any essentials. You have two

minutes. We're going to Noddy's. *Now!*"

While she was getting her things, I went to my bedside table and pulled out my Smith & Wesson 29. The one Dirty Harry made famous. I slipped it in my waistband under my jacket then stood. Maria was watching me. She had a small toilet bag in her hand.

She said, "What's going on, Liam?"

"I don't know yet."

"Is it...?"

"I don't know. I want you safe for tonight. Tomorrow..." I hesitated. "Tomorrow, we'll see what we do."

I called Noddy as we stepped into the elevator. It rang a long while, but nobody answered. In the street the rain had settled into a dark drizzle that twisted the traffic lights into thin trickles of blood across the black tarmac. We climbed into the TVR and slammed the doors.

I handed Maria the phone. "Try him again."

We moved up Church Street and into Notting Hill Gate. The lights were red again, pulsing in the puddles on the blacktop to the rhythm of the rain. When they turned green, we surged forward and made a right at Ladbroke Grove. The cop shop was a black monolith on the corner. I hit the gas and we passed it with the needle touching seventy miles per hour.

Maria said, "There's no answer. Slow down."

The flyover and the railway bridge were like a black tunnel that yawned and swallowed us. I made a right at Cambridge Gardens, left into Portobello and skidded to a halt outside the diner. I could see the lights still on through the plate glass that was spilling amber light onto the wet pavement. There were a couple of customers at the bar and I could see Noddy, talking to them and laughing.

I said to Maria, "Come on."

I got out and crossed to her side as she opened the door. I scanned the street, squinting into the drizzle. I couldn't see anyone except a tramp huddled into his shoulders making his way toward the covered market.

I took hold of Maria and moved her toward the diner. "Let's go."

I pushed open the door to a warm smell of tobacco and damp coats. The sound of conversation and laughter muffled the wet sound of the rain as the door swung closed behind us.

Noddy glanced over and smiled. "Baht time you brought your bird in, you old sod. Awright, Maria, why don' he ever bring you dahrn here?"

Maria drew breath to answer but I cut across her. "Not now, Noddy. Can we talk?"

He could tell by my voice and the look on my face that I meant it. He gave a small frown. "Yeah, sure." He turned to the three guys at the bar who were regarding us curiously and he pointed a huge finger at them. "Watch the place, will ya? And no fahkin' free drinks! All right?"

There was some uneasy laughter. He led us into the kitchen he had at the back of the bar then turned. "What's this about, Liam? You look sick, man."

I reached in my waistband and pulled out the .44. I handed it to him. "It's loaded. I can't explain now. I have to go out for a few hours. I'm leaving Maria with you. Don't let her out of your sight. When you lock up, take her upstairs to your apartment. Keep her with you at all times. Don't sleep until I get back. You understand me? While she sleeps, you sit by her side. Anybody comes near her, you blow their head off."

He stared at me. "What the fuck, man?"

"Don't ask questions. Just do it, Noddy. I'll explain later. Do *not* let her out of your sight. Tell me you'll do it!"

He shook his head, shrugged and spread his hands, all at the same time. His mouth worked and finally he said, "Yeah, man. Okay."

That relieved me a little, so I kissed Maria then left.

I walked out of the diner and into the silver rain. It had stopped drizzling and was now coming down harder, with a damp hiss on the tarmac. I scoured the black mouths of the alleyways for anyone who might be watching or waiting for me to leave. I didn't see anybody. I felt sick with apprehension. Whoever it was, let them come for me, not for Maria.

I stayed in the doorway for maybe five minutes before the Jaguar J-Type pulled in from Cambridge Gardens.

The window slid down then a police officer called over to me, "Mr. Murdoch?"

I stepped over and told him I was as I climbed in the back.

The late-night traffic was sparse, and while we moved through the city, back toward Notting Hill Gate, the rain turned suddenly torrential, like the clouds had overflowed. The streets were pretty much empty, but occasionally a car would pass and its lamps would be like red and amber amoebas of light — swelling, contracting, swimming toward each other and consuming each other, then scattering among raindrops behind the relentless rhythm of the wipers.

We didn't turn down Church Street. We moved east along Bayswater. Up ahead, I saw the flashing red and blue lights of police cars, luminous yellow jackets, an ambulance, police tape. We pulled over at the first gate into Hyde Park.

The driver leaned back and said, "Detective Inspector Grant is in the park, sir. The constables will point you in the right direction."

I pulled up my collar, hunched into my shoulders then pushed through the confusion of cars and vans, flashing lights and milling cops in yellow jackets. The gate to the park had been cordoned off with yellow tape. A sergeant stopped me and I told him Grant had asked me to meet him there.

He summoned a constable. "Tell the inspector Mr. Murdoch is here, will you?"

He watched me as the constable disappeared into the dark, toward a group of arc lights that glimmered through the downpour.

After a moment, he said, "Should have brought a brolly, sir."

"Yeah. Story of my life."

The constable was trudging back through the mud. The sergeant lifted the tape for me.

The constable turned on his heel and said, "Follow me, sir."

Grant was younger than I'd expected, probably college educated and built like a brick khazi. He was wearing a black plastic raincoat that shone in wild, luminous rivers as he moved. He approached through the trees, frowning and reaching out his hand.

"You Murdoch?"

I said I was. We shook and started moving toward an improvised marquee strung with the arc lamps I'd seen earlier. As we drew nearer, I realized it was outside the kids' playground.

Grant said, "Mind me asking why I'm showing you my crime scene, Murdoch?"

I wiped the rain from my face and said, "I don't mind you asking, Grant, but if you want an answer, you should ask DCI Morgan. He's the one getting leaned on from on high."

He pulled the flap of the marquee aside and I ducked in. I was soaked to the skin, but it was good to be out of the rain. That was, until I saw her.

Grant came in after me and stood by my side. We both stared at what was left of a young black girl. She was maybe twenty, a little taller than Eva. She was lying on her back, with her arms and legs symmetrical, like Eva's had been. Her eyes were open and, when she'd been alive, she had been pretty. She had been well-dressed. She had a red rose in her mouth and a Sabatier knife in her heart. Her abdomen had been ripped out, like Eva's. But in this case, the ferocity had been such that her spine had been severed, and she was cut in two.

Grant said, "We've been ordered to assist you in every way we can. The body hasn't been touched. So far, all we've done is preserve the scene and take photographs."

I said, "Who is she?"

"According to her student card, she is Sally Brown, twenty-two years old, of 78B Highlever Road, W3."

For a moment, the name sounded familiar, but it was a common name. I dismissed it and said, "Student? Psychology?"

He frowned, surprised. "Yes, first year."

I nodded. "UCL or Birkbeck?"

He stared. I could tell from his face that I had gone to number one on his suspect list. He said, "Part-time at Birkbeck."

I sank down to look at the rose.

He said, "Feel like sharing?"

"It was a lucky guess. The other victim was a psychology student at UCL."

He didn't believe me. His eyes told me that. He persisted, "How did you know it was Birkbeck?"

I shrugged. "Most first-years are eighteen. She's twenty. She's well-dressed, her clothes aren't cheap. Suggests she's working as well as studying. Birkbeck is the extramural college of UCL." I pointed at the rose. "There are a couple of differences between this victim and the last. There's something on the stem of the rose."

He pulled on some latex gloves and crouched opposite me, with Sally Brown's dead head between us. He gently eased her lips apart and took out the rose. There was a roll of paper wrapped around it. He unrolled the paper and studied it for a moment.

Then he read, "To silence the mocking mouth, to still the arrogant heart, to rip out and steal excitement, hope and regeneration." He raised his eyes to meet mine. "Does this mean anything to you?"

I shook my head and got to my feet. "Not a thing…" I stared at her a moment longer. Sally Brown. Why was the name familiar?

Grant broke into my thoughts. "Do you know her?"

I shook my head again. "I knew the first victim."

He was peeling off his gloves. "I know. I know who you

are, Mr. Murdoch. I did some background reading."

"Be prepared, huh? Were you a Boy Scout?"

"You're an associate of the first victim's father, Peter Rusakov, otherwise known as Russian Pete."

"'Associate' is putting it a little strong. I know him."

"But you don't know this victim?"

"No."

"Know anyone called Brown, Mr. Murdoch?"

I scowled at him. The name was familiar, but I couldn't think…

He went on, watching me. "Where do you like to do a bit of R & R, Mr. Murdoch? Where do you like to unwind?"

"Noddy's Diner —" The blood drained from my face and I felt a hot twist of fear in my belly. I stared at Grant. "Edward Brown, Noddy's real name, and his sister's daughter was Sally."

Grant stepped up real close to me. "So, it seems the victims have two things in common, Mr. Murdoch. They both studied psychology at UCL, and both of them were known to you."

I nodded. He was right. I could see Russell staring at me with his huge black sunglasses. '*If I wanted you, Liam Murdoch, to investigate a murder…of all the people you know, whom would I kill?*' I said, "You're right. Thanks for the hospitality."

I was about to ask for a lift back to Noddy's when my cell rang.

"Murdoch…"

"Mr. Murdoch, it's Juliet Loss."

"Dr. Loss…"

I saw Grant glance at me.

She was saying, "I've seen your missed call and I've read the report. We need to talk. Soon. Can you make it now?"

"I'll come right over. Where are you?"

"I'm at home."

"Where's home?"

Grant was watching me like a cat watching a mouse hole.

Loss paused, then said, "Colville Gardens, number twenty-six. It's in Notting Hill Gate."

"I know where it is. I'll be there in ten minutes."

As I was turning to go, Grant said, "Need a lift?"

I let the smile crawl up the left side of my face. That's the side I use for irony. "I'm good. Thanks. You got an umbrella?"

He didn't.

* * * *

Twelve minutes later, I pushed through the gate into Juliet Loss' front garden. A flagged path led through rose bushes and cypress trees to a broad flight of stairs up to a big, cobalt blue door. Warm light spilled from a bay window into the garden, making the black silhouettes of the trees even blacker in the rain. She'd left the porch light on. Somewhere, water was spilling from a roof or some guttering. The spattering noise somehow made the dull light of the porch look desolate. I climbed the stairs, wiping water from my eyes, then rang the bell.

When she opened the door, she gave a small gasp. "Good Lord, Mr. Murdoch! What have you been doing? Did you walk? Come in, for goodness sake, and get out of those wet clothes. You'll catch your death," she spoke, stepping backward, pulling the door open onto a broad, well-lit hall.

I went in, saying, "Yeah, I walked. I'm going to soak your carpet."

"From Church Street? Never mind that. Take your shoes off and come dry yourself in the bathroom. I'll get you some of my husband's clothes." She was climbing the stairs, speaking over her shoulder as I followed her. "You don't mind that he's dead, do you?"

I glanced at her. She was smiling with what you could only describe as a twinkle in her eye.

I gave her my right-hand lopsided smile and said, "You're still trying to shock me."

We'd reached the landing and she propelled me into a large bathroom. It was IKEA-land, only expensive. A stripped pine set of shelves was piled high with fluffy towels. I dried myself off and, after a couple of minutes, she handed in a pair of jeans, a sweatshirt and a pair of socks. They fit, and two minutes later I joined her in the drawing room. It was what you'd expect, understated, very expensive elegance—old world, new technology. Lots of books and original paintings, two big armchairs and a sofa the size of the battleship Tirpitz. It wasn't cold, but she had a fire going in the grate. She was sitting on the giant sofa and smiled up at me as I came in.

"Before you sit down, why don't you help us to a whiskey each?" She glanced at a tray of decanters on a bookcase and I moved over to it. She added, "Be generous," and something in her voice made me look at her. She was gazing into the flames and seemed drawn.

I handed her a generous tumbler and she took it without saying anything. I sat in a chair opposite her and sipped while I waited for her to speak. I realized I was exhausted. The glowing warmth of the fire and the whiskey were making me drowsy. I wished she'd say something.

Finally, when she spoke, she seemed to be speaking to the hot coals and the wavering flames. "The man you are looking for, Mr. Murdoch, is small, maybe five foot four or five. He is not physically very strong. He is timid and self-effacing, with very low self-esteem. He has above-average intelligence, but his low self-esteem does not allow him to put it to any creative or productive use because he is certain he will be ridiculed and put down by people who believe themselves better than him."

She sighed and sipped, licked her lips then took a moment to think. "He was probably mentally tortured by his mother. He probably endured a childhood of constant criticism, humiliation and put-downs. His response was to withdraw into a world of fantasy. In his fantasy world, he is a genius. He overrates his own intelligence. Here is a profound paradox. He has no confidence in himself, but he has infinite faith in himself. He hates himself, and yet he is a profound narcissist.

"His mother instilled in him what Freud called a 'cruel and punishing superego'. This is the immortal ghost of his mother, haunting his psyche, eternally attacking and humiliating him. And as his self-loathing builds to a crescendo, so he flees into his fantasy world, where he is supreme. He detests authority, because authority represents his mother, and so he defies and humiliates the police by showing them up as stupid and incompetent, and, at the same time, he destroys his mother by killing women."

Now she turned to me. "And here he creates a ritual. You know we all have a reptilian brain within our human one. Reptiles are very ritualistic, like birds. In his ritual, he unconsciously tries to exorcize the ghost of that woman. He places a rose in her mouth to turn the thorns of her words into delicate petals — the symbol of love. You may even find his mother's name is Rose. He places a kitchen knife in her heart, to cut through her dishonesty and lies — the betrayed promise of motherhood — and find the essential, true 'Mother', with a capital M. The womb is about the egg — the kitchen, the warm smell of baking, the offering of food as love. And, finally, he rips out her womb, to attempt — unconsciously — to stop her recreating herself as a monster and so stop recreating *him* as an emotionally crippled, worthless, loathsome lizard he sees himself to be."

She stood up and walked to a low dresser. She pulled open a drawer and got out a pack of Camel cigarettes. She peeled it, pulled out two and offered me one. I took it and we lit up. She sat, blowing smoke at the chimney.

"But that is just the superficial analysis. There were aspects that troubled me. The first was the incongruence that you pointed out, of the attack on the womb and the knife and the rose. Not only did it suggest two distinct personalities — which could be explained by a multiple personality disorder — but the physical strength needed to tear out her abdomen.

"The other was the more subtle point made by Professor Whittering—your friend Russell. It is an extraordinary coincidence that this killer should have chosen, out of millions of possible victims, Eva Rusakov. This suggested two things to me." She was silent then, staring into the fire, as though wrestling with some inner conflict.

I said, "I'm listening, Dr. Loss."

"It suggested, first of all, that he may have been in contact with Eva."

I said, "The kid on the bus..."

She nodded. "He may be associated somehow with the university and he may have selected his victim from the students. This would fit his profile of attacking people he believes to be superior intellectually in order to prove his own superiority—the reality of his fantasy." She hesitated. "If this is so, then we can expect him to attack more students—more female students."

I went to speak but stopped myself.

"The other thing is that the girls may not be his intended target. He may be attacking somebody else through them."

"What do you mean?"

"That attack on the womb suggests an Oedipal element. That would mean that deep, very deep in his unconscious, he is trying to kill not his mother, but his father. So, his actual focus may be a man—a man he hasn't the courage to confront, a man he considers somehow superior to himself. He attacks these women because he sees them in some way as the man's weakness. Trying to hurt the man through the women." Now she turned and stared at me, squinting through the smoke as she sucked on her cigarette. "And that man might—*might*—be you."

I shook my head. "That's nuts. I don't even know this guy."

"But he might know you. Serial killers are stalkers, Mr. Murdoch. He may have come across you in any of a million ways and became fixated, obsessed."

"So, he would have known that I knew Eva—"

"And killed her to draw you into a battle, but a battle in his world, where he can punish you."

I tried to grasp what she was saying. It sounded like bullshit to me. "Punish me? For what?"

She sighed. "Try to understand, Liam…" She hesitated. "Try to understand, it isn't *you* he is punishing. In his obsessive fantasy world, for some reason that does not need to make logical sense, he has chosen you to represent his father. The person he is punishing is his father."

I sat, allowing my mind to assimilate what she was saying. Finally, I said, "So this guy would have a cruel, bitching mother and an abusive father."

She nodded. "And in all probability, his mother fawned over the father, even though he was cruel and abusive to both of them."

I could see it. I had seen it, a thousand times as a kid. And she was right. Boys raised in that kind of family came out badly damaged.

How could you make it out any other way?

My eyes were heavy. I suddenly felt drained. My cigarette was down to the filter. I sat forward and flicked it into the fire. I said, "There was another killing tonight."

She didn't look shocked. She looked sad. "Where?"

"Hyde Park."

She nodded. "A student?"

"Birkbeck. A first-year psychology student."

She closed her eyes. "Oh, no."

"I guess this is one time where it sucks to be right. But there's more. She was the niece of a close friend of mine."

She opened her eyes. Her face was expressionless. Her eyes seemed gray and dead. She said, "You *are* the intended target."

I thought of Noddy and Maria back at his place on the Portobello Road. How did this punk know so much about me? It didn't make sense. And yet, my gut told me it did. I said to her, "What about the strength needed to disembowel these girls? He split this last one in half, for Christ's sake!"

She turned away, glanced at her bookcase then down at the floor. "It isn't impossible. We can't go into it tonight. It's too late and we both need to rest. But there is research, building on the work of Bandler and Grinder and others, Pribram and Bohm, that suggests that the brain can, when in a particular kind of trance state, cause profound physiological changes in the body. There are reliable cases documented of mothers performing extraordinary feats of strength to save their children." She stared down into her glass. "A mother driven by love, a son driven by hate… They are not so far apart."

I stood. "I have to get back."

She stood, too, and came close to me. "Do you want to stay? The weather is awful."

I searched her face for some hidden meaning. I didn't find it, but neither could I say it wasn't there. I said, "No, thanks. I need to get back." I checked my watch. It was two a.m. "It's late."

"Is there somebody waiting for you? Somebody you care for?"

"Yeah."

She closed her eyes a moment. "Take good care of her, Liam…until this is over. You understand?"

I nodded. I understood.

Chapter Seven

She called me a cab and lent me an umbrella. Fifteen minutes later, I was climbing out of the cab outside Noddy's Diner. It was closed and all the windows were dark. I heard the hybrid whine of the cab and watched its red taillights disappear around the corner into Oxford Gardens. Then the street was silent except for the wet splash of the rain falling from the guttering.

I went to the door and leaned on the bell. I stepped back and looked up at the windows. No lights showed there. I leaned on the bell again and hammered on the door. The silence inside the house was a black, physical substance.

One of the bad habits I've picked up over the years — and one which I'll never try to shake — is always carrying a pack of lock picks in my pocket. Picking locks is a skill I have worked hard to perfect over the years, and I am not about to let it go rusty. In thirty seconds I was inside and closing the door behind me.

Apart from the pale streetlight that filtered through the plate-glass windows, it was dark, and the silence was absolute. I moved through the bar to the kitchen at the back. Like the rest of the place, it was still and silent, populated by immobile black hulks. The flight of stairs up to his apartment was a patch of deeper blackness in the pitch. I pulled my pen torch from my inside pocket and switched it on. The thin beam pieced the stairwell, picking out small patches of orange carpet and sage-green wall, making the darkness darker by contrast. I began to climb.

I reached the first-floor landing. The small circle of light from my torch told me it was a chub with a handle. I tried it and found it was unlocked. I stepped in, closed the door and listened. There was nothing — no snoring, no breathing, nothing. I flipped on the lights and went from room to room. The beds hadn't been slept in. The kitchen was clean. There were no used ashtrays. They hadn't even been here. They'd left directly from the bar.

I sat and scrolled through my calls and found the one from Grant. It rang twice and he answered. I said, "This is Murdoch. Is Edward Brown with you?"

There was a pause. He didn't like my tone. *Fuck him.*

He said, "Yes."

"Is Maria Vazquez with him?"

Another pause. "Would that be your partner, Mr. Murdoch?"

"She wouldn't *be*, she is. Is she there or not?"

"She's here."

"And where is *here*?"

"Ladbroke Grove police station."

I hung up. I felt sour. I'd wanted to tell him myself, but the cops had gotten there first. I thought about Maria. She couldn't be much safer unless she was in an army barracks, but it didn't feel that way. I stared at the dull silver and amber raindrops crawling down the black glass. The threat was faceless, invisible and seemed to be present everywhere.

The rain had eased to a heavy, warm drizzle again. I climbed in the Daemon and drove to the Ladbroke Grove cop shop. It was half past two. The desk sergeant showed me to a waiting room. Noddy was there with his sister-in-law and his two nephews. They were all sobbing and holding each other. He glanced at me with swollen eyes but turned away without saying anything. Maria was by his side, a little apart. She got up and came over when she saw me. She put her arms around me and we stood like that for a while, holding each other.

After a while, she looked up into my face. "What's going on, Liam?"

I shook my head. "I don't know yet."

Then Noddy was there, behind her. His eyes were bloodshot. His lip was trembling. I could see his family on the bench behind him, huddled together, their backs turned toward me. Noddy's eyes were resentful.

He said, "Is this because of you, Liam? Is this because of all the shit you get up to? Have you brought this down on my family?"

I had no answer. In the end, all I could say was, "I don't know, Noddy."

He screwed up his face. There was rage, hatred, betrayal. He said, "Go away, Liam. Go away and don't come near me or my family again. Just go." And he turned and went back to his sister-in-law and her remaining kids.

Maria was searching my face, clinging closely to me. "Don't cut me out, Liam. What's this about?"

"I don't know yet, baby. Let's get out of here. I need to think. But, first, I need to see Grant."

I found him in the incident room on the third floor. There were a couple of exhausted cops in shirtsleeves going through papers with tired eyes, drinking what was likely cold coffee from polystyrene cups. Grant was sitting with his ass against a desk, staring at a whiteboard. He saw me come in and watched me approach without moving. Maria moved past me and stood examining the board.

Grant said, "Murdoch. What can I do for you?"

"There are two things you need to know, Grant."

"Just two?"

"First off, Dr. Juliet Loss of UCL —"

"I know of her."

"She is profiling the killer. You should talk to her."

"Thanks. And the other thing?"

"I'm the target."

He raised an eyebrow you could describe as ironic and said, "Oh? Not these girls he's murdering, but you? They are incidental, are they? Perhaps you'd like to explain that to Mrs. Brown out there."

"That's not what I meant and you know it."

He stood and faced me, real close. "I'll tell you what I do know, Mr. Murdoch, without having to talk to Dr. Loss. I know that serial killers often suffer from a form of narcissism which makes them feel they are the center of the universe, and everything revolves around them."

I rubbed my face with my hands and looked into his eyes. Maria had turned and was staring at me.

"Grant, if you want to arrest me for being a narcissist, go ahead. Meantime, the victims have just two things in common. They were both studying psychology at UCL, and they are both connected to me through someone I know."

"I'm very aware of that."

"The killer is trying to get my attention."

"He's certainly got mine. Can you account for your whereabouts at the time of these murders, Mr. Murdoch?"

I stared at him. "When Eva was killed, I was asleep in bed. When Sally was killed, I was alone at home."

He turned to Maria. "While you were signing up for a course in psychology, Ms. Vazquez, at the University of London's Birkbeck College."

She looked at him without answering.

He turned back to me. "Isn't that what they call 'synchronicity', Mr. Murdoch? I say synchronicity, because I don't believe in coincidences."

I shifted my eyes from him to Maria. She was watching me with no expression at all. Then I glanced at the board with the photographs of the murders — the victims, intended to lure me, to draw me, toward…what?

I said, "Neither do I, Grant." I turned back to him. "Talk to Loss. Believe me. If I had done this, I'd have had alibis you couldn't break with a tire iron."

He nodded. "Okay. But don't leave town."

"I won't. I'm going to catch this son of a bitch. My advice is, you catch him before I do."

* * * *

I sat in the car, looking out at the desolate street, with its ineffectual spasms of light where the dying drizzle hit the road in sporadic drips. I offered Maria a cigarette. She shook her head. I lit up and, for a moment, the inside of the Daemon was filled with a dull orange light. I inhaled and tried to gather my thoughts into a meaningful shape. There were too many black gaps where nothing made any sense.

I said, "How long have you known Steve?"

She turned to me and said, "Again? *Now?*" She was mad.

"No. Just answer me, Maria, without flying off the handle, would you? I'm trying to make sense of all this."

She turned away. "Believe it or not, I told you the truth. I met him the day he brought me home on the bike."

"Who else was there?"

She spread her hands. "There were lots of people, Liam. I can't remember all of them."

I watched her face a moment, turned away from me, peering out at the tired drops. "Make an effort, baby. This guy has killed two people close to me. He's been in our apartment..." She faced me and she looked drawn and scared. I went on, "Two gets you twenty that you've been in his company without realizing it."

"Nobody stood out. What does a serial killer look like, Liam?"

It was rhetorical, but I said, "Well, this guy would be small—maybe five-three or four, timid, quiet. He wouldn't have mixed in much, but he would have been in the background, watching—maybe watching you, but you didn't notice."

She rubbed her forehead with her fingertips. "It doesn't sound like anyone there. Liam, I need to sleep. I'm exhausted."

I sighed. "Okay, we'll go to a hotel. We can talk in the morning."

We went to a small guest house I knew in north London. She stared out of the window all the way with her face turned away from me. And when we got to the room, she went to bed without saying anything, and, in five minutes, she was asleep. While she slept, I sat watching the sky turn gray and thinking of Russell and Hook—and Seraphino del Roble and the Brotherhood of the Goat.

* * * *

In the morning, over coffee in the breakfast room, I said to her, "I want you to stay away from UCL and Birkbeck till this is over, Maria. I want to take you down to Russell's."

She didn't answer for a moment, buttering her toast. Then she said, "It's not enough with Eva and Sally? You want to put his life at risk, too?"

I had my cup halfway to my mouth, but I stopped and put it down again. I said, "Maria, if Russell hadn't put *my* life at risk, the Brotherhood would have killed you back at the Abbey of Thelema."

She didn't meet my eyes but she said, "Maybe if you hadn't gone there, my life wouldn't have been at risk in the first place."

"You know that isn't true. Colonel Fermin was out for you because you turned him down. One way or another—"

"I know!" She threw her toast down on her plate and turned away. She shook her head. "But, Liam, everywhere you go! Everything you do! There's trouble, violence, killing..."

"We back here again, Maria? This is the third time. What are you telling me?"

She closed her eyes. "I'm not telling you anything, Liam. I'm sorry."

"I didn't start the war in Spain, baby, but I did get you the safe passage out. Remember?"

"I said I'm sorry."

"Russell has friends who can take care of you. It's just for a few days. Can I rely on you not to—?"

Now she met my eye and smiled in a way you might describe as rueful. "Go off half-cocked?"

I nodded.

"Yes, Liam, you can. She reached across the table and took my hand. "I'm sorry. I am. I've been unfair. But this really —"

I interrupted her. "It really has to be the end of it. I know."

We ate in silence for a bit, but I could feel that the tension had eased.

Suddenly, she said, "I was thinking about what you asked me in the car."

I looked up. "Yeah?"

She hesitated. "It's probably nothing and I don't want to cause anyone trouble."

"What is it?"

"There *was* a young fellow there, but he wasn't part of the group. I don't know who he was and he didn't come to the pub with us. He just sort of wandered in a couple of times. He brought some chairs" — she shrugged — "went to get some markers for the whiteboard…"

"Like a janitor?"

"I don't know. He might have been a student."

I scratched my head. "You were in a class?"

"No, it was a presentation, introducing a new course."

"And he was there helping out?"

"As I say, he brought in a few chairs at the beginning, then he went to get some markers. That was it."

"What did he look like?"

"He was short — about five four, five five — dark hair, rather prominent nose and thick lips. He might have been Mediterranean. Small hands and feet, shabby… He appeared as though he didn't wash too often. A bit spotty, like with acne."

"Did you notice him looking at you, watching you?"

"No, but I wasn't really paying attention. And he was the sort of person you don't really notice, anyway."

I got it. He was the kind of guy who went out of his way not to be noticed. I screwed up my napkin and dropped it on the plate. "Come on. Let's go. I'll take you down to

Russell."

I went to stand, but she didn't move.

She said, "What are you going to do?"

"I'm going to see if I can find out who this kid is. It may be nothing, but we won't know till I check it out. Let's go."

I went to stand again, but she was shaking her head.

"No, Liam. I'm sorry."

"You're sorry? About what?"

"I'm not going to Russell's. I'm staying here, in London."

"Maria, this is not the time. This is not about your independence. It's about—"

"I know what it's about. I'm not leaving you. We have to do this. Okay, fine. We have no choice. So, I'm going to stick by your side. We're a team, a couple, a pair. Maybe you'd forgotten that, or maybe you hadn't realized it till now, but I'm with you, and I'm going to help you. No argument."

I didn't like it, but I knew she meant it. I called Russell and asked him for the loan of a small apartment he had on Mulberry Crescent in St. John's Wood. I had a set of keys and it was understood I could use it if I ever needed to keep a low profile. Right now, I needed to keep a low profile.

Chapter Eight

Five minutes on the phone to the admin department had got Maria the address of 'that nice young man who was helping out at the presentation.' That's because she's a girl—and charming. If it had been me, they would have sent me packing. His name was Anthony Cavra, which made me smile. He lived in a small basement apartment in a 1930s-purpose-built block of flats in Knightsbridge, five minutes from Harrods and just ten from the Albert Hall. The deal was that he changed the light bulbs and unblocked the sinks, and he got to live there rent-free.

The lobby was juniper green with plenty of art deco stucco and mahogany. There were a couple of heavy coffee tables with chairs and two-seater sofas and some lamps that might have been Clarice Cliff or good imitations. The elevator looked original.

But access to Anthony's apartment was not via the elevator. It was through a mahogany door and down a flight of unlighted steps. There was a bare bulb, but the sooty smudge on it told me this was one bulb he had not changed. At the bottom of the stairs, there was another door with a dirty brass plaque that read Boiler, Janitor, in that order. I guess the boiler was more expensive to replace. I knocked.

I could hear somebody moving about inside, but I had to knock three times before he opened the door. He was how Maria had described him, only she hadn't mentioned the cold, secret arrogance in his eyes. The apartment was dark behind him and he watched me from that darkness, holding on to the door with both hands.

He didn't say anything, so I asked him, "Are you Anthony Cavra?"

He watched me a little longer then said, "Why?"

"Because, if you are, I have a message for you."

"Who from?"

I smiled sweetly. "Well, if you're not Anthony Cavra, that's none of your business, is it?"

His eyes shifted away from my face and seemed to scan the floor, like there might be the answer to some existential conundrum down there. Then he said simply, "I am."

"Good."

We stood watching each other a while.

Finally, I said, "Can I come in?"

Now he turned his attention to the door frame, examining it in depth. He said, "Who is the message from?"

I said, "Maria Vazques."

His eyes slowed right down and shifted slightly, so he could probably see me in his peripheral vision. "She sent you with a message for me?"

"Can I come in?"

He thought about it a long time. He didn't like it, but the lure of the message from Maria was too strong. He stepped back and let me in.

There were no windows, and what light there was came from a dull, overhead bulb in a plastic shade. There was a TV and a threadbare sofa in what might once have been beige. There was a steel and Formica table in mottled green, with four chairs. I wondered who sat on the other three. He walked quickly to the table and sat, holding his hands in front of him, like he was protecting his crotch. He stared at the floor to the right of his feet. I pulled out a chair and sat facing him.

I said, "So, you like Maria Vazques, huh?"

He glanced at the tabletop just in front of me. "She's pretty."

I smiled. Two guys shootin' the breeze. "When did you meet her?"

Now he looked up at my face and his eyes were hard as steel pellets. "What's her message? Why did she send *you* with it?"

I shrugged. "It's just the way it played out, Anthony. She wanted me to come and talk to you."

His eyes narrowed. "What's the message?"

I leaned forward with my elbows on the table. "She wants to know if you and Eva were good friends. You did know Eva, right?"

Now his eyes went wild. It was like all hell was breaking loose around him, but only he could see it because it was happening in his brain. His body went rigid and his eyes looked crazy. He turned and stared at the wall, like he was expecting something to happen over there. Then he stared at the other wall, then down at his hands. His breathing was rapid and shallow and he was chewing his lip.

I said, "Hey, take it easy, Anthony. We're just two guys talking. She was cute. I knew her, too. You did know her, right?"

He swallowed three times, then said, "Yes."

"When did you last see her?"

Now he stared into my face. "Are you a policeman?"

I smiled. "Why would you ask that, Anthony?"

A secret smile flickered for a moment on his face. "You're not a policeman."

"When did you see her? Was it on the bus? The conductor said he saw you with her."

The smile came back, stronger. It wasn't a nice sight. "That greasy Italian."

"He talked to her, right?"

"He wouldn't shut up."

"He told me he liked her."

"He wouldn't leave us alone, but she thought he was disgusting."

"Is that why she got off the bus with you?"

He still had his hands in his lap. Now he bent his head like he was going to curl up like a woodlouse and watched his fingers playing with each other. He was going inside, where he was safe.

I said again, "Is that why you got off together?"

"She liked me. She liked talking."

"You miss her."

He was talking to his hands, like I wasn't there. "I don't need to talk to you."

"Who do you talk to, Anthony?"

Now he raised his eyes to meet mine, and there was that same cold, hard arrogance and a smile that was a sneer to give it life. "I have friends. Morons like you haven't the first idea of friendship. I have real friends."

It flashed into my head. His own arrogance made him mad, and, when he was mad, he talked.

I chuckled and said, "Yeah, right...friends." I held up my hands. "Hey, I'm not judging. Each to his own. But me? I never pay for it. Was that where you were that night? With one of your" — I made an inverted commas sign with my fingers — "'friends'?"

He froze and by degrees he looked back down at his hands in his lap.

I scanned the room and gave another laugh. "I mean no offense, Anthony, but Eva was a classy chick, and you're not exactly a Rockefeller, are you? So how come you got off the bus together that night?"

He finally answered, "She is one of my special friends. I have special friends..." His voice sounded strangled.

I felt sorry for the poor bastard, and I was trying not to think of what Pete would do to him, but I said, "Tell me you didn't bring her here. Where would you take a classy chick like Eva? You got somewhere else?"

This time all hell did break loose. He didn't so much scream as roar. He rammed the table into my chest with such force that it winded me and threw me on my back. I was gasping and trying to sit up. He was moving with incredible speed. His chair had gone careening across the room, but he had another one over his head and he was rushing at me. His face twisted with rage. I rolled as the chair smashed against the floor. It must have jarred him, but he didn't show it. I scrambled to my feet and, in one movement, he had hurled the chair at me. It struck my shoulder and I must have shouted with pain.

Then he was rushing at me again. I had no time to catch my balance. I struck out with my foot and caught his thigh with a glancing kick. He didn't even seem to notice. I lost my balance and went sprawling. He was kicking and stamping at me and all I could do was try to fend off the blows and kick back at him. I scrambled away on my back. He was still screaming, chasing me, kicking with his heel. Then I was up against the chair he'd thrown. We both reached for it at the same time. We fumbled and struggled, and he was making a strange, keening sound. I let him have it and, as he went for it, I got on one knee, steadied myself and rammed my fist into his crotch in an upper cut that would have felled a gorilla. Again, he didn't even seem to notice.

He bellowed, lifted the chair over his head then brought it crashing down on me. I just had time to cover my head with my arms, but pain seared through my back and shoulders. I hollered some profanity with the pain as he raised the chair for a second blow. I knew I wouldn't survive it so I put every ounce of energy I had into a savage punch to the side of his kneecap. It didn't knock him down, but it made him pause for a crucial second. Then I was on my feet. I grabbed the chair with both hands and landed a massive kick into his belly. He let go of it and fell back over the sofa.

Too late, I realized I'd knocked him into the kitchenette. He scrambled to his feet, wrenched open the kitchen drawer and pulled out a large knife. I still had the chair. I held it out in front of me to ward him off. But with an agility I'd not expected, he vaulted the sofa, yanked open the door and was gone up the stairs. I made after him, but every muscle in my body was bruised and knotted with pain, and by the time I'd made it to the stairs, he was gone.

I staggered back into the apartment and sank onto the

only chair that was left standing. I needed to think, but my body was doing all my thinking for me. It was thinking that it hurt—everywhere. The kid's strength was unbelievable, as Juliet had suggested.

I surveyed the apartment. It was one room with a kitchenette and a bathroom. The sofa was a sofa-bed. The floor was wall-to-wall threadbare carpet. I got on my knees and looked at the tacks that kept it down. They were old. I pushed the sofa back and found the indentations from the feet. That sofa had been there a long time. Wherever Eva and Sally had been killed, it hadn't been here. The sofa and the carpet would have been saturated with blood. He'd have had to replace both and scrubbed the walls and probably even the ceiling.

And it was when I'd asked him where he'd taken her that he'd gone crazy. I'd touched a nerve. But what nerve?

I searched the apartment from top to bottom on the off chance I might find some clue, but there was nothing. So I closed up, climbed the stairs and made my way, aching, back to the Daemon. I got behind the wheel, slammed the door and dialed Juliet Loss. When she answered, I said, "Tell me about Anthony Cavra, Dr. Loss."

There was a long silence. Finally, she said, "I'm sorry. I can't."

"Is that patient confidentiality, Doc?"

"I shouldn't even tell you that, but, as it's obvious, yes."

"Two women are dead and a third one is at risk. That third one happens to be my girlfriend. If he goes after her—"

"Liam, stop. You can't bully me on this, so don't even try. Tell me what's happened."

I filled her in and when I'd finished, I said, "I need to know where he would go and where he would have taken Eva and Sally."

"You think he has a lair somewhere, Liam?"

Her voice had surprised me. She sounded sarcastic. I frowned, even though she couldn't see me. "Well, what do you think?"

"I think you're making a lot of assumptions."

I felt a sudden twist of anger in my belly. "So, set me straight, Doc. Where'd he go? Where can I find him so we can straighten out this whole *misunderstanding*?"

"Sarcasm won't help, Liam."

I could hear my voice rising. "Why are you being obstructive, Doc? People's lives are at risk."

"You are allowing anger and fear to cloud your vision, Liam. I am not going to tell you where to find Anthony when you are like this. Do you understand?"

I took a deep breath.

After a moment, she continued. "If he is distressed, he is bound to contact me. When he does, I'll see what I can do."

"You'll see what you can do? Are you *serious*?"

"He'll listen to me. If I tell him to hand himself over to the police, he will."

"He is dangerous, Juliet! I was lucky he didn't kill me."

"You need to calm down, Liam, and get some perspective. I won't talk to you while you are in this state. I'll be in touch."

"Don't hang—" I didn't finish because she had. I stared at my phone for a while then dropped it on the seat next to me. I looked at the street ahead of me. The rain had stopped and clouds were drifting across the sun, fading shadows in and out over the red-brick buildings. '*Calm down and get some perspective.*' I could see the sky and the clouds reflected upside down in the windshield of the car in front of me. Perspective. Everything was perspective.

I fired up the big V12 and headed slowly up to Notting Hill Gate. I parked on a back street, bought a broadsheet and made my way on foot to Juliet Loss' place. There was a bus stop a hundred yards from her house and I sat there, reading the paper and waiting. As I expected, about twenty minutes later, a taxi pulled up and she climbed out. She paid the driver, trotted up the stairs and let herself in.

I waited another ten minutes and saw him approaching from the Gate. He walked with mincing steps, with his head tucked into his shoulders, like he was expecting to get slapped across the back of his head. His hands were stuffed into his pockets and he kept his eyes firmly on his feet. He turned in to Dr. Loss' gate and ran up the stairs to her door. It opened before he had time to ring the bell. He slipped in and it closed behind him. It made sense she'd see him here and not at her office, but something else made less sense. I filed it in my brain for consideration later and crossed the road, to where they couldn't see me from the window.

I waited half an hour. I figured that was two hundred bucks worth of Dr. Loss' time and wondered who was paying. Then the door opened again and Anthony Cavra hurried down the stairs and back toward Notting Hill Gate, only now he was wearing a small knapsack on his back. I let him get fifty yards ahead of me and set off after him.

He turned left at Pembridge Road and stopped at the zebra crossing. I did the same but turned away, like I was searching for something on the other side of the road. A black cab passed. I watched it. It slowed and a young woman got out. My skin turned cold and prickled. I watched her look both ways then run across the road. She went through Dr. Loss' gate and ran up the stairs two at a time. I didn't think. I took a step so I could see the door. Loss opened it and they smiled at each other.

They hugged and I heard Loss say, "Maria, darling, come in. I've got the kettle on."

And the door closed.

Chapter Nine

My instinct was to go right back and dangle Juliet Loss out of her fourth-floor window until she told me what the hell was going on. But the blare of a horn brought me to my senses and I saw Anthony running across the road with a driver leaning out of his window shouting abuse at him.

I followed, thinking that if the driver had known how right he was, he might have kept his mouth shut.

The crowds got thicker at the mouth of the Underground and I stayed with him down the steps to the ticket barriers. He went through and headed for the escalators to the Central line. He was either headed west or east. I hung back a bit and observed. At the bottom of the escalator, he went to the eastbound platform.

Five minutes later the train came in. I waited till he'd boarded then got on one carriage back from him. I stayed near the door that connected the carriages where I could keep an eye on him. He sat, with his hands in his pockets, staring at the floor. I knew he wasn't seeing it. He was seeing whatever crazy stuff went on inside his head. I felt sick because I knew whatever that was, it now involved Maria.

Maria…who was at Dr. Loss' place. I heard Loss' voice, '*Maria, darling, come in. I've got the kettle on.*' She knew her. They were old friends.

We stayed like that for twenty minutes — me watching him and him watching his own crazy thoughts. At Liverpool Street, he got off and I got off behind him. He didn't leave the station. He made his way with his weird, mincing walk to the Hammersmith and City line. There he got on a train one stop to Aldgate East.

I followed him out, keeping my distance because there were less people here. He walked quickly, head down. He turned up Tyne Street, then left into Old Castle. He clearly didn't know he was being tailed, but it was like the lack of crowds around him made him nervous—like he felt more visible—and he walked fast.

At Toynbe, he turned left again into a busy street market. I shouldered my way through the crowds, trying to keep him in sight. The smell of curry was powerful on the warm, muggy air, and the shouts and cries in every language but English made me feel like I was in a kasbah. Halfway down the street he moved into a narrow, dark mews. It was a dead end and I couldn't follow him in, but, from across the street I saw him go to a shabby, dilapidated door, pull out a key ring and try two keys before it opened and he let himself in. When it closed, I entered the mews. The number was three Toynbe Mews.

Dr. Juliet Loss had given him a safe house. A hideout. *Why?*

I played with the idea of kicking in the door and asking him, but I knew the timing was wrong. There were too many people, and if he didn't answer, if I had to kill him, a lot of questions would remain unanswered. I knew where he was, and neither Dr. Loss nor he knew that I knew.

Just like they didn't know that I knew about Maria.

I walked back to Whitechapel and hailed a cab. In the back, I looked at my watch. An hour had passed since I'd seen her go into Loss' house. I wondered if she was still there. I wondered it for fifteen minutes before I pressed her quick-dial number. I got a message telling me her phone was switched off. I tried again ten minutes after that. It was still switched off. I got the cab to drop me at the end of the road and tried again. This time it rang and she answered.

"Hey!"

"Hi, you at home?"

"Sure, why?"

"Okay, I'll see you in five."

When I arrived, she opened the door and gave me a warm kiss. I tried to respond but I wasn't feeling warm and she must have sensed it. She managed to smile and frown at the same time as she closed the door.

She said, "How'd it go? Did you find him?"

I went to the fridge and pulled out a cold beer. I cracked it and looked at her a moment before taking a pull. I said, "Yeah…"

She frowned with a little less smile and spread her hands. "So?"

I sat at the table and took another pull. "So, he's pretty crazy. He wasn't surprised to hear that I had a message from you."

"What?"

"I told him I had a message from Maria Vazques. I wanted to see how he would react. He knew who you were and he wasn't surprised."

She went pale. That's something your autonomic system does. You can't fake it. She didn't say anything. She just stared at me, like she was wondering what the hell to say.

I said, "Do you know him?"

Now there was no trace of a smile in her frown. "Of course not! Why ask such a stupid question?"

I spread my hands and shook my head. "I'm sorry, Maria. I'm just trying to understand what the hell is going on. This guy attacked me. He is very violent and very strong. He knocked me about like I was half his size. And if he killed Eva and Sally, you are next on his list."

She swallowed and sat slowly at the table opposite me.

I watched her a moment, trying to read her, then I went on, "He knew who you were. He wasn't surprised to receive a message from you. He was surprised that it was me bringing the message. Now, I'm going to ask you one last time. Do you know this guy?"

She stared at me a long time before answering. "Liam, I don't know what the hell is going on, but whatever it is, we cannot let it come between us or damage our trust."

I nodded. "Okay, you're right." I took another swig and hated myself for setting a trap with my next question. "What did you do this morning, babe?"

She smiled. It was a feeble smile. "Don't be mad at me. I know you said I should stay in. But you remember I told you I'd made a friend? Well, I felt so frustrated and upset, and I really needed to talk to someone. She is an amazing listener and she called and asked if I wanted to have tea. I couldn't resist. So I went over. I was really careful—"

I cut across her. "Your friend is Dr. Juliet Loss?"

She burst out laughing. "Don't be ridiculous! No, she's a dear old lady called"—her face went blank and she hesitated.

I put the bottle on the table and rubbed my face. I was getting mad and trying to control it because I didn't know who to be mad at. I said, "She called you and asked you to go over? Let me tell you something. You missed Anthony Cavra by about two minutes. After he beat seven bails of shit out of me, he went to see her. They were together for half an hour, and I was just tailing him to a safe house she gave him the keys to, when you turned up."

We were quiet for a moment.

Then she said, "That means—"

"How long before you arrived did she call you?"

She put her hand to her mouth. She looked scared. She stared at me. "About twenty minutes."

"While he was still there."

"Liam... What the hell?"

"Let me ask you something. This course you were looking into. Who runs it?"

"Dr. Loss... She does..."

"How did you meet her, baby?"

She shook her head. "I..." She frowned. "We got talking at the whole food shop on Portobello Road."

"Did she approach you or did you talk to her?"

"I don't know."

"Think, honey. This is important."

She shook her head again. "I don't know, Liam. I can't be sure." She stood and walked away to the window. "No! This is crazy! I refuse to believe it." She turned to face me. "She is a sweet, caring, lovely lady. I *won't* believe it!"

"Believe what?"

For a minute, it seemed as though she didn't know what to say. Finally, she said, "That she is somehow involved."

I sighed and took a while pulling a Camel from my pack and lighting it. I blew out a stream of smoke before answering her. "Baby, she *is* involved. That isn't the question. The question is, how? *How* is she involved?" I thought for a moment then asked her, "What did she talk to you about?"

She shrugged. "Nothing... Chit-chat... How I was getting on... Liam?" Her face was drawn. She was frightened.

I stood and went to her and took her in my arms.

She said, "I'm frightened. What's going on?"

"I don't know, babe, but I plan to find out." I pulled back a bit and held her face in my hands. "Meantime, we have got to be much more careful. And by that, I mean *you* have to be much more careful."

"What are you going to do?"

I went over and fell into an armchair. I took a long drag and let the smoke out slow. "There are too many uncertainties. Is it one killer or two? Is it Anthony Cavra or not? Is Dr. Loss involved or isn't she? Are the victims chosen to draw me in or not? Are you a target or aren't you? There isn't one single damned thing I can pin down as a certainty." I thought for a moment then crushed out my half-smoked cigarette in an ashtray. "So tonight, I am going to pin down at least one."

Throughout the afternoon, the sky had turned black and the thermometer had risen to thirty-eight Celsius. As evening fell, it had started to rain again, torrential sheets, like there was an army of avenging angels up there with giant hoses. Maria had sat herself in front of the TV with a vat of Ben & Jerry's, occasionally picking up the remote and flicking to a different channel.

At one point, I kissed the top of her head from behind and told her, "Hey, it's going to be okay."

She'd smiled up at me and said, "I know." It was the sweetest lie she'd ever told me.

She was watching the news. It was a special report on an Anglo-American initiative on clean energy and the fusion reactor they were building in Wales—the one del Roble had tried to kill so he could control Europe's energy through Andalusian oil. The Minister for the Department of Environmental Regeneration was talking.

"The reactor at Llyn Celyn will not only provide us with clean energy well into the next millennium, it will put us in a position to sell energy – totally clean energy – to the whole of northern Europe. Naturally, the EU wants to be a part of that, and that's why they want to write the software. But, sorry. The fact is that we want to do what is best for Britain. And best for Britain is that the software is written in Silicon Valley by the Institute for the Climate and the Environment. They happen to be the best, and we want the best – the best for Britain."

I zoned out and looked at my watch. It was seven-thirty p.m. I put on my Driza-Bone coat and hat, kissed Maria and told her not to open the door for anyone, then made my way down into the deluge.

The streets were practically empty. You had to be crazy or desperate to be out in this. Maybe I was both. I drove slowly, and the wash from the tires was like the wash from a tanker in the night. It took me an hour to get to Spitalfields. I turned off Whitechapel onto Castle Street. The light from the street lamps seemed to hang above the road, without ever penetrating down into the shadows. I crawled up as far as Tyne Street and turned in. When I could see into Tyne Mews as far as number three, I killed the engine and the lights. The drumming of the rain on the soft top was deafening, and the water spilling over onto the windshield made it impossible to see. I cracked the window far enough so I had a clear view of his house. Down the road, that water had gotten into one of the lamps and it was buzzing and flickering like it was about to die. I peeled a fresh pack, stuck a Camel in my mouth, lit it and waited while I thought.

Loss was his therapist. I knew that much. Cavra's broke and he can't pay her, but she's a dedicated pro, so she lets him work at the college in exchange for therapy. Then Eva gets killed and I show up asking questions. She profiles the killer at my request, having seen the forensic report, and, after Sally gets killed, she knows he fits the profile like a glove. What does she do?

The simple fact was that I didn't know. I figured she'd had a session with him, but what had gone down in that session was anybody's guess. What I did know was what had happened when I'd called her and told her I'd found him. She'd called him and told him to meet her at her house. Once there, she'd given him the key to this place. Why? And while he had still been there, she'd called Maria, the third girl, and told her to come over for tea. *Why?*

They were questions I couldn't answer without more information. And what I couldn't decide on right now was the best way to get that information. My instinct was to go in and beat it out of him, but with a crazy like Anthony, that could just drive him deeper into his own craziness. The other option was to wait and follow him. But if Maria was his next prey and he didn't know where she was, there was no telling how long I'd have to wait before he made a move — unless I used her as bait. And there'd be icebergs in Hell before I did that.

So, that left a third option. Go in, grab him by the scruff of his neck and take him to Dr. Loss and have it out with both of them, right there in her house. She could give him up and have him sectioned, or I could hand him over to Russian Pete. Her choice.

I flicked the butt out into the rain and climbed out of the car. The water was almost ankle-deep around my boots and beginning to spill onto the sidewalks. I waded through the discarded trash from the market with the dull, flickering light from the street lamps twisting and breaking on the ripples. I walked into the mews, fishing my lock picks from my pocket. It took me fifteen seconds then I entered silently.

There was a narrow hall with a flight of stairs straight ahead and a door on the right. I got out my pen torch and shut out the rain behind me. The door on my right led into a small living room littered with boxes and bags and old junk that had once meant something to somebody. Now it was here because it didn't mean anything to anybody, but no one was ready to throw it away yet. I pushed past an empty printer box and a clown on a bike then through a door into a kitchen with a linoleum floor. There were no dirty plates or glasses. The sink was dry and the whole place smelled of musty rot. I made my way back to the top of the stairs.

They creaked. All stairs in old English houses creak. And even if you try to step on the outer edges, they creak. These creaked loudly in the dark, and after two steps, any hope I had of surprising him was gone. I paused and listened. There was not a sound in the house, except the patter and splash of the rain outside. I climbed the remaining stairs to a small landing with three doors. There were two bedrooms and a toilet. I guessed the back room would be his. I stepped in and flipped on the light. It was a single bulb in a fly-blown orb that gave a depressing, pallid glow. The bed had been lain on. Two of the drawers were taken up with a pair of jeans, two sweatshirts and four pairs of socks. The third drawer held three scrapbooks. Each had a name written in thick black marker pen — Eva, Sally, *Maria*.

It was too easy. I opened each one and looked through them. There were photographs of the girls taken at the college, in the street, outside their homes. Shots taken from far away as well as close-ups of their faces, where he must have used a telephoto lens.

I sat on the bed and began to go through them in order. They started out with pictures taken at the college, usually with a group of people. He'd written some sentimental poems, idealizing them. Then the pictures were in the street, mostly from a distance, at bus stops or Underground stations.

There was Eva going into Pete's apartment block, getting into her dad's car and, beside these pictures, poems about how their love—Anthony and Eva's—would set her free from her prison. Then there were pictures of her at the Albert Hall bus stop and in Hammersmith, going in to Mark's house. A picture of Mark and Eva kissing near the river, looking radiant and happy then the tone of the poetry changed. It was about how she was blinded, unable to see the truth, but how he knew that his love would soon set her free. How her words were, unwittingly, like barbs that tore at his heart. How her own heart was frozen, but his love would melt it.

And the last page was horrific. Close-up pictures of her face, scrawled over in red felt pen—*bitch, whore, slut, betrayer of love, die.*

The Sally scrapbook was pretty much the same. It started out with fantasies of a relationship of love between them that would set her free, though he never said free from what. Then—as before—the tone changed. She was blind to her own love of him, but it wasn't her fault. He would save her, open her eyes and her heart to her own love. And, finally, with the realization that it was nothing but a fantasy, the horrific outpouring of hatred and violence.

I picked up the scrapbook titled 'Maria'. I didn't want to open it. There was a hot, smoldering pain in the pit of my belly that flared into a hot rage when I turned to the first page. She was there, talking to Steve, laughing. She was putting on a helmet to get on the back of his bike. The poetry was the same, badly written, naïve, self-indulgent. The next pages were of Maria entering Dr. Loss' house and standing on the stoop, talking to her, then at the front door of our apartment block on Church Street. The poetry was still at the stage where she was blind to her own feelings, but his love would liberate her.

I was finding it hard to think straight. All I wanted to do was find him and put the poor bastard out of his misery. Instead, I dialed Loss.

She answered, "Dr. Juliet Loss." Her voice was cool.

I didn't waste time. "I'm at number three Tyne Mews looking at Anthony's scrapbooks. The way I see it, I have two choices. I tell you to come here now and explain to me what this is all about, or I call Russian Pete and tell him to come here so I can explain to him what I think it's all about."

There was a long pause. "Where is Anthony?"

"Where are you?"

"Have you done anything to Anthony?"

"I'm waiting, Doc. What's it to be?"

"I'll get a cab. Wait for me there. Please, don't do anything stupid."

I hung up.

I picked up the scrapbooks and started going through them again, more slowly, searching for content, for details. I noticed sometimes the poems were written especially for a particular photograph, but sometimes they were reused. That seemed odd. Eva, he called a slut and a whore after he had seen her and photographed her with Mark. But there were no photographs of Sally with another guy. In fact, there was no indication at all of what had made him turn against her. Maybe he'd spoken to her and she'd rejected him. But when I tried to imagine Anthony talking to a woman about his feelings, it didn't gel. And that got me thinking about Anthony on the bus with Eva. How the hell did he persuade her to get off with him? And where the hell had he killed her? That got me thinking about timing. I pulled a Camel from the pack and sat staring at it. The timing... There was something wrong with the timing.

A noise downstairs made me put the thought on the back burner. The door closed softly and the stairs creaked. I glanced at my watch. Forty minutes had passed since I'd called Loss. A couple more creaks and the door pushed open.

She stood in a wet rain mac and hat, dripping water on the floor and staring at me. She said, "I do not appreciate being ordered out on a night like this and threatened with violence, Mr. Murdoch."

I wasn't in the mood for being a wiseass. I said, "You want to explain to me why you gave Anthony Cavra a safe house? You want to explain to me why you phoned Maria and told her to come and have tea with you, while he was still in your house collecting the keys? And while you're at it, Juliet, you want to tell me why you befriended her and encouraged her to go to Birkbeck to study psychology, where you had Anthony running errands for you and selecting his victims, and you never told her who you were? You want to explain all that to me, Juliet?"

She sighed and shook her head and pulled her waterproof hat from her head. "Oh, please, don't be so melodramatic."

"You can explain it to me, or you can explain it to Eva's father. He's got a real taste for melodrama. It's your choice."

She narrowed her eyes at me and for a moment seeming real mad. "Don't threaten me, Murdoch!"

I stood, stepped over to her and looked down into her face. "I just did, Juliet, and I'm waiting. Are we going to talk or are you going to talk to Russian Pete and his friends?"

She just stared up at me.

I took a step closer, so we were touching and our faces were just an inch apart. "And, while we're on the subject of threats, let me tell you something. If you or Anthony hurt Maria, I will do things to you personally that would make Pete break down and weep like a little girl. Do we understand each other?"

She broke out of her stare and sighed again. "I need a cup of tea."

She turned and left the room. I followed her down to the kitchen, carrying the scrapbooks. She flipped on a switch that made the kitchen look like a morgue, put on the kettle and found some tea, a stained paper bag of sugar and a couple of mugs in a cupboard. She opened the fridge, smelled a carton of milk and emptied it down the sink.

When she was stirring the tea, she said, "Anthony is my patient. You may not know it, Liam, but I am the world's leading authority on Freudian psychoanalysis, and I would stake my reputation on Anthony's innocence." She leaned her ass against the sink and blew into her tea. "He is deeply neurotic and he has borderline personality disorder, but he is not a killer."

I didn't say anything.

She went on, "I know all about Eva's father. Believe me. He is a far better candidate for homicidal psychosis than Anthony will ever be. When you phoned me and said you had found Anthony and he had attacked you, I realized what serious danger he was in. What Eva's father and his thugs would do to Anthony doesn't bear thinking about. I couldn't let that happen, so I gave him the keys to this place." She regarded me with distaste and added, "I should have realized that a man like you would track him down."

"I guess I am not supposed to take that as a compliment."

"No." She sipped her tea and was silent for a bit, seemingly staring at a patch of air. Finally, she said, "I met Maria at the Grain Shop on Portobello Road. She struck me as a delightful, intelligent, creative young woman. We had coffee." She glanced at me in a way you could describe as mischievous and said, "You won't be surprised to hear that I am a very good listener. It goes, as you would say, with the territory. She ended up telling me that she was with a man she absolutely adored, but who was obstinate and extremely arrogant and couldn't see that she was wilting and withering away in London with nothing to do." She shrugged, shook her head and stared at me like I was a mental retard. "I gave her simple, common sense advice. I told her to check the courses at Birkbeck because that is the college I know best for extramural classes. She seemed interested in psychology. I didn't tell her who I was because it would have seemed arrogant and presumptuous. And, if you weren't so fixated on blaming Anthony for these murders, you would see that.

"Why did I call her while Anthony was there? Because we had agreed to meet soon for tea. I knew the poor girl was home alone *again*, and, as far as I was concerned, having given him the keys, Anthony was leaving." Her face suddenly contracted with annoyance. "And, frankly, Liam, *you* think it's odd because you are convinced he is a serial killer. But *I* know he's not! So, there was nothing odd for me in calling her while he was there."

We looked at each other in silence for a while.

I was leaning on the doorjamb and I said, "He exactly fits the profile you gave me of what our killer would be like. You know that."

She shook her head. "Superficially, yes, but Anthony is actually a kind, caring person who has no repressed rage or feelings of violence toward anyone. He *likes* women. He doesn't hate them."

I reached out and handed her the scrapbooks. "Have you seen these?"

She took her time going through Eva's, examining the pictures and reading the poems. When she reached the last couple of pages, she went pale. She searched Sally's and Maria's in silence.

I said, "No repressed rage? No hatred?" She didn't answer and I went on, "I'll tell you something else, Doc. You were talking about the physiological changes the brain can make when in a particular kind of trance. I'm a big guy and I've been in my fair share of scraps and usually held my own. This kid knocked me around like I was a ninety-pound weakling. He fits your profile to a T."

She leafed through the scrapbooks again, shaking her head and repeating, "I can't believe it. I just can't believe it."

I said, "Where is he, Doc?"

Chapter Ten

"Where is he, Doc?"

She raised her eyes from the scrapbook to look at me. "I don't know."

I said, "Phone him."

She suddenly appeared drawn. "Please, Liam."

"Believe me. It's better you do this through me."

She pulled out her cell and sat staring at it.

I said, "I have Pete on speed dial. How long do you need to think about this?"

She scowled at me and dialed. After a moment, she said, "Anthony, it's Juliet, where are you?"

There was silence and I mouthed at her to put it on speaker. She glared at me and shook her head, then stood and stepped away with her back to me. "You should come home. We need to talk."

I stood also.

She was listening, kept shaking her head and starting to speak, "No... No... Anthony, listen to me... No, Anthony..."

An undefined anxiety was beginning to twist my gut. I started to ask, "What's he...?" but she held up a hand, shaking her finger at me.

"Anthony, you have to listen to me. Listen to my voice, Anthony. Are you focusing on me? Anthony, please *listen!*" She made an inarticulate sound then stared at the phone, like it should explain itself to her. Then she said, "He hung up on me."

I could feel the anger building in me. I said, "What did he say, Doc?"

She took a long, ragged breath. "He says he is going to

your apartment to find Maria."

I stared. "And how long were you planning to wait before telling me this?"

"I've just hung up, for God's sake!"

"*Which* apartment? The one on Church Street?"

She closed her eyes and sighed. "No. he says he knows you have moved. He says—"

I grabbed her shoulders and shook her. "*What*, God damn it?"

"*Liam!*" She pulled free and took a step back. "He says Maria told him where it was."

I swore under my breath and ran. She was right behind me, half stumbling down the stairs, shouting at me to wait. I wrenched open the front door and ran out into the downpour. The rain was torrential and spilled in my eyes, blinding me. I was vaguely aware of Loss' voice behind me, shouting at me to wait. I grabbed the keys from my pocket and thumbed the button as I ran. The lights on the Daemon flashed through the sheets of black rain. I wrenched open the driver's door and heard her scream, "You need me! Liam, you *need* me!"

I froze and she stumbled up, drenched and wiping water from her eyes. She faced me across the roof of the car and shouted above the din of the downpour. "You need me to talk to him! He will only listen to me."

I growled, "Get in." And when we were in and had slammed the doors, in the muffled silence I gunned the engine and pulled away. I said, "If he has done anything to her, if he has hurt her or touched her, I want you near. You are going to wish it had been Pete who found you and not me. Now, call her and hand me the phone."

She gaped at me in the darkness. "Liam! It's not my fault—"

"You brought them together. You allowed him to get close to her. You protected him. You concealed him… Now quit stalling and *call* her!"

I drove like a thing possessed. The rain was like

bloodstained steel blades in the streetlights and traffic lights that streaked by. All I could see was the blackness that was swallowing my world and the black terror that was twisting my gut, thinking of Maria and what might be happening to her. The road was interminable, and though I was doing over seventy, the car felt sluggish, wading through oceans of heavy, leaden water.

She dialed in silence. She put the phone on speaker and I could hear it ringing, but there was no reply. She looked at me. "She isn't answering."

"Try *again!*"

This time the phone was dead. At one point, she said, "Liam, you have to slow down or you'll kill us before we can get to her."

I snarled, "Tell me to slow down again and I'll break your neck and throw you out of the car."

After what felt like hours but was only thirty minutes, we screamed into Mulberry Crescent, skidded and my trunk smashed into a parked Mercedes that started flashing and wailing its alarm into the rain. I screeched to a halt in front of the apartment block and was already out and running up the stairs before Loss had undone her seatbelt. I was reaching in my pocket for the keys while I ran, but I could see the street door was already open.

Ours was the first-floor apartment and I was screaming out her name as I scrambled up the stairs, fumbling in my pocket for the keys.

But the door was open. There was a dark smear on the latch on the doorjamb, and I knew without looking that it was blood. There had been a struggle in the drawing room. Two lamps lay smashed on the floor. An armchair was on its side and the coffee table had been thrown against the wall. An ashtray lay broken in half. Cigarette butts and gray ash littered the carpet.

I knew it was pointless, but I checked the bedroom. The bed had been badly rumpled, the quilt had been pulled back and the cushions were on the floor. I felt dizzy and sick.

I was fighting to stay cold, to think. There was no blood except on the doorjamb. If he had killed her, there would have been more blood. *The scrapbook.* In the scrapbook, he had not reached the homicidal stage. Why had he changed his pattern? Why had he come here? Why had he said that Maria had told him where we were?

I went into the bathroom and stood staring. Everything was as normal, but scrawled across the mirror in red lipstick was a message for me.

Time to start feeling the heat, Murdock.

Then I heard Loss calling to me. I heard her feet clattering up the stairs, irregular and unsteady.

She was crying. "Liam… Oh, Liam… Oh, God, Liam…" And she was sobbing.

The room swayed and I seemed to be walking through a fish-eye view of a tunnel toward the front door. I was lightheaded, like my mind was floating above my body. It was unreal. The whole thing was unreal. I stepped out of the door onto the landing and looked down the stairs. Loss was holding on to the banisters, staring up at me. Her eyes were like two huge black holes and her mouth was sagging open.

She said, "Liam… Liam, you have to come."

She turned and staggered, unsteady, down the stairs again. I was paralyzed. I didn't want to go. I didn't want to see what she had found, because I knew. As I'd run in, there had been a bulk, a large black bulk on the small patch of lawn on the flowerbed by the wall. I had ignored it. It hadn't been important then. My mind had been fixed on Maria, on Anthony, on the apartment where he was with her.

But he wasn't.

I snapped out of it and ran down the stairs two at a time to the street door and out into the rain. The short footpath was awash with the light from the lobby, writhing crazy in the ripples. To the right and left there were small plots of garden. And in the right-hand plot, bundled against the wall, crushing the flowers into the mud, was a large, black bundle. Loss was standing next to it, staring at me over her shoulder. I couldn't tell if she was crying because the rain was streaming down her face. I wiped my own eyes and realized my hands were shaking.

Then I realized I was mumbling to myself, "Oh, no, please, God, no…"

My legs seemed to move of their own accord. My feet sank into the sodden turf. I crouched down and saw that the dark bulk was covered in a dark-blue woolen coat. I could feel Loss by my side. She seemed very tall and very still. I took hold of the body and brought it toward me. It was heavy and rolled with a small thud. I pulled back the coat and saw the great, gaping wound in the belly, with the rainwater pooling in among the blood. I saw the knife handle and the rose. Then I burst into uncontrollable, convulsive sobs.

Because it wasn't her. It wasn't Maria.

I stood and stepped back. My head was reeling and my mind spinning. I stared down at the face, struggling to find meaning. It was Anthony. The ground around him was saturated, not just with the rain, but with blood and gore. His face was waxy and expressionless. I could see the edge of a note wrapped around the stem of the rose. I turned to look at Loss. She was staring at me. There was absolutely no expression on her face.

I said, "What does it mean?"

She shook her head. "We have to call the police."

I stared down at the body. A voice in my head was screaming at me to get a grip, to react. To do *something*! I said, "Where is Maria?"

She was still looking at me, occasionally wiping the back of her hand across her eyes. She said, "Why did she tell him to come here?"

I thought of the message on the mirror. I said, "It doesn't make any sense."

We stood, staring at each other, with the water falling around us.

Finally, she spoke. "To somebody it does. To somebody it makes perfect sense." Her voice was a strange, strangled, almost a hiss.

* * * *

Two hours later, I was sitting in an interview room at Ladbroke Grove police station. The door opened and Grant came in, holding two paper cups with small plastic sticks poking out of them. A constable closed the door behind him and he sat on the chair opposite me and placed a cup in front of me.

"The machine says it's coffee. Personally, I doubt it." He shrugged. "But it's hot and it's a drink." We watched each other a moment and he said, "Dr. Loss confirms you were with her most of the evening. Apparently, you were at Anthony Cavra's place."

I sighed and rubbed my face with my palms. "Not exactly." I filled him in as much as I could. Something made me stress Loss' role as Anthony's therapist and play down her relationship with Maria.

When I'd finished, he sat stirring his coffee for a while.

Finally, he said, "So this Dr. Loss is the one you said I should have a talk to."

I nodded. "Yeah."

"Because she's an expert profiler on serial killers."

I smiled in a way you could describe as rueful and said, "Only this isn't a serial killer, is it?"

He studied his little plastic stirring stick and said, "What makes you say that?"

"Serial killers have one motive for killing—the desire to kill. But they desire to kill a particular type of person. It might be a woman of a certain physical type, or gays, or prostitutes. Whatever it is, it will be a certain type of person."

I picked up the paper cup and looked at the black liquid inside it. I thought about drinking it for a moment but abandoned the idea. I put the cup back on the table and said, "These three victims only had one thing in common."

He was watching me carefully.

He said, "Go on."

"Me."

He raised an eyebrow and drew breath to speak.

I went on before he could. "Eva was killed in the certain knowledge that Pete would pull strings to get me involved. You know yourself that Pete carries weight in high places. Sally was killed because she was the niece of one of my closest friends, to let me know that whoever it is can get close to me and to deliver me the message on that scroll of paper." I quoted, "'To silence the mocking mouth, to still the arrogant heart, to rip out and steal excitement, hope and regeneration.' And the note in Anthony's mouth— 'To silence the arrogant mouth, to still the proud heart, to eviscerate Man who has brought upon himself the heat of Hell's punishing fire.' Those messages were directed at me, not at Eva and Sally. And Anthony was set up as a scapegoat—a red herring to let me know Maria was a target, but to lead me away from whoever it is who wanted to take her."

Grant snorted and shook his head. "I'm sorry, Murdoch, but that is a very unlikely story. It just isn't credible."

I nodded. "I agree, but when you think it through, it is also incontrovertible. And whoever it is that killed Anthony, also took Maria and wrote on my mirror, 'Time to start feeling the heat, Murdoch.'"

He was pensive for a bit. Then he said, "Well, if you're right, it means one of two things. Either you've *really* pissed off some total nutter who is prepared to go to ridiculous lengths to cause you grief…"

"Or?"

"Or you've pissed off someone who is so rich and powerful that these lengths don't seem ridiculous to them."

I nodded. He was right.

After a moment, he said, "Can you think of anyone like that, that you have *really* pissed off?"

I looked him in the eye and lied. "No."

Chapter Eleven

We were on the Chichester Channel, drifting slowly toward the ocean. The air had turned fresh. The molten weight of the heat had gone, and the meringue clouds against the blue sky were light and cool. A soft breeze made small waves on the water and carried us toward the Isle of Wight.

Russell was pacing the deck. He paced carefully, like he was counting his own steps. We were on Hook's forty-foot cutter. He was leaning on the helm, just back from the hatch, with his sight lost in the distant haze on the sea. But I could tell from his eyes that he wasn't really seeing it. His inner eye was seeing his thoughts. I was sitting on the deck holding a cold beer, studying the grain of the wood, thinking about Maria.

No one had spoken for a while, and my mind had gone back. Russell's flat was a crime scene. It had been sealed off with yellow tape and the cops were all over it. I'd returned to my place in Church Street and taken a bottle of Bushmills into the bedroom. There I'd sat on the bed, staring through at the empty bathroom where Maria should have been preparing for bed. But the light had been stark and dead and the bathroom silent. The empty mirror had looked back at me with no particular expression, just tiles and a shower cubicle. Cold. Dead.

Cold. The word had resonated in my head through the whiskey fumes. *Cold.* But that wasn't what the message had said. The message had said that it was time to start feeling the heat.

'Time to start feeling the heat, Murdoch.'

HEAT.

And as I had sipped at the whiskey and stared at the smoldering tip of my cigarette, I had remembered Russell, sitting in the sun in his white linen, with his huge insect sunglasses, saying, '*I see the Monopolies and Mergers Commission has allowed the HEAT Corporation's bid for the Llyn Celyn fusion reactor. That will bring problems.*' Then, '*The High Energy Atomic Technologies Corporation. HEAT. It pleases us, doesn't it, when an acronym amounts to an actual word.*'

He'd known all along.

He'd phoned me while I'd been staring at the mirror. The cops had contacted him to tell him his apartment was a crime scene. I'd sat staring at the screen as it rang, looking at his name, 'Russell'. Then I'd pressed green and said, "It's del Roble, isn't it? He's back."

"Don't talk. Come down. Now. We'll talk here."

I'd gone to the wardrobe and pulled out my Smith & Wesson from where Maria had made me store it. I'd loaded it and slipped it into my waistband, then put a spare box of slugs in my jacket pocket. The game had changed. I wasn't looking to find anyone anymore. I was planning to kill somebody.

I had driven through the dark hours, racked by despair and terror for what might have happened to Maria and by waves of sickening, bestial rage. I'd arrived at Russell's house in Fishbourne, as the eastern horizon was turning a pale blue-gray. I'd parked by the mill pond and looked at the rickety silhouette of his ancient house against the dawn. I had seen see warm light through the leaded panels of his ground floor windows. He had been up and about.

I'd climbed out of the Daemon. The slam of the door echoed dull in the early morning. Somewhere an owl called out into the dying night. My feet were loud on the blacktop, and the blind windows of the sleeping houses seemed to scowl at me. I pushed through the gate and saw a crack of light as the front door opened and an anonymous silhouette was framed in the amber glow. It wasn't Russell. My skin prickled and the hair on my neck stood up.

My hand slipped to my waistband, but a voice I recognized said, "Please don't shoot me, Murdoch. I'm afraid you might come off worse."

I dropped my hand and allowed myself a left-handed smile. "Brigadier, I had a hunch you might be here."

"Russell is in the kitchen frying bacon and making *carajillos*."

I stepped into the warm light of the house. The smell of bacon and coffee was rich on the air.

He closed the door behind me. "I'm not sure if you're familiar with them — black coffee improved by the addition of a generous slug of whisky or brandy."

We'd eaten bacon and drunk *carajillos*, but when I had tried to talk to Russell about Maria, he had waved me to silence. Now we were on Hook's yacht and Hook was saying to the horizon, "Even with today's cutting edge technologies, water tends to sod up listening devices, and here" — he gestured at the vast open spaces around us — "it would be difficult to set up a listening device."

I nodded. "Who? Who would be listening, and, more to the point" — I shook my head and spread my hands — "why?"

Russell stopped pacing and stared at me from behind his huge, black sunglasses. "My dear boy, are you in complete denial? Have you forgotten what happened to you in Spain?"

I looked away, at the black shadows under the trees in the woodlands on Bosham. No. I had not forgotten. I would never forget. I had wanted to believe — Maria and I had both wanted to believe — that if we forgot it, if we put it behind us like it had never happened, it might all go away. I said, "No, Russell, I haven't forgotten."

He kept staring, like he couldn't get over his own disbelief. "Have you any idea just how powerful del Roble is?"

A worm of irritation twisted my gut. "What do you think, Russell? Do you think I realize?"

He frowned, a rare thing for Russell. "Well, apparently not. If del Roble wielded enough power to control some of the most powerful governments on Earth, how bloody powerful do you think his masters are, Liam?"

I rubbed my face and said into my hands, "I try not to think about it, Russell."

His voice rose a little. "So, you never stopped to think that they might be just a bit annoyed with you?"

I stared at the boards under my feet. "So, what? This is punishment? They've set up this whole, elaborate thing just to punish me?"

He sighed and resumed his pacing. "Nothing is ever that simple with them, Liam."

Hook said, "You can be sure that is a big part of it. But they will have integrated it into some larger plan—part of something."

That made me uneasy. I said, "Like what?"

Russell said, "We can't be absolutely sure, but the messages they left you—the scrolls and your mirror—seem to confirm what I was beginning to suspect. They are punishing you and the HEAT Corporation is the hub of their activities now."

A seagull wheeled overhead, screaming something that sounded like 'Oh fuck!' We ducked into a small trough and spray leaped up from the bow. Russell made his way to a large cane chair by a round table then sat.

"You will recall poor Rupert's Uncle Hugo," he said, once he was sitting.

I nodded.

"Del Roble's interest in him was the fact that he had designed a workable fusion reactor. The reactor at Llyn Celyn is the very one that Hugo designed, and, though initially it was a government project, the HEAT Corporation moved in and took over, with the help and collusion of certain government officials."

I listened. For some reason the lapping of the small waves against the hull and the cry of the seagulls seemed to grow intensely clear. I had a hollow pellet of fear in my gut and my skin seemed to prickle. He sighed and went on.

"We just don't know who the HEAT Corporation is. We know there are a couple of very high profile investors, household names to most people, but a couple of the key investors are anonymous. Hook's chaps have done some digging and it seems at least possible that the Brotherhood have a controlling interest. And, through them, del Roble."

I was quiet for a while. Then I said, "And you think that the message on the mirror was intended to let me know that the Brotherhood was behind the killings and Maria's..."

Hook said, "It's almost certain, just as it's almost certain that she's still alive."

I squinted at him through the sun. "Why?"

"My guess is that this is a personal vendetta. He wants to make you suffer as much as possible. Simply killing her wouldn't satisfy that." He paused and turned his head so he was facing me. His expression was cold, utterly ruthless. "So, you need to get to her before he does whatever he is planning to do, Liam." He took a swig from a bottle of beer he had by his side and stood a moment, studying the label, like he had his lines written there. "Equally," he said, still looking at the label, "it won't be enough for him to just punish you."

For some reason, he looked at Russell, who was nodding.

Hook went on, "He will need to show his power. You humiliated him, Liam. You didn't just scupper his plans. You brought him to his knees, made him beg and humiliated him—this man, this creature! Whatever he is has a huge ego, and he will need to show you his power as well as punish you."

Russell quoted in a monotonous rhythm, "'To silence the arrogant mouth, to still the proud heart, to eviscerate Man who has brought upon himself the heat of Hell's punishing fire.' That's why he is using the HEAT Corporation."

Maybe for the first time in my life, I suddenly felt completely helpless. I looked at them both and said, "How the hell am I supposed to get to her? I don't even know where she is? I don't know where del Roble is? He wouldn't be stupid enough to go back to Çalares. So, where the hell do I search for him?"

There was a long silence. The slap and wash of the water against the hull of the yacht, the cry of the gulls above, seemed to wash over the silence without disturbing it. In my mind, I could feel del Robles' dark mind leaning out of the vast sky — watching, turning everything dark.

Russell spoke suddenly. "He wants you to find her. More to the point, he wants you to find *him*. Because when you find them, he will exact his punishment and take his revenge. So, the clue lies in everything he has done and said. What *is* the message he has sent you?"

I spoke without thinking, like the knowledge had been there all along, just below the surface of my mind. I said, "He has her in Wales, at Llyn Celyn. He has her at the HEAT Corporation."

Hook nodded. "I agree."

Russell sighed. It was the first time I had ever seen him appear really worried. He said, "Liam, there is something you need to be aware of. The Brotherhood, or whoever these creatures are, appear to have three main areas of interest."

I frowned. "Yeah?"

"As we have discussed before, they seem hell-bent — literally — on increasing the CO_2 in our environment and making the planet hotter. They also have a huge interest in developing AI — artificial intelligence — and information technology, probably as a means of mind control…"

I frowned harder. "And?"

He looked at me and seemed to wince. "And genetics. For about sixty years, possibly a lot longer, they have been running a program of genetic research and manipulation."

I said, "The hybrids…"

"Among other things. You need to be aware of that."

I nodded once. I didn't know what he meant, and something inside stopped me from asking.

We emerged into the English Channel. The Isle of Wight rose like a black behemoth on our right, to the south and west. The breeze picked up suddenly out of the northwest and the yacht surged, crashing through a roller and sending spray exploding high into the air. Hook hollered something, but I knew what to do. I scrambled to my feet and, for a while, there was a rush of activity, with Hook setting the course southeast and me releasing the boom so that she was dove-winging with the wind behind us. When I'd secured the sheet, I went and stood by Hook's side at the helm. Russell had his hands on his belly and seemed to have gone to sleep in the midst of all the action.

I said, "How does he do that?"

Hook smiled. "They could write volumes about what we don't know about Russell."

Something in his voice made me glance at him. "How long have you known him?"

"Since prep school."

"He was a kid once, then."

He laughed out loud. "I didn't say that. He might have been one of the masters."

He raised an eyebrow at me and I smiled. I turned, leaning my elbows on the hatch, looking back over the stern at the small sails, white, intense blue, crimson, all heeling and darting with the wind.

I said, "I'm going to Llyn Celyn, but I have no idea what I'm going to do when I get there."

He spoke to the horizon. "That isn't the issue. The issue is what you do before you go. He will dictate what you do once you're there. All you need to do is let him know you're going." He glanced at me. "Have you ever done any martial arts, Murdoch?"

"No, not unless you count getting beaten up as a kid on the streets of LA." I shrugged. "I improvise."

"Have you even been up against a professional assassin? An expert?"

I looked away, back at the darting sails shrinking behind

us. "Yeah. Once."

He seemed surprised. "And you lived to tell the story? I'm impressed."

"Don't be. I was lucky. He should have killed me several times over."

He nodded. "You can't rely on luck. She is fickle. There is only one thing to do when you face an opponent who is stronger and more skilled than you."

"What's that? Shoot him?"

He chuckled. "If you can, that will help. But if he's that good, he won't give you the chance." He shook his head. "No, go with him. Let him lead. In a word, yield." He sensed I didn't like the word then glanced at me and smiled. "Whatever your balls are telling you, Murdoch, winning is the prize. So, you do what you have to do to get the prize."

I didn't say anything and, after a moment, he went on. "Everybody has a vulnerable spot. Homer taught us that. If you are attacked by a superior force you cannot resist, yield, and, while you yield, study your attacker and find that weak spot. And when you find it, strike with devastating lethal force."

I studied the grain of the wood on the deck. He was right. My enemy was largely unknown and invisible, but what I did know of them was that their power was incalculable. I was outgunned and outclassed in every way. Almost.

I spoke to my shoes, mulling over each word as I said it. "So, I let him—del Roble or whoever it is—know I am going to Llyn Celyn. How?"

His tone became brisk, professional. "He has eyes and ears on the ground here. That much is obvious, because he has been leading you till now. So, tell the people who have been involved so far…"

I looked up at him. "Russian Pete, Dr. Loss, Grant…"

"Tell them you need a break. You need to get away from it all and come to terms with what has happened."

I took over. "When word makes its way back to del Roble—or whoever—he'll know what I'm really doing is going after him."

"Exactly as you were supposed to. And here, by going with him, you expose his first weakness — pride, arrogance. It has clouded his vision and he has underestimated your intelligence and your intelligence network."

"Okay." I nodded. "I hear you. So, I book a room, where?"

"Not too close. Go to Pembrokeshire. There's a village there, on St. Brides Bay, called Little Haven. Stay in a bed and breakfast there. It will give the impression you are trying to keep off the radar. Drive up to the reactor. See if you can go for a guided tour. Ask impertinent questions.

"They have an office in Wrexham. Drop in for a visit. You know the drill. Pretend you are trying to keep a low profile, but you're not a pro, so you're making a mess of it."

I watched the seagulls wheeling overhead, screaming their ugly, mournful cry to the empty sky. I said, "And wait for them to make their move, show me what the next stage of my punishment is."

"Exactly."

"What if the next stage in my punishment is where... where he does to Maria what he — ?"

He cut across me and his voice was like a slap in the face. "*Stop!*"

I turned to face him and his eyes were the hardest, most ruthless thing I had ever seen.

He barked at me, "*Focus.*" He studied my face till he knew I was focused, then he said, "For reasons I can't share with you, we know that is highly unlikely. In any case, there is no point thinking about things you can't do anything about. Focus. Focus on drawing del Roble out and finding his weak spot. That is all you can do."

Then Russell was climbing to his feet. He came and placed a hand on my shoulder. He took off his giant insect glasses and let me see his eyes. They looked ancient but full of power.

He said, "Your enemy sees that he has rendered you powerless to move, but you see that he has focused your mind on victory. You win. Now, luncheon, my boy. Food!"

Chapter Twelve

I had told Grant I needed a few days to get over the trauma of Maria's disappearance, and I'd given him the address and phone number of a B&B that Hook had provided me with. He'd just stared at me and told me not to leave the country. I'd told him I wouldn't and left.

I'd tried to contact Pete, but he had been unavailable, so I'd left a message with Melanie, who seemed to have been promoted to his personal assistant. She'd said she'd let him know. Then I'd called Dr. Loss and she'd said she thought it was a very good idea and asked me to stay in touch. If I needed anything, to let her know.

Then I'd tried to call Noddy. His phone had rung twice and gone dead.

Now I was standing on the cliffs above Little Haven, looking out at Stack Rocks, floating like some bizarre ghost-ship among the sea mist on a day the TV had called the hottest day in recorded history. I was watching a small group of men walking about. They seemed to be busy doing something, but at that distance, I couldn't make out what. In any case, my mind wasn't really on them. I wondered absently how they'd gotten there, but I was thinking about Maria and my next move. Believing she was still alive was an act of faith, but I had no choice. Imagining a world, a future, without her in it was not an option.

But faith in what, or in who, I had no idea.

I was about to turn and make my way back to the Daemon when I noticed one of the guys had stopped and was standing, peering up at the cliff. He was too far away for me to be sure, but I had the weird feeling he was looking at me.

I stepped up close to the edge and shielded my eyes from the sun, trying to see the men more clearly. They seemed to be wearing jumpsuits. Some were crouching down. Others seemed to be walking, scanning the ground. This one guy suddenly mirrored my action and raised his hand to shield his eyes. I dropped my hand and, after a moment, he dropped his.

I watched him a couple of seconds longer, then turned and made my way down the footpath to where I'd parked the TVR.

Google told me it was slightly more than three hours to Llyn Celyn. I reckoned I could make it in two and three-quarters. I fired up the big V12 and crawled through the narrow roads, shielded by eight-foot hedgerows and steep banks, toward the A487, which would pretty much take me all the way.

The heat was fierce and the humidity was off the charts, but instead of putting the air con on, I put the top down and let the speed cool me.

I'd been on the road half an hour when I saw it. For a moment, I thought I'd driven through a time-warp. Up ahead in the slow lane was a VW camper. It looked original '69 or '70, painted in vivid orange and yellow psychedelic designs. Hendrix figured large, as did details from Santana's *Abraxas* album. Che was there, too, and big bulbous letters with the legends, *All You Need Is Love* and *Your Love Is Here*. It made me smile, and as I drew level, the driver, a guy with long hair and big shades, waved at me, laughing and calling something that sounded like, "Follow the love, man! Follow your heart!"

As I pulled past, I saw in the rear-view mirror the front of the van was painted with a big golden apple and the word *Kallisti* written across the top.

Kallisti, the goddess of chaos. The golden apple from the garden of the Hesperidies—Hesperus, Venus, hope. Something in my memory told me that Spain—*España*—was a corruption of Hesperus, and meant 'hope'. Russell would know. I dismissed it and drove on, watching the throwback shrink and vanish in the mirror. As I did, I glimpsed the plate — KAL15T

It was noon when I reached Snowdonia National Park and started snaking down into the Afon Tryweryn river valley, toward Lake Celyn. Wales is probably one of the most beautiful countries on the planet. It isn't the insane beauty of Switzerland or Peru, which blows your mind. Like England, Wales manages to take prettiness to a level that makes you wonder how anything can be that perfect. The lake was stretched out, deep blue-black, reflecting the sun in sudden flashes. Surrounding it were the green hills of the Afon Valley, segmented and broken up by long, uneven hedgerows, like slow streams of billowing green smoke. On the western end of the lake, massive, gleaming and sterile white, was the monstrous shape of the Llyn Celyn fusion reactor — the generator of limitless clean energy that would lead humanity into the new millennium, into the New Order and the New Age.

My mind went back to the hippies and to Hesperus. I wondered what it was about us as a species that made it so hard to adapt to our own planet. Of all the creatures on Earth, we were the only ones who could not be satisfied with what the planet gave us. We needed clothes, buildings, go-faster vehicles, more energy. We behaved like a virus in an alien organism. We needed hope, all right.

Then I sighed and shook my head. Next thing, I'd be wearing sandals and eating lentils.

Ten minutes later, I was pulling into a large parking lot outside the huge white dome of the reactor. A flash of yellow and orange caught my eye and caught me up short. The VW camper I'd seen on the road — or an identical one — was parked a few rows ahead, near the outer fence of the reactor. I ignored a couple of empty lots and cruised to a space near the van. I parked, climbed out of the TVR and strolled over to the VW. I put my hand on the grill. It was cold, which meant it had been there a while. Hendrix was watching me from the side, and Che, in psychedelic negative, was advertising a revolution he would probably have preferred to suppress with guns and electrodes. I closed my eyes and tried to recall the registration plate. It had been some kind of joke.

KAL15T. It was the same van. I hadn't stopped and I hadn't dropped below seventy mph. Most of the way, I'd been doing more than one hundred and twenty. How the hell had they got ahead of me?

The voice came from behind me. It was as hard to believe as the VW camper that was sitting in front of me. "Hey, man, you diggin' the love bus? Is she beautiful? She has beautiful karma, man."

The only way to describe the way he walked was 'sloping'. He sloped toward me on the longest, skinniest legs I had ever seen on a human being. He was smoking a joint and had a headband holding his long, dirty hair out of his eyes. I recognized him as the guy who had called to me on the highway.

I nodded and said, "She's beautiful. What have you got under the hood, a dilithium crystal?"

He did a thing that sounded like a car with a half-dead battery trying to start. I realized he was laughing.

"You got it! Yeah... Dilithium, man."

I pressed the point. I was thinking he was familiar, but not just from the van. I said, "My ride has a V12 with three hundred fifty horsepower. I overtook you doing a hundred and thirty miles an hour. How'd you get here ahead of me?"

He smiled apologetically and moved the hair from his face with the backs of his fingers. "Actually, dilithium crystals are only in fiction. This is more like Adams' improbability drive." He laughed, like what he'd said was silly. "Only we don't use cups of tea!" He did the dying battery thing again.

I didn't laugh. I tried to hold his gaze, but his shades kept reflecting extremely vivid images of the lake and the hills behind me.

I said, "I'm serious. How'd you do it?"

He laughed some more and shook his head then said, "Oh, man," a couple of times. Then he extended both hands toward the camper and said, "Do you want love? If you want love, you can come with us. Love is waiting for you inside, man!"

I told myself some things in life were just inexplicable. I shook my head and said, "Thanks. I'm fine," and left him standing by his flower-power re-enactment machine. I made my way through the car park in the glaring heat, to the barrier. There was a uniformed guard with a platinum crew cut and eyes as blue as the kind of ice you stick to when you touch it. He was six foot six of solid muscle. He was Frederick Nietzsche's wet dream and his face said he knew it. In fact, that was about all I thought he did know. That, and the fact that he'd spent his life expecting trouble, and I was the trouble he'd been expecting.

He looked at me like he'd enjoy watching me drown and not care while he did it, then said, "Thus us a restricted area." He had a heavy South African accent.

I said, "I heard they did guided tours. I came all the way from London." While I was talking, I noticed he had a sidearm, which is unusual in the UK.

He eyed me up and down and said, "Hev you booked?"

I shook my head. "No."

His eyes smiled unpleasantly without letting his mouth in on it. "What's your nem?"

"My nem? My name's Murdoch, Liam Murdoch. Why?"

I could feel a hot pellet of excitement in my belly. My gut was telling me I had found something, but I didn't know what. This guy had been expecting me. I knew it.

He said, "I'll put your nem on mah list and we'll contect you for the next tour. Where are you staying?"

I pulled a face, like I wanted to be evasive. "I haven't found a room yet. I might stay in Wrexham. I can call back."

His face took on the kind of stony expression, like nothing much is happening. He said, "You should book."

I smiled. "Yeah…" I shrugged a few times, pulled a face and thanked him for his help.

His eyes smiled frost at me again and he said, "We'll see you again, Mister Murdoch. It's easy to book."

I'd gone four paces when he called after me, "Mr. Murdoch?"

I stopped and turned.

He said, "Try the Dragon's Head at Ysgol Bro Tryweryn. Ah've heard they give a very"—he smiled like a hungry wolf that thinks your cries for help are amusing—"*warm* welcome. Ah think you might find what you're looking for there. You can book the tour from there, too."

I nodded and left.

The Dragon's Head was an old inn a mile southeast of the lake. I drove there thinking everything had been too easy. It was like Russell and Hook had written the script and it was being acted out for my benefit.

I pulled into the gravel parking lot and stepped through to the cool shade of the wood-paneled reception. There was a counter with a brass bell. I thumped it and, after a minute, a small, plump guy in a tank top came out, dabbing his mouth with a napkin.

Before he could swallow, I said, "I'd like a room for the night."

He danced his head around a bit, smiled apologetically and chewed fast while he tapped at a computer. He said, "Yumph, be haff ung womb avaiwable," and swallowed. "Three-o-four, on the top floor, with views of the lake."

I told him that would do fine, took the key and climbed six flights of stairs I recognized from a Tim Burton movie to the third floor, where I found four doors.

The room was small, with an en-suite shower room you had to squeeze into and a sloping ceiling. There was a sash window that gave a view across green hills and hedgerows, with tall red-brick chimneys poking out of them like masts in a green sea fog. In the distance was the harsh, silver sheen of sun glaring off Lake Celyn. I suddenly felt exhausted. My body ached with stored anxiety about Maria. Her certain death suddenly loomed in my mind. I had to fight it off. He would not kill her. I had to believe that. If I let the shadow of her death enter my mind, I would go under.

I threw my jacket on a chair by the window, pulled off my shoes and socks then took off my shirt. I lay on the bed and closed my eyes. A voice in my head kept repeating the phrase. *If I let the shadow of her death enter my mind, I will go under.* I could see the shadow entering through the bedroom door and moving into my head. And I would go under. I could see myself going under. But under what?

There was darkness, deep and impenetrable. It was cold and dense, though it moved like water. A voice in my head told me it was quicksilver. It felt cold and metallic, like quicksilver. I was naked and standing in it up to my waist. And if the shadow of Maria's death entered my mind, I would go under, into the cold metallic darkness of quicksilver.

The door opened a long way off on my right. A wedge of yellow light leaned into the room and there was a shadow silhouetted in the light. The shadow was watching me and Maria's voice said, "Liam?"

I tried to call her, to tell her I was there, in the darkness, but my mouth was paralyzed with weariness and I could only make a moaning sound.

It was not loud enough for her to hear and she said again, "Liam?"

The door opened a little farther and her shadow warped and twisted and contorted in the yellow light. She was walking toward me – urgently, purposefully.

"Liam?"

I was in bed, stripped naked. The bedcovers were tucked in tight and I couldn't move. The light from the open door had gone but there was a milky white glow in the air. She said, "Liam," then leaned over me. Her face was so close it was almost touching mine. Her hair was loose and fell across her cheeks. I wanted to reach up to her and touch her, but the covers held me back. She smiled and stroked my face with her hand.

I said, "Where were you?" but no sound came out of my mouth.

She smiled and stood and I thought I heard her say, "Everything is fine, Liam. We will be so happy now." She unbuttoned her blouse and dropped it on the floor. Her skin looked cool and milky. She pushed down on her jeans and wriggled out of them like a snake. I heard her say, "We are going to make love."

Then she was completely naked. The bedcovers were gone and I was naked, too. I looked down and saw that I was stiff and rock hard. I had a crazy feeling in my head and in my body. I desperately needed to feel her skin on mine. I tried to reach for her but my arms wouldn't move.

Then she was climbing on top of me, lowering herself onto me. Her hair was on my face and her lips and her breath moist on my ear.

She whispered, "But only biting. No kissing. No licking. Just biting."

And her teeth sank into my neck. A tickle of electricity ran through my skin and I arched to her. Our skin touched. Her belly was on mine and her breasts skimmed my chest. I groaned. The pleasure was too intense. Somehow, I knew that as long as our skin was touching, I could move. My head was pounding and my breath was hot and ragged. I put my arms around her and crushed her to me too hard. She whimpered in my ear and the hair from her bush brushed against me, then pushed.

I bit her shoulder. It tasted salty. I sucked hard, clenching my teeth. She arched, pushing, grinding her hips into me. Her teeth were on my neck – biting, digging deep, dragging across my skin. The pain was sharp, but it surged and ran through me like electricity, becoming a pleasure that was intolerable. I moved my mouth and bit her neck. The bite was savage. I wanted to draw blood and, as I bit, I screamed into her muscles and tendons.

Then she was sitting astride me, clawing slowly at my chest. She bent forward and bit savagely, dragging her teeth over my flesh. I roared with the pain that was pleasure. I wanted it to stop but I needed more. I sat up and hurled her on the bed. She laughed. I fell on her and plunged my head between her legs, taking big, sucking bites at the tender white flesh of her inside thigh, moving to where her legs met. I grabbed her ass in my palms, like a great drinking bowl, and buried my face in her bush, taking huge, soaking mouthfuls of her. She screamed. She tore at my hair and I bit harder with a feverish madness hot in my head. Her thighs crushed me so I could hardly breathe. I was sinking, sinking into her, and she was engulfing me. Then she was thrashing and writhing like a snake. She was wrapped around me, crushing my whole body. I raised my head and saw her looking down at me. Her body seemed to enfold mine in a warm, moist, suffocating envelope. She sighed. The quiver of a pulse ran through her. She screamed and the pulse quickened to a spasm, and I came. We came, biting at each other with quick, pecking bites. And it wouldn't stop. The stronger the electric, pulsing spasms grew, the more savagely we bit, until we were clenched to each other and screaming. Then we collapsed and lay, drenched in sweat, with an exquisite, stinging, moist burning, where I was still hard inside her.

I was in blackness. I could feel her skin under my hand. I murmured, "Where were you?"

She breathed in my ear, "At the power station."

I tried to open my eyes. I said, "How come you're here? How...?"

She laughed and said, "She's not."

My heart thrashed. I struggled to sit up and open my eyes. She was by the window. Outside, there was the dark light of a moon glowing on her skin. I couldn't make out if she was inside or outside the window. She was naked and her skin was smooth and milky. Her face was a gentle triangle and her eyes were slanting and luminous blue. Her hair was short and blonde. I knew her but I couldn't remember how.

She said, "Under the power station."

Then there was absolute blackness.

I woke up in a wild panic. My heart was pounding hard and a sharp pain was constricting my chest and my breathing. The room was dark, but a faint glow of dusk was filtering in through the window. As my breathing slowed, I made out voices. Laughter. Conversation. The chink and clatter of plates and glasses. I was at an inn — The Dragon's

Head. There were people dining downstairs and drinking.

I switched on the light. It was stark and harsh. Stupidly, I looked around for Maria—or the woman with the weird blue eyes. There was nothing. It had been a dream. Checking my watch, I saw it was eight-thirty. I'd slept for six hours. I swung my legs off the bed and realized I was naked. My brain ached and I struggled to remember. I was sure I'd lain down with my pants on. After getting to my feet, I walked unsteadily to the bathroom, feeling groggy. I turned on the shower and caught a glimpse of my reflection in the mirror. There were big bruises on my neck and shoulders and four parallel scratches down my chest.

I stepped into the shower and turned the water to cold.

Chapter Thirteen

The place was busy, with the warm noise of people talking, eating and drinking. The dining room, which had been closed and dark when I'd arrived, was now open and bright with art deco lighting, and across the busy room a bank of French windows stood open onto a lawn with more tables. I figured people must come from a long way to eat here. The guy in the tank top was at reception and I stopped to talk to him.

"When I go up, can you have someone collect my clothes and have them cleaned by morning?"

He smiled and made a note. "Of course, sir."

I was about to walk away when I saw a stack of brightly colored leaflets. I picked one up. It had a big picture of the Llyn Celyn reactor on it and was advertising guided tours. There was a paragraph about cutting-edge technology and their latest generation eye-scanning security systems. Below the phone number it read 'Call any time to book a tour. Twenty-four-hour answering service.'

I studied it a moment then made to move toward the dining room. The receptionist was watching me, smiling.

I said, "Thanks."

He pointed to the dining room and said, "It's a wonderful night, and we have plenty of free tables outside."

I nodded, crossed the dining room then stepped out into the garden. It was a broad lawn surrounded by flowerbeds, with flaming torches placed at intervals around the dining area. The moon was rising over the hills to the east and I could just make out its translucent glow on the water of the lake to the west. Most of the tables were taken, but I could see a couple that were free. As I was about to move toward one, a waiter in a burgundy waistcoat with a bow tie approached me.

"Table for one, sir?"

"Yeah."

He indicated with his hand and led me to a table near the flowerbeds. Two tables away there was a couple seated by one of the torches, their faces half hidden by wavering shadows. The waiter was talking to me. He was asking if I would like a drink.

I frowned at him a moment then said, "Yeah. A Martini, very dry."

He went away and I stood looking at the couple. The woman caught my eye and smiled. She was the woman who had been in my room — in my bed, in my dream, if that was what it had been.

The man was Serafino del Roble.

She said something to him and he turned to me.

He smiled in a way that was not a smile and gestured to a chair opposite him at his table. "Mr. Murdoch, what a pleasant surprise. It has been far too long. Won't you join us?" His Spanish accent was there, but his English was flawless.

I began to pull out the chair and paused. "How do you manage to make everything you say sound like a cheap line from a tacky movie?"

He ignored me and gestured to the woman with him. "Allow me to introduce —"

I interrupted him, "We've met. Back then, she was called 'Maria'." I turned to her. "What's your name now, sugar? Let me guess. Cherry Brandy? Peachy Bonds? Or maybe the more subtle Amber Truelove?" I turned back to Serafino, pulled out the chair then sat. "How about you, Serafino? You still Serafino del Roble? Or are you now Ben Dover or Neil N. Takem?

Serafino's face was a picture of distaste, but the woman was giggling like a kid.

He said, "That is quite enough, Murdoch. Your jokes are in very poor taste."

I pulled a Camel from the pack, flipped the Zippo and lit up. I allowed the smile to ride up the right side of my face as I breathed out smoke through my nose and said, "Fuck you."

He seemed genuinely surprised then shrugged as though I had confirmed his opinion of me. He turned to the woman and said, "You see what I mean? He has a total disregard for social convention."

She nodded, looked back at me and smiled. She said, "I had noticed the same thing."

I said, "What? While you were biting me?"

She smiled. "You don't recognize me."

I said, "I recognize you." But she was right. Her face was familiar, just like the hippie's had been. Her manner and her voice, too, but I couldn't place them. I turned back to Serafino. "As we are observing social conventions, let's catch up. Whatever happened to Catherine Howard? You have her killed?"

His face darkened. "That is none of your business, Murdoch."

I smiled. So, she had gotten away, with Sinead Tiernan. If he'd killed them, he would be gloating. The waiter appeared with my drink.

Serafino said, in a way you could describe as urbane, "Put it on my bill, would you, Peter?"

My lip curled. "Thanks. I can pay for my own drinks."

He raised his hands and laughed. "Please! I insist. It's the least I can do after all the inconvenience I have caused you."

That stopped me. He dismissed the waiter with a flick of his fingers and sat waiting for me to talk.

I said, "Okay, you got me here and you've got my attention. What's with the psychotropic drugs and the free strip-o-gram? Couldn't you have just phoned?"

He chuckled. She watched me, smiling, like I was an interesting specimen. He said, "You caused me a lot of pain, Murdoch. I have to admit it." He blustered a moment, shaking his head, shrugging, spreading his hands. It was real Spanish. "Our project is vast. Far too big for one simple simian to stop it. But you caused us serious inconvenience. And the loss of the Çabra Stone…" He shook his head, and he seemed gray and drawn. "That's unforgivable."

I exhaled smoke through my nose and said, "Good."

He looked amused, opened his gold cigarette case then extracted two cigarettes. He handed one to the woman and lit them both with a fine, gold lighter. When he was done, he squinted at me through the smoke and said, "Really? Good? Two innocent girls and one wretched schizophrenic have died horrific deaths because of you. And, at some point in an indefinite future, Maria, the woman you profess to love, will die in a far more horrific way. So, do you still think it is good?"

I flicked ash on the lawn and said, "What do you want, del Roble?"

He smiled then laughed out loud. A couple of people glanced at him.

"Oh," he said, "wouldn't you just love it to be that easy!"

A hot pellet of anger built in my gut. I said again, "I asked you what you want."

He stared at the tip of his cigarette like there was something interesting and amusing there. He said, "Let me ask you a question, Murdoch. You hairless simians, what do you want with all your nature reserves?"

I narrowed my eyes and fought the desire to take a butter knife and stick it in his heart. I said, "What?"

He waved his hand around, like he was showing me all the nature reserves in the world. "You hairless simians, you have practically eradicated nature from the planet, and, in its place, you have created thousands of nature reserves, as though you could *reserve* nature. What are they for? What do you use them for?"

I shook my head. "I'm not in the mood, del Roble."

"For what? For playing games? And yet that is precisely

what your nature reserves are for. Games. You even call the animals 'game'. What does the most powerful species on the planet do when it has achieved ultimate power? What does it do with the lesser species? It studies them, and it plays games with them — the elephant, the lion, the fox, the bull..."

I crushed out my cigarette and sipped my Martini. "Is that what you're doing with me? Is that what you're telling me? That you're playing a game with me?"

He raised an eyebrow. "Because I can. It has been very easy for you so far, but it is about to get much harder, Murdoch. I have been feeding you clues, leading you toward your own punishment, and you have followed them all to here."

I interrupted him, deliberately offensive. I said, "Harder? Really? Lady Deepthroat here told me, 'underneath the power station.' That's harder?"

There was a flicker of something in his eye that I couldn't place. He smiled. "And you believed her."

It wasn't a question so I didn't answer it. I said, "Come on, del Roble. How stupid do you think I am? I'm a hairless ape, but I get the game. You feed me easy clues that are good intelligence. Then you feed me a false clue, I fall in your trap and you crucify me as punishment for stealing your fucking stone. The game is, I have to guess what the false clue is when it comes along. And the prize if I guess is that you kill me in a different way. So, the next clue is, 'under the power station.'"

As I said it, my eye caught the leaflet under my pack of Camel. I took the pack, shook out a cigarette and lit up. When I put down my Zippo, I picked up the leaflet, folded it then put it in my pocket like I didn't want him to notice. He did, but looked at the tip of his cigarette, like he didn't want me to notice that he had noticed. I sucked smoke and blew it out through my nose like I hadn't noticed that he'd noticed. Then we sat smoking and admiring the night sky.

Finally, he said, "Whatever you may think of us, Murdoch, we are not like you. If you find Maria before our hybrid kills her, you may keep her. If you don't, then you will both become part of our genetic research program, and you will be destroyed."

Then he said to the woman, "I'm hungry."

She said, "Me, too," and del Roble turned to me, obviously enjoying himself.

"We were about to order when you showed up. Will you join us? Balazs is a superb chef. He does a rare steak which is" — he smiled smoothly — "literally to die for."

I picked up my cigarettes and my lighter and said, "Thanks. I've lost my appetite. Enjoy your evening."

I stood and went to walk away, but I stopped and put my hand on the back of the woman's chair. I leaned across her toward del Roble. She had a curious, musky smell, which was familiar.

I spoke softly, "Del Roble, before I go, I want to tell you that this time I'm going to kill you, and you're going to stay dead. Do you understand that?"

He met my eyes and didn't answer. I like to believe that he was thinking I might be right. After a moment, I blinked real slow and turned to the woman. Our faces were almost touching.

I said, "You, too, sweetheart." I said it real quiet.

I saw her swallow, then I walked away.

At reception, I stopped by the stairs and pulled out my cell. I made sure Tank-Top Man was in earshot and turned away like I didn't want anyone to hear me. I dialed the number on the leaflet. It rang twice and a chirpy voice answered.

I said, "Hi, I'd like to book a guided tour of the Llyn Celyn fusion reactor."

"Oh, yes, sir! No problem! When would you like to come? Would it be just you, sir? Or would you be bringing your family?" She sounded really pleased, like she had a vested personal interest in making that happen for me.

I said, "My family were all killed in a freak marquee accident at my best friend's wedding. It will be just me.

139

How soon can you make it?"

There was a moment's silence while she tried to decide whether I was the unluckiest man in the world or a wiseass. She gave a small, single giggle and said, "Well, we have a guided tour of the Llyn Celyn reactor tomorrow morning at half past nine, if that would suit?"

I said, "That will be perfect. Thanks." I gave her my name then hung up. I asked Norm the Tank Top to send me up a steak and a bottle of Martini, and have someone collect my clothes for the laundry. I laughed like I was a hopeless disaster and wasn't that just hilarious? "I wasn't planning on staying over, so these are the only clothes I have!"

He smiled sympathetically. Over his shoulder, I spotted that rooms three-o-one to three-o-three had their keys in their slots. There was nobody home.

Once upstairs, I figured I had fifteen minutes before the steak arrived. I chose three-o-three at random, picked the lock and went fast to the wardrobe. I was lucky. The room was occupied by a couple. I snatched a pair of pants, a shirt, a jacket and a pair of socks and left the room, closing the door quietly behind me.

In my room, I put the clothes in a laundry bag, tucked a fiver in the top and left it outside the bedroom door. Then I waited.

After twelve minutes, there was a knock and a voice called, "Room service!"

I said, "Leave it outside the door, will you? Your tip's in the bag."

"Thank you, sir!"

In a moment, I heard his feet rattle down the ancient stairs. I stepped out and collected the tray. The steak was as good as del Roble had promised, and I followed it with two stiff Martinis. Then I turned out the light and lay on the bed to wait.

By eleven, the voices outside the window started growing quieter and the clatter of glasses and plates more sporadic. By half eleven, there were only a couple of tables left, and, by twelve, the sounds were those of the waiters cleaning up for the night. By one, there was total silence.

I swung my legs off the bed and leaned out of the window. There was dense ivy up the side of the building, like there is on most British houses from that period. It's pretty tough stuff and I hoped it would hold my weight. I took the Smith & Wesson from my bag, slipped it in my waistband, then leaned out and grabbed hold of the creeper with both hands. I eased myself out. It held firm. A few seconds later, I dropped onto the lawn and stayed squatting, immobile, for five beats. There was absolute stillness and silence. The moon watched me, and I swear she was smiling. Her light was turquoise and washed everything with a strange translucence that made it hard to judge distances. The shadows under the nearby trees were bloated and diffused. I made a quick sprint for them.

Remote Wales at one-twenty a.m. is quiet. Like most of the roads in the area, the road to the power station was bordered by high banks and hedgerows that blocked out the moonlight. It was like walking through a dark tunnel of trees with a faint blue-green glow overhead. Rustles and snuffles crept on the cool night air, from obscure places below the brambles where small animals played out their own life and death dramas. The moon didn't care. It was all a game to her.

It took me ten minutes at a steady trot to make the station. When I got there, I strolled across the car park to the barrier. Light was filtering out of the cabin and I could see a uniform inside watching a portable TV. He looked up when I leaned in and wished him a good morning. He wasn't the 'Seth Efrican' from earlier, but he was from the same gene pool.

He gazed at me with no expression and said, "Who are you? This is a restricted area."

I hesitated a moment and that made him stand up and step out of the cabin.

I said, "My name is Murdoch. I have an appointment with Serafino del Roble here at one-thirty."

His forehead clenched into a painful knot. "An appointment..." He reached for the walkie-talkie on his hip.

I scratched the back of my neck with my left hand and said, "Yeah, I know it's an odd time," and, as he looked down at his radio, I put all of my two hundred and twenty pounds into a perfectly executed uppercut to the tip of his chin.

It would have laid out a rhino. This guy had the courtesy to wince and stagger and his eyes glazed. He dropped the radio and reached for his piece.

However tough you are, there are some parts of the human anatomy you are never going to make any stronger than they were created. I took a small step to my left and delivered a kick worthy of a Shire horse to his nuts, and deprived the world of at least one perfect Arian baby. He made a noise like air escaping through a small hole in a balloon and sank to his knees. I have never pretended to be honorable or noble. I kicked him again, in the head, which was neither.

I grabbed him under his armpits and dragged him back into the hut. I rifled through his pockets and found a pass card for first level security access. I knew it would need a PIN, and second and third level would use laser iris recognition. I stripped him of his uniform and put it on. Then I hefted him into his chair and pulled out my penknife. I made a small incision in his wrist and let the blood flow a bit. I slapped him a few times to wake him up and, as I saw his eyelids flutter, I pressed hard with my thumb on the cut.

He came around. His pupils were dilated. He tried to focus, first on my face, then on his wrist.

I said, "I just sliced through your vein, pal. All the way through. When I let go, you'll be dead in a couple of minutes. Tell me the PIN for your pass card, and I'll call an ambulance."

His face drained and he gaped at me. He was struggling to make sense of what had happened between his decision to call his superior and having his vein cut open. I didn't let him.

I snapped, "You have no choice. Do it!"

He moved his mouth and swallowed.

I said, "You are two minutes from being dead. React!"

He burbled, "Hash seven two six five four three eight hash." Then his face crumbled and he added, "Oh, shit!"

I made him repeat it and memorized it as he did. Then I let go of his wrist and stepped behind him. He stared dumbly at the small flesh wound.

I said, "Sorry, pal. I lied." Then I took hold of his head and broke his neck. "It was less than two minutes." Like I said, I am not honorable or noble. Besides, the world was probably a better place with him doing something useful, like feeding maggots.

What I did next I had never done before, and I hope I never have to do again. I pressed my thumb into his eye socket and pulled out his right eye. I severed the optic nerve with my knife and wrapped the eyeball in my handkerchief. You have to wonder about the direction your life has taken when you find yourself putting somebody else's eye in your pocket.

I walked across the forecourt toward the main building and followed the wall around, away from the main entrance, hoping there would be at least one side door. There was, and it had a keypad beside it with a slot for the card. I slipped it in and punched in the number he'd given me. A green light came on and the door clicked. I pushed in.

I didn't know what I was looking for. Knowing these freaks, there could be a big red sign saying, 'Murdoch, this way to the dungeon.' There wasn't. It was a very normal institutional corridor with a very normal institutional carpet and no signs. I knew the main entrance was right, so I turned left. The corridor did a full circuit of the building. There were a couple of doors that were not particularly interesting. One led to a library, another to the station manager's office, and the passage eventually took me to a large atrium with a security desk at the bottom of a broad flight of steps.

The guard at the desk looked bored, but he frowned at me as I trotted down the stairs and he said, "I don't recognize you."

I stepped over with a big smile on my face and said, "Tomorrow they'll ask you my name."

He frowned and stood. "Huh?"

I nodded, like it was obvious. "Yeah. You can tell them it was Murdoch."

He wasn't as tough as the guy outside. He went down easy. I still broke his neck, though, so he wouldn't be telling them anything tomorrow. I made my way back along the passage to the first door. There was no keypad, but there was a laser scanner. I fished out Superman's blue eye and let the laser scan it. The door opened. It was too easy, but it was always going to be a fifty-fifty chance they were expecting me, despite the laundry bag and the telephone booking. I pushed open the door then stepped in.

I was on a plain concrete landing with a bare rail of steel tubing. To my left, the landing became a flight of steel stairs that followed the curve of the wall down into semi-darkness. Above me, the ceiling domed into shadows. I couldn't see the light source, but it was dull and ineffectual. I heard a soft clang behind me as the door closed.

Unconsciously I reached back and touched the Smith & Wesson in my belt. It was good to know it was there. I began to descend the stairs into the vault. The farther down I went, the more the vast size of the place became apparent. Every step, however softly I tried to tread, seemed to scrape off the metal and echo around the huge cavern, multiplying into a thousand reverberations as it went. The air was dank and cold, and, though it wasn't pitch black, the light was gray and visibility was poor.

I must have descended a hundred feet before I saw the bottom, then climbed down another twenty to get there. I was in a vast, concrete vault. The ceiling was too high to see, and the far walls were lost in tenuous shadows. About thirty yards away and slightly to my right I could see the hulking forms of steel containers, like the ones you see on transport ships. There must have been a hundred of them, stacked on top of each other. For a moment, I wondered how the hell they'd gotten down here, but I shelved the thought.

The ghost of a voice came rolling through the half-shadows and dissipated in the cavern. It was answered, but the words were indistinguishable. I gently pulled the revolver from my waistband and inched along the wall on my left. Ahead of me, it fell back and I could make out, maybe forty or fifty yards away, some kind of porter cabin. Beyond it, the cavern was lost in darkness. I flattened myself against the wall and inched toward the cabin. I saw a guy come out, turn, then say something that was again lost in echoes. There was laughter and he walked away among the reverberations of his feet, till he was swallowed up in darkness.

It took me a whole minute to cover the distance without making any noise. By then, I could see there were no windows on the thing, just a door that stood open. I peered in and wondered why it was that whenever you leave a slob on his own, he starts watching porn. He had a burger frozen halfway to his mouth. He'd stopped chewing and all his attention was concentrated on the two women who were making out naked on the screen. That's why he didn't hear the hammer click, and that's why he didn't notice me till the muzzle was pressing against the back of his neck.

I said, "You know why I'm not going to shoot you in the back of the neck?"

His hand went limp as the burger hit the floor with a ketchup splat.

I took that for a 'no' and said, "Because it wouldn't hurt. You'd never know about it. I'm going to shoot you in the kneecaps instead. That hurts."

He made a little squeak. One of the girls on the TV was saying "Yes? Yes?" like she was answering the phone. I gave him a moment and thought about the strange mixture of emotions he must be experiencing. I was getting deep like I do sometimes.

Then I told him, "But I don't have to. We can do a deal. You tell me what I want to know, and I don't blow off your kneecaps. You think we can do that?"

He made a noise that might have been affirmative. I thought he could learn something from the girl on the TV. She had it down pat. She was saying it over and over, no problem.

I said, "Ask me what I want to know?"

He said, "Wha…what do you want to know?"

I smacked him hard across the back of the head and kicked the chair out from under him. It was an office chair on casters and it went spinning across the room then crashed into a filing cabinet. Slob hit the ground hard, covering his face with his arms. I put one knee on his chest and leveled the gun at his face.

I said, "I'll ask the questions, motherfucker! You give the answers."

He looked at me like I was being unreasonable. He was right. I was.

I said, "There's a girl here—petite, pretty, dark. She's a prisoner. Where is she?"

His mouth was trembling, so it was hard for him to talk, but he managed, "I don't see 'em. I don't know what they look like."

My eyes narrowed. I wanted to shoot him right there and then. I said, "Them?"

He swallowed. He knew he'd said something wrong, but he didn't know what. He gestured toward where his pal had disappeared a couple of minutes earlier. "In the cells. But I don't know—"

"Who would know?"

He swallowed again. It was something he wasn't finding

146

easy. "Don?"

I couldn't help it. I snarled. "Are you telling me or asking me?"

His face went gray. He said, "Don."

"That the guy who just went down there?"

He nodded. "He takes care of the...cells."

I shook my head. I was having trouble wrapping my head around it. I said, "This is a God damn power station! Why the hell have you got cells?"

He shrugged with his eyebrows. He didn't know. He was just the hired help.

I pointed at the containers. "What's with them? The containers?"

He was confused. He hesitated then said, "That's how they ship them out — in the containers?"

"The *girls?*"

He nodded.

"Where to?"

He shook his head. "I don't know. Honest. I just sit here. I don't get involved."

I stood and pulled him to his feet. I said, "For once in your miserable life, it's going to pay off for you. Turn around."

He turned his back to me and hunched his shoulders. I couldn't kill a guy that pathetic.

I said, "For your own sake, when they question you, tell them you never saw me. You were taken by surprise."

I put him down and left, along the passage and toward the cells.

Chapter Fourteen

I followed the passage for maybe thirty or forty yards. The light got dimmer as I moved along. Soon I came to an iron grill. Beyond it the passage turned right and descended a flight of steps into blackness. There was an iris scanner on the grill. I showed it Superman's eye and the grill opened.

The stairs led down through half a spiral. There was no light in the stairwell, but there was a dull glow filtering up from the bottom. I came out at a small antechamber with another grill. On the other side was a wide passage with seven metal doors evenly spaced on each side. I was sure these were the cells. Each of the doors was open. There was no sign of Slob's buddy.

I took the Superman's eye and used it one more time. No one was there. There were two bunks in each, which made a total of twenty-eight girls. I wondered what the hell they were using them for. Genetic experiments were a recurring theme with these people. The thought made me sick.

I explored each of the cells on the right-hand side in turn. There were empty and half-drank plastic water bottles and fast-food containers were strewn about. By the quantity, I figured they had been there for maybe four or five days. So, if Maria had been here, she would have been the newcomer.

The left-hand cells told a similar story, until I came to the fourth one. There were the usual water bottles and pot noodles, but one of the pots was unlike the others. I almost missed it, but a slight difference caught my eye and made me look again. The lid had been left on and there was a corner of cloth poking out from under it—the sort of thing you would only notice if you were trying to find something. I picked it up and pulled out the cloth. It was a corner torn from Maria's blouse—a desperate attempt to send a message on the off chance that I might find this crazy place. I felt a savage twist in my gut that I couldn't give her hope—let her know I was on her trail.

At the end, the passage made a T-junction, and from each branch more passages ran off with more cells. There must have been a hundred and forty cells, at least. Maybe there were more and I hadn't found them. Either way, all the ones I'd found had been unoccupied. It had the feel of a place that was only starting to gear up to some full use in the future. I could still hear Slob in my head, telling me they used the containers to ship the girls out. Where the hell did they send them? And for what? I needed Slob's pal, but there was no sign of him.

Until I came to the end of the right-hand branch of the T. There was a grill, which Superman's eye opened, and a flight of stairs similar to the last, which curved up to the right. I could hear sounds filtering down. Canned laughter. At least it wasn't porn, unless they'd come up with a new genre that I didn't know about. Sit-com porn. The possibilities were rich.

I climbed the stairs slowly, keeping my back to the outside wall and the Smith & Wesson held out in front of me. I got to the top of the stairs without meeting Friend of Slob. There was a landing that turned sharp left. The sound of the TV was loud and the show was recognizable as a repeat. I could hear rapid knocking and a voice saying, "Penny... Penny...Penny..." Laughter.

I edged around the corner. I was face to face with a wall. The wall was pale-green plastic from the floor to about three or four foot high. Above that, it was glass or Perspex up to the ceiling. There was a normal door on the right, with a normal handle. Through the glass panel I could see Friend of Slob sitting gawping at a TV, like a clone of his pal. He had a dirty plate on the desk by his side, and occasionally, his gawp turned into a loose smile and he laughed along with the canned laughter on the TV, even when what they said wasn't funny. He was a true child of the Zombie Revolution.

I kicked in the door. He clambered to his feet and I slammed my fist down into his gut. His eyes bulged and he went "Whoomph!" I slapped him twice back-handed, and, while his ears were ringing, I grabbed him by his synthetic clip-on tie and threw him on his back. I kneeled on his solar plexus and shoved the barrel of the .44 into his mouth.

I said, "You have heard of Dirty Harry..."

His eyes went wide.

"Then you know all about the Smith & Wesson 29. It won't hurt, but they'll be picking bits of your skull out of the concrete for months. It will be very upsetting for your mother."

A nasty smell made me look down. His pants were slowly turning dark at the crotch. He was going to be very cooperative.

I smiled at him. "Talk to me. Tell me everything I want to know, and you will live to see the dawn. But you have to promise me you'll get a real job tomorrow, okay?"

He nodded and tried to talk around the barrel. It sounded like, "I onging—"

"Where are the girls?" I removed the barrel.

He swallowed hard. "They shipped out, about two hours ago. There wasn't many. Only twenty-eight."

"I am looking for one girl in particular. She's not tall. She's dark, looks Mediterranean."

He was nodding. "Yeah, I know the one. She's different to all the others. I noticed. They always go for the tall blonde ones. But she arrived last minute. She was short, dark, cute—"

I curled my lip and snarled at him. "Watch your mouth. Where are they being taken?"

He went pale and started to sweat. "I don't know. Middle East, North Africa, maybe... They don't tell us nothing. But the driver..."

He hesitated and I cocked the piece.

He gabbled, "Waitwaitwait! When he saw your...the woman you're after, he said they had plenty of them. They liked the blonde, Western ones."

I stared at him. "This is a *white slaving operation?*"

He was sweating and shook his head. "I don't... I don't know. I don't fink so, but some of the girls—"

I cut across him. "License plate of the truck!"

I saw his eyes flick to the desk. He saw me follow his gaze too late. I stepped over. There was a dispatch form. I shook my head. How crazy were these people? There was the name of the driver, Hassan Marabet. The destination was Port of Dover, the plate was KAO05S. I had a flash of Maria, sitting in a darkened container with twenty-seven other women—cramped, terrified and abused. I turned to Friend of Slob. He was on his knees, staring at me. Suddenly I was filled with hatred, revulsion and a fury I couldn't control.

I put my revolver on the desk and stepped away from it. I nodded at it. I said, "Go ahead. Take it."

His expression turned a nasty mixture of predatory and crafty. He eyed the gun sideways, swallowed, looked at me then back at the gun. He lunged. He should have got to his feet first. He might have made it—maybe.

I waited till he had the gun in his hand, till he was actually a threat. Then I stepped over, grabbed his arm with my left, levered the barrel around with my right, and pressed his finger on the trigger. At that range it blew his face off. That was for calling Maria 'cute.'

I took the dispatch form. There was a back door to the cabin and I kicked that open, too. I was being stupid. I wanted them to hear me. I wanted them all to come for me. I wanted to punish them for what they had done—what they were doing—to Maria.

But nobody came. In my bones, I knew they wouldn't. I was still playing his game. I followed the passage for another few minutes then came to a set of double doors on my right.

I pushed through and found myself in a large lab. There were no technicians. The rows of benches and the apparatus were all empty and still, except for a bank of eight-foot glass tanks across the wall, maybe forty feet away. There must have been a hundred of them running the length of the room. The glass was tinted green—or the liquid in it was green—but the tanks were transparent and you could see clearly what was inside them. People—mostly women—but there were some men and children, too.

I felt a sick twist in my gut. I inspected each one carefully, but Maria wasn't there. I knew they had been left there as a message to me. This was just part of what was in store for her—and for me. They had known I was coming, all right. They didn't mind me killing a couple of guards. They were expendable and replaceable, but lab technicians, scientists? They were more valuable. There were none of those for me to go primal on.

I walked out and followed the passage to the end. It led me back to the containers and the long staircase to the top. Nobody stopped me. Nobody intercepted me. I got to the atrium in the reception and walked out of the main door. At the barrier, I left Superman's eye on his desk in case they wanted to bury him with it.

I headed toward The Dragon's Head at a fast trot. I got into the Daemon, fired up the big V12 and burned rubber for Bala, the nearest town big enough to have a public phone box.

I made it in two minutes and almost killed myself five times on the way. At the entrance to the town, there was a major intersection with a broad patch of lawn and a car park on either side of the main A road. I was going too fast to slow and stop, so I cut across the lawn and the A road and skidded to a halt in the far car park. By the time the Daemon had stopped moving, I was already half out of the door and running. I'd spotted a payphone by the entrance.

I stuck my card in the slot and dialed Russell. It rang for about twenty years before I heard his voice. It had that pillow sound.

"Yes..."

"I have a truck with a container on its way to Dover. It left the station...you understand? The station—"

His reply sounded peeved, like I thought he was stupid. "I understand the *station*, yes..."

"Okay, it left the station about two hours ago. Final destination North Africa or the Middle East. Registration number, KAO05S."

I heard him chuckle. "Cute... 'Chaos'. Our friend is the chairman of the Kallisti Corporation, which owns the controlling share of the station."

"Russell, I need—"

"Don't talk, we don't want any trigger words. Just listen. We haven't long. I take it the virgin is contained, so to speak."

Virgin, Mary, Maria... "Yes."

"She'll be met, but they won't have a tin opener. You understand?"

"Yes."

"Reggie's friends will house a pigeon on the coop."

"*What?*"

"Think, boy! And Tom will meet you at the docks with a baited glove."

"Russell, I have no idea—"

"I take it you are driving your monstrous machine..."

"Yeah."

"Just go. Go to the Dover Docks, Union Street car park off the big roundabout. And make haste, boy. Go!"

I climbed back into the TVR and barked "Dover Docks!" at the GPS. It blinked at me and told me it was three hundred miles of freeway, what the Brits call 'motorway', and would take me five hours and thirty-five minutes. I laughed.

I filled up at a gas station and hit the highway at a hundred and twenty mph. Then I began to hit the gas. When the Brits decide to make a mean car, they make it mean, and the TVR Daemon is the meanest SOB of a car ever made. It sounds like a Harley on steroids and will do zero to sixty in three seconds. It accelerates like a jump jet, will do two hundred mph without breaking a sweat and it doesn't give a fuck if your heart can take it or not. It's *mean*.

There was very little traffic at that time of night. I averaged one hundred and eighty miles per hour. Sometimes I hit two hundred. While I drove, I tried to relax and think about what Russell was trying to tell me. A pigeon and a baited glove. He would house a pigeon on the coop and give me the baited glove.

It came to me suddenly. A homing pigeon. Reggie was placing a homing device on the truck. The baited glove was what the pigeon would return to. The tracker. His guy was going to give me the tracker.

An hour and fifty minutes after I'd left Bala, I was pulling off the Prince of Wales roundabout and into the Union Street car park at the Dover Docks. I parked, got out of the car and planted my ass on the trunk while I lit up a Camel. The place was floodlit, but there was a feeling of desolation. Occasionally, you could hear the mournful call of a foghorn answered by a confused seagull that didn't realize it was nighttime. Bill Bryson once said that if you got more than two Brits together, whatever time of day or night, before long, they started laughing. It's true. But it wasn't true that night at the Dover Docks. What people I could see were dark shadows in dead, orange light. If they spoke to each other, it was in muted tones. Their footsteps echoed and were lost. Somewhere, it seemed very far away, the sea sighed.

I blew smoke into the night air. It took on an amber hue for a few seconds then vanished on a cool sea breeze. I saw a dark Range Rover approaching at speed along the viaduct from the Clarence Place. It pulled up next to me and a tall guy with blond hair and the loose, military bearing of a professional killer climbed out. He had a black leather jacket and SAS written all over him. He smiled at me.

He said, "Harry? I'm Tom. Richard asked me to give you

something."

Tom, Dick and Harry. Cute. I gave him my best lopsided smile and said, "Cool."

He yanked open the back door and pulled out a kitbag, which he dumped on the back seat of the Daemon. "You've got your tracker in there and a few other goodies, courtesy of his nibs. You're booked on the next ferry to Boulogne. Departs in half an hour." He glanced unconsciously at his watch. "Twenty-seven minutes. I'll take you to the VIP departure lounge so you can look at your birthday gifts." He gave the Daemon the once-over. "Nice motor. V12?"

I nodded. "Yeah."

"By the time you get across, Hassan will have six hours head start on you. He has a co-driver and they may do twenty-four hour stretches." He jerked his head at the hood. "She should allow you to catch up, but don't get too close. Hassan's a pro. He'll spot you. Your brief is to observe and report." He smiled like he was telling me something real nice. "Try not to kill anyone."

I raised an eyebrow at him. "I'll do my best, Tom."

He smiled a different kind of smile then that made him oddly human. He said, "I know you won't. I wouldn't."

I followed him back in the Daemon the way he'd come. The ferry was loading and a small, wiry Scots guy that I guessed was one of Tom's colleagues, grabbed my keys and loaded the car. Meanwhile, Tom took me to the VIP lounge. It was deserted. I guess very important people don't travel at four in the morning.

I said, "Can I get a drink?" and dumped the content of the kitbag on a sofa.

He said, "Sure. Irish is your tipple, isn't it?"

I stared at him. The bar was deserted, but he was behind it pouring two generous measures. I said, "Who told you that?"

He came around and handed me my drink. "We know a lot more than what you like to drink, Murdoch. But I'll let his nibs explain why when the time is right."

I felt suddenly mad. I said, "Maybe I think the time is right now."

He held my eye as he sipped. They were mild, like his voice when he spoke, but they were the eyes of a killer. No mistake. "I'm on your side, Murdoch. Don't take it out on me." He pointed at the stuff on the couch. "What have you got?"

There was a short note. I glanced at it but left it on a cushion while I had a look at the rest of the gear. There was a thing that seemed like a cell phone and fit in the palm of your hand.

I picked it up and Tom said, "The other part of that is stuck under the container. That's your monitor. You'll have to configure it. It uses voice recognition and, once you've programmed it, it will only respond to you. You switch it on with the word 'track' and 'off' is off."

I nodded, put it down on the note and turned to the other stuff. There was a Sig Sauer P226 Tacops 9mm with a threaded barrel and four twenty-round magazines. I tested it. It was nice and comfortable but felt light after my cannon.

Tom said, "A tad more sophisticated than your 'Big Bertha'. It has night-vision sights, a silencer and it's made of a carbon polymer that makes it undetectable to border security. You might need that if you go beyond France into North Africa or the Middle East. I shouldn't think you'll be hunting rhino, so I suggest you leave your monster here. I can get it to Russell, if you like."

There was a state-of-the-art hand-held GPS, a pack of water-sterilizing tablets and a small, high-resolution camera. I examined everything and put it back in the kitbag. I took a pull on my whiskey and lit a Camel. I said, "How much do you know?"

He shrugged. "I don't know what I don't know, so I can't tell you."

"Cute."

"I know enough. I've discussed it with Reggie. I know about del Roble."

"Is he still ahead of us? Are we still playing his game? Or did we just steal a march on him?"

He heaved a deep sigh and studied the whiskey in his glass, like it contained a map of the future. "That's very hard to tell, Murdoch. I'd say he wants you to follow the container, so, as far as that goes, you're still playing his game. Does he know we're involved? Your guess is as good as mine. As a rule of thumb, I'd say, once he starts trying to kill you, you'll know you've stepped out of his game plan." He glanced at his watch. "Time to board, I think."

We stepped out into the cool dawn air. Over in the east, the sky was turning a pale, mournful gray. A light drizzle had started. Somewhere in the North Sea a foghorn moaned and overhead a seagull cried out and seemed to laugh. I didn't know why. I couldn't see anything to laugh about.

Chapter Fifteen

There was nothing but scorched sand as far as the eye could see. It wasn't yellow, the way you see it in the movies. It was gray, rust-red and black under a white sky. I was headed south and east into the heart of Algeria. That had been more than ten hours ago. Now I was rattling down a road in my Daemon that I could barely make out in an endless ocean of dirt and dust.

The heat was insane. The rocks, the sand and the chassis of the Land Rover were all too hot to touch. The air con had given up the ghost coming out of the Atlas Mountains, just south of Beni Boussaid, and I had all the windows open and my shirt undone. But it was still scorching and I was running sweat.

In Boulogne I'd waited for the shops to open and bought myself a couple of shirts, some linen pants and some desert boots. I'd had a hunch I'd be needing them. By the time I was done, they had an eight-hour lead on me and the tracking device was telling me the truck was nearing the Pyrenees. It looked like they were aiming to cross into Spain at the eastern end, via Cerbère, which suggested they were making for North Africa via Ceuta. They had a good start on me, but I hadn't been too worried. I figured if I didn't rest too much, I'd catch them before they reached Algeciras.

But they'd hammered the truck and had driven, as Tom had suggested, a full twenty-four hours nonstop, and by the time I crossed the mountains, they still had a good lead on me. It had cost me three hundred euros in fines, but by the evening of the second day, I'd closed the gap on them. At three o'clock in the afternoon, I pulled into Algeciras, where my tracker told me they had dropped the container at the docks. I'd caught up with them.

I'd cruised down and parked near the port, climbed out of the TVR then took a walk along the nearest docks. From what I could see, there was an armed cordon around the container parks. In an economy as crippled as Spain's after its recent civil conflict, it figured that any foreign trade would be heavily protected. Looking at the tracker, I could see roughly the area where the container was. The thought of Maria being so close and kept in those inhumane conditions had made me sick to my stomach, but getting to her in broad daylight, with fifty or sixty armed guards around her, was going to be impossible. I would have to wait till nightfall. Late.

I was ready to drop and would probably have been useless anyway. I'd climbed back in the car and set about searching for a *posada* where I could eat and sleep. I ended up at the Alborán, just off the main drag and a short walk from the docks. I took my luggage out of the trunk, had a Martini and a steak, a long, hot shower and slept for nearly eight hours solid. By the time I'd got up and showered again, it was midnight. I dressed and went downstairs.

The hotel was pseudo Moroccan tacky in the way only pseudo Moroccan tacky can be. There were lots of eastern arches and cushions that loudly disagreed with each other but weren't prepared to do anything about it except shout. It managed to be sumptuous without being luxurious and, by the way the receptionist assessed me as I crossed the lobby, I knew the most he could get me on the black market was a ticket to a depressing cabaret involving bored women in nylon veils.

I climbed into the Daemon and drove the short distance to the port. It's a cliché, but the night was sultry. It was hot and humid and the air was full of possibilities you really didn't want to happen. Everywhere you looked there was cheap sex on offer among the ruins of recent war. Bombed-out buildings stood like broken teeth in a leer of death.

Groups of soldiers—seemingly too frightened and too young to play with guns—patrolled the streets, eyeing the cheap whores who called to them in listless provocation.

The container park at the Algeciras docks is on an island just off the port, which you get to via a long bridge. There was still tight security and, at the entrance to the bridge, an armed sergeant demanded to see my pass and my ID. My ID was my passport and my pass was a fifty euro note I'd accidentally left in the back. He pocketed the fifty, handed back my passport and jerked his head in a move-on gesture. I guessed nobody was expecting an American in a swanky English sports car to start busting open containers. I'd play it along like this as far as I could, then I'd try to lose myself in the shadows.

I crossed the bridge and drove along the north side of the island, where I finally pulled up into a desolate, concrete car park and took the tracker out of my pocket. I hadn't checked it since four that afternoon. I didn't give a damn what Russell and Hook expected of me. If Maria was here, I was going to blow the lock and get her out.

But I also knew the container would have a shipping number stenciled onto it. Whether I could get her out or not, I could use that number to find out when it was shipping, with what company and to where. That kind of information could put me—and Russell and Hook—one step ahead of the game instead of playing catch-up all the time.

I switched on the tracker. It took a few seconds to connect to the satellite, then it told me what I didn't want to know. The container had shipped while I had been sleeping. I swore under my breath. It was halfway across the Alborán Sea, heading toward Morocco. By the looks of it, toward Ceuta. I swore again, more loudly, climbed back into the Daemon and hammered across the bridge. A left at the roundabout took me to the passenger port. Everything was closed. A timetable on a public information board told me the last ferry had gone at eleven p.m. The first in the morning would be at four a.m. If it was going beyond

Morocco — and it almost certainly was — the container, with its cargo, would be hundreds of miles away long before I'd had my first coffee.

And that created a whole new problem. The Daemon. On highways and motorways, I could hit the gas and close the gap pretty fast. But I couldn't take the Daemon into the Sahara. It just wasn't built for that kind of terrain. I would need a good 4X4, but that would reduce my speed by two-thirds or more. I was looking at averaging thirty to fifty miles per hour most of the way. I'd be matching their speed, topping it by twenty miles per hour at best. That meant that before I'd caught up with them, the container would deposit its cargo and head back toward London. I'd cross my tracking device on the road, returning, without an exact location for where the girls had been dropped. It was a disaster.

One of the few things I've learned in life is that you play the hand you're dealt, and there is no point worrying about things you can't fix. So, I found the long-term car park, locked up my TVR then went to look for a restaurant and a whiskey.

Algeciras is one of the ugliest towns on Earth, on the inside and on the outside. Nighttime didn't make it any less ugly. All that changed was the ugly people who slept through the daylight hours came out in the dark, like geckos, to lurk on the fringes of dull streetlamps, waiting for something weaker than themselves to come along so they could prey on it. I didn't look weaker than anyone I saw on my way back from the docks, and, if I spotted more than three in a group, I made sure they got a glimpse of the Sig in my belt. When they did, they understood I was the meanest son of a bitch in their particular valley and gave me a wide berth.

I found a late-night joint that didn't look too bad. I had a steak and two large whiskeys and went to my room for another two hours' sleep.

* * * *

The ferry pulled into Ceuta just after five as the eastern horizon was turning a dirty, grainy gray. It was already getting warm and there were damp patches showing through my linen shirt. I found a Hertz car rental manned by a guy who seemed determined to grin too much, even though he was already at work at five a.m. I rented a Land Rover Defender, which is the best 4X4 ever built, bought twelve liters of water then climbed into the cab.

When I was behind the wheel, I checked the tracking monitor. They had six hours on me and they had made them count. They were in the Atlas Mountains, approaching the border with Algeria.

Now, ten hours later, I was crashing out of the mountains and hurtling into a broad plain where all I could see was dust, heat-mirages and desiccated emptiness. My head ached, my neck ached, my whole damned body ached, but I couldn't stop. Ahead of me, to the south and east, I could just make out the black rim of a mountain range on the horizon. The Illizi Highlands. I glanced at the clock on the dash. It was four o'clock. The hottest two hours were ahead. I wiped sweat from my eyes and wondered how much longer I could keep going before I had to rest. I took the tracker from the seat beside me and snapped, "Track!" It told me they were in the Grand Erg Oriental Desert, headed toward the Tassili N'Ajjer Mountains, the black rim I could see to the southeast. The road straightened out ahead of me and I floored the pedal in top gear. The big V8 struggled to eighty miles per hour and stayed there. It was the most it was going to give me.

I kept up that rate for the next two hours. At six o'clock it started to get dark. Night falls real fast in the desert, and by six-ten the west was a blaze of orange and purple, and the east was a deep, midnight blue. My eyes were aching and I was thinking I needed to pull over for an hour to have a sleep, when something caught my eye in the distance, away in the south-east. It was like a flash of silver light, like a distant headlamp, only above the horizon, in the air.

I looked again, but it was gone.

I drove another five minutes, trying to eke out every mile I could before resting. Then it hit me—a flash so intense that the desert and the sky disappeared. I hit the brakes and heard the tires scream. The Defender slewed on the sand and dust on the blacktop. There was a loud 'whoomph' and next thing the flash had passed and I was staring out into the deepening darkness of the desert. In the sky to my right, I could see a small red light moving slowly. It seemed to stop and hover. Then it began to flash red, yellow, blue and green. I hit the gas and realized the Defender had stalled. I turned the ignition but nothing happened. It was totally dead. I swore under my breath and tried again, keeping an eye on the light.

It seemed to swell and pulse for a moment. Then the flash again, so intense everything vanished and I covered my head with my arms. Again, the sound, 'whoomph' and the Land Rover rocked on its suspension. The light vanished. I raised my head. Outside, it was still and dark. No dust had been whipped up by a slipstream. There was nothing, only the stillness of the desert. I tried the ignition. Nothing, not even the choking cough of a dying battery. I climbed out of the cab and stood looking around me. I found it over to the east, winking red and yellow and blue and green, sitting maybe two hundred feet above ground, watching me. I couldn't tell how far away it was, maybe a mile or two. Maybe more. Then I noticed it had begun to creep closer. A cold prickle of fear skimmed my skin.

Soon I could make out that the colors were a kind of rainbow prism of intense light around a solid object. It was maybe fifty foot across, saucer-shaped and featureless. It was completely silent in its movement and didn't seem to disturb the air around it. There were no eddies, currents or slipstreams. At three hundred yards, the winking, swirling prism went out and left a dull, silver glow. The object was metallic. I knew what I was looking at was the classic UFO flying saucer that the crazies were always talking about on conspiracy sites. I thought of Russell and Hook and their crazy theories and I felt sick.

Then it was over me, filling the whole sky. Now I could hear a faint humming sound and my skin tingled. My heart was pounding high up in my chest and I was struggling to breathe and keep a cool head. There was another, massive flash of white light and I found myself curled up in the dust with my arms over my head. The sky was empty and completely still, apart from the distant, frozen stars. The dust was chilly under my hands as I pushed myself up. I scanned the sky for the red light. It was gone. I turned to stagger toward the Defender and saw its headlamps were on and the engine was idling.

I clambered into the driver's seat and fumbled for a Camel. I flipped my Zippo, lit up and sat smoking, staring out of the windshield. Had it happened? Had I had a hallucination brought on by fatigue? I rubbed my face with both hands. That was what I wanted to believe and it was what I chose to believe, but I knew damn well what I'd seen was as real as the Land Rover I was driving. I put the Defender in gear then pulled off the road. I killed the engine and allowed myself two hours' sleep.

I awoke with a start. It was still dark. Outside there was absolute stillness in the desert. The stars were winking like tiny particles of ice. I was aware they had changed their positions. I was also aware the horizon had changed. The mountains were higher. The lay of the desert was different. The road was in a different place. I looked at the clock. Exactly two hours had passed.

I swore violently, hit the ignition, put the engine into gear and hit the road. While I was driving, I fumbled for the tracker and shouted, "Track!" The container was at rest, maybe a hundred and fifty miles away. I pushed the Land Rover to eighty miles per hour. My headlamps were on full beam and all I could see was the coned funnel of light ahead of me in the blackness. The road was straight and there was a kind of craziness to the way it was rushing at me. A voice in my head kept telling me I had seen a UFO and somehow been transported almost six-hundred miles in two hours. But the thought was too crazy and I pushed it away. What I needed to focus on was that the container had stopped and was within my reach, two hours away. I didn't know how, but it was, and I had to grab that opportunity with both hands.

I'd been hammering the road maybe ten or fifteen minutes before it turned sharp right. I slowed as much as I could to take the corner and began to accelerate out of the bend when I was blinded by a sudden flood of intense light. A voice in my head swore and said, "Not again!" I slammed on the brakes and shielded my eyes with my left arm. Through the glare, I saw uniformed figures with submachine guns slung across their chests. They were jumping around in front of me, holding up their hands and shouting at me. I screeched to a halt feet away from their barrier.

I was as mad as a bear with a hornet up his ass and was bellowing at them and punching the wheel. It wasn't smart. A captain marched up to the driver's door with two grunts and wrenched it open. He was screaming something at me in Ugly. I shouted back at him but then all three of them were grabbing at me and dragging me onto the road. As I stumbled down, I saw three more grunts training their weapons on me. One of them caught me by the back of the neck and another was twisting my arm. The captain was pointing his pistol at my head, still bellowing at me like an angry fishwife.

Then some future hero of the People's Revolution smashed me in the kidneys with a rifle butt. I bit back a shout of pain and someone, probably the same SOB, kicked me in the back of the knee and I went down. Then the whole world was a rain of kicks, boots and rifle butts. All I could do in a moment like that was to sacrifice my dignity to the fetal position and hope the beating ended soon. After a bit, the pain stopped being intense and became a generalized, dull ache. I picked up a few bruises on my back and legs but managed to salvage my good looks.

Next thing, two of Algeria's finest were pulling me to my feet and pushing me toward an open-top Jeep. The captain was still pointing his weapon at me and yelling as he took swipes at my face. They pushed me in the back and the captain climbed in the front and turned to keep his pistol trained on me. I noted it was a Desert Eagle and was glad I was beginning to think and react. I didn't look at the Land Rover. I didn't want them thinking it contained anything but my luggage. I really didn't need them finding the Sig or asking me what the tracking monitor was. But, as we pulled away, I could see two guys climbing in, like they were searching for something.

We drove at speed, heading south. After five minutes, we hit a roundabout and crossed it without pausing. Then the road bore left at a gas plant illuminated by vast spotlights, like a giant football field. A road sign said *In Amenas* and next thing we were driving through a squalid, desolate town where nightlife was a frightened, timorous crime against authority, and the streetlamps revealed nothing but empty pavements and dark, silent doorways and windows.

There was no traffic and we hurtled through the town doing forty miles per hour. Then we were out in the desert again. Up ahead there was a glow of light from some kind of complex. I'd spotted the wings on the captain's collar and I guessed it was an air force base. I was beginning to put two and two together, but I was scared I was making five instead of four.

I eyed the captain a moment and said, "You speak English? I'm an American."

His answer was to pistol-whip me across the face and scream at me in Ugly again.

In less than five minutes, we were pulling into an airbase. As we cruised toward the main admin buildings, I caught sight of the field and the runway. I saw one small plane, a lot of military helicopters and a real long runway — the kind of thing you'd need for a Jumbo 747. I wondered how many

747s they had landing out here in an average week.

We stopped outside a row of one-story buildings. Double glass doors gave onto a small lobby lit by strip neon lights. I was pushed through the doors and the captain strode ahead to a set of fire doors that led down a passage with offices either side. I thought about demanding to see the colonel, demanding they respect my rights under the Geneva Convention, but I knew the best I'd get from that would be another pistol-whipping — if I was lucky.

The captain knocked on the door at the end of the passage and opened it. He exchanged a few words with somebody inside then turned and signaled the grunts to bring me in. I had a hot pellet in my belly because I was pretty sure I knew what was coming next. The grunts pushed me in. They closed the door and stood on either side of it. There was a guy in uniform in a chair behind a desk. By his insignia, he looked like a colonel. He was about sixty with graying temples. He watched me a moment with mild disgust.

Finally, he said, "You are Jewish!"

I shook my head, "No."

"Israel! Jewish pig!"

"I'm an American."

"Israeli, Jewish pig, American…all the same. What you are doing here?"

I'd been thinking about that question since Dover. I still hadn't come up with an answer I liked, but I did my best.

"I'm writing a book about the Fennec, the Algerian desert fox. It's unique. It's one of the natural wonders of the world, and it is practically unknown. I am researching it. The examples at Illizi are the best in the world."

"You are naturalist." It wasn't a question, but it was full of ironic disbelief.

I shrugged and sighed and said, "Yes. I am."

"Where is camera, film, notebooks, notes?"

"My bag was stolen."

"Where?"

"Ceuta."

167

"Ceuta? You come from Morocco?"

"Yes."

"Why? Why not fly to Algiers?"

"It was cheaper to fly to Malaga and rent a car in Morocco."

Outside, I watched a Jeep skid to a halt. The door at the end of the corridor slammed open and boots tramped down to the office. There was a loud knock. The colonel barked in Ugly and the door opened. A grunt handed him my bag and an explanation. He was dismissed and he left. Colonel Brain poured my stuff onto his desk. The tracker was there, but the Sig wasn't. I figured they had made only a perfunctory search and hadn't felt under the dash. That might mean nothing, or it might mean they weren't out searching for me, in particular. They didn't know who I was. They'd just hauled me in because I was a Yank driving around the desert at night for no good reason.

He picked up the tracker and turned it over in his fingers. He was looking for the On button. He showed it to me. "What is this?"

"It's my voice recorder. The battery is dead. The charger was in my other bag, the one that was stolen." He watched me and I thought I detected doubt in his face. So, I pushed. "And before you start laying into me again, Colonel, I am an innocent citizen of the United States of America and I am protected by international treaties and international law. So take it easy, will you?

He put down the tracking monitor and walked over till he was standing in front of me. I knew I'd overplayed my hand and I was ready for the backhander when it came. But it still hurt like hell and left my head ringing. What I wasn't ready for was the right cross that sent me crashing to the floor, half-unconscious, or the vicious kick that followed.

The beating lasted maybe two minutes, but it was enough to leave me badly bruised and weakened. I knew a couple more of those would incapacitate me. I had to avoid any more beatings, and clearly the US citizen card was no ace of trumps in this neighborhood. The same grunt who had kicked me to the ground earlier now grabbed a handful of my hair and dragged me to my feet. The colonel, panting from his exertion, shoved me back into the chair.

He thrust his face into mine, just an inch away, and screamed, "You American Jewish shit! You shit! Shit! You're nothing here! Nothing but shit!"

And I knew in that moment I was going to kill him—him and his grunt.

I had the iron taste of blood in my mouth, and I could feel my lip and the side of my face swelling. I said, quietly, patiently, "I am not Jewish. I am not religious. Life is complicated enough without bringing gods into it. I am just a naturalist who loves your deserts and your wildlife, nothing more." Then, promising myself I would put a bullet between his eyes, I added, "I am very sorry if I have offended you or your country with my behavior."

He stood erect and looked down at me. The contempt was palpable, like slime. But he'd liked the apology. It had fed his ego. "Prove!" He spat the word at me, literally, and I felt his saliva rain on my face. "Prove you are not Mossad spy!"

I was sure now they had no idea who I was, and I was getting a pretty good idea of why I was here. I frowned at him. "How can I prove a negative?"

"Who you work for?"

I spoke without thinking. "I work for the University of London."

"University of London? Prove!"

"Okay, call the head of my department."

I gave him Russell's number at UCL. He stared at me a long while then barked at his grunts in Ugly and I was dragged away. They took me out of the building and across a yard to a place that was little more than a shack next to some hangars. They unlocked the door and threw me in. I dropped to the floor, rolled on my back and listened to the door lock behind me.

Chapter Sixteen

I lay for half an hour, nursing my wounds in the dark and allowing my eyes to adjust to the absence of light. I had no idea if the colonel would buy my UCL story or how Russell would react when he received a phone call asking about me. Either way, my first priority had to be escape, but the state I was in, I didn't know how I'd make it.

After a time, I dragged myself to my feet and had a look around. It was a plain, empty room with a wooden door and a window. The window had metal bars and the door had a simple Yale lock—a cinch if I'd had my picks. But they were duct taped under the dash with the Sig, if they hadn't been found. There was nothing in the room I could use for a weapon, either.

I slid down the wall and curled up on the floor. If there was nothing I could do right then, my best plan was to sleep and try to recover some of my strength. I was pretty sure I was going to need it.

They came back about an hour later, the one who'd hit me with the rifle butt and another one. They didn't put much enthusiasm into it. They kicked me around for a few minutes, but they'd obviously interrupted a cheap porn movie or a speech by their favorite political leader to come and see me, because they finished up quick and left. But enthusiasm or not, they left me more badly bruised and aching, and, what was more important, in even less of a fit state to make a run for it. I tried to find a place on my body that didn't hurt so I could lie on it, but there wasn't one. So I thought about Maria and the container instead. It had stopped moving and had presumably unloaded its cargo.

If I wanted to check out their operation and get Maria out of there, I needed to get to it by morning, before it took off back to London again. And I didn't know how I was going to do that. I doubted I could even stand right then, let alone run.

One small consolation was that my arrest didn't seem to be part of del Roble's plans. If I survived, it might just give me an edge of surprise.

Then I heard boots tramping outside and I groaned. They were coming back for more. I pushed myself up against the wall and prepared to try to stand. I was out of options. I was going to have to either kill them or die.

The door opened and the two grunts came in, followed by the colonel. They'd brought an old, rickety wooden chair with them for him to sit on. He sat and produced my tracking monitor from his pocket. His manner had changed subtly. He was what you might call dangerously courteous.

"What is this?"

"It's a voice recorder."

"Why have you brought it here?"

"I use it as a notebook."

"Why can't I switch it on?"

"The battery is dead."

"Because you left your charger in the bag that was stolen in Morocco…"

It wasn't a question but I said, "Yes."

He turned it over and showed me the back. He was showing me the battery cover. It was a cell—the sort you replace after two years, not the sort you recharge. I looked at it, then met his eye.

"What are you showing me? It's a cell. I know. You haven't got that here yet? It's new from Apple. Next year, you'll be able to recharge your watch."

He closed his eyes, like he was sad. "I don't know what you are doing here, Mr. Murdoch, but you are not studying desert foxes. We haven't the facilities here, so I am going to take you to Illizi. There we can make you talk very quickly."

He jerked his head and the two grunts grabbed my arms. The colonel walked out and I made my play. I made a feeble attempt to shake free of the grunts.

I snapped at one of them, "I can walk!"

He didn't like my tone and he curled his lip, swore at me in Ugly and shoved me hard. I stumbled and fell onto the wooden chair. As I'd expected, it splintered underneath me and I crashed to the floor. They were screaming at me and kicking me and I made a big show of cowering and covering myself as I crawled away from them. By the time they'd dragged me to my feet and out of the room, I had my weapon hidden in my pants. It wasn't much, but a long, jagged piece of wood is as good as a Samurai sword, once it's inside you.

I was thrown into the back of a Jeep again, and it was no surprise to see the colonel being driven away in a black Audi. We took off after him, back toward In Amenas. When we got there, under the flood of light from the gasworks, we turned south and accelerated into the blackness of the desert. The grunt who'd hit me with the rifle butt was sitting in front, half turned toward me with a service automatic in his hand. I had a grunt on either side, each holding an automatic weapon. Then there was the driver. From what I could see, he was a sergeant. This wasn't the time, and besides, I was getting a free ride to where I wanted to be.

But, for the hell of it, I eyed Rifle-Butt Man up front and said, "You speak English?"

He sneered and spat something at me in Ugly about English American Western Satan Jewish Pig. I smiled.

I said, "Good. Tonight, one of us is going to die, and two gets you twenty, it's going to be you."

He showed me his nostrils again and gave me some more crazy talk. I looked away and smiled at the racing blackness around us. We drove for maybe an hour and a half, and over to the right I began to see the glow of some kind of facility in the desert. After a while, the Audi up ahead swung right off the road and we followed it. Ten minutes later, we drove into the base. The guard on duty at the barrier must have known the colonel's Audi because he glanced at it and saluted without stopping it. We sailed through in its wake.

Before we hit the main offices of the base, the Audi turned off the blacktop and we moved across the dirt toward a collection of huts and low buildings set aside from the main complex. I figured these were the colonel's 'facilities'. I had a nasty pit in my belly that I knew was raw fear. This was it. *Now.*

We headed for one of the huts. The door was open and light was spilling out onto the yellow sand. The Audi was parked out front with its two near-side doors open. We pulled up behind it and they dragged me out by my arms and my hair. Then they pushed me through the open door into the hut. I saw a small desk with the colonel sitting behind it. In the middle of the room was an autopsy table and next to it was a trolley with lots of cold, steel blades on it. Beyond, there was an iron frame bolted to the wall. There was also a tap, like a garden tap, with a bucket next to it.

The colonel looked at me with eyes that were bored of seeing suffering. He had seen human beings reduced to their most pitiful, broken state and he'd gotten used to it. He said, "I spoke to your Professor Russell Whittering. He was annoyed at being woken so late, but confirmed everything you said."

I frowned. "So I can go?"

He smiled at his desk and shook his head. He pulled out the tracking monitor and laid it in front of him. "This is not Apple technology. There are no plans to recharge your watch for next year, Mr. Murdoch. You—and Professor Whittering—are lying."

The pain in the back of my legs was like nothing I had ever felt in my life. Before I could fall, I was being dragged backward and I was thinking, *Not the autopsy table! Not the autopsy table!* That was when I saw the pulley in the ceiling. The room went upside down. My head smashed against hard concrete. Rope bit into my ankles. My face scraped on the cement then I was swinging, being hoisted upside down. It stopped when my head was three or four feet from the floor. Then a wooden chair was pulled in front of me and the colonel sat with his face maybe a foot or eighteen inches from mine.

"First," he said, "we will castrate you. Forgive me if the blades we use are not quite razor-sharp. We are just a humble, third-world country without your Western resources, so we don't replace our scalpels very often.

"The scrotum is, as you know, a very sensitive area with many nerve endings. The pain, Mr. Murdoch, will be beyond imagining. And the psychological impact will be profoundly destructive, on a psychic level.

"Your death, however, will not follow quickly. We will do things to you that go beyond horror, but we will make it linger. If you talk now, I can promise you a quick, painless death. If you talk a lot and you are of interest to us, I may even be able to spare your life and send you back home."

I ignored what he was saying. I had to. All I could think of was that I needed him to turn away for just a moment. Rifle Butt had stepped out to take the air. Maybe he was squeamish. The other was sitting by the door looking bored, like he wanted to fast-forward to the good bit.

I said, "Are you crazy? You can't just arrest random researchers and murder them because they have voice recorders! There will be political repercussions."

"You are wrong, and I think you know you are wrong. We can do anything we like."

"Yeah? Like Lockerbie?"

He smiled and shook his head, "No, *we* can do anything we like."

I stared at him, but my head was beginning to throb. *We? Who's we?*

"You don't know?"

I lost patience. "Oh, for crying out loud. You are fucking crazy. This is insane. For fuck's sake, show me the damned recorder and I'll show you how it works!"

He raised his eyebrows, stood then moved to the desk. Every muscle in my body was screaming, but I forced myself and doubled at the waist, reaching for my pockets. With my fingertips, I found the four-inch piece of wood I'd taken from the chair and slipped it into my palm. The colonel came and stood over me. He had the tracker in his hand.

"What are you doing?"

"Colonel, this is insane. Let me down!"

He sat and leaned forward. His eyes were soft and brown. I saw every pore in his skin.

He said, "When we start cutting, Mr. Murdoch, it will be too late to turn back."

He didn't get any further. What he said next was just gurgles. I had plunged the piece of wood into the soft flesh behind his jaw. His eyes bulged as his throat filled with blood. I pulled hard with my right arm, till his face was an inch from mine. With my left hand, I released his pistol from its holster. It was a good, reliable Colt 45 automatic.

"Let me introduce myself, Colonel," I said, and it must have looked weird to him, my face upside down and swollen from hanging there. "I am the meanest son of a bitch in this fucking valley." I put the muzzle in his eye and blew his brain out of the back of his head.

I turned and saw the grunt gawping at me, fumbling for his piece. It's hard to aim upside down, so instead of hitting him in the chest, the slug tore out his balls. Juliet Loss would have said there are no accidents and my unconscious had done it deliberately. Maybe she'd be right about that. Either way, he let out a weird, high-pitched sound then passed out. The other grunt came crashing in. My favorite, Mr. Butt. I made a hole in his thigh and, as he went down, I aimed at the ropes around my ankles. I was lucky not to blow my foot off, but the next moment I was on the floor, winded but alive. I staggered to my feet and turned. Butt was half out the door, leaving a trail of blood behind him. He thought he was going to raise the alarm. I took two strides with an energy that was pure adrenaline fueled by hatred, kneeled on his back and put a .45 round through the base of his skull. I'd have liked to have made some wiseass comment to him, but you can't always get everything you want.

I collected the tracker from the colonel then stepped outside. The main airbase complex was about five hundred yards away and brightly illuminated with spotlights. It looked quiet. Over to my right, in the shadows, was my Land Rover. I figured they'd brought it to make a thorough search of it. I opened the cab and felt under the dash. They hadn't done the search yet. My Sig was there, with my picks. My bag was on the back seat, with my two-hundred Camels and my Zippo.

I grabbed my things and slung them into the Audi, closed the smoked windows then drove out of the airbase, like I was heading out for a breath of air. As I turned onto the highway, headed south, I shook free a Camel and lit up, inhaling deeply and gratefully. Then I laughed — a lot and a bit crazily but figured I was justified.

I drove for half an hour, not knowing where I was going, not checking the tracker, trying to be as random as I could. Eventually I saw a faint glow beyond some sand dunes and took the next dirt track in that direction. After ten minutes, I saw a small, ramshackle town in the distance. I pulled off the road and behind a low hill. I figured I had maybe four hours before first light. I was asleep in seconds, with the Sig on my lap. Any son of a bitch who tried to arrest me that night was going to die.

Chapter Seventeen

Dawn came at six a.m. The first thing I did was pee in the dirt, make a paste and plaster it on the license plates so they were covered in desert dust and grime. Then I fired up the Audi and made my way into the town.

It wasn't much of a place, maybe thirty houses and a couple of tea shops. I noticed the buildings were all new, but there was no factory or plant that I could see, and there were very few plantations of crops. I wondered what the purpose of the town was. I stopped on a dirt esplanade in the shade of a palm tree, where the car's plates wouldn't be too visible. Then I climbed out and walked over to an inn that doubled as a tea shop that was just opening. The guy was wearing a *djellaba* and had a face like a desiccated date. He watched me with caution but no interest, which was odd, because I must have looked as though I'd just gone ten rounds with a grizzly on steroids.

I smiled as I approached. "You speak English? Coffee?" I made a drinking motion. "Breakfast?" I made an Italian gesture at my open mouth.

He turned toward the open door and shouted a lot then carried on setting out tables and chairs like I wasn't there. A few seconds later, a boy of about fourteen came out, wearing a grown man's moustache.

He went into a frenzy of grinning and said what sounded like, "I am Habib. You are from Gh'listicor? You would like coffee and breakfast? You are hurt? You want doctor? I can get doctor for you."

I said, "Slow down. Coffee and some breakfast sounds good. I don't need a doc. What is...?" I made a noise like

I was trying to remember the name of a Scottish lake and squinted at him.

He grinned harder, if that were possible, and said, with great deliberation, "Ghal-isti-cor. You are from them?"

I looked like I suddenly realized what he was saying and nodded. "Yeah! Yeah, that's right. Bring me a pot of coffee and some *ktaif* or *m'hancha*, would you?"

He went away and I sat searching at the dirt road and the hills, wondering what Ghal-isti-cor might be. Then I got a flash of a hippie VW camper van and the license plate of the truck I was following. Kallisti. The goddess of chaos. The Kallisti Corp.

The kid Habib came out with a big pot of coffee and a plate with two *m'hancha* on it—'snake cakes'. He put them down in front of me and I handed him a months' wages. His eyes popped.

I smiled and said, "Listen, Habib, maybe you can help me. I have an important job at the Kallisti Corp. They were expecting me yesterday. But"—I laughed like a stupid Westerner who knows someone as smart as Habib would never do anything this stupid and said—"but I got lost in the desert, and I was mugged."

"Muckt?"

"Some men tried to steal my things."

His eyes and his mouth made three perfect Os. I let him catch a glimpse of the Sig and winked. "They didn't get anything, but I am lost. I need to find the Kallisti Corp. You know where it is?"

He nodded vigorously and waved his hands about a lot. "Yes! Yes! Many people here working there. Is near!"

"Tell me."

He jumped into the road and made a manic motion like he was throwing a spear in the opposite direction from where I'd come. "You go down, down, down, down…"

"Okay, I go down the road…"

Then he started dancing, throwing his arm over to the right, "Then you go, there, there, there…"

"I turn right."

"Yeah, the road turning, turning, turning"—he danced like a baby trying to rock'n'roll—"and, maybe ten minutes, you come."

"I come…"

"Yuh, big fence and soldiers."

I thought about it for a minute then nodded. "Okay. Give me a room for the night. I'm going to have a shower and a sleep, then lunch. Okay?"

He beamed. "Okay, mister!"

I slept like the dead, only without the decomposition. I awoke at half two, expecting the place to be overrun with soldiers all shouting in Ugly. But it was quiet, except for the sound of the old guy outside sweeping the sand. I guess it made sense to him. That was what my life is all about, trying to get things to make sense.

I showered, ate a lamb *tajin* and drank a couple of gallons of sweet mint tea. Then I stepped out into the heat and the dust. I drove along the dust road, going *'down, down, down, down,'* until I came to a junction. It was the only place on the whole plain where I could turn right, so I took it. The kid had been right. The road became a wide track, winding among sand dunes that grew bigger as I went deeper. I followed the track for seven minutes, driving slowly, trying not to raise too much dust, then pulled off the track and parked behind a couple of dunes. Then I set out on foot.

The heat was like nothing I had experienced before. It must have been well over fifty Centigrade. There was no smell to the air except the warm odor of toasted dust. The sun burned and the occasional breeze was more of a hot wind that dried your skin and made it feel hotter.

I struggled over the dust and loose stones, clambering up and down hills and dunes for about five minutes, which in that kind of heat and terrain feels more like half an hour. Then I came on it suddenly. I had reached the top of a hill, and I saw a broad plain stretch out in front of me. It was probably twenty or thirty miles square. The earth was a pale gray, almost white, with sparse, stunted shrubs, but nothing else—save rocks and stones—to relieve the dead tedium of the landscape.

But in the hot glare of the sun, I noticed something in the middle of the plain that made me drop and crawl to the crest of the hill on my belly. It was probably no more than two or three hundred yards away, and once you knew it was there, it was easy to see. But I figured that from the sky—or to a satellite—it was all but invisible.

It was a series of twenty-five hangars set out in a series of concentric pentagons. They were painted the same gray-white as the earth, and the space between each concentric set of hangars was draped with a pale-gray camouflage cloth. It was hard at this distance to see what was beneath the cloth, but I thought I'd caught glimpses of green, as though they were crops of some sort. There was a perimeter fence with five watchtowers and barbed wire, and I could see armed soldiers patrolling the area with dogs. I took the tracker from my pocket. The container was there, by the looks of it in one of the outer hangars. But that didn't tell me where Maria was. She could be anywhere by now.

I lay there for about twenty minutes, getting heatstroke, and counted a total of twenty guards. There were Jeeps and Toyota trucks. They all had army insignia. This was obviously a joint operation between the Algerian government and the Kallisti Corporation. And that was going to make breaking in hard.

I scrambled down the hill and made my way back toward the car. I was beginning to hallucinate about frosted tankards of ice cold beer and big chunks of cucumber and watermelon. I knew I was becoming dehydrated and it was time to head back to the inn.

I switched on the air con as I pulled back onto the track. The circulation helped, but my mouth was dry, like I'd been eating dirt. I made myself focus on what I needed to do next. The engine whined and complained as I bumped onto the track. It was cool inside, but outside the glare was fierce. I told myself I had two clear short-term objectives. I had to get Maria out, and I had to get a message to Russell and Hook, telling them where this place was. We had been really quick to jump in, but we had not thought about an extraction strategy. "Just observe," Tom had said, but he'd known I couldn't do that. So had Hook. The million-dollar question I couldn't answer was whether we were still playing del Roble's game or whether my arrest had thrown them off. If we were playing del Roble's game, my cell was being monitored, and if I called Russell or Hook, he would know about it.

I thought about driving to the nearest town and mugging some random guy to use his phone, but it would take too long. And it was a safe guess all the cells in the village were being monitored, so I couldn't use any of theirs — *if* we were still playing his game.

I turned it over from every angle, but as I pulled back into the village and parked, I was still no nearer a solution. If I got Maria out without a good extraction plan, we were as good as dead — or worse.

Habib was sweeping when I stepped into the shade of the building. I was about to head up the stairs when, thinking about that ice-cold beer, I said, "Habib, is it possible, for the right price, to get a cold beer?"

He gave me a big, leering wink and said, "Go up! Go up! I bring! Often I bring bosses at Gh'listicor."

I went up. My head was splitting, but the shutters were half-closed against the heat and the room was cool. I threw my clothes on top of the kitbag that was laying on the chest of drawers then stepped into the bathroom for a cold shower. The cool water brought me around and cleared my head and I stood for two whole minutes letting it run over me, thinking of nothing. It was while I was toweling myself dry that I heard Habib knock.

"Mister? I come in? I bring?"

I wrapped a towel around my waist and opened the bathroom door, calling, "Come on in!"

He had a six-pack of Carlsberg and a bucket of ice. His hands were full and he was looking around for somewhere to put it all. He spotted my clothes on the chest of drawers and made a beeline for it, babbling as he went. "Oh! Excuse me. I put off and make a room."

Before I could stop him, he'd stuck the beer in the bucket and grabbed my clothes and the kitbag and slung them onto the bed. The Sig dropped out at his feet and, next to it, the note from Hook.

He glanced down at them, grinned at me and said, "Sorry, sorry…" Then he put the bucket on the dresser and went to leave.

I said, "Wait." I picked up my pants and pulled out a ten-dinar note. I gave it to him and winked. I said, "Thanks, Habib. You're a good kid." He had seen the Sig that morning and it hadn't fazed him. But it couldn't do any harm to keep him sweet.

After Habib left me, I bent down, picked up the note and realized I hadn't read it yet. Things had moved so fast. I cracked a beer, drained half then sat on the bed. I opened the note and cursed myself for a damned fool for not having read it in the beginning.

It was brief, with instructions on the use of the tracker and the Sig, all of which Tom had covered back in Dover. What he hadn't covered was the last, two-line paragraph.

When you need extracting, call this number. Say something meaningless. We'll call you back. We will be untraceable. You say nothing. Just listen.

The number followed. I memorized it, tore the note into small pieces and flushed it down the pan.

I drained the remains of the beer. Then I opened the shutters and sat with my feet on the wrought-iron railings of the small balcony.

I dialed the number and an efficient female voice said, "Albion Counsel, how can I help you?"

I said, "Hey, babe, it's me. I'm missing you, sweetheart. I want to come home and make sweet love to you tomorrow, but I don't know if I can."

She was good. She wasn't fazed. She said, "Thank you, caller. We'll get back to you shortly."

I said, "Oh, babe, don't hang up—" but it was too late. The line was dead.

I cracked another beer and sat for ten minutes, sipping it, looking at the burned, gray landscape outside. Then the phone rang. I said, "Yeah."

It was Hook. He said, "Simple 'yes' or 'no' answers. Understood?"

"Yup."

"Have you got the girl?"

"No."

"Will you have her in the next twenty-four hours?" .

"Yes."

"Sooner?"

"Yes."

"Does it look like a research facility?"

"Yes."

"I assume you're going for her tonight. Take the tracker with you. Switch it on. Be well out of there by o-nine-hundred hours. Is that understood?"

"Yeah, but—"

"Shut up!"

I was silent.

He went on, "Steal vehicles. Head west to Morocco. Suggest Igli, Madkha Meski, then north to Meknes and Ceuta. Then Spain. Our man will intercept you. Is that understood?"

"Yup."

The line went dead. I said, "Thanks, doll. I feel better already."

I spent the next few hours dozing, rubbing ice cubes over my bruises and drinking beer. At six o'clock there was a knock at the door. I slipped the Sig in my waistband behind my back, put on a shirt then opened the door. I guessed we were still playing del Roble's game. It was the dame with the triangular face from Llyn Celyn. For some reason, I wasn't surprised to see her. Before I could speak, she smiled. It was a cute smile, almost apologetic.

She said, "Hello, Murdoch."

I thought about romantic but went for accommodating instead and said, "What do you want?"

"Aren't you going to let me in?"

"I let you in once before, remember?"

She was short. She ducked under my arm and was inside. I closed the door and turned to face her. Her smile had changed. It was still cute but now it was mischievous instead of apologetic.

She said, "Are you going to tell me you didn't enjoy it?"

"Sure, I enjoyed it. I thought you were somebody else. If I'd known it was you, I wouldn't have enjoyed it."

She laughed. It was a pretty laugh. She said, "We both know you're lying, Murdoch. You are a decent, honorable man."

"Bullshit!"

"And you are faithful to your lady. But all of that..." She stepped over real close to me, so our bodies were touching, and placed one finger on my temple. "All of that is in your head. Biology will not be denied, Murdoch, and your body wants me. Admit it."

I wanted to deny it but I couldn't because she was rubbing her thigh against the hard evidence while she was talking.

I held her gaze and thought of Maria, imprisoned in the container, trapped right now in the complex in the desert. I thought of her eyes looking at me, calling for help. The hard evidence wilted. I asked, "What do you want?"

A flash of anger contracted her face and she stepped away from me toward the French windows. The sky had turned pink outside and somewhere some goats were bleating to a dull bell.

She said, "Del Roble knows you're here."

"Yeah, I'd got that far on my own, sister. Do I have to ask you again or shall I just throw you over the balcony?"

She looked back at me over her shoulder. "You need an ally. I can help you."

"This is the last time I'm going to ask you. One more bullshit answer and you are going over the balcony. What do you want?"

She smiled. "Everything they say about you is true." She walked back to me and placed both her palms on my chest. "I want you to take me with you."

Chapter Eighteen

I laughed out loud. "How stupid do you and del Roble think I am?" I shook my head. "And how fucking *bored* are you?"

"It's not a ploy, Murdoch. If he knew I was making this offer, he would kill me…"

"So where the hell does he think you are right now?"

She appeared irritated, like I was being dense. "You may not have noticed, bright boy, but this is the only place around here you can get a beer. We often come here for a cold beer when we have time off."

It was so weirdly normal it was probably true. I shrugged. "Okay. So?"

Her eyebrow twitched and she glanced away. "He knows you have to make your move tonight or tomorrow. You can't risk waiting any longer. He will make it possible for you to get in and, once you are inside, he will close the trap."

I said, "Then?"

She looked at the broken green tiles on the floor. "Then he will do horrific things to you and to Maria. You will be an example."

"An example?"

She walked over and sat on the bed. "Catherine Howard and Sinead escaped. They betrayed him and they escaped. The Brotherhood tried to suppress it, but the rumors got out." She held my gaze. "Not all of us are happy, Murdoch. Not all of us support their method of doing things. Some of us believe there is another way. But if you betray them…"

I said, "But Sinead and Mary-Jane escaped…"

She nodded. "So, you and Maria have to pay the price, to be an example to the rest of us. Especially people like me."

There were two beers left in the ice bucket. I cracked them and handed one to her. "People like you?"

"I'm a hybrid."

I took a swig and rested my ass against the chest of drawers. "What does that mean?"

She stood and walked around so she was sitting on the near side of the bed. I had the window behind me and a cool breeze sent a chill down my back. The desert can drop to freezing during the dark hours.

She said, "Yes, I'm genetically modified. I'm only part human."

I gave a laugh like I didn't believe her, made as if I checked my cell and looked out of the window while I clicked 'record'. The dark was closing in fast. I said, "I didn't believe that crap the first time I heard it. I still don't believe it now."

She frowned. "But you saw it with your own eyes."

I cut across her. "I saw what? I was shown a lot of smoke and mirrors, and I was given hallucinogenic drugs. Under those conditions, you can make people believe anything you want. I don't believe in aliens. I don't believe shit!"

"We…they…are not aliens. They were here long before you were."

"Cut the crap, sister. You wanting out of this mess does it for me. The bullshit about aliens doesn't."

She seemed mad for a moment then sighed. "Fine, aliens or not, they have a huge genetic research program. I am a product of the program. I am a Seraph, like Serafino, with all the privileges and…" She shook her head. "I am a Seraph. Let's leave it at that. The point is that they have declared war on humanity, and there are those of us who feel it is wrong. Since Sinead and Mary-Jane's escape, there is a different mood among us — a feeling that our masters are not that powerful, after all."

"Your masters?"

"The Ael."

I sighed. "Look... What's your name?"

"Joanna."

"Look, Joanna. I'd like to believe you and I'd like to help you." I shrugged. "But what reason have I to believe you, let alone trust you?"

She stared down at the green tiles again. "None."

"This is just another one of del Roble's stupid, over-elaborate ego trips."

She raised her eyes to meet mine. There was laughter in them. "You're right. It is exactly the kind of stupid thing he would do. But think it through, Murdoch. What would he gain from it? You're going there tonight or tomorrow, anyway."

I spread my hands. "The game..."

She gave a small shout of laughter. "The game would be to trap you in the research facility after you have cut your way through the barbed wire. Or to hunt you through the desert and drag you back, kicking and screaming to be..."

I said, "To be what?"

"Never mind. There would be no sport in catching you this easily, and besides" — she shrugged and echoed my own gesture, spreading her hands — "he's too intelligent. He knows you would never go for it."

It had gotten dark while we had been talking. I stepped over to the bed and switched on the bedside lamp. It gave a soft glow. We were real close.

She was looking up at me. She said, "Do you know what drives us?"

I shook my head. "No..."

"We can't feel the way you do. We are... It's hard to explain, but we are different. We are not exactly of *this* world. We call ourselves *Asuras*. We are of this planet but not of your world. And that means we can't feel the way you do, with the intensity that you feel. But we are hungry for it."

My heart was pounding. She was doing something to me.

My belly was on fire and I was fighting hard to resist it. I said, "I don't need to know this."

She reached out and took my hand, then let her fingers slip down to my thigh. "The other day, at Llyn Celyn, we were together for hours, and I almost felt the way you do. We call it *rupa*. It's a transcendent state, when we feel like you. It changes us."

I said, "Stop it!" But my voice sounded thick. I moved away from her, back to the window and stood staring out at the night. It was black as pitch with a trail of stars making a broken path across the sky. I said, "Supposing I gave it a try. How would this work?"

I turned to face her.

She was watching me carefully. She said, "He is expecting you to approach by car, the way you did earlier today."

"You saw that."

"We have satellite surveillance. We have access to every satellite orbiting the planet. We knew you were coming, so we were watching. He expects you to return the same way, cut through the barbed wire, take out the guards then storm the hangars." She smiled. "He knows you only take sophistication so far, then you go barbarian."

I didn't smile. I was pissed that he was right—and that she was, too. I said, "So?"

"So, throw him a curve ball. Let me take you in. You'll be my prisoner and you'll be in my charge." She stood and came over to me. She pressed her body against me and touched my face with her fingers.

I didn't want her. I didn't want to touch her, but my body was on fire and there was an insane hunger for her in my belly.

"When the time is right, I'll release you and we escape together."

"What about Maria?"

"Forget her. What do we need her for?"

I pushed her hard. She gave a small cry and fell back across the bed. Her dress crawled up her thigh. I turned away. My breathing was coming hard and fast. It wasn't the only thing about me that was hard.

She glared at me. "When have you ever experienced anything like what you felt with me? I can be anything and anyone you want. Look at me!"

I turned. She had taken off her dress. She was in black lace pants and a black lace bra. Her waist was small, her hips were round and smooth and her breasts were full. I could see her nipples through the lace, hard and erect.

She said, "You know I can take you places you have never even dreamed of. You know I can give you pleasures you can't even imagine right now.

I went over, gripped her hard by her shoulders and pulled her to me. She gave a small whimper and I felt her naked thigh push between my legs. She eased closer and began unbuttoning my shirt with her small fingers then raking her long red nails down my chest.

She whispered, "Kiss me. I can do things with my tongue…"

I snapped, "No!"

She scratched my chest again and the pain was a spasm of pleasure. "Stop fighting it, Murdoch. It's what you want. You have always just taken what you want. Take me now." And she ground her crotch against my thigh as she said it.

My voice was thick and my breathing was shaking. I said, "All right, but we do it my way."

She pushed her arms around me and squeezed. She was strong, stronger than a woman her size should be. She buried her face in my neck and whispered, "Tell me your way. Tell me what you want. Anything…"

I wrenched her arms from around me and pushed her savagely. She hit the bed and sprawled on the floor. Her eyes were wide. Spread-eagled in her lace underwear, she seemed vulnerable and small. I felt sudden pity for her, but I had to keep up the act. My life and Maria's depended on it.

I snarled, "I go in from the south, alone! I take the Audi

across the desert as far as it will go. Then I dump it and go on foot to allow del Roble to believe I'm coming from the north..." I let my voice simmer down then stepped to the window. I spoke to the blackness outside. "I'll need at least a couple of hours. Expect my attack about midnight. I'll take out a few of your men to make it look good, so have plenty there to take me. Then you come and claim the arrest."

I turned to face her. She was still on the floor, but now she had one elbow on the bed and she seemed to be listening hard.

I said, "Whatever happens, Maria goes free. If she's hurt, I'll kill you."

Her eyes narrowed. "You still want her."

I shook my head and my breathing was hard. "I want *you*. She goes free. I owe it to her. Where is she?"

Her eyes were like frosted glass, so was her voice. "In the labs."

I felt sick but I didn't show it. "Where?"

"In the central hangars at the center of the Pentagon."

I nodded and I repeated, "She goes free. I get del Roble. Then you are mine. From now on, I own you. Do you understand? You want *rupa*? You're going to get more *rupa* than you know what to do with."

Her eyes were shining and she was smiling. She started to get to her feet. She started to speak, "Murdoch—"

I snapped, "Save it. Get your damned clothes on and get out."

Her face went hard and I knew I was over-playing my hand.

"You don't get something for nothing, Murdoch. Not from me."

I got to her in two long strides as she stood. I grabbed her arms and pulled her close. My voice was a hoarse whisper. "You listen to me, you little gray lizard..."

She made an act of struggling, of being mad, but I yanked her tighter so our bodies were pressed up close and my lips were almost touching hers.

"I told you I own you, and if I say leave, you leave."

Her eyes were telling me she'd do anything I said except leave. I'd put myself in a corner and there was only one way out. This was where I stopped playing del Roble's game. This was where del Roble lost control, but it was where I had to betray Maria so I could save her life.

I put my head on one side and spoke through my teeth. "You want *rupa*?" Her breathing quickened and I saw her pupils dilate. My muscles tensed. I knew I was losing control. I knew I had to lose control. She had to believe what was coming next. If she was going to believe it, I had to, too.

It wasn't difficult. I knew she was doing something to me. I didn't know what it was, but I had to use it to my advantage.

I growled, "You want goddamn *rupa*." I bit hard into her neck.

She cried out and her body quivered. I chewed and sucked hard, until I tasted the salt trickle of blood. She trembled, and I knew it was hurting her. She wanted human feelings and she was going to get them. If I was right, it was the one way to make sure she was hooked.

I picked her up, threw her on the bed and ripped off my clothes. I was stark naked and sweating. I had the hardest erection I'd ever had in my life. The cold desert air touched my back. I knew I was going crazy, but knew I had to go with it. I climbed on the bed and straddled her with my arms and legs. I lunged and bit her shoulder, hard, then her throat and her breasts, in quick, savage bites. I felt her nipples through the lace, growing hard between my teeth. I could hear myself making whimpering noises. I moved down and bit hard into her waist and her belly, then her hips.

I gripped her ass in hands, bruising her soft, white buttocks, then tore a hole in her lace panties with my teeth. I gnawed and bit and licked like a wild animal at a bloody carcass until she was screaming and pushing into my face.

Then I grabbed her hips and rolled her onto her belly and straddled her ass with my legs.

I pushed Maria out of my mind and silenced the voice that begged her forgiveness. I had to be here and now and do this like I wanted it.

I grabbed her hair with my right hand. I could feel her smooth, soft buttocks on my inside thighs. My head was wild. I felt crazy, like I had been drugged. My erection was insane, like iron. She was writhing, grinding her ass into me. I gritted my teeth and clawed her back, leaving livid red scratches. Then I positioned myself. She resisted, tight and hard — cried out, groaned and gasped. Then her passage dilated, she came to me and I pushed inside her. I bellowed, shouting like I was mad, as I sank deeper, deeper than I imagined possible. Then we were grinding in a frenzy, her ass hard against my hips, her small waist twisting and arching. I felt her clench hard on me then she was making strange, weird bird-like noises and the spasms hit me like waves of electricity that racked my body.

I fell forward onto her — clutched her, feeling her breasts in my hands. She was thrashing, and with every move she clenched harder and the orgasm shook me deeper. Her skin was smooth, wet with sweat, and I bit her shoulder from behind, tasting the salt on my tongue. Then we lay still.

I was shattered. She was trembling softly against me. I pulled away and swung my legs off the bed. I was also shaking and I felt weak. I stood and picked up the bucket. Most of the ice had melted. I put the rim to my mouth and drank deeply, then tipped the remaining half-bucket of iced water over my head. The shock was violent on my burning, sweating skin and made me shout. But it was good and brought me back to my senses.

I heard her move in the bed but ignored her and made my way to the shower. Standing under the cold stream, I scrubbed hard with soap, trying to wash her off my skin — trying to wash the memory of her off my skin.

Finally, I toweled myself dry and went back to the

bedroom. She was lying in only her bra, with the white sheet tangled around her legs.

I said, "Get out. Go and do what you have to do."

She said, "Why are you like this? What we just did —"

"Can it. You own me now. You know it. I'm as addicted to you as though I'd been mainlining horse. But I own you, too, baby. We own each other. That doesn't mean I have to love you or even like you." I gave a nasty laugh. "Hell, you wouldn't know what love was if it bit you in the..." I faltered.

She smiled and raised an eyebrow. "I think it just did."

I said, "Get dressed. Get out. Be ready for me." I checked my watch. It was half-eight. I said, "I'll be there, at the south perimeter fence, in three or four hours."

She got off the bed and started dressing. She glanced at me sidelong. She looked almost like a timid teenager. "Then we can be together?"

I threw the towel on the floor and pulled on my pants. I had a sour taste in my mouth. I said, "I told you. We own each other...if we get out of this alive." Then I stopped and stared at her, aware I was taking the gamble of my life. "You keep your end of the bargain and I'll keep mine. You'll get all the damned *rupa* you can handle."

She smiled like she'd been promised her favorite toy for Christmas then left, closing the door behind her. I heard her tripping down the stairs, and a minute later, her car door slammed in the silent night and her engine roar, whine and fade.

Then I was running down the stairs, calling Habib at the top of my voice.

Chapter Nineteen

He appeared at the reception desk with alarmed, sleepy eyes, still in his *djellaba*. "Yes, mister! Yes! I am here."

I said, "Listen to me. This has to be fast, okay?"

He nodded. Fast.

"I need a Land Rover. Does anybody in this village have a Land Rover?"

He nodded furiously.

I barked, "Who? Where?"

"Salim! Back of…here, here!" He pointed to the back wall.

I got the idea. I pulled five-hundred dinar from my wallet and gave them to him. "I am going to buy his Land Rover, okay? I haven't got time to ask him. You explain to him in the morning. You understand? I'll send another two grand by DHL. You give him what you think is right. Got it?"

His eyes were like soup plates, looking at the cash.

I grabbed his shoulders and gave him a small shake to make him meet my eyes. "Look at me."

"Yes, mister."

"Keep silent until twelve o'clock tomorrow."

He nodded more slowly, weighing the risks. The odds were good, and he said, "Okay…"

"Last thing, Habib… Wire cutters. I need wire cutters."

Now he appeared a bit sick. "Okay. You come."

I followed him to the kitchen. On the way, he locked the money safely in a cashbox. The kitchen smelled strongly of cumin, cinnamon and mint. He rummaged in a drawer then pulled out a pair of wire-cutters. He still looked sick. He handed them to me and said, "Wait, please."

Then he reached over and picked up a big meat cleaver

with his right hand. He braced himself on straddled legs and, with his left hand, he pointed to his chin. He said, "Now, please, mister. Make good…"

I said, "You're a pal, Habib. Be safe." And I smacked him hard as I could on the jaw. I may have broken it. I hoped so. Either way, it was hard enough to convince any investigating cop.

I went back to my room, put on my shoes and a dark shirt then slipped the Sig in the back of my waistband with the silencer and the night-scope attached. I put all my stuff in the kitbag and took it downstairs.

The night was freezing. It might have been zero — or one degree. I was trembling and my teeth were chattering. I loped around the back of the inn and up a short hill. There were a few mud houses set back with walled front gardens. They had palm trees for shade and one of them had a chicken shack. Next to the chicken shack there was a Defender.

It was easy to break into. Before I fired it up, I checked a couple of things. It was gasoline, not diesel, which in North Africa is not so surprising. It was also good news. And in the back, he had two twenty-five liter cans that were also full. Also good news.

I released the hand brake and put it in neutral, then pushed it gently out onto the hill. I put it in second, depressed the clutch and it free-wheeled down to the dirt track that passed for the main drag here. When it hit the level, I let out the clutch, hot-wired it and hit the gas. The old brute roared to life and we were away. And Salim still had a good five hours' sleep ahead of him.

I took the road out of the village, away from the complex, for about ten minutes, then turned off-road, into the desert. There was no moon and I had the headlamps off, so I was driving blind. It felt like I hit every pothole and rock in the desert. But after fifteen minutes, I began to see a faint glow ahead and to my left — south and east. I knew it was the complex and I headed toward it. Another fifteen minutes and I could make out the watchtowers and the barbed-wire fence with the hangars maybe sixty or a hundred yards beyond it. The whole area inside the barbed wire was floodlit.

In the faint glow from the spotlights, I made out some dunes and pulled the Land Rover in behind them then killed the engine. I climbed out and opened the back. The desert air was freezing and it was hard to control my fingers. I emptied the kitbag and stuffed one of the petrol cans in it. Then I strapped that to my back. I closed the door quietly, hit the ground and began to crawl.

I'd told Joanna I was coming in from the south. Between them, del Roble and she would have all their men focused north and south. I was coming in from the west. I crawled for five minutes, till I was right up to the wire but still in the shadows of the desert. There was one watchtower near me. If I went under the wire, the guard would see me. I figured the shot at fifty yards. It wasn't easy, but it wasn't impossible. I knew I'd hit him, but I couldn't be sure where. I aimed for the middle of his body and double-tapped. The two slugs tore through his chest. He leaned for a moment on the rail in front of him, like he wasn't sure why he felt dizzy all of a sudden. Then he slowly lay down. That was the end of his story.

I took off the kitbag, rolled onto my back and laid it next to me. Then I began to wriggle under the wire, cutting as I went, dragging the bag next to me. The wire had a depth of seven feet. It took me three minutes to get through, which, when you're on your back, under barbed wire and expecting to be shot at any minute, is a long time.

Then speed became more important than keeping hidden. I knew I wasn't in the field of vision of the two next towers, and I figured the CCTV would be focused on the hangars, so I ran. I ran twenty-five yards, half the distance to the nearest hangar. Then I dropped, pulled the fuel can from the kitbag and propped it up with a couple of rocks. After that, I was up and running again, oblique, headed for a large rock forty or fifty yards away, that was casting a shadow away from the spotlights. I dropped on my belly in the shadow of the rock, took careful aim at the gas can and pulled the trigger. The silencer made a soft *phut!* sound and, half a second later, the can exploded.

Twenty-five liters of gasoline makes a big explosion, and right then, Joanna would know I had betrayed her. I took fifteen seconds to cover myself in dust and dirt then lay motionless, listening to the shouts and hollers and the tramping of running boots. They passed close, but they saw what they expected to see – a rock surrounded by dirt. Besides, all their attention was on the burning, smoldering can, fifty yards away.

Then I was up and running again, heading for the hangar and scanning the wall for CCTV cameras. I spotted two, dropped to my belly again, took my time aiming, *phut!* And again, *phut!* And the two cameras were out of action. I knew I now had seconds. I made it to the corner, took out two more CCTV cameras that were watching the front of the facility where the road passed through a main gate to a parking area. The entrances were a sheet-glass façade and two large plate-glass doors. I didn't run. I strode purposefully and pushed through the two doors, bellowing like a sergeant major whose first coffee of the morning has been disturbed.

"What the *fuck* is going on here?"

There were six men. They all stared at me in shock. None of them was carrying anything more dangerous than a clipboard. Each one of them died, wondering what was happening. There was a set of double doors in the back wall that had to lead into the central areas where I had seen what appeared to be green crops. I crossed the floor, burst out through the doors and stopped dead. I was standing in the shade of what felt like a vast forest, only they weren't trees. They were cannabis plants, twenty and thirty feet high. Their fan leaves were maybe five or six feet across, and they were hung with buds that looked like cabbages, oozing a thick, white slime in dense threads across the clusters of fruit. The stench was overpowering, sickly and heady.

The plantation was maybe a hundred feet across, with five giant plants abreast in rows of maybe thirty trees. I paused for only a moment, staring agog. There was a stone-paved path that crossed the plantation to the next pentagon. I ran then pushed through the doors.

I was in another broad passage. The walls were brilliant white. I kept going toward the double doors opposite. I heard feet, boots running — at least six pairs. I hammered through into another cannabis forest and stopped. I knew what I was going to find on the other side of the next set of doors. More men. I was being funneled into a trap.

It's a golden rule. If you are being led into a trap, do something different. It might not work, but at least they won't be searching for it. I turned, faced the doors and kneeled with the Sig held in both hands straight out in front of me.

The doors exploded open. They'd expected an empty corridor. They'd planned to charge straight through. They stumbled and froze for three precious seconds. Two on the left... *Phut-phut!*...straight through the heart. Two on the right... *Phut-phut!* Then the two in the middle... *Phut-phut!*

Neat.

Without pausing, I hurled my back at the left door. It slammed open and I had a clear view of four soldiers in uniform, all looking surprised. They'd expected me to barge through the middle with six soldiers behind me. Right now, they were trying to readjust to the fact that I was about to shoot them.

I figured there were four more behind the door who couldn't see me.

I knew I had at least two seconds. I closed in methodically from the sides — left right, left, right. *Phut-phut! Phut-phut!*

Don't stop! Keep moving!

I let my legs go and rolled. There were four guys in uniform. They were in disorder, trying to see where I was going to wind up.

Phut-phut! Phut-phut!

Neat.

I stood and hesitated.

Do the unexpected.

They assumed I would go barging through...she'd said, like a barbarian. So, I should circle around and approach from the side or the back. But *that* was what they would expect me to do. What they wouldn't expect was this.

I hammered through the next four sets of doors. Another cannabis forest. Another corridor. Empty. Another cannabis forest. Then I crashed through the next set of doors and froze.

It was a lab. It was a pentagon, following the same pattern of the outer hangars, but there were no inside walls. Instead, there was a pentagonal garden, maybe fifty feet across, like a small woodland of giant cannabis plants. All around it the lab was a broad, deep gallery, furnished with benches, advanced chemical apparatus and high-tech electronic equipment that meant nothing to me.

What meant something to me were the thirty-odd men and women in lab coats, standing, looking at me with absolutely no expression on their faces. And the five large green-glass or Perspex tubes that stood against the far wall. All but the middle one were filled with only gently bubbling liquid. The middle one had Maria in it.

I heard the door crash behind me and the running tramp of military boots. I ignored them. Maria was suspended somehow. She was naked and her hair was covering her face, but she was unmistakable. I knew it was her. I took a couple of steps forward and heard the rattle of maybe six automatic weapons being cocked behind me. I kept walking until I heard del Roble's voice.

"I will not say you are disappointing, Murdoch. You are never that. But you are predictable."

He was on my left, leaning his ass against a bench with his arms crossed. Joanna was next to him. I turned and started toward him. I didn't know what I was going to do, but I knew I was going to end it now.

He watched me without moving till I was three strides away, then he said, "She will die."

I stopped.

He watched me a minute, then said, "She can live or she can die. It's up to you."

"I have your word on that, have I, del Roble?"

The sarcasm was palpable and Joanna laughed.

Del Roble sighed like he'd suddenly grown bored and said, "Come..."

He levered his ass off the bench and went toward the big tank where Maria hung suspended in what looked like a green gelatinous liquid. He stopped a few feet from it and did that thing Spaniards do, where they shrug and pull down the corners of their mouths.

"This is your love, the thing you live and die for." He gestured at it with his hand. "A lump of meat...animated by flows of excited particles." It was like he was talking to himself instead of me. He shrugged again, a couple of times, the way only Latins can. "Why? What is she? Why suffer and die for this?"

I laughed. It was short and humorless. "You want to understand love? Forget it." I reached in my pocket and found a pack of Camels. I peeled it and pulled one out. I spoke as I poked it in my mouth then lit it. "You'd have to be human, and even then, you wouldn't get it."

He turned and smiled at me. "Do you?"

"No."

"And yet—"

I cut across him. He was getting on my nerves. "What do you want, del Roble? We are irrational, hot. Maybe we're crazy and contradictory. Who gives a fuck? It's what makes us *us*, and we like it that way."

He narrowed his eyes and there was an angry hunger in them. "Do you know how old I am, Murdoch?"

I watched him while I let smoke out through my nose. I

was fighting the desire to smash his face into the glass vat. I said, "Old enough to know better?"

Joanna surprised me. She had come up beside me and said, "It's an important question, Murdoch."

"Important to who?"

He dismissed my question and said, "I am three hundred and fifty years old."

"Bullshit!"

"All these years I have lived among you, maintaining this form, trying to understand you, trying to fathom your feelings. Your irrational, confused, *stupid* emotions..." He turned back to stare at Maria and muttered, half to himself, "These hungers that drive you. This heat."

I looked at Joanna.

She gave a small smile. She said, "*Rupa.*"

Del Roble turned to her, a little surprised, nodding. "Yes," he said. "Yes, *rupa.*" He turned and gestured at the whole lab around him. "It's what this is all about. This facility, Llyn Celyn, when it goes online... Thousands, tens of thousands of years of research. You have no idea."

I sighed and glanced at the tip of my cigarette. It was halfway down. I reached in my pocket and made a show of searching for the pack. I found my phone and once again pressed record, then pulled out a second cigarette and lit it from the first. I said, "You're boring me."

He seemed slightly disgusted. "You are the lowest form of thinking life. Yet you are uniquely gifted in the universe."

I smiled. "Who? Me, Doc?"

"Your species!" He was suddenly all passion and intensity. "You are so finely balanced between the animal and the Seraph, that you are capable of heights of emotion and feeling, capable of feats of consciousness that we—"

Joanna cut across him, "Seraph!"

He glanced at her.

I looked at them both and laughed. "So you grow giant cannabis plants to help you feel? Good luck with that."

I saw him glance at Joanna. "We develop hallucinogenic

chemicals. This is not cannabis, as you know it." He stepped over and took hold of one of the cabbage-sized buds, dripping with a mucous like slime. "These buds—"

"Seraph!" It was Joanna again.

He hesitated, then shrugged. He settled on, "They contain secrets you cannot imagine."

I thought a moment while I sucked on the cigarette. As I let out the smoke, I said, "You really want to tell me, don't you? But she won't let you. What's that about, del Roble?" I turned to her and scanned her face for a bit. She was still expressionless. "You the senior officer here?"

He looked from me to Joanna and back again. He said, "We have many projects in the fields of genetic development. Ultimately, our aim is to discover the nature of consciousness itself. It is the principle that binds and defines the whole universe, yet nobody knows what it is. It is not predicted by relativity or quantum mechanics, yet it is central to understanding both."

I sighed. "You're still boring me."

He smiled and raised an eyebrow, like he knew I was lying and trying to provoke him. "Modify a genetic code and you modify the intellectual potential of the organism. You modify its capacity to be conscious."

I knew what he was driving at but I asked, "What's your point?"

"You know perfectly well what my point is, Murdoch. We are searching for a perfect hybrid. A vehicle that will allow us to retain the clarity and perfection of the Ael's mind, while having the sentient capacity of the human. We want to genetically code Enlightenment. We want to breed enlightened beings. Create, finally, the true—"

I couldn't suppress an incredulous laugh. "Illuminati?"

He glanced at me, then at Maria suspended in the slime. He changed the subject. "You have the capacity for growth."

I frowned. "Growth?"

He stared at me and his face was full of dark anger and hatred. "Apparently. Didn't you 'grow' when you first felt love for this woman? It's all you humans ever talk about—growth. Some metaphor to do with a change in consciousness."

I had suddenly lost patience. I dropped the butt on the floor and said, "It's all bullshit to me, del Roble. So, you have a genetic program where you are trying to create the perfect cross between an angel and a human. You aren't crazy. You're just plain stupid. What else are you doing with all this shit?"

He didn't get the pun. He smiled in a way you'd call thin and said, "When we have isolated and reproduced the code for growth toward perfect consciousness, we will rob you of the only thing that makes you remarkable."

I raised an eyebrow at him. "You will?"

"Nature gave you this ability to touch the divine and the bestial with your minds. We are going to remove that from you. We will turn the human species into a gray, amorphous mass of organic robots. You will serve us in every way, and we shall live, as you live, feeling your appetites and conflicts, but with our higher minds."

I nodded. "This is your obsessive pursuit of *rupa*. You know, del Roble, I have to hand it to you. Every time I meet you, you're a little bit crazier than the last time—"

Joanna cut across me. "Crazy? Why? For seeking all the feelings and experiences you take for granted? Isn't it exactly what you do? Do you have any *idea* how much money you humans spend each year on food, alcohol, sex and violence? Every ounce of your effort is invested in exciting these feelings. It is what you live for. Do you know what happens to people who are deprived of excitement and stimulation? They becoming psychotic and suicidal. Your entire existence as a species is focused not on survival, like every other species in nature, but on stimulating sensations of excitement and pleasure. And you call us insane for wanting the same."

She had a point.

I frowned at her, "How can you not feel? If you don't feel,

how come you're frustrated? That's a feeling."

She drew breath to answer, but del Roble was talking over her. "Of course we feel, but not as you do. It is impossible for you to understand. We do not occupy three-dimensional space as you do, so..." He spread his hands and shook his head, defeated by the impossibility of communicating with a hairless ape. "Imagine that you live permanently in a dream. You see, you hear, but your *feelings* are dull, muted." He rubbed his fingertips against his thumbs. "Not full, not *real!*" He glanced at me. "Can you imagine that? Living permanently in a dream, without ever experiencing real touch, real taste and smell, real *feeling?*"

I thought about it. For a moment, I kind of understood what he was saying. "So your whole thing is to create a hybrid that can think with cold-blooded clarity and feel with hot-blooded intensity?"

"That is part of it." He rapped hard on the glass of the huge vat.

I saw Maria twitch and move.

He said, "She is alive. She is sentient. She is in a dream, like us, but she has no control."

I said, "What are you going to do with her?"

He pointed a finger at her. "Her... We have taken genetic material and we will use her for the hybrid program, to make docile slaves who are free from motivation or disquiet." He glanced at me. "She will be happy. Her clones will be happy. The original, we may release back to London with certain modifications."

Then he turned to face me and there was real hatred in his face. He stabbed his finger on my chest. "But you? You, Murdoch, will die a slow, miserable death and your seed will be dispersed and diluted and degraded and you will be the father of a race of mindless slaves. And, before you die, you will experience every shade of pain and humiliation right down to the loss of your limbs until your very ego begs for annihilation."

I inhaled deeply while he was talking then blew a stream

of smoke in his face. I said, "And your problem is you don't feel intensely, right?"

"Yes." It was Joanna. She was smiling at me.

There was a strong, burning pain in my arm. The walls moved sideways and the floor surged up to smash me in the face.

Chapter Twenty

I woke up and everything was wrong. Everything was upside down. I felt as though somebody had been pumping insulating foam into my face—and I had a headache. When I tried to put my hands to my head, I realized they were tied behind my back. Then the operating table started to come into focus.

Maria was on it.

I ignored the pain and the nausea and raised my head to look at my feet. They were chained together, and the chain was over a hook suspended from the ceiling, also on a chain. It was Colonel Ugly all over again, only this time they'd thought it through.

I squeezed my eyes and tried to see clearly. Her hair was clean and dry, so she had been out of the tank a while. Her eyes were closed and she seemed to be resting peacefully. She was covered in a white sheet up to her neck. There was a trolley next to the table with an array of cold, steel instruments on it. I noted there were several scalpels. I gave my body a shake in the vain hope the chains might be loose. They were solid.

Then I heard a small laugh behind me. It was oddly familiar. I twisted my body, tried to turn, and the laugh came again as a slow giggle.

"Are you uncomfortable, Mr. Murdoch? Pain is inevitable in the world, but the Buddha tells us, suffering is optional."

I twisted again, trying to see where the voice was coming from. I knew the voice but I couldn't believe it. I said, "Rinpoche?"

The voice was moving slowly, one step at a time.

"Rinpoche… Rinpoche…" Then it went high with childlike amusement, "*Why* always Rinpoche?"

He came into view on my right. I went cold, from head to foot.

I said, "Steve…"

He wheezed and nodded. "Stephan. What to do? What to do?"

He went to the operating table and stood over Maria. He had a strange expression on his face, like he didn't know what she was and wanted to understand. He said, "She was faithful to you, Murdoch. I tried…" He leered down at her then turned the leer at me. "I tried to fuck her and kiss her, but she only like her fucks from you, yeah?" He clenched his fists and thrust his hips forward. "Dr. *Love!*"

"What the fuck? I smashed your windpipe! What the hell did they do? Give you a new head?"

He closed his eyes, shook his head and doubled up with laughter. "Man! You are soooo primitive…" His voice had changed again.

I knew the voice. It wasn't Rinpoche. I struggled, but he was talking again.

"Be hip, man. Be cool. Things are not what they seem, cat. Free your mind. Get on the magic bus."

I said, "The VW camper… That was you. I thought I recognized you."

He was still wheezing a slow laugh, pointing at Maria, looking at me. "And she was in the van, man, all the time! I told you, get on the magic bus and find your love, but you ain't listening, baby." He stopped, doing a weird mix of nodding and shaking his head. "You are stone stupid."

I screwed up my eyes. "How do you do that? Who are you?"

His face went cold and hard. His eyes were like pale-blue slits of ice. "What to do? I just like fucking with your head." He leaned against the wall, watching me.

I thought my eyes were losing focus from the blood pressure caused by being upside down. But I realized he was changing, turning a pale shade of gray. His hair was kind of withdrawing into his head and his face was becoming featureless.

He said in that same neutral voice, "I'm a chameleon, Murdoch, just like Dr. Loss." He glanced to his left. There was a door there. He said, "I think they're coming now."

The door opened and Dr. Loss came in with del Roble and a big, powerful man in heavy horn-rimmed glasses and a white lab coat.

I said, "Dr. Loss? It was you, all along?" My head was spinning and things were beginning to make sense. Steve, Cavra, Loss...

She glanced at me but didn't say anything. They were talking in muted voices and ignored me, like it was normal to have a man hanging upside down in their office. They gathered around Maria and started prodding her face and her skin like she was a roll of beef. A crazy rage was beginning to well inside me.

Del Roble glanced at me briefly then looked at the guy in the glasses. "Professor Banks, will you please tell us what will be your first procedure."

Banks nodded and Loss smiled at del Roble like she was thinking he was a bastard and that was funny.

Banks was flexing his hands. He stripped back the sheet and exposed Maria's body, naked and motionless. I could feel my heart pounding hard.

Banks spoke. He said, "First we will go in through the vagina and take scrapings from the uterus and the womb. Then we'll take biopsies of the ovaries. We assume she is fertile, but if she is not, we can do it artificially." He had a mild South African accent.

He started moving around her, feeling her thighs and her calves.

Del Roble spoke to Banks, but he was smiling at me. "Who were you thinking of using to inseminate her?"

Banks stopped and looked at him like he thought he was stupid because they had already talked about this.

209

He gestured at the chameleon and said, "Stephan, as you suggested." He moved up to her head, bent then peered into her ear. "We'll drill through the top of the skull and insert the implants directly into the hippocampus. They will take root there very successfully."

I could feel the sweat dripping down my face and running into my eyes. My pulse was racing. I needed to get out of the chains and I had to do it in seconds.

Banks glanced at me then turned his attention back to Maria. "And what will we do with the male?"

Del Roble was enjoying himself. He was smiling openly now, observing me. He could see the state I was getting into. It clearly fascinated him and also obviously gave him a peculiar pleasure. He said, "Oh, I want him seminal to the beta program. But we are going to remove bits of him and study the emotional impact, Professor Banks. He has a very strong personality. He is very resilient. I want to know at what point he will break down emotionally."

Banks was studying him with interest. He said, "There are many studies on that subject, most of them from Mengeler."

Del Roble had stepped over to me and was smiling down into my face. He said, "I know. Nevertheless, I am interested in this subject. I think today we'll remove the left hand. No need for anesthesia."

Banks turned back to Maria. "As you wish."

Del Roble said, "I think we'll do it first. Now. Let's observe the conflict. His struggle over which hurts him more, the emotional pain of seeing what happens to the woman or his own physical agony and loss."

Banks shrugged. "Yeah. Yeah, that is interesting. Yes."

Loss giggled. It was a weird thing to watch.

She said, "This is the downside of feeling so intensely, I suppose. Isn't it, Murdoch?"

I held her gaze. I said, "You may be wrong."

Del Roble gestured to the chameleon Stephan and said, "Golika! Come, help."

The chameleon seemed to acquire color and shape as

Rinpoche and walked over to stand at my left shoulder, while del Roble stood on my right. Loss came and stood in front of me. There was a strange, moist sound and I realized she was licking her lips.

She smiled into my face and said, "You don't mind if we taste some of your blood?"

I held her stare. Something bad was happening inside me. I was aware I was being pushed past a limit I didn't want to cross. But I also knew we were past the point of no return. She blinked and I noticed with disgust that she had vertical eyelids in her eyes under her normal ones. I felt del Roble grab my wrist and start undoing the cuffs.

Golika-Rinpoche, the chameleon, grabbed my other wrist and Banks selected a scalpel and said to Loss, "Get a bowl to collect the blood. We'll all have a drink."

She moved off to get the bowl and del Roble held my right arm tight. I let it go limp. Golika wrestled my left arm around to the front, with my hand turned palm up. I was making a show of struggling, but I could feel panic as well as hatred welling up inside me.

Banks said, "I must get a tourniquet."

Del Roble smiled and said, "No, we want pain, Professor. Use the blowtorch. We want to see how far we can take him."

Banks nodded and raised a finger, like he was thinking. "Ah, yes, splendid idea."

There was a kind of banal normalcy to what they were doing that was making me crazy.

He raised his voice slightly and said to Loss, "Oh, Doctor, could you bring the blowtorch?"

Then he stepped over and looked down at my wrist, palpating the joint with his left hand, finding the right place for the incision. I could hear my own breathing. It was loud and shaking. Loss came back with a steel bowl and a propane blowtorch. She put the bowl on the trolley.

Del Roble said, "Light it."

Banks said to Golika, "Hold firm."

I did the only thing I could do. I opened the floodgates and let the panic take over. I screamed at the top of my voice like a thing gone crazy. I whiplashed my body and wrenched my left arm forward, twisting and grabbing Banks' wrist as I did so. Golika staggered. I used Banks as purchase and all my wild panic to give me strength. I twisted my right arm and grabbed del Roble's face. I was still screaming but I could hear del Roble's cry of pain louder than mine as I pushed with all my strength against his face and Bank's wrist then thrashed and whiplashed my body again, up toward the ceiling.

It was a forlorn hope, but it was the only one I had, and it paid off. I managed to raise myself the two inches I needed and kicked my chains off the hook, then all my two hundred and twenty pounds came crashing down toward the floor. Del Roble pulled his bleeding face away from my hand. Banks felt his arm torque, dropped the scalpel, staggered and fell forward with me, and Golika-Rinpoche collided head first with him as he came down, too.

I had no idea what was behind me. I didn't really care. I figured that whatever it was, it had to be better than what I had in front of me. It turned out to be five trolleys, two lab coats and a wide assortment of lethal instruments. As we fell, I could see Rinpoche's face, his eyes bulging, his teeth gritted and his neck swollen to twice its size. He was scrabbling for the scalpel where it had dropped between two overturned stands. Banks had fallen on him. He was heavy and strong. There was a shout and a grunt. My hand found the scalpel. Rinpoche clawed my face. Banks tried to scramble to his feet, pushing on Rinpoche. Rinpoche sprawled. The trolley went flying and I slipped between them, but I had the scalpel. I didn't aim. I just rammed it in Golika-Rinpoche's face. Hard.

The scream was horrific. His skin turned ash-gray. All his features disappeared and his skin seemed to ripple in scale-like folds. He was like a huge gecko on its hind legs, lurching back, clutching at the scalpel that was stuck, wedged in his cheekbone.

Banks was holding his head, swearing and spitting at me, "I am going to kill you!"

Del Roble was clutching his bleeding face and cursing, "*Me cago en su putisima madre!*" and Loss was staring from one to another of these three heroes. I leaned forward and loosened the clasp around my ankles. Then I was on my feet and people were going to die.

I didn't think. I grabbed a trolley and smashed it across Golika's head. He dropped and stopped screaming. Loss was next on my list, but as I turned, I saw her hitting Banks over the head with the propane canister. He went down when del Roble looked up. His eyes bulged as he stared at Loss. She swung and bashed him on the temple.

We stood staring at each other. She threw the propane bottle down and her skin crawled and shifted like Golika-Rinpoche's and she was Joanna. My head was spinning. I wasn't thinking. I just wanted to kill.

She snarled, "Stop fucking staring at me and help!"

Before I could move, she had turned and pulled the sheet up over Maria's face. I said, "What the —"

She snapped, "Put a lab coat on. Fast!"

I bent and seized a scalpel from the floor. I took two steps toward her, throwing twisted trolleys out of the way. I was going to gut her right there and then, but she held my eye as I approached. She didn't flinch.

I hesitated and she said, "You love her. Whatever that is, I get it's a big deal for you. If you want her to live, get with the program. Drop the fucking knife."

I snagged a lab coat and put it on. I said, "My things —"

She pointed. "The chair. Move!"

I grabbed my Sig, my cell, my Camels and my Zippo. I left the tracker where it was on the chair. I turned to her. "I need photographs. And videos…"

She stared at me like I was crazy. "*What?*"

I barked at her through gritted teeth. "Listen, sugar. Maybe you don't give a shit, and I'm no saint, but in my book, massacring and enslaving nearly eight billion people is something you shouldn't do. And all it takes for you motherfuckers to get away with it is for *me* to do nothing!"

Her face flushed. She rasped at me, "We need to get *out* of here."

I kicked a trolley out of the way, leaned across Maria's motionless body and captured a fistful of Joanna's throat. "To *where? Where* are you going to go? Where are you going to *hide?* And for how long before it's all over?"

She held my eye and croaked, "Let go of me."

I gripped harder and yanked her close so our heads were touching. I could see her inner eyelids and the weird formations of her pupils. I growled, "I need *proof!*"

"Okay! I can give you proof. Now for God's sake, let's get out of here."

I shoved her and she staggered back, crashing against the wall. I said, "Go to hell."

I pulled the Sig and cocked it. She held up both hands in front of her. She looked genuinely scared.

She said, "No! Wait! Okay, we'll get photographs and films. Just calm down." He skin was turning a weird gray, like Golika's had. She said, "There's an underground loading bay. The road takes us out into the desert near the main highway. We'll go down there and steal a truck. On the way, I'll take you through the labs..."

My mind was racing. I said, "What proof can you provide?"

She shrugged, clearly feeling on safer ground. "Anything you need."

"You a senior officer?"

She frowned. "Pretty senior..."

I jerked my head toward the door. "Let's go. Get something to put on Maria. I'm not taking her out of here naked."

We pushed out into a long, empty corridor in absolute silence. Joanna grabbed some work garb from a nearby storage closet. We hurriedly dressed Maria, then we moved along at a quick pace.

Joanna glanced at me and said, "Will you stop looking at everything? You're like a damned tourist. Keep your eyes on the trolley and do as I say."

We came to an elevator and waited a minute. The doors slid open and we rushed in. There was a guy who appeared to be in his sixties. He smiled at Joanna and looked down at the trolley. Apparently, I didn't exist.

He asked, "DH?"

Joanna shook her head. "BC implant."

He raised his eyebrows and pursed his lips, nodding. "Export?"

She said, "NWDS."

He smiled. "Exciting."

The elevator doors hissed open and we hurried out into a corridor that might have been the one we'd just left. I followed her a moment and she reached back with her right hand, not looking at me.

"Give me the clipboard from the end of the trolley. We are going into a lab. If there is a supervisor, do *nothing*. Understood? If there is no supervisor, you can film and take photos."

I glanced at my watch. It was six-fifty-eight. We would soon be running out of time. She nudged the trolley and we pushed through a set of fire-doors into a long room with maybe a hundred people, men and women of varying ages, sitting at desks in front of screens with earphones plugged into their monitors. The screens were playing all kinds of images, and the viewers were staring at them intently. There appeared to be no supervisor. I glanced at Joanna and she pointed to a bank of larger screens at the end of the room.

"Film me." She waited while I got out my cell. When I was recording, she pointed to the bank of screens on the far wall. "Those screens monitor the electrical and chemical activity of each of their brains..."

I walked over and filmed several of the screens. They showed 3D representations of the subjects' brains rotating east to west and south to north. In the margins and below, there were annotations about neurotransmitter levels and synaptic activity, as well as other notes I could not understand.

Joanna was by my side. "Film a couple of the subjects."

I glanced at her and began to walk down the aisles, filming the people at the monitors. "Their subjective functions — visual, auditory and kinesthetic — are all being dictated by the input data. As they visualize, create auditory hallucinations and trigger chemical, emotional anchors, they generate neural networks which govern their behavior."

I closed in on one of the screens. It looked like a newsreel. I said, "You are mapping their brains?"

"Generating maps in their brains." She smiled then snorted. "The beta version went live in 2000. We have been developing it as cells, tablets and TVs."

I felt sick. I said to her, "So, how do you control the chemicals in the brain? What is it? Water supply? Food?"

She shrugged. "Industrialization has made that kind of thing much easier, but we actually do a lot less of that than you'd think. The brain is a chemical factory. By controlling the images, narratives and dialogues you have in your head, we can make you produce the chemicals we want you to produce." She smiled. "Lots of dopamine and lots of serotonin to keep you volatile and dependent."

I stared at her, trying to assimilate the magnitude of what she was saying. Finally, I said, "So, the giant cannabis trees?"

She shook her head. "Come on. Let's go before we're seen."

I followed her out and along the passage again. I had the uncomfortable feeling that she could be leading me anywhere, but I kept telling myself she had her own agenda, and for now it seemed to be compatible with mine.

We came to another elevator. This time we rode it alone, and as we were descending she said, "Those weren't hybrids that you saw. Those were people, normal people. We pick them up at random. Some we take for a night. Some we take for a week or a month. Some we take for a lifetime. Most of them we take repeatedly, on a regular basis. They are experimental subjects."

The elevator stopped and when we stepped out we were in a vast, cool, underground chamber. It was dark, but through the gloom I could see a dense forest of cannabis trees, maybe thirty-feet high. There was a sighing, rustling sound from the giant leaves, and somewhere you could hear the trickle and splash of a stream. I looked up but the roof of the cavern was lost in shadows. I said, "What the hell is this place?"

She seemed not to hear. She continued talking as though I hadn't spoken, and I followed her, pushing Maria's body down a winding track through the trees.

"Most of them never know they have been taken. In many, we implant memories that are actually close to the truth. They believe they have been taken by a superior, alien race, and they must encourage humanity to accept the aliens, to save the environment."

I said, "Abduction syndrome."

She gave a weird scream of laughter. "Those very aliens who are feeding your greedy governments and industry all the technology they need to destroy that environment." We were approaching large steel doors set in the wall of the cavern. "Aliens! *You* are the *fucking* aliens!"

The doors slid open and we were in a vast lab. There were a hundred people, maybe more, in white coats—men and women, working quietly at benches, moving to and from electronic equipment and bench-mounted test tubes and what looked like microscopes.

Beyond them, the lab opened out, as though it had no back wall, into a second vast cavern. Here, instead of giant cannabis trees, there was a forest of tall, glass cylinders, maybe ten feet high and five feet across, like the one that had held Maria. Each one was filled with green liquid and each had a body suspended in it.

"Take your films and your photographs!" she spat the words at me.

I stared at her a moment then began to film.

I said, "Is this where you develop the hybrids?"

She nodded. "We grow them. They start as buds. She pointed out at the forest. "Those are mainly Seraphs. Upstairs, there are Grays and experimental strains."

I froze and felt my skin crawl. "Those buds... Those cabbage things..."

She nodded. "They will grow into bodies that we will store in vats like these. When you killed Golika, who you called Rinpoche, it was easy to transfer his brain, which was largely undamaged, into another body. In this way, we can live for centuries, replacing our bodies every fifty years or so. The knowledge and wisdom we accumulate are beyond your imagining."

We stared at each other a minute. The hostility was palpable.

I said, "Are you sure? How would you know? You still want to be like us, don't you? But, you know, we wouldn't really want to be like you." She didn't answer, just stared.

I said, "Where is this damned loading bay?"

She turned away without saying anything then led me through the lab into the chamber with the tall, slim vats. Each one emanated a soft, green light. Plastic tubes ran between them, feeding into them, an endless network of artificial roots. Soft sighs and gentle bubbling noises whispered and echoed around the cavern. I filmed as we went. It had a strange feeling, like an alien forest—or a cathedral built to an alien god.

After a few minutes, we came to the other side and passed through an arch to a broad ramp that descended, turning gently to the left. She took hold of the trolley and we eased it down the ramp into a large loading bay. A truck with a container was pulling out, accelerating away down a long tunnel.

The scale of the place was surprising. To the left, a bank of hydraulic elevators opened onto a raised platform that must have been at least two hundred feet long. Beyond it was an open area where I could see a fleet of trucks. They were painted with the livery of several well-known corporations. She pushed the trolley to the right and we began to move toward a line of smaller vehicles, vans and saloon cars.

I said, "What the hell is this for?"

She said, "It's the invasion of the body snatchers, Murdoch, only much worse."

We had pulled level with a white van and she slid open the side door.

Then she paused, studying my face. "We are taking you and modifying you. We take you in and ship you out — by the millions. We make politicians, civil servants, actors, directors, whores — lots of those. You name it, and we make it."

She pointed down the tunnel. "That was a shipment bound for London, pleasure models for an exclusive club. Del Roble and Banks will be there to enjoy them — only they won't. The girls' memories will be implanted. They will never know where they came from."

She turned back to me. "This is not the only facility, Murdoch. We are changing you into submissive drones. We are jealous of you. We hate you because you can feel and love and grow, and we are stuck in hell. You know what hell is, Murdoch?"

I shrugged, shook my head. "Pain?"

She smiled. "No, pain is just a very strong motivation. Hell is not being able to move, to grow. Some of us have lived a thousand years and more but never changed. We assimilate information, but it doesn't change us. We are stuck. We want what you have."

I helped her slide the trolley into the van and secure it. She slammed the door shut and stood close to me with her hands on my chest.

"Take me with you, Murdoch. I have felt things with you.

219

I came so close…"

I touched her face. "What about her? What about Maria?"

She gently held my hand and rubbed it with her cheek. "We'll take her back. She'll be okay. She won't remember anything. I can help you. I can provide facts, evidence, names and dates, and in exchange you can help me to feel, to grow, to be like you."

I cupped her face in both my hands and kissed her. I said, "You know you own me. I have felt things with you I have never felt with any other woman. But I need to know what you have implanted in her brain."

She faltered. "We got out before—"

"Don't lie to me. Tell me the truth and you have your ticket out of here."

She closed her eyes and spoke without opening them. "It's a hard habit to break for us."

"Lying?"

She opened her eyes. "Loyalty to the Seraphs. It's a biochip."

"What does it do?"

"It's connected to her handler. She will unconsciously transmit information to him, and he can control her actions and her behavior."

"Only her handler?"

She nodded and shrugged. "Yes, it's personal to the handler."

"Who's her handler?"

She smiled. "Was. Her handler *was* del Roble."

I glanced at my watch. It was just after eight. I said, "I'll drive. You keep an eye on Maria."

We climbed in. I pulled out of the parking lot and headed into the long tunnel out to the desert and the long highway that led to Algiers in the north.

Nobody tried to stop us.

Chapter Twenty-One

We exploded into the morning. The sun was low in the east, but there was already a heat haze on the hills. The tarmac gave out and we were on a broad dirt track, moving fast toward the black ribbon of the highway maybe a mile or two away. I heard Maria moan in back.

Joanna turned instinctively to look at her and said, "It's okay. Rest. You'll be safe soon."

Maria seemed to settle, and I smiled at Joanna.

"You know what? You might make a decent human being after all," I said.

She gave a small laugh.

After a moment, I said, "You bring everybody in and out by road?" I shook my head. "The logistics would be impossible."

She laughed again. "No. We have ships. We have technologies you only fantasize about in your science fiction." She turned to face me. "You remember when you were driving down here? You had fallen behind at Algeciras…"

I nodded. "Yeah…something weird happened in the desert."

Her laughter was like the crowing of a bird. She said, "You were abducted by aliens. That was one of the ships. Don't ask me to explain how they work. We have reached heights in particle physics you can't even imagine."

"Not even in our science fiction?"

Something in the tone of my voice made her glance at me. I swung the wheel and we rattled off the dirt track, half sliding down the side of a hill toward a shallow valley about half a mile away, where two low hills cast a pool of shade in the morning light.

She said, "What are you doing?"

I said, "Bear with me."

Maria had started moaning again.

Joanna turned in her seat and muttered, "It's okay, baby. You're going to be safe soon."

We hit the floor of the valley and I started to accelerate toward the two hills. I could just make out the shape of the Land Rover in the shadows. The van was bouncing like it was about to fall apart.

Joanna frowned at me. "Take it easy. What the hell are you doing?"

I glanced at the clock on the dash. It said eight-forty a.m. I slammed on the brakes and we skidded to a halt in a cloud of dust six feet from the Land Rover. I said, "Get out. Fast."

She climbed out. She was looking around her, a bit wild, like a person who feels she's losing control.

I said, "Help me."

I ripped open the side door to the van and started dragging Maria out. I could see by her face that she was fretting.

Joanna grabbed her and helped me pull her from the trolley, muttering, "It's okay, baby. It's okay." To me, she frowned and snapped, "What the hell are you doing, Murdoch?"

I said, "There's no time, Joanna. Shut up and help." I dragged Maria around to the Land Rover and bundled her in the passenger seat.

Joanna kept repeating, "What are you doing? What are you *doing?*"

I said, "I'll explain as we go. Help me at the back." I half ran to the back of the vehicle and ripped open the door.

She came around behind me and saw me grabbing the spade. She just had time to frown and say, "Wha?" before I smashed her between the eyes with the handle. She staggered back a few paces. I took the spade with both hands and swung it like an ax, over my head with all my strength and let out a bestial roar. The blade split her head in two, right down to her collarbones. Her legs twitched and danced for a second then she dropped to the sand, soaking it with a pool of thick, glutinous blood. I beat her head a few more times until her brains were mashed and mixed in with the sand. I fired up the van and positioned it over her so she was under the fuel line. Then I crawled under and cut it so the fuel tank started to drain out onto what was left of her head.

I climbed into the Land Rover and saw that Maria was awake. She had her eyes open and was staring out of the windshield. She didn't look at me or say anything. I fired up the truck and drove away from the van, about thirty or forty feet. Then I stopped, climbed out and took careful aim with the Sig.

The tank must have been full. The van leaped five feet into the air. The flaming body was tossed up the side of the hill where it lay twisted and smoldering, the shattered stump that had been the head blackened and in flames. I climbed back in and closed the door. We took off, headed west across the desert. After about five minutes, we crossed the highway and plunged on into the desert.

At eight-fifty a.m. I saw six black specks appear over the horizon in the northwest. In seconds, they had turned into low-flying Typhoon FGR4s. The sky tore open with a terrible shriek of jet engines as they thundered overhead, tearing up the sand from the desert and rocking the Defender on its suspension. I braked, opened the door and leaned out. Ten seconds passed and the earth shook. It shook six times in rapid succession. Huge billows of black smoke mushroomed into the air, spilling blackened dust into the upper atmosphere. I watched the Typhoons fan out, curl around in the darkening air and come in for a second run.

The second lot of explosions were more muted, but you could feel the tremor in the ground, like a distant earthquake, and I guessed they were using deep penetration bunker-busters. As I climbed back in the cab, they were coming in for a third attack. I slammed the door, put it in gear and plowed into the desert. Maria was sitting with her elbows on her knees and her hands over her head.

I gave her a minute, then asked, "Are you okay?"

She didn't answer.

We drove for an hour in silence until I saw some steep rock cliffs on my left, about four or five miles away. I headed for them, found a shallow cave and parked inside, where it gave us some shelter and shade and we would be hidden from view until sundown. Then we would move on. Maria curled up on the ground and went straight to sleep.

* * * *

At just after six, the sun touched the horizon and began to sink. I woke Maria and told her to get in the Land Rover. She was so groggy that I almost had to drag her to her feet. It gets dark really quick near the equator, and as I started the engine, the sunset was draining into blackness.

I watched her a moment and said, "Are you up to talking?"

She was silent for a couple of beats then nodded. "I don't remember. Why are we here, Liam? Why are we in the desert? Who have I been with?"

I'm not ashamed to admit that I had to bite back tears right then. I said, "We'll come to that, baby. Right now, let me tell you what we're going to do. We're going to head north toward the N107, maybe lose the Defender in Ghardaia and take the 107 west toward Morocco. We'll cross the border south of Tlemcen, then catch a flight to Heathrow or Gatwick from Rabat. Okay?"

She stared at me. Her cheeks were sunken and she had deep shadows under her eyes. She was struggling, trying to read my face. I just wanted to take her in my arms and tell her everything was going to be okay, but I knew I couldn't. Not yet. I had to be sure.

I pulled out of the cover of the cave and headed west. I glanced at Maria a couple of times to see if she had registered the direction, but all she did was close her eyes and try to get comfortable.

I drove west for about ten hours. We made occasional pit stops, but we had no food and little water, so the stops were short and we didn't talk. It was back-breaking, but finally, about four in the morning, I began to see a faint glow of light on the horizon. It was a town called Igli. We wouldn't stop there. I didn't think they'd be expecting us, but I was pretty sure two Americans—one a girl—in a Land Rover would arouse some interest if we were seen. No, Igli was good news, not because we could stop and get food and water—we couldn't—but because it was just eighty miles from the border with Morocco. And Morocco was one step closer to escape.

If there was ever any escape.

I noticed Maria was awake. She was staring dully at the haze of light on the horizon. She said, "Is that Gardaia?"

I said, "Yeah. We're on the second tank and it's holding out. So, I'm going to give it a miss and hit the N107. I want to get as close to the Atlas Mountains as I can tonight. We'll cross the border tomorrow, at Maghnia."

She didn't answer. She just stared ahead. After a few minutes, she said, "You killed Joanna so ruthlessly. It was as though you felt nothing. How could you do that? What did you feel?"

I went cold and my skin prickled. I said, "How do you know about that, baby?"

She gazed at the dash a long while. Eventually I realized she wasn't going to answer.

I said, "You were asleep. What do you remember?"

I glanced at her and saw she was watching me.

She said very quietly, "I'm not sure…"

A few minutes later, we crested the hill and there, maybe twenty miles away, was Igli. It was as dull and dead as every other place I had seen in this forsaken, blasted desert, but I wasn't planning to go searching for hot nightspots. The N6B passed close by on the south, and that's what I was looking for. That, and the Moroccan border that lay just beyond it.

Behind Igli, the land rose steeply into a rocky tableland. Climbing the rock in a vehicle would be slow and difficult, so for this stretch I needed to risk the road. I figured that at four in the morning, four-hundred miles from where they probably expected me to be — if I was right about Maria — I could risk the road for half an hour.

We descended the sandy, rocky slope at a bone-rattling fifty miles per hour and hit the N6B just south of the town. We passed a couple of small residential areas that seemed more like barracks, then turned a sharp left, with the brakes squealing in the gray, predawn silence. I was scanning left and right, searching for a suitable prey. I had very little time in which to act, but I saw what I was looking for as we approached the exit to the town.

Hook's state-of-the-art GPS had told me that Igli was a commune that depended heavily on agriculture. Agriculture, especially in this kind of terrain, meant one thing — 4X4s. We had some real rough terrain coming up. I knew the Defender could handle it, but we were about to run out of gas, and we couldn't afford the time or the risk of refueling. Now I smiled to myself, eased off the gas and swung in among some cypress and palm trees by a house with a broad front garden. There in the drive was what I had been searching for. Another indestructible, indomitable Land Rover Defender.

I pulled my lock picks from my bag, said, "Stay here," to Maria then sprinted silently to the house. The Defender may be the best 4X4 ever made, but they are not sophisticated. I was in after three seconds. I loped back, grabbed the rucksacks and some water then pulled Maria from the passenger seat. She came with me like she was sleepwalking. We got in. I hotwired the engine and we were out of there, climbing steeply through sparse woodland into the bare stone of the highlands. I followed the road up in a broad sweep, turning right and west. All the way, I kept my eyes glued to the mirror, searching for any headlamps or movement. There was nothing, just the still, empty highway.

Twenty miles south of Igli, the N6B joined the N6 going north and west. I turned onto it as my watch hit five a.m. Then I floored the gas pedal for the next sixty miles. It was a strange drive through the darkest hour before dawn. There was empty desert all about us. Not sand, but bare stone, rolled like a petrified ocean. The funneled beams of the headlights searched out the few yards of blacktop ahead of us, while the stars drizzled ineffectual light out of an impenetrable sky.

Suddenly, Maria spoke out of the shadows. "These are not the Atlas Mountains, are they?"

"No."

After a silence, she said, "Why did you lie to me? Why don't you trust me, Liam?"

I was silent for a long time, fighting back the tears of rage, knowing I had to tell her but hating myself for it. Finally, I said, "They put a biochip in your head, babe. I think I killed it, but I don't know for sure. It may still be active and I don't know what it's programmed to do."

I felt, but didn't see, her turn to face me.

"What have they done to me?"

"I don't know."

"I remember things that have never happened to me. I know things…"

I glanced at her. She was staring out at the blackness racing past.

I said, "What things?"

But she didn't answer.

At six a.m. the sky started to turn a grainy gray color. Up ahead I saw we were approaching a dogleg junction. The nearest turn-off doubled back south and west, the farther one turned north and east. I didn't take either. I just kept straight on, off the road and into the desert sands again.

The next four hours were some of the most exhausting

I have ever lived through. We hammered across dry sand and stone, rarely dropping below thirty miles an hour. For two-and-a-half hours, I just kept the Defender pointed northwest, slamming through ruts and dips, shaking the chassis and rattling our bones, kicking up clouds of dust into the early morning sun. At some point, after the second hour, I knew we'd crossed the border into Morocco, and about half an hour after that, the ground began to slope down in a vast sweep that must have been ten miles across. On the other side of the slope, a wall of rock rose steeply out of the sand. We were almost there. I began to bear left, half-driving, half-sliding across the sand, headed ever down toward the river Ziz Valley below, and the Errachidia Road that would lead us, by and by, back to Ceuta.

We hit the road after ten minutes, just south of Douira, where the river valley suddenly lays a rich, fertile area of palm-tree plantations over the dry, yellow sand of the Sahara. We drove for another twenty minutes through dusty, dilapidated settlements, set among palms and cypresses, following the river until we came to an old fortress, half-buried in the sand, and a bridge that crossed the river to Aufous. Here the woodland became pretty dense. So I crossed the bridge and pulled off the road, in among the trees.

Maria was staring at the palms outside the window like she wasn't seeing them. She said, "We're in Morocco."

I climbed out then went around and opened the door for her. I helped her down.

She said, "Now what?"

I said, "Now we get you some decent clothes, check in to a hotel, have a shower, a meal and a sleep."

She studied my face a moment. "You dare to fall asleep with me around? I might cut your throat, or call Banks or del Roble." There was an edge of bitterness in her voice.

I half smiled. "I'll have to take my chances. Let's go."

And we turned and walked out of the palm grove and into Aufous, toward the Hotel Maison Vallee Du Ziz — and who knew what.

Chapter Twenty-Two

I told the receptionist we had been robbed. He smiled sympathetically while his eyes thought about something else then asked if we had credit cards. I told him we had managed to hang on to those and we wanted a suite for a week. He engaged his eyes, smiled and inquired whether we wanted him to call the cops. I said no, we'd deal with it ourselves. He made that weird 'as you wish' gesture French speakers make with their head and handed over a key.

"Room three-twenty, on zee top floor. Anysing you need, *monsieur*, just let me know."

I told him I wanted a bottle of Irish whiskey and two hundred Camel cigarettes. He rang a bell and we left.

The view was like a view of a Martian landscape, with a few palm trees thrown in just to confuse you. There was no air con. I opened the rickety, slatted terrace doors and a small breeze wafted in, didn't like what it found then left again. The air was hot and dusty and seemed to be paralyzed by the molten light that leaned down out of the near-white sky.

There was an en-suite bathroom that might have seemed new in the nineteenth century, but I didn't think so. The pipes groaned and rattled like The Canterville Ghost, but after a while, hot and cold water came out of the faucets and it looked mainly transparent. I propelled Maria in and told her to get a shower.

While she was undressing, there was a knock at the door. A young kid with a mustache and over-sized ears handed me a bottle of Jameson and two hundred cigarettes. I gave him a handful of change and he seemed happy and left.

I peeled a pack of Camels and poured myself a generous measure of Irish. Then I sat on the edge of the bed, sipped and inhaled gratefully while I watched Maria in the shower, glistening wet with thick suds running down her skin.

She probably had the most perfect body I had ever seen, but right now as I observed, it couldn't have been less sexy. All I could think was that buried inside that beautiful head might be a transmitter feeding information to del Roble and Banks – because I'd bet they hadn't been killed, either by Joanna or in the raid. And what else might they have programmed into the chip? It would fit del Roble's twisted mind perfectly to program Maria, the object of my love, to be my executioner – for me to rescue her and for her to carry the irresistible impulse to kill me.

She came out, toweling herself. She looked a little more alert.

I said, "Hungry?"

She shook her head.

I said, "Get some sleep. You need the rest. We'll be moving on soon."

"Is that another lie?"

"Maybe. I'll play it straight with you when we get that chip out of your head. Now, get some rest."

I locked the door and took the key into the bathroom with me. I stripped and stood under the hot water, letting it wash away the sweat and the dust and ease the aches from my muscles. I kept an eye on Maria from the shower while she slept. She didn't move. After I'd dried off, I sat and watched her sleep some more while I had a second whiskey and tried to think.

My killing Joanna had been a game changer for them. They had expected me to take Maria and Joanna back with me. What for, exactly, I couldn't be sure. I had an idea, but it wasn't a cert. But now, with Joanna dead, what would they do? The way I read it, del Roble had two aims. First, to implant Maria with a chip and put her and her handler, Dr. Loss – later Joanna – on me. For what reason, I could only guess. And second, to punish and humiliate me.

Now the plan was blown, and I had Maria. No plant, no punishment. And, to cap it all, I'd killed another one of their precious Seraphs. He was going to be mad as a bull at a communist rally. By the time I'd finished my whiskey, I had no doubt they were coming after me. Maria knew where we were now, so I had to assume they did, too. I couldn't be sure but I had to assume it. Sooner or later, they'd show.

I dressed, stepped out and relocked the door. I took the elevator down to reception and told the guy with the French accent, "I want to rent a car. Can I rent it through the hotel?"

"Of course, *monsieur*. For when do you want it?"

"Soon as you can get it. This afternoon?"

"*Pas de problème.*"

He gave me some papers to sign and, while I was doing that, I asked him, "As a matter of curiosity, is there anywhere else in town that does car rental? Hertz, Avis?"

He looked at me curiously for a second then said, "In ze town, there is an 'Ertz, but we can arrange everysing here."

I nodded. "Sure."

We concluded our business and I stepped out into the heat and the dust and started walking into town. As I walked, I pulled out my cell and called Russell. He answered almost immediately.

"Where are you?"

"I need you to do something. Get Hook to Google Hertz Aufous, Morocco. Reserve a car for me. Something with a bit of grunt. I want it today, as early as possible. As soon as you've booked it, let me know at what time it'll be available. I'll collect it from the office. Tell him he needs to make the booking as dark as he can. Untraceable. You understand me?"

"Of course, I understand you."

"Good. It's great to hear your voice."

He was about as stiff upper lipped as the Brits can get, but he knew what I meant. He was silent for a moment, then said, "Be careful," and hung up.

The town wasn't big, and I soon found the Hertz office on a street corner with a handful of cars on a parking lot. There were a couple of big French saloons and a Merc sports model. I don't like German cars, but I guessed out of what was available, the Merc would suit me best.

I headed back to the hotel.

I checked on Maria. She was still asleep. I locked her in again and headed back downstairs. The receptionist from last night had gone off duty, so I told the girl who'd relieved him to let me know if my wife called down from room three-twenty, then I went into the dining room and had a lamb *tajin* and two ice-cold beers. Russell's message came through as I was sitting over coffee. The earliest the car would be available was four-thirty that afternoon. I swore under my breath. That was too late. It was cutting it too fine. If Maria was in touch with them through some bio-chip, that would give them plenty of time to reroute and get to us here. But there was damn all I could do about it. I just had to play the hand I had been dealt.

I finished my coffee and returned to the reception desk.

"I ordered a hire car this morning. Can you tell me when it will be available?"

She tapped something out on her computer and told me it would be available from three in the afternoon.

I smiled my most charming smile and asked her, "How long would it take to drive to Rabat from here?"

She batted her long eyelashes at me. She was kind of cute if you weren't expecting intellectual stimulation. She cocked her head to one side and said, "Maybe sree hours?" Like she was asking me.

I held her gaze a little too long then asked, "Is it worth a visit?"

"Oh, many monuments and much 'istory."

"How about interesting things that are not historic?"

She leaned her elbows on the counter and held my stare right back. "Many interesting sings in Rabat. What kind of sings you are looking for?"

I gave a small laugh. "You know what? My wife is into history, old things. Me? I'm more interested in young things, interesting experiences. You know what I mean?"

She gave a cute laugh to go with her cute eyes. "'Istory can be very boring."

I pulled out a Camel and lit it. Through the smoke, I said, "You got that right, sister."

She watched me a minute, still smiling, "You can't smoke in here, Mr. Murdoch."

"Call me Liam."

"You can't smoke in here, Liam."

"I have to take my wife to see a bunch of old stuff in Rabat this afternoon. But tomorrow she's going to visit friends in Casablanca for a few days. How about I take you to Rabat and you show me all the interesting stuff? You could be my guide. What do you say?"

She gave me the once-over before she answered. "I say you are a very bad man, Liam. My name is Yasmine. I'm free the day after tomorrow. Can you wait zat long?"

"I'm sure it will be worth it. I'll have a couple of cold showers in the meantime. I'll be down at three to collect the car."

I went back up and found Maria in the shower again. When she stepped out, I threw her a towel and said, "Get dressed. We're going out for lunch."

She dried herself and put on her clothes in silence.

As we were leaving the room, I said, "We're going to Rabat."

She looked at me like I was crazy as we waited for the elevator. When she stepped in, she said, "We're going to lunch in Rabat? How far is it?"

I punched the button and the door closed. I said, "No, I told the receptionist we're going for lunch. But we're going to Rabat. I hired a car. I told her we're touring the area. You're into history. We're going out for lunch, have a drive around and back for dinner. But actually, we're going to

Rabat."

We stared at each other till the elevator stopped, competing for blank expressionlessness.

As she stepped out, I said, "I'm trusting you. Okay?"

She paused then and looked up into my face. I was serious, like I really meant it.

She nodded and said, "Thank you, Liam. I won't let you down."

I stood close over her. As the elevator doors closed behind us, I smiled and pecked her on the lips. "I know."

I caught Yasmine's eye as we went out and winked at her. She smiled back like she was a real bad girl. I felt a twinge of regret that I would never find out just how bad.

I linked Maria's arm in mine and we walked through the sweltering glare of midday heat like we were a couple of totally besotted lovers who were fascinated by Moroccan history and loved nothing more than baking in desert sand for their holidays. I led her to a teashop I'd seen on my previous walk. It was dark inside, with a warren of rooms leading off a large, central patio where a fountain played endless wet music into the heat of the afternoon. The owner and his wife were a little too solicitous and courteous, but as long as they remembered us, I could live with that.

I had a light second lunch of skewered lamb and sweet mint tea, but Maria was famished by now and had a chicken *tajin* with enough couscous to bury Casablanca. When the owner came over to clear away our plates, I asked him if he had a map. He said he didn't, but where did I want to go. I noticed Maria go stiff and I smiled at her and put my hand on her knee.

I said, "Chill. No one knows we came here." To him, I said in my worst schoolboy French, "*Nous voulons aller à Rabat.*" We wanted to go to Rabat.

He explained at length the best way to get there. Maria was real tense and I noticed that he noticed. When the guy had cleaned the plates away, I checked my watch. It was three.

I turned to Maria, "Try to relax, will you? I'll order you another mint tea. Wait for me here. I'm going to get the car."

She didn't answer but I felt her eyes on me all the way out.

I collected the car from the hotel, gave Yasmine a very handsome tip and told her I was looking forward to our trip the day after tomorrow. She seemed to be happy. I climbed in the car and drove a couple of minutes down the road, following the river upstream. The afternoon was at its hottest. The whole world seemed to be composed of glaring heat, yellow sand, panting dogs and flies that were too hot and tired to fly. They just sat there waiting to be swatted. There were no people in this world of heat. So there was no one to see me turn off into the palm grove and lose the car in the thickets on the river bank.

It was a slow, hot walk back and I'm pretty sure I lost about ten pounds just through sweat. I made it to Hertz. A generous surcharge ensured I got the Merc. Before driving back to the tea shop to collect Maria, I drove down to the river and parked a couple of hundred yards from the Maison Vallee Du Ziz. I smoked three cigarettes and nothing happened. No black Audis turned up. No Golika-Rinpoche. No del Roble. No Banks. So, I drove back to the tea house by way of a supermarket where I bought a rucksack and filled it with provisions for the journey ahead.

She was still at the table. She watched me come in and pay the bill at the bar without reacting.

Then I walked over to her and said, "Okay, let's go."

We headed out on the Madkhal Meski road, following the river upstream. I drove fast, not because I wanted to escape anymore, but because suddenly I was sick of the game and wanted to get back to my own turf. Maria seemed more alert now but kept her eyes on the desert, like she was waiting for me to say something or do something.

After a while, I spoke. I said, "Are they coming after us?"

She stared at me a while, chewing her lip. She said, "Yes.

He has to punish you and eliminate me. But more, he knows you have evidence. The photographs, the films…"

How did he know that? He could only have gotten that through Joanna.

I thought for a minute, then shrugged. "They prove nothing. Who'd believe they were real? Even without Photoshop, any special effects man could make up those sets — even more believable ones…" I glanced at her. "What would I do with them? Take them to the cops? The MOD? The Pentagon? Would I post them online? Upload them to some conspiracy theory website? He knows as well as I do that I'd join the ranks of celebrated nuts like David Ike and Steven Greer before you could say 'gray alien.' And that would be a more effective way of silencing me than killing me ever would."

She shook her head. "Then why did you take them in the first place?"

I nodded. "That's the question, isn't it? That's the million-dollar question."

She turned away. "What do you mean?"

I barked a laugh. That had been the game all along. "Come on, Maria! I know, you know and *they* know that those pictures and videos are useless on their own." I glanced at her again. She was still staring out of the window. "Unless I have somebody to look at them, who will *believe* them? And the million-dollar question is, who? Who did I take the pictures for? How did I find this damned place, anyway? How did I track the container? Who sent me?"

She was real quiet, staring at the scorched desert.

I went on, "You were both plants, designed to gain my trust and get on the inside, find out who was behind me, who their enemy in the shadows was, who screwed up Çalares's operation. That's what Joanna hoped to find out. That's what you're here to find out. And when you do, that's when you'll kill me."

We drove in silence through the sweltering heat for maybe fifteen or twenty minutes.

Finally, I said, "That's the billion-dollar question for them. The billion-dollar question for me is, is that bio chip in your head just a program or does it also act as some kind of radio transceiver? Do they hear everything I say to you? Have we been left alone because they don't know where we are? Or have they just been holding back, giving you time to draw information out of me?"

She didn't answer for a long while, but eventually she said, "The honest answer – the *only* answer – to all your questions, is that I simply don't know." She turned to face me. "I don't know."

I thought about the elaborate set-up I'd left behind me. If they turned up at the hotel, the receptionist would tell them we had gone to Rabat. They'd find we'd hired and collected a car for that purpose. If they dug deeper, they'd find another layer – that I had misled the receptionist into believing we were coming back. A simple misdirection. While they wondered whether I was coming back or not, they forget to wonder whether I actually went to Rabat.

But no one had turned up at the hotel by the time we'd left. There had been no black Audis. No search party. Was that because Joanna was the transmitter and I was the smartest son of a bitch in the valley, or because they had me hooked, and they were playing me? Whatever the reason, it was about to become irrelevant, because the whole game was about to change.

I figured we had about four hundred miles to go. On good roads, the Merc could get us there in less than four hours. But about two-thirds of the way was winding mountain roads – winding *Moroccan* mountain roads. It was going to take us eight hours to get back to Ceuta – at least. I could keep her guessing about our destination for about half the way. But as soon as we hit the Rabat turn-off at Meknes, she would know. She would know we were headed for Ceuta again.

I glanced at my watch. It was coming up to five. That put us at Meknes at about ten and Ceuta about one or two in the morning. If they were coming after us, that's where they'd do it.

But something was telling me they weren't—and they wouldn't. They were after a bigger prize than me.

Chapter Twenty-Three

It was dark. We'd been driving down out of the mountains for over an hour, among bare rocks and boulders. The sun had gone down suddenly, as it does in these latitudes. Then it was night, and the car became a dark cocoon enfolding us against the blackness outside, hurtling forward, toward an elusive safety we might never reach. Maria spoke suddenly, after two hours of silence, not looking at me, but looking at the amber beams that penetrated the night ahead of us.

"If I have, as you put it, a transceiver in my brain, then they are aware of everything I tell you and you tell me. You believe I have been planted here to get information from you about who sent you." She paused and shrugged. "And maybe you're right. You probably are. And if you give me that information, I will probably kill you. So, it seems to me the answer is simple. Don't give me that information. Let's both state it very clearly for them to hear. You are not going to give me that information, and if you try, I will refuse to hear it."

She was quiet, watching me. I was thinking hard.

After a while, I said, "If we do that, what happens?"

She didn't answer. She said, "I'll go further. I'll tell you everything I know about them."

I frowned at her. "What *do* you know about them?"

"I told you, Liam. I seem to have memories. Dr. Loss formed some kind of link with me. I don't know how it works. I think she started it back in London and finished it there, at the plant. Our minds, our experiences, linked somehow. I have memories, knowledge, that belonged to her. I think she had the same with me."

My head was reeling. Things were beginning to make sense. I said, "You didn't answer my question. If you do this, what happens to you?"

"If I kill you, the biochip has run its program and dies. If I don't… I'm not sure. I might have a psychotic break. It might kill me. I don't know."

"Are they hearing all this?"

She spread her hands. "I don't *know*, Liam! But I am willing to take the chance." She sounded exasperated.

At half ten we came to the Rabat Meknes junction. Instead of turning west toward Rabat I cut across the roundabout and kept going north, toward Tangier, Tetouan and Ceuta. She saw it and glanced at me. Neither of us spoke. We drove through Meknes then we were out among fertile, agricultural land and semi-suburban villages. The road wound among small, well-lit towns for a few miles, with silent cars parked in silent lots and clusters of male youths standing in pools of sad lamplight, likely talking about punishable dreams and hateful pleasures. Then we were back into the dark, moving north.

I said, "Okay, let's do it. Who are these people? What are they doing? What the hell was the facility all about?" Joanna had told me, but I wanted to hear it from Maria.

She rubbed her face with both hands and sighed deeply. "She told you it was about mind control."

"Mind control for what? By whom? To what end?"

"Shut up, Liam! Just for a minute, shut up and listen and stop attacking me."

My skin went cold. Her voice was different. I stayed silent, driving.

She waited, drew a breath then began to speak again, but it wasn't Maria. It was Joanna. "You believe that you are the only intelligent species inhabiting this planet. You are not. Get your head around that, because that is just the tip of the iceberg. Not only are you not the only intelligent species, there are many — *many* — among you whom you think are human, and they are not. Many of them don't even know that they're not."

I snapped, "Come on, Maria! What are you talking about?"

"I'm talking about a program of hybridization, involving millions—tens of millions—of human beings who don't even know that they are part of the program."

She reached forward to the glove compartment and pulled out a pack of Camels. She lit two and handed me one.

I said, "Pull out the Irish, will you? I need a drink."

We took a slug each and drove on, punching through the night.

"Are we talking about aliens? What is this? Are you asking me to believe we are being invaded by extraterrestrials? Because that just doesn't hold water."

She was shaking her head before I'd finished. "No, Liam. Understand this, once and for all. *You* are the aliens. If anyone on this planet is an invader, an alien organism, it's *you!*"

I stared at her.

She said, "Eyes on the road."

I looked back and swerved around a bend, narrowly missing the barrier.

I said, "*What?*"

"Just read Professor Lovelock. Look at the way you behave in this environment. You are like a damned parasite. An alien organism ravaging and destroying, consuming everything until you kill the host. You are in constant war with this planet, talking of *conquering* nature…" She paused, sucked on her cigarette, then went on, "For hundreds of millions of years the environment of this planet was scorching hot. The natural CO_2 levels were off the chart. It was a paradise."

"A *paradise?*"

"Yes, for reptiles and Saurians, it was a paradise. They thrived and evolved on their world, and one of their species developed intellectually. They evolved mentally well beyond what humans have achieved."

I sighed. "The Ael."

She looked surprised. "Yes, at least, they would eventually

become the Ael. A long time ago, a very long time ago, there was a catastrophic event, and the environment and the climate changed. It became much colder and the levels of CO_2 fell dramatically. There was a mass extinction. Most of the Saurians were wiped out. Only a very few survived by going underground."

"That was *sixty-five million* years ago!"

She was quiet for a long time. Then she said, "They don't experience time the way we do."

We had been climbing steadily into low sierra and now we were passing Chefchaouen. I began to see signs for Tetouan. I glanced at my watch. It was close to midnight. We were behind schedule, but still no sign of del Roble, Golika-Rinpoche or their pals.

I said, "This is bullshit, Maria. You want me to believe that all of this is somehow rooted in a meteor that fell sixty-five million years ago?"

She was quiet for a bit then said, "That was when the Saurians went underground. They continued to evolve. They bred very rarely and have lifespans that are incomprehensible to us. To humans, they are like gods. They have appeared in mythology as gods or demons. But they are not gods."

"But they are demons?"

She ignored the question. "For a very long time, the planet evolved and developed in peace. The surviving Saurians evolved into different branches, with the Ael at the top of the evolutionary tree. Others were able to come to the surface in certain regions where it was hot and dry. But then, about a million years ago, when the current ice age was at its peak and the Saurians were in retreat underground, there was an event that was to change the destiny of this planet forever."

I waited. She was just staring at the road ahead.

I said, "What?"

"Earth was invaded by an alien species."

I said, "Don't tell me, the Grays." I couldn't keep the irony from my voice.

She gave a humorless snort. "No, Liam. The Grays, as you call them, are not aliens. These invaders came from a neighboring planet within the solar system. They had a problem. Their planet was just a little too small and its gravitational pull was not enough to hold their atmosphere. It was, literally, draining slowly into space. They were an intelligent, aggressive species and they had developed crude technology capable of taking them off-world and to their nearest neighbors'. Technologically, they were about where you are now."

I pulled over into a lay-by. I killed the engine and stepped out of the car. We were in the sierra, surrounded by pine trees. It was chilly and dark, and the stars above were like tiny flakes of ice. There was no moon. I went and leaned against the hood of the car. I heard the door open and close behind me. Then she was standing next to me, offering me the bottle of Jameson. I took it and put it to my lips. The warmth was good inside me. She was lighting two more Camels and handed me one.

I said, "You're talking about Mars."

"I don't know the whole story, Liam. I know the Saurians, under the guidance of the Ael, had been going to Mars for a long time. But as the ice age began to bite, that stopped. There was mammalian life on both planets—had been for a long time. The people of Mars knew that Earth offered them hope, a new home. To them it was a paradise...an Eden."

I said, "It's bullshit," but I didn't believe me.

"There was war. It's in all the mythology. You won."

"We won." I stared at her. I couldn't keep the resentment from my voice. "Why do you keep talking as if you were one of them?"

She closed her eyes. She looked drained. "Because this is Joanna speaking to you. Like all victors, you skewed history and mythology to reflect *your* version of what happened. Yahweh, the angels, the gods... They were all human. The Naga, the devils, the evil ones... They were all reptiles, snakes, dragons who lived underground in Hell. You created an empire that spanned the equator. Its hub was in the Caribbean. You took possession of the surface. Your methods were, and always have been, aggressive, intelligent, systematic—military."

I smoked and took another drink. The chill in the air made me shudder. The sky looked vast and the woods dark. I said, "And their methods?"

She shrugged. "Subtle. Humans are pack animals. Saurians and reptiles tend to be solitary, individual. They tried reason—" She laughed. "Remember the story of Adam and Eve? Lucifer, the bringer of light... He didn't offer Eve an apple. He offered her the fruit of the Tree of Knowledge. In return, you nuked them."

"Stop." I said it quietly. I'd had enough.

I had another drink and finished my cigarette. Then we drove on in silence, toward Ceuta.

There was no attack. They didn't come for us.

We reached Ceuta at two a.m. I ditched the car in a back alley and we got a room at a filthy hostel where I told the guy at reception that Maria was my whore. I paid cash—no credit cards, no passports, no ID.

* * * *

It was pitch black and there was a dead weight on my chest. I could feel my heart racing. I tried to move my arms. They were immobilized. But there was something worse. I couldn't breathe. I was suffocating and I couldn't shout. Something was smothering my face, pushing down. I tried to thrash and kick but I was pinned, trapped. Then I realized what was happening and I allowed myself to panic. Because I knew if I didn't, I was going to die. I arched my body, thrashed and hurled myself sideways. There was a loud thud. The darkness thinned. I gasped then threw myself away from the direction of the sound. I was on the end of the bed. The darkness shifted. I heard wood splinter.

The old chair by the window. As my eyes adjusted, I saw the pale glow of the streetlights outside on the panes. Then a black shadow loomed. There was an inhuman sound and the blackness rushed at me.

Broken wood tore at my shoulder. Nails gripped at my neck. Instinct told me the broken wood was coming for my face. I grabbed a wrist, felt the wood tearing at my arm. I lashed out with my right, connected with a body then punched again. Warm blood was running down my other arm as the wood bit deeper. I heaved with all my strength and the body fell back, screeching. I lunged for where the door should be, for the light switch. Something caught my ankle and I fell hard on the tiled floor.

I broke my fall with my hands and felt slippery blood under my left fingers. I heard movement on my left and rolled right. Wood stabbed and splintered on the floor. I was on my knees, then on my feet, kicking out with my right foot. Claws ripped at my ankles, clutched at my leg, pulled hard. I fell on a body, grappling with it, clutching at invisible hands and arms. I was thrown hard on my back by incredible strength, pinned down. I groped. Two hands held the broken wood, forcing it down toward my neck and chest. I held both wrists in my hands but the force was too much and I could feel the jagged stake inching toward my windpipe. I knew I was near the door. I knew the rucksacks were there. I twisted my neck away, gripped hard with my left and groped out with my right, searching for the bags.

Only tiles. Cold tiles. The sharp, broken teeth of the wood were brushing my skin. I was losing my strength. I couldn't hold. Then I felt the rim of a bag with my fingertips. Too late.

I yanked the bag to me. My left arm gave. The wooden stake plunged, going deep. I gasped and moaned, went limp and stopped breathing.

There was absolute stillness. A long time seemed to pass with the black body sitting heavy on my chest. Then a voice. A whisper.

"Liam?"

I didn't move. I made no sound.

"Liam?" a little louder. Then growing frantic, "Liam? Liam, speak to me! Liam, please, wake up! Liam!" She was on her knees next to me, slapping at my face, holding my shoulders and shaking me.

I heard her scramble to her feet and head for the light. When it snapped on, she saw me on my back, staring with sightless eyes at the ceiling, the blood-smeared chair leg sticking out of my throat at a grotesque angle, clutched in both my hands.

She thought I was dead.

And the program in her brain would die, its purpose fulfilled, as she'd explained it to me.

She sank to her knees sobbing, wailing and repeating over and over, "Oh, God... Oh, God, no... Oh, God, no..."

I gave her a couple of seconds to fully assimilate that I was 'dead'. Then I sat up and pulled the chair leg away from my neck where it had been buried in the fabric of the rucksack. She was staring at me, her mouth twisting as she released ugly sobs and her face drenched with tears.

I said, "It's okay. You're okay now."

I pushed myself across the floor till I was next to her, then I took her in my arms and held her for a long time while she sobbed and cried out by turns, clinging to me. After maybe half an hour, I settled her on the bed, wrapped her in a blanket, found a tooth mug in the bathroom and poured her a stiff whiskey. She drank it in silence, trembling, holding the plastic mug with both hands.

Finally, I crouched in front of her and made her meet my eyes. I said, "It's over. The program ran its course. Now it's dead. You're free."

She stared at me with uncomprehending eyes. Her face creased like she was going to start sobbing again, but she said, "Oh, God, Liam, I thought I'd killed you."

"And when you thought that, so did the biochip. It had done its job and that cell died."

Her face cleared. "So?"

"So, it's over."

"But, what—?"

"Now we see what happens next."

"Why did I—?"

"They must have triggered it because of the agreement we made in the car."

She nodded, thinking.

I went on, "Which means there was, maybe still is, something in you that transmits to them somehow."

"Joanna?"

"Maybe."

"So what do we do now?"

"We wait and see. We wait and see what they do next."

Chapter Twenty-Four

The Balearia ferry didn't depart till eight in the morning. We left the hostel at first light and found a café on the dock where we had coffee laced with Spanish cognac and toast doused in olive oil. By ten past nine, we were pulling out of the port, pushing through the still waters of the Mediterranean toward the distant hulk of Gibraltar.

I got some polystyrene coffee, took Maria by the arm then led her up to the deck. The sun was hot, even at that time of the morning, and the glare off the sea was blinding. But there was a strong breeze off the starboard side. It battered our clothes and whipped her hair across her face. We found a plastic table and chairs in a sheltered nook on the port side and sat in silence awhile, looking out toward the vast, dark Atlantic. I kept asking myself if I was sitting with Maria or Joanna. I needed to know.

Finally, I said, "I think you're bullshitting me." I turned to face her.

She kept staring at the ocean beyond the Pillars of Hercules.

I kept at her. "You said you'd give me information about this organization — whatever it is — and all you did was spin me a cock-and-bull story about dinosaurs and something that happened sixty-five million years ago."

Now she faced me and held my gaze. "You told me to stop, remember?" It was Joanna.

"We have less than an hour. Tell me something I can believe before we reach Algeciras."

She pulled a face and shook her head. "I can't guarantee you'll believe it, Liam. This whole thing exists because it's unbelievable."

"Try me."

She sighed and let her gaze move back to the West. "I'll try to keep it to what you believe is relevant."

"I'd appreciate that."

"This Martian race, because they were better suited to the cold environment on the surface and because of their systematic, military mentality, established their dominion and created an empire that spanned the globe around the equator. This was during the height of the ice age, when the north and south of the planet were covered in vast ice sheets. The equator was a lush, temperate zone. Their principal state was in what is now the Caribbean, stretching from Belize to Martinique, bounded by Cuba and the Dominican Republic in the east, and Honduras and Nicaragua in the west."

I rubbed my face with my palms. I was getting antsy. "You're talking about Atlantis, Maria. You're doing it again."

"Just shut up and listen, Liam." She turned to face me and looked pretty antsy herself. "Not everything in this world fits into the nice, neat boxes that have been made for you. A couple of days ago you were taking photographs of people growing on giant cannabis plants, remember? Under the surface, Liam, this is a weird, fucked-up world. Now, do you want me to tell you how it is, or do *you* want to tell *me* how it is?"

She had a point. I stared into my coffee. It was very black. I said, "Go on."

She snapped, "Every Native American civilization, surrounding the Caribbean Sea as far as Mexico, has a tradition of a nation that sank below the ocean, with a name like Atlantis. The Toltecs, Nahuatlacas, the Aztecs— and *all* the races that settled Mexico—trace their ancestry back to Aztlan or Atlan, located in the Atlantic. You know what happened to this place? It sank after a great flood." She leaned forward and her face flushed with anger and tears spilled from her eyes. "What a fucking coincidence that Plato put Atlantis right there, and it sank right at the beginning of the interglacial period, when the fucking ice caps were melting! Does that have a familiar fucking ring to you, Mr. Bullshit?"

"Okay…"

"Maybe you'd like to explain to me, Liam Mr. Fucking-Know-It-All-Murdoch, how Solon, two-thousand five-hundred years ago, knew that the Atlantic was a vast ocean and beyond it lay another vast continent. And how he knew that ten thousand years earlier the interglacial had begun."

"You made your point."

"Then please *shut up* and *listen!*" She glared at me, her breath coming heavy. "You *demand* the truth over and over, but you *ignore* it when it stares you in the face!"

I didn't answer and we were quiet for a while.

Then she said, "Their empire lasted for millennia. They reached a level of technological advancement similar, perhaps a little more advanced, than what you have today. But they were constantly at war, with each other — just like you, and also with the Saurians. Their great genius — your great genius — is the ability to organize systematically and attack in packs. Those Saurians who had remained on the surface — or visited the surface — were decimated and driven below, but at a cost."

She sipped her coffee and sat thinking.

I said, "What cost?"

"They began to produce CO_2, just like you. The population of the world was far less, and the volumes were far lower. But the climate was also a lot colder and, over time, it only took a few degrees, coupled with the natural cycles of Earth, to cause a catastrophic collapse of the ice sheets. The amount of ice that melted is inconceivable. Trillions upon trillions of tons of ice fell into the Atlantic. Sea levels rose, there was torrential rain and there were hurricanes that devastated the planet. Not only that, but the massive displacement of the weight of the ice caused Earth's crust literally to spring back, triggering earthquakes that would have measured ten and twelve on the Richter Scale."

"This is the origin of the myth of the Flood."

She nodded. "It is universal. Atlantis, the Flood... There is not a culture on Earth that doesn't have it. The human race was decimated and the culture was all but lost, along with its military might. You can imagine what happened next."

I looked at the stark, blue-white sky. Seagulls were wheeling overhead, crying their weird, desperate cry across the sea. I said, "The balance of power shifted. Some of the" — I felt embarrassed using the name, but I shrugged — "some of the Atlanteans survived. They retained some of their science, but they had lost their industrial and military base."

"Manu, Noah, Jehovah, Deus... The names are all there if you search for them. As the climate began to settle, what emerged was that temperatures had risen substantially. The elite who had survived withdrew into mountain refuges, just as before them the Saurians had withdrawn to underground refuges."

"Agarte..."

"Yes, to name but one. The event had been traumatic and there were those, like Manu, who believed that humanity needed to rethink its relationship with the planet and with the Saurians. They formed a counsel. They called it the Seven Sages, others called it the White Counsel. The name is irrelevant.

"There was one among the Saurians who agreed with them. His name will remain unspoken for now. The important point is that the bulk of surviving humanity was reduced, in a few decades, to primitive, savage tribes, struggling day to day simply to survive. They stayed that way for nearly five thousand years. In that time, a new war began. A different war. A war for their minds and spirits."

My coffee was now very black and very cold. I knew what she'd meant but I decided to ask, anyway.

"Lucifer? The Garden of Eden?"

She ignored me, as though I hadn't spoken, then went on, "As the climate warmed, so more and more Saurians began to make sorties to the surface. Many simply vented their hatred on the warm-blooded, savage race who had taken their world from them. They stole and ate their babies, stalked them in the night, became the stuff of nightmare and legend. Others tried to bridge the divide by teaching and by giving spiritual guidance. Inevitably, this deteriorated among your ignorant tribes into superstition, cult and, eventually, religion.

"Meanwhile, the human elite who had established themselves in mountain refuges in the Himalayas and the Andes began to echo the activities of the Saurians. They would kidnap young girls and boys that grabbed their fancy, breed with them and tell them they were the beloved of the gods. Soon religions sprang up around them, too. They became Thor and Odin, Zeus, Apollo, Krishna, Yahweh…

"But where your gods grew decrepit, we did not. About ten thousand years ago, we began to help your tribes to cultivate the land and build cities. We taught them the basic skills of metallurgy…"

She went quiet, staring toward the sea and the ridges of white foam that gradually moved away from us in oblique lines. I pulled out a pack of Camels and began to peel it. I lit two and handed one to her. She glanced at it, then at me, took it and stared at it a while before taking a drag.

I wasn't sure if I believed her or if I thought it was all a crock of bull. But something inside was telling me that somehow, in a way I could not explain, it was true. And besides, I was curious about where it was leading. I was also aware that she'd reached a point in her narrative that she thought was important.

I said, "So what happened?"

"The highest Saurians, the Ael, wanted to teach more. Remember that Eve did not eat an apple. She ate the Fruit of the Tree of Knowledge that was offered to her by a serpent.

This was deliberate. The Saurians knew well the nature of humanity, and they knew what they would do with this knowledge if they were not taught also to love and respect their new home." She took a deep drag then examined the burning tip while she tapped away the ash. "Remember that the Saurians do not think in years, as humans do. They measure time in centuries and millennia. And they knew that human greed and avarice — and their war-like nature — would lead them again to the excesses of Atlantis. But this time they would do it all over the globe, unconstrained by the ice age."

"What are you saying?"

She seemed not to hear my question. "I don't know what happened to your 'gods'. Over the centuries, they faded and were replaced by one — Yahweh, also called Allah. Yahweh, who banished the serpent. Perhaps they died. Perhaps they were killed. But your civilizations flourished, and with them, your wars and your empires. In the end, the Ael and their Seraphs despaired of you, and as your empires came and went, they began to guide and nurture them in a different way.

"The first to receive this new attention was Rome. With Rome, your technology advanced by leaps and bounds, founded on the law of five, the Eden Cypher, and directed at ever more efficient ways of slaughtering each other. And, finally…"

She turned to stare at me, almost as though I disgusted her.

I waited then said, "Finally, *what?*"

"Three times you were given the chance — Greece, the Renaissance and the Enlightenment. Each time you sought power over wisdom, and finally, you came at last to where you were always going to wind up — in the Industrial Revolution. Guided by the scaly hand of the London Masonic Lodge, you set about building factory after factory after factory, all over the globe. From London, you had already sent forth the Founding Fathers to America —

the new Atlantis—to build more factories and yet more factories, all making…what?"

I shook my head. "I don't know. Shoes? Cars? Steel? Weapons? I don't know! What are you getting at, Maria?"

She was shaking her head long before I'd finished. She leaned forward, stared me in the eye and half whispered, "C…O2!"

I don't often gape, but I think I gaped. "Are you *kidding* me?"

"No, I'm not kidding you, Liam. It was the most effective weapon ever created against humanity, and you manufactured millions of tons of it yourselves, to satisfy your own unbridled greed. Let the damned humans gorge themselves and sate their lust. Let them ravage their home and murder each other over plots of land they want to rape and pillage. Let them rob each other and sack each other's cities and homes, if all the while they are pumping CO_2 back into the atmosphere on a scale the Saurians would never have been able to manage. Because that way, Liam… That way they will—in *typical* human fashion—make the world uninhabitable for themselves, but eminently habitable once again for the ancient masters of this planet—the Saurians."

I was in disbelief. "Are you seriously telling me…?"

"Am I telling you that for the past ten thousand years your history has been guided and directed by Saurians masquerading as gods, demons, prophets and Enlightened Beings, directing your steps toward the Industrial Revolution? Yes! That's what I am telling you. And since then, there has hardly been a major public figure who was not either a hybrid or a puppet of the Saurians." She sucked on her cigarette and blew smoke aggressively into the wind. "They have given you chance after chance to learn, and every single *fucking* time you blew it! Every conspiracy theory you can think of, from JFK to the Illuminati, from Roswell to the Bilderberg Group… Every one of them is a smokescreen for this one simple conspiracy."

My head was reeling again. It was too much to take in.

All I could think to ask was, "But… But what happened to the…what you called the human elite?"

A twisted distortion of a smile made her look suddenly ugly. "Why? You think Yahweh might come back and save you?"

I shook my head.

She barked a nasty laugh. "Shall I tell you something, Liam? It is your oh-so-human leaders who are *begging* us for the technologies that will destroy your environment. Your oh-so-human leaders *fully support* our plan, either to turn you into an army of brain-dead androids, or, when you are wiped out by the coming holocaust, replace you with walking vegetables, so that they can rule as princes under the Saurian emperors. If you want anyone to save humanity, Liam, don't expect humans to do it."

I stood and walked to the rail and stared down at the churning ocean. I could see Algeciras approaching and the vast rock of Gibraltar to the West. I was hit by a wave of desolation. How do you save an entire race of intelligent beings who seem hell-bent on their own destruction? The grind of the engines changed as we began to pull in toward the port. The gulls were screaming overhead. I was trying to put everything she had told me together, trying to make sense of it, trying to decide if I believed any of it, some of it or all of it.

She came and stood beside me, looking down at the churning sea.

I said, "So, the purpose of the facility, the purpose of this whole project, the trees, the labs, the ships…"

She was nodding. "Yes…"

"The purpose of all that is to provide a contented slave race for…" I was shaking my head, shrugging, spreading my hands.

"Not for the Saurians, Liam. Not for the Ael, they have never used slaves. They have never needed or wanted them. They are individualists and loners. Slaves are a human thing. This slave race was commissioned from us by humans in nineteen forty-seven by your political masters, when they realized it was too late to turn back climate change. We already make millions of them, mainly for the sex industry. You, and your human hunt for feeling and sensation."

There was a blast from the foghorn above our heads. The gulls wheeled crazily against the scorching sky. The sea churned and eddied beneath us. Ahead, Algeciras, the gateway to Europe, bustled. Cars sped back and forth, trains screamed in steel agony, planes roared into the heavens, factories billowed black and gray smoke, and five-hundred million Europeans lived their lives like ignorant sheep, staring into their phones, tablets and computers, passively having their brains programmed, shuffling steadily, obediently, toward their enslavement and eventual slaughter.

Chapter Twenty-Five

We took the Autovía del Mediterráneo out of Algeciras then headed east. I could have headed north to Jerez and Seville, aiming to cut over western Spain and cross the border at Irun into France. But being the obvious thing to do, I chose not to do it. The second most obvious thing to do would be to follow the Autovía del Mediterráneo all the way up to Barcelona and enter France through Cerbère, on the French-Catalan border, but I didn't do the second most obvious thing, either. I was pretty sure Golika-Rinpoche and del Roble were going to find us, but I didn't want to make it too easy.

I headed east in the Daemon toward Malaga. The heat was oppressive. The thermometer in the car was showing fifty degrees Centigrade. But with the hood down and cruising at a hundred miles per hour, it was tolerable. By midday, we hit Benalmádena, with it's crazy Stupa flashing golden light under the sun, and ten minutes later, before we hit Malaga, we peeled off onto the AP46 and took off north, toward Cordoba.

We didn't talk. We didn't even look at each other. It was good to be in Europe. It was good to be driving in the sun and the wind, pretending for a couple of hours that we were back in the real world. Back from Godzilla in wonderland. But inside, I was growing tired of Joanna. I had killed her to save Maria, and now she seemed to have taken possession of her, and I was wondering if I would ever get Maria back.

It was after two when we crested the hill and saw Cordoba spread out below us. As we drove down into the city and crossed the Bridge of San Rafael, from the South Bank to the north, the heat was fantastic. I glanced at the thermometer and it was showing fifty-two degrees Centigrade. I knew that in inland Andalusia in the summer, temperatures peaked at four and five in the afternoon—in another two or three hours.

We cruised up the main avenue, past the old Alkazar, then turned right into the shade of the trees in the Jardines de la Victoria. I wound down a couple of narrow streets onto the Avenida Dr. Fleming and pulled into a car park that had been built into the old city walls. I took our bags from the trunk and we stepped out into the blazing heat.

I glanced at Maria. She was pale.

"We'll find a hotel, eat, rest, buy some clothes, get a few hours' sleep and move out about four in the morning. You okay?"

She nodded. "Okay."

There was a plaza set against the old city wall. It was like a small Roman theater with a fountain in the middle, surrounded by cafés and terraced restaurants. In the wall, there was a giant, mediaeval archway that led into a maze of narrow, cobbled streets. My instinct told me to go to ground there. So we ducked in past two *mesones* that looked like medieval taverns, a club where they did the dance of the seven veils and a labyrinth of tiny streets that hadn't changed since the wheel had been a controversial novelty.

After a couple of minutes, we came out to a cobbled square dotted with orange trees. It could have been a Hollywood film set for a kasbah in an Indiana Jones movie. Thousands of people milled, spilling off narrow sidewalks. There were jewelers on every corner, selling silver filigree. There were bars and ice-cream parlors with chairs and tables sprawling across the road, and cars, motorbikes, horse-drawn carriages, taxis, gypsies selling tired, nicotine-stained dreams and tourists renting vicarious freedom by the week. All were jostling, gazing, competing for space.

We pushed through the crowd and suddenly the narrow street opened into a large esplanade, and there was the most bizarre building I had ever seen in my life—the mosque-cathedral. It was a vast, sandstone construction with a great tower rising over one hundred and fifty feet into a stark sky. There was a giant Arabesque door set in the base of the tower that led into a square, maybe two-hundred feet across or more. At the far end was the main body of the mosque-cathedral, with its great arches and the huge dome of the cathedral rising above it. At first glance, it was Spanish renaissance, but when you looked closer, you saw that it was just renaissance twiddles on top of Arab architecture that was probably over a thousand years old. As I stared, I became aware that Maria was talking to me.

"It was built one thousand three hundred years ago by Abd-al Rahman I, a Umayyad prince from Syria, nicknamed the Umayyad Hawk. He was descended from one of Mohammed's cousins. His whole clan was massacred by Abu Abbas as Saffah, in Palastine. Abd-al Rahman was only fifteen. He was the only one to escape. He crossed North Africa on foot with his faithful servant, Badr, and after seven years he finally landed at Torrox, age just twenty-two. He raised an army and took Cordoba in a single battle. Throughout his reign, he refused to build a mosque. His life had taught him to be an atheist, not to believe in the god of his ancestors. But he was persuaded by his advisors, just before he died, that for political reasons, for the sake of his dynasty, he must. So he did. He built this. It is the only mosque in the world that faces southeast instead of east. A small act of defiance against Allah, Yahweh, Mohammed and religion."

I stared at her. "How do you know that?"

She smiled without much humor. "He was six foot tall, red-haired and blue-eyed. He was a hybrid, like all his clan."

We were standing under the minaret tower, in the vast archway that gave onto the Patio de los Naranjos—the patio of the orange trees. She began to walk away, into the glaring sunlight of the courtyard. I followed her. There was an ancient stone fountain set among the orange trees and she headed for it. The sound of its splashing, trickling water was cool in the heat. I caught up with her as she bent over and drank from her cupped hands. She straightened and spoke without looking at me, wiping the water from her chin.

"You should never come here without drinking the water."

I said, "What do you mean, 'he was a hybrid, like all his clan'?"

"I told you that all the men and women who have shaped history have been guided and influenced by the Saurians. A number, perhaps the most important, have been hybrids."

I pulled a face. "And this guy was important? I've never heard of him."

She raised an eyebrow at me and moved on, crossing the square toward the far exit, with slow steps. "Few people have. But he created an empire of learning, poetry, art and religious tolerance. He paid a pension for life to any scholar or scientist who would settle here. While Europe was in the grip of the Dark Ages, mathematicians, scientists and scholars from all over the world were drawn to his kingdom. Muslims, Christians and Jews all lived here together in peace."

We had reached one of the many great doors in the wall and she stopped again to look at me.

"But, more important than that, the present-day conflicts in the Middle East, the fundamentalist movements in Islam, even the Crusades, all have their roots in the Umayyad massacre by Abu Abbas and Abd-al Rahman's escape to the West. He was told in a prophesy, you know, by a Jewish astrologer, that he would save his family by going to the West, to the Land of Hope. Hesperus, España. And he did."

I said, "Why are you telling me this?"

She stared at me a moment then turned and walked through the great door out into the crowded street. I followed. We were on a corner, and just to the left was the

Hotel Marisa.

We were lucky. They'd had a cancelation and we were able to get a double room. We climbed the stairs, threw the bags on the bed and took turns to shower. While Maria was in the bathroom, I stood at the window. Our room overlooked the mosque, and to the right I could just see the dome of the cathedral. Below, the street was teeming with people. I searched for Rinpoche but there was no sign of him or of any black Audis.

She came out of the bathroom, naked and toweling herself. We watched each other a while. She smiled.

We had some food sent up and, at about seven, we went out and bought some clothes. The ones we had were pretty rough and attracting too much attention. We changed in the toilets at the Corte Inglés superstores and had dinner at a restaurant in town. All the while, I was keeping my eyes peeled for any sign of Golika-Rinpoche and his pals, but there was nothing. Not a hint.

At eleven, we walked back through Las Tendillas, the main square of the town. In the amber lamplight with the crowds and the fountains playing, you could almost imagine that everything that had happened in the last couple of weeks had been a dream. A weird nightmare. This happy, beautiful city was reality, not the facility in Algiers, not the Saurians or the hybrids. Not the madness of the slaves, the mind control and the killings.

She stopped me and placed her hands on my chest, looking up into my face. For a brief moment, she was Maria again and my heart thudded with hope. I could hear the water from the fountain splashing in the warm night air. Somewhere some kids laughed, a motorbike revved and the traffic hissed and hummed under the city lights. Her eyes seemed to gleam with hope. With a dream.

She said, "Liam..."

I held her face in my hands, wanting to believe I could get her back, that she would come back to me.

She said, "Can't we just escape? Can we just lose ourselves?

Change our identities, run, find some place where none of this is real? Just you and me?"

Was it Maria talking? My belly burned with hope.

I bent and kissed her then whispered in her ear, "I love you, Maria."

We half ran, half stumbled back through the lamp-lit alleys, suddenly laughing like teenagers. We ran up the stairs to our room and surged through the door, kissing and undressing each other. We fell on the bed, tangled in each other's arms and legs, kissing, biting and gripping like we were going to fuse into one single, crazed being. My whole world was her skin and her face against mine. I was inside her, biting at her neck and shoulders, biting her lips, seeing Maria's face, hearing Maria's voice, knowing it was Maria. And my mind was full of her sighs, her voice and her cries as crazy spasms racked our bodies over and again until we collapsed, exhausted and sweating, in the heat of the night. Then there was stillness and silence.

I had been sleeping. I didn't know how long. I could feel Maria's body close to mine, with her back to me. There was a restlessness in my mind. I was wide awake. I rose from the bed and went to the window. The sandstone walls of the mosque were floodlit in amber, making the cobbles of the street look like burnished bronze. There were no people. The city was asleep.

Then I saw him. He was just a black silhouette, down in the street, leaning with his shoulder on the wall of the mosque, looking straight at me. I stepped back from the glass. He had tracked us and that meant just one thing. I listened to Maria's breathing. As far as I could tell, she was asleep. I dressed quickly, slipped the Sig into my waistband then peered out of the window again.

He was gone.

I moved to the door and eased it open. The landing was dark and quiet. I could hear voices downstairs, the guy on reception speaking softly but firmly. Golika-Rinpoche's voice, smiling, wheedling. Then silence. The main door opening and closing. Then there were feet on the steps. I counted three, maybe four sets. I slipped out of the room and closed the door behind me. In the light filtering up from reception, I could make out the shadows of four men stretching out and dancing on the wall as they climbed the stairs.

The landing made a dogleg opposite my door. I stepped across and flattened myself to the wall on the corner and waited. The footsteps stopped. They had reached the landing. There was some muttering. Then more footsteps and two hulking shadows passed me and stopped at my room. The other two must have stayed at the head of the stairs.

I heard the soft click of the lock. The door opened. The two hulks moved and blended into the shadows of the room. Then I moved fast. I slipped around the corner. They were both looking down at the reception. Three strides got me to them. A shot fired with the muzzle of a gun pressed against a body makes no sound. The body acts as a silencer. I grabbed the nearest guy by the hair, pressed the Sig into his neck, aiming at the second guy. I fired. The bullet tore out his vertebra and smashed into the second guy's throat. Neat. They'd both died in silence.

As they slumped, I had a good look at them. Neither of them was Rinpoche. I headed back to my room. I walked in quickly and quietly. Maria was sitting up in bed. I couldn't see her face. The two goons were staring down at her.

Then Maria gave a little squeal. "*Liam!*"

They spun to face me. I raised the automatic but the nearest guy grabbed my wrist and slammed his left fist at my floating ribs. I swayed and dropped my elbow to deflect most of the force, but I was off balance and we fell in a heap on the floor. He tried to straddle me, but I gripped his collar and head-butted him in the nose. I heard him grunt, then there were powerful hands grabbing my shirt and my hair from behind and pulling me to my feet. As I came up, the guy I'd head-butted was on his knees spilling blood from his nose. But before I could follow up, the goon who'd grabbed me started wailing into me with his right fist, while yanking at my hair with his left to keep me off balance.

Most of his blows hit my arms and my shoulders. Keeping me off balance was also making me a moving target, but a couple of his punches hit home. He was a big guy and strong and I was feeling it. I still had the Sig in my hand, but everything was happening too fast and I couldn't take aim. Then I stumbled on one of our bags and fell. He came with me and planted his knee on my chest. His left hand had my right hand pinned down with the Sig in it and his right fist was drawn back for the killer blow.

Then something shattered around his head. There was a shower of shards. He swayed for a moment then keeled over to one side. Maria was standing over him, staring at me. I looked at the other guy. He was staggering to his feet, still holding his nose.

Maria was saying, "We have to go!"

I heaved myself up, my head spinning with sick pain, and swung a big kick between the guy's legs. It wasn't his day. He whimpered and sank back to his knees. We scrambled. I snatched my wallet, my cell and my car keys. Maria was grabbing clothes and pulling them on as she made for the door. I could hear a wheezing voice from the floor saying something about a motherfucker. I took that to be me. I didn't take offense.

I went through the door first. I was saying, "Rinpoche is here. I think he's downstairs..."

"Rinpoche?"

"Yeah, Golika, your pal Steve... Just stay behind me."

I stepped over the bodies at the top of the stairs and peered down. There was no sign of anyone in reception. I went halfway down and saw the receptionist slumped over the counter. His throat had been cut from ear to ear. Rinpoche wasn't there. Nobody was there. I took the last few steps two at a time and peeked out of the door. Nobody. I signaled Maria to follow.

I said, "We need to make it to the car, fast."

I stepped out into the street. Even at this time — in the small hours — the air was sultry. Across the road, there was a big iron street lamp bolted to the sandstone wall of the mosque. Inside it, I could see three geckos on the glass. I peered down the street to the right. Pools of dull yellow light made the shadows look darker. At first I couldn't see anyone, but then, maybe a hundred yards away in the direction of the car park, something shifted in the dark then resolved itself into two shapes moving our way. Then I heard staggering footsteps behind me. The goons were coming down, and they'd be real pissed. I cursed myself for not taking them out when I'd had the chance.

I took Maria's hand. "Come on! Run!"

Instead of running right, toward the car park, we ran straight, down a long, cobbled road that descended at a gentle gradient into shadows. Behind me, I heard a couple of shouts then the thud of running feet. I had no idea where we were going, but I figured I'd make it up as we went along. One thing I knew, we had to move.

At the bottom of the hill we hit a T-junction, with the mosque making the corner on the right, leading to a large, open square and a winding alley climbing to the left. It made sense to go left, so I turned right and ran like all hell was on my tail till we came into the open, cobbled square. Then we ducked left into the shadows.

We were by the river. I made a mental note that the car park was to my right. In front of me there was a big arch, like the Arc de Triomphe, only smaller, and just beyond it was the old Roman Bridge, spanning the river Guadal Quivir. Everything was quiet. The only sound was the sigh of the river. Old, wrought-iron lamps cast a dull, orange glow over sandstone walls and cobbles. On the bridge, Victorian street lamps stood like black wraiths, and in the pool of light under the nearest, a single black figure watched us.

I said to Maria, "We'll make for the bridge, try to get across and lose ourselves on the other side."

She hesitated. "That figure—"

I smiled on one side of my face. "We'll cross that bridge when we get to it."

By the look on her face, she didn't think it was funny. We ran.

Behind me, I heard a smack like someone dropping a heavy hardback book on a tiled floor. Then there was a smack and a whine. As we ran through the arch, the bridge became visible again. The yellow sandstone seemed to glow golden in the diffused lamplight. There was another crack and another ricochet. The figure I'd seen before was moving toward us and resolving itself into Rinpoche.

I scanned behind me. There were five men, fanning out, running at us.

I grabbed Maria's wrist and shouted at her, "*Run!* Run for the bridge!"

It was a desperate plan. It wasn't even a plan. It was just desperate. But it was all we had.

When we emerged from the arch, the silhouette was standing, legs straddled, blocking our way. Behind us, five pairs of feet were pounding the cobbles. Angry voices were shouting, but I wasn't listening. I knew just one thing. I had to get Maria past Rinpoche and onto the bridge.

Then all hell broke loose. The five goons were on us. I heard Maria scream and her wrist was wrenched from my hand. As I turned, from the corner of my eye I saw Rinpoche run. I pulled the Sig and tried to aim. There was a flash and a crack. Somebody screamed. Maria was stumbling. Two guys closed in on her as she fell. A guy behind her collapsed. I ran for her and there was a blur in my peripheral vision. I lashed out and kicked one of the guys in the head. As he went down, I shot him. Maria was on her hands and knees and the other guy didn't know whether to go for her or me. While he thought about it, I shot him between the eyes.

Then six tons of brick hit me in the back. I sprawled and my chest went into spasm so I couldn't breathe. I rolled over and saw Maria scrambling over to me, screaming for them to leave me alone. Rinpoche was laughing, doing a little Bruce Lee dance. Two guys were watching him, panting. Two. I looked around. I saw three guys were down, dead. I had shot two.

Rinpoche thumbed his bottom lip and smiled. "Time to die, Murdoch. What to do, huh? What to do?"

I grabbed for the Sig. I was slow. My chest felt like I had an iron bar through it and my hand was shaking. The speed of his movements was terrifying. He spun and his heel smashed into my hand, sending the Sig spinning across the road.

He was maybe four feet from me, smiling his idiot smile, and he had death in his eyes. "Now," he said. "Time to die, now."

Then he gave a start, froze and frowned down at his chest. There was a dark patch there that was spreading. I heard two *phut!* sounds and the two guys who were watching him keeled over. Footsteps echoing behind me in the dark and another *phut!* Rinpoche gave a little shake and slowly sank to his knees. Maria was staring behind me. I struggled to my feet. My savior looked at me. Behind him, maybe twenty yards away, I saw my Daemon idling by the sidewalk. Now Tom was watching Rinpoche, who still looked confused.

He said, "You were early, old chap." And he put a third bullet in his head.

Rinpoche died.

Again.

Tom turned to me. "I hope you don't mind, I hot-wired your car. Shall we go? The Brigadier is anxious to talk to you."

Chapter Twenty-Six

Tom had given Maria a sedative and she had curled up and gone to sleep in the back. Then he and I had taken turns driving. He drove fast and with impressive skill. In twelve hours, we'd reached Calais, by way of Madrid, Irun and Paris.

When we got to Calais, Maria began to stir and Tom gave her another shot.

He'd smiled apologetically at me and said, "Let's just keep her confused for the while, shall we?"

We'd taken the ferry to Dover then he'd driven us to a nondescript suburban house in St. John's Wood, North London. We arrived about six in the evening. He'd let us in with a key and locked and bolted the door behind him.

He'd pointed at Maria and said, "You're downstairs, in that room." He indicated a door on the other side of a small drawing room. Then he pointed at me. "You are upstairs, first floor, first door on the right. There are sandwiches and beer in the kitchen if you're hungry, but get some sleep. Professor Whittering and His Nibs will be here in a couple of hours."

Maria went straight to her room without saying anything. I gave Tom my cell, told him what was on it, had a couple of sandwiches and a beer then collapsed into bed and slept for three hours like I was dead.

* * * *

I woke and showered at nine. There were fresh, clean clothes on a chair by the window. I dressed and went down. I found Russell and Hook in the dining room. They were having soup. They looked up as I came in and Russell dabbed his mouth with a large linen napkin.

"Liam. Good to see you alive. Take a seat. Soup?"

I sat and shook my head. "No, thanks, Russell."

He poured me some white wine and a girl came in and took away the soup plates.

When she'd gone, I said, "Where's Maria?"

"She's still sedated."

I nodded. "How did you find me?"

Hook smiled. "The same way you found them. We put one tracker on your car and another in the Sig. I guessed you'd ditch the car in Algeciras, but it was a fair bet you'd hang on to the Sig for dear life, wherever you went."

I nodded again. "Fair bet. Did you know what I was going to find in Algeria?"

Russell glanced at Hook. The brigadier stared at his glass and pursed his lips. Then he shook his head. "No. Not really."

"Not really?"

"We've downloaded the information from your phone. It was excellent work. We need to debrief you. We have some idea what they are about, but we have no idea how they are doing it. Maria could be very valuable to us if she has information."

I drained my glass. The door opened. The girl came in again with a trolley bearing a silver platter and a couple of silver dishes. She served us sirloin steak, potatoes and two veg, then poured a powerful Burgundy from a crystal decanter.

Then Hook said to her, "All right, Margarita. Leave the decanters on the dresser and you can retire."

She thanked him, brought in a tray of whiskey and port and left.

Over the steaks, I told them the whole story with every detail. When I finished, they were quiet for a while. Russell stared at his glass. Hook was studying the backs of his hands and chewing his lip.

Finally, he said, "You have strong feelings for Maria. Can you be objective about her?"

"I can be objective about her." I started cutting my steak. Then I laid down my knife and fork and said, "How much of what Maria told me was hogwash? Are they serious about all this Atlantis crap? I know we've talked about hybrids and reptiles before, but this is crazy."

I was saying it, but again, in my gut, I knew the answer.

Hook raised an eyebrow at the back of his hands, like he could see my face there. "Crazier than growing people on giant cannabis plants?"

Russell chuckled and shook his head. "Things are crazy, Liam, until we see them and live them, then they become mundane. You've seen this Golika, the chap you call Rinpoche—rather inappropriately, I might add. You've seen their craft. Good heavens, Liam! It must be clear to you by now that something out of the ordinary is going on."

I drained my glass and began to peel a pack of Camels. I said, "Yeah, and I'd like to know what it is, but I'm sorry. I don't buy fifteen-thousand-year-old Martians and sixty-five-million-year-old dinosaurs."

Russell levered himself to his feet and stood a moment, leaning on the table, his eyes lost in thought. Then he sighed and said, "Well, whether you buy it or not, there may be more truth to it than you care to believe." He made his way to the sideboard, speaking absently as he went. "Who'll join me in a Bushmills?"

We both said we would and he brought a decanter and three Waterford tumblers to the table. While he was pouring, he said, "We have access to archived material that most people don't even know exists." I saw Hook look at him sharply. "There are secrets that are known and accepted within…" He paused while he pushed the cork back into the bottle. "I wouldn't call them circles, exactly, Liam. Perhaps I should say, at certain levels of power."

Hook handed me a glass and kept one for himself.

Russell sipped and went on. "One of those secrets is the existence, fifteen thousand years ago—though by then it was already ancient—of a great civilization, technologically as advanced as our own, or more so. That civilization had its hub in the Caribbean. It was destroyed by global warming and rising sea levels."

"Atlantis. You're telling me she was telling the truth about that."

He nodded. "Yes… We also know that they were at war."

I couldn't keep the acid from my voice. "With intelligent dinosaurs?"

"In all probability, yes."

Hook drew breath, hesitated a second then spoke. "In any case, Liam, at this stage it really doesn't matter if it's all an elaborate deception or the truth. The fact is that there are some very powerful people out there with access to extraordinary technology. And for whatever reasons they may have, their intention is that our environment should change catastrophically—very soon—and become largely uninhabitable for us. I think you have to ask yourself, why would they want to do that?"

I looked at him a long time. "Us?"

There was a flash of irritation on his face. "Yes, Liam, us. Humans."

I sighed and sipped my whiskey. I was about to ask them the billion-dollar question. "And what can we"—I gestured around the table—"a professor of mathematics, a brigadier in the SAS, and a ne'er-do-well grafter like me, do about it?" I turned to Russell. He was watching me impassively. I went on, "You asked me to track Maria's abductor. I did it and I wound up in a subterranean lab where they grow human vegetables… Come on, Russell! You want me to believe you and trust you? That's a two-way street. It's time you came clean and stopped keeping me in the dark. Who the hell are you and what are you about?"

He nodded. "You are quite right and I apologize, but we are plagued by difficulties, Liam. Nothing is clear-cut and we have enemies everywhere. And our most dangerous enemies are in our very own governments, in the highest offices. Some of them are hybrids themselves, as you've heard. Yet others are human, working against humanity in exchange for the promise of vast power in the New Order." He paused, frowning at his glass. "Haven't you ever wondered why, when humanity is confronted by the real and present threat of extinction, the world's governments are *so* reluctant to do anything about it?"

Hook took over. "Our" — he hesitated — "let's call it a Council, for now, was established just before the Second World War. Certain individuals who shall, for the moment, remain nameless realized that powerful government and public figures were being manipulated and controlled by a shadow organization, apparently for the purpose of changing the climate and the environment. We were formed to work against them."

I interrupted. "You're talking Dan Brown Illuminati bullshit."

His voice was real quiet when he said, "I think you owe us a little more respect than that."

I sighed. "I'm sorry."

He pressed on. "I'm surprised what you've seen already has not made you more open-minded."

Russell said, "It's a lot to take in, Liam, but unfortunately we haven't got much time. And what makes it worse is that the enemy is made of smoke and mirrors. They appear, change, transmute, vanish and reappear somewhere else, as something different. They are extraordinarily powerful, and they are masters of illusion. Robert Anton Wilson's Illuminati is a better comparison than Dan Brown's."

He stared at his whiskey a while, like he was seeing all of the world's history in the spirits in his glass. There was total silence at the table. Then he said, "You know that Adam Weishaupt founded them in Bavaria, the very same day that Washington declared America's independence."

Hook spoke as though he hadn't heard. "Speaking plainly,

we need you, and Maria, to join us. This project you have described is immensely dangerous. If they pull it off, the consequences are unimaginable."

I held up a hand. "Wait…." I shook my head. "Let's take this one step at a time. What has this to do with Llyn Celyn and the fusion reactor? What the hell do you mean by 'join you', but, before that, I want to know where Maria is and what Joanna did to her. I want to know what the hell is going on with her."

Russell said, "She's in Wiltshire. She's under observation. She's agreed to help us to" — he frowned and hesitated — "help us to understand. Technologically, we are vastly outgunned by them. They are way ahead of us. But we are beginning to understand how they work, and with her help we can go a lot further. It seems somehow she is still linked to—"

I said, "To Banks and del Roble."

"Yes." He sighed. "It seems as though they somehow mapped Joanna's neural 'codes', for want of a better word, into Maria's brain, so Joanna is" — he spread his hands and shook his head — "quite literally a part of Maria. It's as though she has two people living in one brain."

Hook said, "From what our boffins can gather, those codes are sustained by some kind of link, rather like a radio, with del Roble and Banks."

I said, "Can they fix it?"

Russell looked drawn and gray. He said, "They're not sure. There are signs… It's possible that if we can't break the link, her own brain might start to…to die away, a bit like Alzheimer's."

I felt sick and my head seemed to swim.

Russell took a big pull on his drink then said, "But to answer your first question, del Roble's purpose has always been to kill the fusion reactor program. The last thing they need is clean energy. They need us to keep pumping out CO_2.

"But perhaps more than worrying than that is their

continued growth in power. Politics is the art of accruing and retaining power, nothing more. And power means one thing — control. Their whole research and development program seems to be aimed at one thing, control. Control of human behavior, of the human mind. It seems Llyn Celyn is to be a front for that research here in Britain. At the highest levels of power, politicians and high-ranking military are abdicating to them in droves, buying their seat at the high table, while the bulk of humanity is sentenced either to death or to spiritual and mental slavery."

I said, "But they want to keep us human. They are fascinated by our ability to feel. They kept telling me their greatest drive was to learn to feel like us. I think Joanna really was prepared to jump ship on the promise of learning to feel."

He and Hook stared at each other a moment. He refilled my glass and passed it back to me.

Hook said, "Yes. Fortunately, until now, they don't seem to have been able to get it quite right."

Russell began to speak suddenly. "In 1947, what was taken to be an alien spacecraft crashed in New Mexico near the Roswell Air Force Base. The American military recovered the craft and the crew. Most of them were dead. Two survived. One was shot and killed by a trigger-happy soldier. The other was taken into captivity. This was not the first craft to crash, but it was the first to be recovered largely intact. And it was the first time we were able to capture one of them alive."

I raised an eyebrow and said, "We?"

He paused. After a moment, he said, "Let's just say for now, Liam, that the independence of Western governments is more apparent than real. At the highest level of political power, in the West, we are all, effectively, one."

He watched me.

I shrugged and said, "Okay. If you say so."

"I do. Very few people know what really happened at Roswell, but the important point is, it marked a turning point in our relationship with 'them'." He sipped his drink and replaced it carefully on the table. "You have to understand that until 1947, our relationship had been a distant one. They had connected with certain individuals for the purpose of guiding us toward the industrial revolution. But during the warm, they became more active, more involved, observing us more closely, perhaps because of the rapid advance in our military and industrial technology, particularly that of the Germans, perhaps because they were guiding us into the Cold War and the arms race, and unprecedented emissions of CO_2." He paused, watching me a moment. "As I say, nobody knows exactly what happened at Roswell, but since then their contact with certain members of the IT and defense industries and certain political figures has gotten much closer and much deeper. And it seems that with the crashed craft, the US industrial-military complex had at its disposal technologies that had been, until then, undreamed of.

"And with these new technologies, it became essential to create a department whose function would be to reverse engineer the technology recovered from the crash. To that end, General Hap Arnold, Jimmy Doolittle, Donald Putt and Hoyt Vandenberg all strong-armed President Truman into creating an independent Air Force, separate from the Army. This had been an ambition of the US Air Force's for a long time, but, after Roswell, it happened almost overnight — on the 18th of September, just two months after the crash. Then, in the face of fierce opposition from the Air staff, on the 23rd of January, 1950, just two and a half years after Roswell, the Air Research and Development Command came into being as a separate, independent organization. Its function, in theory, was to research and develop weaponry for the Air Force. Its *actual* function was to develop technology from the captured craft."

I said, "Why would that cause fierce opposition?"

Hook answered. He said, "Because, despite its name, the ARD Command put the research and development of weapons under the control of a desk at the Pentagon. That desk was not controlled by the Army or the Air Force—or even the President."

I took a slug of whiskey and lit another cigarette. I asked the question, but I already knew the answer. "If it isn't under the control of the military or the President, who controls it?"

He smiled at his whiskey. "Who do you think, Liam?"

I stared into my glass. "The Federal Reserve... So, basically you're telling me that the Military and Air Force Research and Development desk at the Pentagon, which is charged with the reverse engineering of a spacecraft recovered in 1947, is run by the world's biggest private banking cartel."

"Yes. The R&D desk is used to filter reverse engineered technology into the private sector. Who are the big names in the Federal Reserve, Liam? Who were the names behind the corporations that drove the huge military advances post 1950?"

I shook my head. "I don't know."

"Think, Liam. The Roth banking empire, the Bank of England, the Rockford family... The House of Saude, the bin Abbasids..."

I stared at him.

Hook said, smiling, "Strange bedfellows, don't you think?"

I thought a moment while they watched me. Something inside me was telling me I knew all this was true. I said, "And the technology that has come out of this has not been solely military, has it? There has been another, more important technological advance."

Hook nodded his head at his whiskey. "Oh, yes, Liam, there has. The microchip. The technology of the great zombie apocalypse. The information revolution that, ironically, has led to the most ill-informed, uneducated, unquestioning generations in human history."

"Mind control."

"Yes."

I said, "Okay. I'll join you, and I'll do whatever you want me to do, but on one condition."

Russell said, "I suspect your condition fits very snugly with our aims. Name it."

I told them what it was. Russell smiled and nodded, and Hook burst out laughing.

Chapter Twenty-Seven

I was in Maria's bedroom. They had been keeping her sedated. She didn't know it, but we were in Wiltshire, at Russell's family home. The window was open and a cool breeze was stirring the edges of the curtains. Two oblongs of light lay twisted across her bed, but her face was in shadow. She had just opened her eyes and was watching me, watching her.

She said, "Where am I?"

I put my hand on her knee. "Everything's fine, baby. We're going home."

She blinked. We were quiet for a moment.

Then she said, "What about —?"

"It's over. Del Roble is dead. Banks is dead. Joanna — Dr. Loss — is dead." I gave a small laugh. "You remember this whole thing started with a serial killer?"

She nodded, not smiling.

I said, "That was Golika, the guy I called Rinpoche, literally bred for the job. He's dead, too, baby. It's over."

She gave an uncertain smile. "I still have this knowledge. I still feel her inside my head."

I nodded. "Russell has talked to the best neurologists there are." I sighed, like a school teacher explaining a difficult lesson in simple terms. "You have to understand, honey. It isn't her in there. They mapped her neural networks into your brain, but they're not really yours. And they will decay with time. They will fade and die. I promise."

She smiled for the first time like she might mean it. "Really? You promise?"

I took her hand and squeezed gently. "I promise, baby.

You're going to be fine."

She said, "I don't remember much. We were in Cordoba—"

"You've been unconscious. They've been doing tests, looking for the biochip."

"Where are we?"

"We're in Scotland. It's an MOD training camp they're letting us use. Hook pulled some strings..." I shrugged and smiled, covering my misdirection. "He has friends in high places. They have the same school tie."

She smiled down at her hands and made small folds in the quilt. She seemed wrecked. She had deep shadows under her eyes and I knew that what she had in her brain was slowly killing her.

She said, "When can we go?" Then she looked up at me and there were tears in her eyes. "When will we be back to normal?"

I moved closer, took her in my arms then kissed the top of her head. She wrapped her arms around me and I felt her tears soaking through my shirt.

I whispered, "Real soon, baby. Real soon."

After a bit, she pulled back and I took her face in my hands. It felt small and frail.

I kissed her lips real softly and said, "I have some things I have to take care of, here in Scotland." I shook my head. "Some debriefing stuff, but Tom and Hook are going to take you back home, and Tom will stay with you until I get back. Okay?"

She frowned. "How long will you be, baby?"

"You'll be home this evening, and I'll be with you by tomorrow evening. It's over, honey." I kissed her again. "It's over."

She smiled and stroked my face. "My hero. You rescued me from Hell."

I laughed. "Yeah..."

* * * *

Rinpoche had dressed himself in a woolen hat, a brown vinyl jacket and old jeans. In London, that made him totally nondescript. He hung around the corner of Vicarage Gate as evening fell, smoking rollups and flicking stumps into the gutter. He knew they thought he was dead — he and the Seraph and Banks. In his left hand he held a rose. It still had the thorns on it. At seven p.m., he saw the black Land Rover pull up and a big blond guy get out and stand on the sidewalk looking up toward the Gate, then back down the hill again. He had SAS written all over him.

Two more guys got out, with a woman supported between them. He was too far to see her face, but he knew it had to be Maria. She seemed weak. Without Joanna to support her, the chip was killing her. He smiled in a way you'd describe as thin. He was going to get there first. He wanted Murdoch to experience, first-hand, the total destruction of a person he loved.

He felt a slight stirring in his belly, a warmth, but nothing more. Rinpoche had never experienced horror or dread or sheer sexual arousal. He knew Joanna had come close, and he hungered for the experience. Like del Roble, and Joanna before she had been destroyed, he found Maria and Murdoch strangely fascinating. There was an intensity about them. Maybe tonight, with Maria, he would get close to *rupa*.

* * * *

Maria had had an early lunch with Russell and Hook in her room. They had talked and Russell had reassured her that all the research they had done proved pretty conclusively that Joanna was indeed dead, and that the strike on the facility in Algeria had eliminated del Roble and Banks. There was no sign of them anywhere. As for Golika-Rinpoche, Tom had seen to him in Cordoba. They'd given her a mild sedative and told her to rest and that a car would collect her shortly and take her down to London.

Hook and two of his men would accompany her.

The car had arrived just before two. She had been very sleepy and she had sat in the back and dosed fitfully, aware of the occasional murmured conversation from the front and the swift flitting countryside as dusk had fallen and had turned to evening.

She was aware, then, of the stop, start of city traffic – of the lights, amber, green, red, that occasionally flooded the car as it idled at crossings, in busy streets.

Finally, it stopped and the engine died. There was more murmured talk as she opened her eyes. She felt exhausted. All she wanted was to sleep – to sleep forever. The door to the Land Rover opened and Hook leaned in. He was there, smiling, with another guy. They helped her out and between them walked her across the pavement to the entrance to the building.

Hook was saying, "You're home now, Maria. You're home. Everything is going to be fine now."

She said, "I desperately need to sleep."

He put an arm around her shoulder and supported her. "Don't worry. We're nearly there. We'll pack you into bed and before you know it Murdoch will be back with you."

She leaned against him, struggling to stay awake. "When? When will he be here?"

Hook stroked her head. "By tomorrow evening, he should be back. Here we are."

The elevator stopped and they half-carried her to the front door.

Hook was gently patting her cheeks. "Stay with us a few minutes longer, Maria. Stay with us. We are nearly there."

He unlocked the door and they carried her through the darkened apartment to the bedroom. There, they took off her coat and her shoes and put her to bed. The guy with Hook stepped out and switched on the living room light. Maria saw it as a halo around Hook's head as he smiled at her.

"You are home safe now, Maria. You can go to sleep.

Murdoch will be with you by tomorrow afternoon. The boys and I have to step out for a bit, but we'll be back in a couple of hours. You'll be fine. You're safe now."

Then he, Tom and the other guy left, and Maria drifted into a deep sleep.

* * * *

Rinpoche watched the men step out of the building and climb into the Land Rover, which took off at speed toward the Gate. He felt a hot jolt of excitement in his gut. It was a new feeling and he liked it. He smiled and licked his lips. "What to do?" he said to himself. "What to do?"

He stepped into the road and loped through the traffic. There was no one in the lobby and the elevator was still down and open. Rinpoche stepped in and punched the button. As the doors closed and the car began to rise, he thought of Joanna, trying to explain to them what she had felt with Murdoch—the insatiable appetite, the hunger for feeling in her skin. He wanted to know that feeling and saw himself in the room with Maria. She would be weak and vulnerable. She was dying. He thought of her eyes looking up at him, the heavy handle of the knife in his hand and the feeling of pushing the hard steel blade into her belly. It was nice. Maybe he would hold her close as she died and try to love her, as Joanna had begun to love Murdoch.

It was a nice thought. He would enjoy that.

The elevator stopped and the doors slid open. The passage was dark. He didn't turn on the lights. He didn't need to. The front door opened easily. He paused. He could hear that she was sleeping deeply. They had sedated her. They didn't know how easy they had made it for him. She would wake up. Once the adrenaline kicked in, she would be wide awake.

He closed the door behind him with a soft clunk. The apartment was very quiet. His night vision was superb, as was his hearing. He could hear her breathing in the bedroom. It was surprisingly heavy, but the sedatives would do that.

The curtains in the drawing room were open, allowing light from the street below to filter in. He stood in the open bedroom doorway with a pale blue and amber glow of light behind him. He had the knife in his hand, and the large blade caught the light and reflected it. He stepped close to the bed, where he could see Maria's bulk under the quilt. He was possessed suddenly by the desire to feel her skin against his, to kiss her lips and her pink nipples—to do those things that he had watched humans do. He scanned his body for a stirring, for a passion of excitement, but the burning in his belly died, even as he searched for it, and there was nothing.

Only the rage of frustration and the desire to kill, to rip out her entrails and eat them, devour them whole, as he had with Eva and Sally, then silence her mouth and still her heart, as Joanna—Dr. Loss—had taught him to do. Rituals were important, she had said, to understand how humans feel. To reach *rupa*.

He leaned down close to her hair and whispered, "Wake, Maria. Now it is time to die."

* * * *

The Sig is an awesome weapon. I had enjoyed using it. But I am not a subtle, sophisticated man. I am a brute. I know it and I don't care. My weapon was always the Smith & Wesson 29. It's not a hand gun. It's a canon. And, as Rinpoche pulled back the covers to reveal me lying in my bed where he expected Maria to be, that cannon blew his Golika balls clean off. He dropped the rose and the kitchen knife to the floor for the last time. He let out a strange, whistling whine then staggered back, away from the bed, clutching his groin. I flipped on the light and watched his skin turn gray and ripple, as it had before. Long, thin claws sprang from his fingertips and a strange fan tried to rise from his shoulder at the back of his neck, but he was weak and bleeding profusely. He dropped to his knees.

I kneeled in front of him and looked him straight in the eye. I said, "You know what I did to Joanna? I'm going to do that to you."

He shook his head. "Get me to the Golden Apple in Mayfair."

I laughed, loudly. I said, "Really? Seriously?"

He reached for me with his right hand. The claws were covered in thick blood. "They have facilities there. Don't let me go, not yet."

He stared into my face, trying to make sense of what was happening, trying to give it a meaning.

I helped him. I said, "I'll do a deal with you, Rinpoche. Tell me where del Roble and Banks are, and I won't kill you. I'll even leave the phone so you can try to call your pals to come and take you back to the cabbage farm. How's that?"

He was nodding, still reaching for me. "They are at the Golden Apple. Please don't let me bleed out. I am so close." His pupils were dilating. "I felt excited today."

I stood looking down at him looking up and me, still reaching for me.

"You, you and Maria, you stimulate feelings in me. Joanna felt the same. I was excited about killing her, Murdoch, for a moment…"

I said, "Thanks for sharing, Rinpoche." I picked up the phone from the bedside table and placed it next to him. I smiled in a way you could call humorless then said, "Be quick, Rinpoche. I think it's time to die."

He frowned and shook his head. "No. You said… I have to get to…"

I stood and stepped to the bedroom door. There I stopped. I looked back at him and said, "That's fine by me, Rinpoche, but I think Pete and his friends have a different idea. What to do, huh?"

As Pete pushed in with his guys, I put a hand on his

shoulder. I said, "Remember, the brain. And clean up good afterward, okay?"

He nodded. "*Da.*"

I paused. "And Pete?"

"What? I heff business…"

I shook my head. "I never want to see you again. You understand?"

He went serious, put a hand over my hand and nodded. "Okay, Murdoch. I will miss you but is okay. I agree."

I managed to get out of the building before the screaming started.

Three hundred and forty miles away, in Edinburgh, Maria slept.

Chapter Twenty-Eight

I stepped into the Golden Apple in Mayfair. I had showered and shaved then dressed in the kind of cream tuxedo Russell told me was vulgar, unless you're in the tropics. I figured if Rick didn't mind in *Casablanca*, why should I give a damn? The Golden Apple was on the ground floor of the Royale Palace Hotel. It was supposed to be the most expensive club in the UK. The idea was that by charging prices nobody would ever pay, it would attract billionaires who liked to pay ridiculous prices for things. To me, it looked like a club for self-indulgent narcissists who'd run out of thrills in their five-star Michelin lives. As I stepped through the door, I was thinking maybe I could help them with that.

A guy dressed in a purple general's uniform with more gold braid than Colonel Gaddafi bowed and asked me if I needed valet parking. I told him my chauffeur would pick me up and he bowed again and asked me to have an enjoyable evening. He made it sound like it meant a lot to him. I gave him fifty bucks just for being so good at being fake.

I found the bar. The room was heaving with expensive people, and the mix of voices and music was deafening. There was an Australian kid in a purple waistcoat behind the bar. He leaned forward and shouted, asking me what it would be. I said it would be a Martini dry, and, for the hell of it, I told him to make it shaken, not stirred.

While he was shaking it, I told him, "A friend of mine, a Russian guy called Yulian, said the Golden Apple had the sweetest dames in London. What do you think?"

Like most young Aussies, he spoke in questions. "Personally? I think the sweetest chicks are Kiwis? But that depends what you're looking for." He poured the drink and dropped an olive in it. "If you're looking for a wild night on the town, then maybe you need to talk to Salim? I've heard his girls will give you a night you'll never forget. But he is exclusive and expensive, even by our standards?"

"Yeah?" I sipped the Martini. It was good. "Expensive isn't a problem. Where can I talk to Salim?"

"Take a seat. I'll see if he's around."

Salim didn't take long to show up. He was in an evening suit that Russell would have approved of. He sat next to me at the bar and selected a Balkan Sobrani from a gold cigarette case. I pulled a Camel from a cardboard one. He lit his with a gold Cartier. I lit mine with a brass Zippo. I felt glad I wasn't him.

He watched me a moment with expressionless black eyes and said, "You are a friend of Yulian's?"

"I wouldn't go that far. We've met. We were introduced by Russian Pete. You know him?"

He nodded. "The billionaire club is a small one. I know Pete."

"I told him I was coming to London on business. He said Yulian could put me in touch with some girls who wouldn't be worried by my...special tastes."

That made him smile. "Special tastes are expensive."

"That's not a problem."

"May I ask what line of business you are in, Mr....?"

That made me smile. "No, Salim, you may not. My name is Smith. John Smith. And what I do pays far too much for me to talk about it. Are you going to introduce me to some nice girls?" I held up my Amex Black and added, "I'd like to tell Pete you were very accommodating."

He spread his hands. "Any friend of Pete's is a friend of mine. Please..."

He gestured with his hands toward the back of the club. I followed him through the press of dancing, laughing bodies to a door padded in burgundy leather. He opened the door onto a silent stairwell with a burgundy carpet and wood-paneled walls. Nobody had frisked me yet, and I wondered if they would.

We came to another leather-padded door at the top of the stairs and Salim punched a code into a pad by the jamb. I was either into the inner sanctum or I was dead.

We went through to an elaborate, over-luxurious lounge, like something out of the Belle Époque in Paris. He closed the door behind us and pulled a tasseled cord.

He said, "Drink, Mr. Smith?"

I shook my head. "I've had a drink. I'd like to get down to business now."

An Asian woman in an expensive black cocktail dress came in from a passage at the end of the room. She smiled at me but didn't say anything.

Salim said, "Our purpose is to give you a night you will never forget, Mr. Smith. What, exactly, are you looking for?"

I dropped the butt of my cigarette into an ashtray on an occasional table. I watched it smolder a moment and said, "I want a bitch I can slap around." I watched her for some reaction. There was none, but she didn't meet my eye. I said, "But I don't want some dame who's used to it and enjoys it. You understand me? Yulian told me you had new girls on a regular basis. I want a girl who's never experienced this. I want to see real fear in her eyes." I said all this to the woman, who was staring at the floor and smiling. I knew why she was smiling. She was going to be watching, and she liked the sound of the movie.

Then I turned to Salim. "I've seen real fear, Salim. I know what it looks like. And I know a fake. Can you deliver?"

He smiled. And, like the Asian woman's, it was genuine. "Oh, yes, Mr. Smith, we can deliver."

The woman said, "Please follow me," then led me down the corridor from which she had appeared. It was a dogleg with half a dozen doors. She led me to the last one. Just beyond it was another, smaller lounge. It was less luxurious, and there were two big guys with tattoos drinking beer from cans. They watched me go into the room. The Asian woman said to me, "Please wait. Your lady will be here in a moment."

The room was luxurious in a way Russell would call vulgar. It was all reds, purples and pinks—and over-stuffed. There was a big bed, a drinks cabinet and a bucket of ice with a bottle of Cristal in it. I poured myself a Scotch single malt and waited. After three minutes, the door opened and a pretty young girl stepped in. She was maybe twenty, blonde and slim, with a nice figure. She was wearing a white milkmaid blouse and tight jeans. She had a pearl choker around her neck. She seemed terrified, and it was real.

I said, "Hi, sweetheart. What's your name?"

"Whatever you want it to be." She was English, middle class. Up till a few weeks earlier, she had likely been naïve and young. Now she was old and scared. Her voice shook when she spoke.

I said, "What did your mother call you?"

She struggled a moment with her feelings and said, "Emma."

"Come here, Emma."

She stepped up to me. I took her face in my hands and kissed her gently on the lips. I felt her tremble and I buried my face in her neck, like I was kissing it, but I whispered to her, "Don't react. You're terrified. Stay terrified. I'm here to get you out. Play along…"

I let her go and smiled at her. I said, "You like intense experiences, Emma?"

She was trembling. She said, "Yes…if you want me to."

I laughed. "I am going to take you to heights of intensity you never dreamed possible." I went to the drinks cabinet and poured her a whiskey. I handed it to her and said, "Drink it, babe. You're going to need it." She drank and I started kissing her neck again. "In a minute, I'm going to

290

throw you on the bed, face down. Then I'm going to get on your back. I'm going to ask you questions. Scream like you're terrified and in pain. And answer my questions in a whisper."

She was shaking like a leaf. She was having trouble breathing.

I stepped back and shouted, "Are you *deaf*? Get on the *fucking* bed!" Before she could react, I grabbed her and hurled her onto it.

She screamed and I climbed on her back, making like I was pounding her and slapping her head. I was giving the bastards a good show.

I took a fistful of hair in my left hand and pressed my mouth to her ear. "How much muscle is there? Is it just the two guys, or are there more?"

"Just the two..."

I sat up, straddling her, and snarled, "Yeah, you like that, huh? You want it harder?"

She squealed something and I bent down again like I was biting her shoulder and her neck. She thrashed and screamed like it hurt and I whispered, "How many of you?"

She writhed and pounded the bed. Maybe it was the whiskey going to her head or maybe she was getting into the spirit of the game. She whispered while she thrashed, "Twelve of us."

"I need you to be strong, sweetheart." Again I shouted, "Stop struggling, bitch!" I slipped my arm around her throat like I was choking her and put my lips to her ear. "When I go out of this room all hell is going to break loose. I need you to run, get the other girls and get the fuck out of here — through the lounge, down the stairs and out through the club. Run for your lives. There'll be a van waiting for you outside." I sat up and screamed, "Understand, bitch?"

She screamed, "Yes! *Yes!*"

I got off the bed, went to the door then wrenched it open. The two thugs glanced up.

I strode toward them and, when I was three steps away, I

bellowed, "Run! Run! *Run!!*"

The first one was on his feet, appearing mad and confused. My instep connected with his balls and he stopped looking mad. He doubled up, making a weird keening noise. The other swung at me, but there was a coffee table in the way. I took his wrist, pulled and twisted hard then slammed my left forearm into the joint. I heard it crunch just before he screamed. As I pulled him across the table, I felt Emma running past me. The hulk tripped on the table and fell on his face. I stamped on the back of his neck and he stopped suffering.

The other guy was staggering to his feet. He had a long knife in his hand. Unless you are really good at knives, they are not a good idea. I kicked him in the head and sent him halfway to gaga land. I bent and took the knife from his fingers, slipped in between the second and third vertebrae in his neck and sent him the rest of the way.

It had taken a few seconds, but in that time, pandemonium had broken loose. Emma was running up and down the corridor screaming for the other girls. A handful were standing in the corridor looking lost, staring at me in horror. I counted five, plus Emma. Doors were opening and girls were peeking out, scared and confused.

I was shouting, "Get out! Get *out!* Now! *Run!*"

I made for the nearest door, wrenched it open and hauled the girl stumbling into the passage. I pushed her and sent her hurtling toward the lounge. "Get out! *Get out!*" I yanked open the next door.

Emma was leading them toward the entrance and the last four girls came out and ran after them.

I followed, shouting, "What the *hell* are you waiting for? Get out of here!"

Then I saw Salim and the woman. She was pale and he had his hands to his head. I have a special ceramic knife I keep for occasions like this one. I reached down and slipped it out of the scabbard I had strapped to my calf.

Salim was walking toward me, his hands held out, "What

is this? What are you doing? What is going — ?"

I guess he was going to ask me what was going on, but I interrupted him and took hold of his throat with my left hand. "You have no heart, right, Salim? So this shouldn't hurt."

Ceramic knives are real sharp and real hard. It slid in under his fifth rib easy. His eyes went wide and I felt his whole body spasm before it went limp and slipped off the knife into a crumpled heap at my feet. The Asian dame was backing away, with both hands held up in front of her. It was an easy throw. Nobody ever looks as startled as they do when they have a blade buried three inches into their forehead.

Emma and the girls were in the lounge area. I loped after them and yanked open the door. I grabbed Emma by the arm. "Go down. Cross the club. A man called Tom will meet you outside with a minibus. Do everything he says. You're going home. Go!"

Wherever the hell home is.

They ran.

I heard the voice behind me. I knew I was going to hear it. It was the reason I was there.

"But they're not going home, Murdoch, and neither are you. We finish this here, tonight."

I turned. "Banks."

"Close the door."

I closed it. "This time you stay dead."

He came at me like a puma. The speed was insane. Then he was in the air and his right leg flashed. The pain was impossible to describe and I felt myself smash against the wall behind me. My head was ringing. I couldn't stand and I couldn't see straight. I felt his knee press on my chest and his left fist grab my collar. I knew what was coming next and, when I felt him tense, I let gravity pull my head to the side. His fist smashed its deathblow into the wall and I heard him curse. He stood, gripping his hand and swearing.

Then he did something that made me real mad. He

sneered and from my waistband he pulled my Smith & Wesson and leveled it at me. "Tonight, you die with your own gun, Murdoch!"

I'd fallen against a small table and there were spasms of pain going through my back where I'd hit it. But through the pain I saw a marble lamp overturned on the floor. My gun exploded at me, but at the same instant I lunged and grabbed the lamp. I levered myself to my feet and came at him as he was turning to finish me off. If I'd swung the lamp, he would have blocked it. But it is deeply ingrained in me — stab, don't slash. I rammed the lamp straight into his face. He staggered back, covering his eyes, and he dropped my gun. I leaped forward and rammed again, into his chest. He screamed and I did it again and kicked him in the nuts for good measure. I picked my Smith & Wesson up off the floor. He was ten times the fighter I was and I needed a weapon.

By the time I'd picked it up, he'd rolled, jumped to his feet and was coming back at me in a flying, spinning back kick. I managed to weave and roll, but his heel caught the edge of my jaw and I staggered. He landed feet wide, knees bent, and delivered two power punches to my belly. I doubled up, retching, but the only thing in my head was *don't let go of the revolver!* His right uppercut smashed into my nose and I went down on my back. As I hit the floor, he jumped with both knees up. He was going to slam down into my chest with both heels and I was going to die.

I found a strength I didn't know I had, and I can't explain. I just knew I couldn't let him win. I raised the Smith and Wesson and emptied it. Everything Dirty Harry said about the Smith and Wesson 29 was true. The magnum rounds spun him in mid-air and he fell in a bloody heap. I slowly got to my feet. I pulled a box of rounds from my pocket and reloaded. I put two rounds into his head at point-blank range. If any of his neurons survived, they were going to be real lonely. Then I put two rounds into his neck and pretty much decapitated him. The last four rounds cut him in two at the waist.

I said, "Banks, tonight *you* die with my revolver."

After that, I made my way down the passage to where the two goons had been sitting. I was remembering. There had been a door — the door Banks had come out of — a door I was going through. And I knew what I was going to find on the other side. The door was open. There were more carpeted stairs leading up to another level. I climbed them, feeling my whole body aching, my legs screaming with pain at every step. There was no door at the top, just a landing that expanded out into a large, open space. There was a sofa and there were two armchairs arranged around a coffee table.

They were not expecting me. They were expecting Banks, and they went pale when they saw me reach the top of the stairs, bleeding and disheveled, with a look on my face they could not have misread if they had wanted to. I intended to kill them, and they knew it.

Chapter Twenty-Nine

Del Roble rose slowly to his feet. His thick glasses were flashing in the lamplight. Maria sat motionless, expressionless. Del Roble said, "Murdoch? Who the hell *are* you? What do you want?"

"Who am I?" I must have looked like spawn from Hell. I could taste the blood from the gashes on my face trickling into my mouth, and it was making my belly burn. "I'm a human being, del Roble, and I'm the meanest son of a bitch in this fucking valley of yours. What do I want? I want answers."

He was shaking his head. "There is no way you can begin to understand."

I took three long strides and backhanded him. He staggered and fell across the sofa, blood trickling from his nose. I leveled the gun at him. "Next time you say that to me, del Roble, I'll blow your fucking head off your shoulders."

I turned to Maria. "Who is the woman I know as Maria? If she is you—if she is one of you—why did you kidnap her?"

She sighed and covered her face. After a moment, she dropped her hands and began to speak. "She is me in a way you can't under—" She stopped herself and rectified, "In a way that is hard to explain. Our constant goal is to find a way to bridge the gap between our masters and humans. That is the main purpose of all our hybridization programs. Maria is an experiment in that program."

I snarled. "What the hell does that mean?"

"You and Maria fascinate us, Murdoch. Especially Dr. Loss—Joanna. She found you both utterly intoxicating. She came very close to *rupa* with you. When we took Maria, we created me with her, so that we could tap into her feelings and thoughts." She smiled. "But you knew that, or at least suspected it. That's why you are here."

"So, you are a hybrid... And Maria?"

"I am a hybrid but Maria, like you, is human. When you are together, the feelings you arouse in each other are very powerful. They are almost impossible for us to conceive." She turned to del Roble. "I can feel myself dilating, Seraph. I could come in *rupa* right now."

"So you used her to punish me, to try to destroy me, but also to explore this damned *rupa* you are obsessed with" — I turned to del Roble — "and, at the same time, have a spy you could use close to me and my employers."

He looked bitter. "That was the idea. How did you *do* this?"

I turned to Maria. "But she's linked to your mind. And you can transmit to her and receive her."

She smiled. "I *am* her, Liam, in every meaningful sense of the word. We are one." She frowned. "But we need to help her. She is dying."

"Is she connected to anybody else?"

She frowned, shook her head and said, "No...only through me." And, as she said it, she realized it was the wrong answer.

All it took was a single shot to the head and Maria's problems were all over. If I was right about the link — and I knew I was — back in Edinburgh, she would be smiling in her sleep and resting peacefully for the first time in months.

I turned to del Roble. "You're coming back with me. You have a lifetime of explaining to do, pal."

He burst out laughing. "You must be insane! You think I'll come with you? How incompetent do you think we are?"

I looked at Maria then turned back to look at the stairwell, with all the ruin and dead bodies behind it. I turned back to del Roble and his mad eyes. "Pretty incompetent, del Roble. Now, we can walk out quietly, or I can blow your kneecaps off and drag you out. You choose, but one way or another, you are coming with me."

He raised his wrist and touched his watch. "I have to make a call."

"Your goons are dead, del Roble, including Rinpoche, the Dharma Golika. It's over. The fat woman has sung. Stand up."

He stared at me. There was something kind of manic in his stare. Then he was laughing, a horrible, harsh mixture of a bark and a scream. Then it wasn't del Roble. There was a spray of color, a crest of spines and flashing, scaly skin behind his head. His face was the face of a Komodo dragon, and his hands were claws. He rushed at me and spat. I raised my hands instinctively and felt the searing of acid burning through my sleeve. Something lashed out. I wanted to believe it was his arm, but I was pretty sure it was a tail. The pain in my leg was excruciating and, when I tried to move, my legs were paralyzed.

I fell. I rolled onto my side. My vision was blurred. For a moment, I saw a giant lizard on its hind legs. But then it was del Roble, bending over a briefcase. He loomed over me and kneeled, and he was sliding a package under my head. He was saying, "I hit you with a paralyzing agent. It will wear off in ten minutes. In seven minutes, this incendiary bomb will go off under your head. It will burn slowly but very hot to start with, then it will explode. It will destroy any evidence of our having been here, but it will also provide you with a very painful death." He smiled and gave a small laugh. "I wish I could experience some of your terror, Liam. I really do. You think you have stopped us, but you are so, so wrong. Nothing can stop us now. It is too late. We are past the tipping point, past the point of no return. Goodbye, Liam. It really has been a privilege. You are extraordinary."

I acted without thinking, with the last of my strength. The acid he'd spat at me was still burning in gobbets on my sleeve and on my revolver. I swiped at his face. It was a feeble blow, but it was enough to spread his own, vile toxic spit over his eyes. I watched him, warped and sickening, stand, yelling and clawing at his face. He staggered back and fell, sitting against the wall, screaming at first, then just whimpering, with two smoldering red holes where his eyes should have been.

I tried to call out. But I hadn't the strength and only a soft moan came from my throat. There was panic inside me, but I couldn't use it. I wanted to live and feel, but it was like I was dead inside, and I wondered if that was the way they lived, every day of their lives — the undead — and they were trying to make us like them, while they tried to make themselves like us. I looked at him, blind and sobbing, as the paralysis took hold of me, and I felt pity.

I sagged. The device was hard under my head, like a pillow of death. I didn't want to die. Most of all, I didn't want to die like this, numb and unable to fight back. I battled inside to overcome the paralysis, but I couldn't. My body was not my own. From the corner of my eye, I could see the digital timer. There was a minute and fifty seconds left. My heart was pounding but I couldn't feel and I couldn't move.

A minute and twenty seconds. There was a figure in the doorway — motionless. A minute and fifteen seconds. I tried to shout, to call out, but only a soft murmur came from my throat. The figure moved and disappeared. Panic gripped me, but still I couldn't make a sound. A minute and five seconds.

Fifty-nine seconds and hands gripped my ankles and I was sliding along the floor, the device behind me. Blind, gibbering del Roble was also back there. I was through the door. Halfway down the passage, I saw a flare of white-hot light in the room. I grunted and there was some feeling in my fingers.

Then there was an arm under my shoulders, and a voice in my ear. "Come on, old chap! Can you stand?"

I tried. My legs buckled. I tried again. He'd said ten minutes. But Liam Murdoch is the meanest son of a bitch in the valley, right? I heaved and managed to get to my feet. Strong arms held me up, guiding me toward the door and the stairs and behind me the sound of roaring, searing flames.

We squeezed through the doorway and began to stumble down the steps at a half-run.

I whispered, "Hook…"

He said, "Shut up. There's a good chap. Now, run!"

We burst through the door into the heaving bodies and the blasting music. We pushed and elbowed. Slowly my strength was coming back, but the noise and the airlessness were splitting my head and making me sick. The entrance seemed a million miles away, a small amber rectangle dancing in swarming, sweating, blearing darkness. Hook's voice kept repeating, "One more step, one more step… Come on, old chap, just one more step," and we were at the door and out into the blessed, cool night air. And we were staggering toward a car.

He dropped me in the passenger seat and folded my legs in. Then the driver's door slammed. He was firing up the engine, and we were pulling out of the lot, into the traffic.

I said, "Is Maria okay?"

"Sleeping like a baby."

I smiled. She was safe.

Epilogue

There was a stillness in the room. I don't mean that nothing was moving. There was a lace curtain that was rippling with a small breeze. And there was a cat, part tabby with a white bib, lying in a patch of sunlight on the orange and red patchwork quilt, and his tail was twitching sporadically. It wasn't silent, either. Birds sang outside, and there was the occasional squeak of the gardener's wheelbarrow and the clip of manual hedge trimmers. But the small, wafting movements and the small sounds seemed to accentuate the stillness and the quiet.

She watched me come into the room and sit by her side, by the window. She was sitting up, with her back resting against three or four pillows, with the patchwork pulled up to her chest. She smiled. The bags had gone from under her eyes. She looked like a different person. She looked like Maria.

"Hi... You seem well. How you feeling?"

Her eyes seemed to glaze and she shifted them to gaze out at the trees in the sunlight. "I'm not sure. Something happened. I'm not sure what, but it was as though somebody pulled the plug on a huge, noisy machine that was making devils and demons in my head." She turned to look at me. "It suddenly went quiet, and I slept. I slept like a baby for the first time in..." She trailed off and shrugged. Then she shook her head.

I said, "That's good. It might take time to adjust. But it will all make sense...eventually."

She gave a little frown, watching the lace curtain moving like a lazy fish in the breeze. "You killed her, didn't you?

That's why—"

"Yes,"

"That night… They never took me to London."

"No, they took you on a long drive to Edinburgh. They set up an apartment to replicate ours. In your sedated state, you believed it and transmitted it. It lured Rinpoche to our place, where I was waiting for him."

She nodded. "Thank you." Then she spread her fingers on the quilt and seemed to study them. "Russell asked me if I would help them—if I thought I could help them. I was so confused. It was as though Hell had taken up residence in my head. But this morning I have so much more clarity, Liam. I will help. We will help together, won't we? I don't know how yet, but we will." Then she raised her eyes and seemed to see right inside me, to dark corners I didn't even know I had. And she smiled. "Their plans cannot be allowed to succeed, Liam."

I said, "I know."

And we kissed for the first time in an eternity. And it was good.

* * * *

We found Russell in the garden, drinking tea. He had his giant sunglasses on that made him look like an albino ant with black eyes. He seemed to be staring toward the maze. Maria sat in an old, green wrought-iron chair in the shade of a cherry tree. She had no sunglasses on and watched me with a small frown, which might have been a squint because of the sun. I sat and Russell turned his eyeless glasses on me. "Cup of tea?" Before I could answer, he turned to Maria. "Will you be mother?"

She poured us a cup each and handed one to me, watching me with amused eyes.

Russell said, "You did very well, Liam, but I don't understand why you killed Joanna. She would have been a great asset to us."

I shook my head. "She was very credible. She almost had me convinced. But a few small things didn't add up."

Maria asked, "Such as?"

I sipped the tea and set down the cup. A blackbird started singing on a chimneypot. "Such as… Their initial plan was to lure me to the facility, kill me, then send you back as an unwitting spy. But when I broke free, she improvised and changed her strategy. She decided to go along with me. We'd ditch you and she would become my woman. She could do invaluable research on *rupa* and transmit it back to del Roble, while secretly being your handler. And, above all, the most important thing was, between you, you could find out who my employers were. She really thought she had me hooked."

I turned to Russell. "After we got out, I noticed she was real good at soothing Maria. She called her 'baby' and it was enough for Maria to hear her voice for her to relax and sleep. I put two and two together and made four. Loss had been grooming Maria from the start, and the implanting process had started back in London. And if that was true, her story about wanting to escape with me was bull." I shrugged. "And if *that* was true, then her telepathic link with Maria had to be destroyed. So I destroyed it."

He sipped his tea. "You certainly did that."

We were quiet for a bit, listening to the safe, gentle sounds of the English countryside.

Finally, I said, "So, what now?"

"We keep watching, waiting and working behind the scenes to try to stop what is happening…if it isn't already too late."

Suddenly Maria said, "What about Anthony Cavra? Did he want to kill me?"

"No. He was deeply neurotic, but he wasn't a killer. Loss was using him as a decoy, fueling his fantasies and encouraging his crazy beliefs. Eva befriended him. That's the kind of girl she was. And Loss and Steve — Rinpoche — used him to lead her to Rinpoche's apartment, where he killed her. When he went to you that night, the poor kid was trying to warn you."

The blackbird was singing his long, complicated song into the aging, burnished afternoon. A bumble bee was humming around a red rose in the flower patch, and in the east, the dusk was thinking about bedtime. Deep shadows were gathering under the ancient trees and hedgerows, where small animals rustled and chattered quietly among the first dry leaves.

We sat in silence for a while, and finally I asked Russell, "Who are you?"

He looked surprised and stared at me through his huge black glasses, with the afternoon breeze moving his very white, fine hair. "Why," he said, "I'm Merlin. Hadn't you realized?"

And his laughter rang out under the sun, across the maze, across the fields and the oak trees and the yews. And, above our heads, the blackbird leaped into the great blue dome of the sky.

A Love to Kill For

Excerpt

Chapter One

I parked my TVR Daemon outside Noddy's Diner on the Portobello Road, put my 'Doctor on Call' sign on the windshield, loped through the gray rain and pushed through the door. Chandler once described a woman as the kind who'd make a bishop kick holes in a stained glass window. This one would have had him burning down the Vatican with the Pope strapped to the roof of the Sistine Chapel. It wasn't just that she was a drop-dead looker. She was. She had all her curves in the right places, bobbed black hair, crimson, Cupid's-bow mouth and slow sea-green eyes. But more than that, she managed to look vulnerable and lethal at the same time in a way that stirred your primal urges till you had smoke billowing out of your sphygmomanometer. Yeah, look it up.

In my book, all women are bad news. They make you feel

this thing called 'love', so you'll let them chew you up, suck you dry then spit you out before they move on to their next victim. But even by those standards, I could see this lady was the kind of bad news they interrupt regular broadcasts for. Fortunately, I'm immune to bad news.

She and Noddy both saw me as I pushed in, but I noticed his eyes pleading in a way I had never seen before. I ignored him and eased onto a stool next to the vamp, pulled out a Camel and asked Noddy for a Martini, dry. He stared at me like he was astonished I wanted that drink instead of another and said, real urgent, "This is Caffrin, Liam. Caffrin 'oward. I told you abaht her."

I nodded that I knew and he went to get the Martini. While he put it together, I flipped my Zippo and lit up. She watched me do it the way a cat watches a fly — cute and patient, and ready to eat it alive the minute it gets close enough. Finally, I blew smoke and said, "Noddy thinks I can help you. Want to tell me how?"

She made a slow, green blink. When she spoke, she had that absence of accent the English call cut glass, but husky with it.

"I'm being blackmailed, Mr. Murdoch. I've arranged to make a payment and collect the incriminating material, but I'm afraid that when I do, I may be murdered."

I'm not easily fazed and this didn't faze me, but I wasn't expecting it. I took a moment to study the olive in my Martini. It floated, so I bobbed it up and down a few times. I took a sip and, as I put the glass down, I said, "So you want me to get murdered for you."

She didn't even have the decency to blush. Whether she said yes or no, it was going to be the wrong answer. So she said, "Not exactly, Mr. Murdoch. I'd like you to make the drop and collect the material. I shall pay you very well for that. Clearly, I don't want you to get murdered." Something like a smile played across her face. "That wouldn't help anybody, would it?"

I nodded. "Especially me. You want to give me some

background?"

She hesitated and pointed at my glass. "Can I have one of those?" While Noddy fell over himself in four different directions assembling a second Martini, she gestured at my cigarettes. I nodded and pushed them along the bar with the lighter. It's hard for a woman to make a Zippo look graceful. In her hands it was triple-X-rated exquisite. She let the smoke drift out through red lips and read my face for a while. I put a blank page there. After a moment she said, "I used to work as a high-class prostitute. I had highly placed clients. I was expensive…"

I said, "Class usually is."

She blinked sea-green at me and carried on. "I didn't waste the money. I put myself through university. I read biology and did a master's in business. Just over a year ago I bought myself into a biotechnology research and development company as a partner." She sucked on the Camel, frowning at the ashtray. "There are films and photographs. They're held by a man. We used to call him the Don. He used to be my…" Her look turned resentful, like it was the ashtray's fault she'd once had a pimp. She tapped a little ash into its mouth and said, "Manager. I bought myself out a couple of months ago, but now he wants money for the films and the photographs. If I don't pay, he'll send copies to the board."

I took a long drag on my cigarette and squinted at her through the smoke. "I've known a few pimps in my time, Miss Howard, and a few blackmailers too. Most of them weren't smart enough to know a biology degree from an amoeba's ass, but most of them weren't dumb enough to kill a goose that laid golden eggs, either."

She tilted her chin and smiled. Her voice was so husky it could have pulled a sled across Alaska. It was getting to me. She said, "You don't believe me."

"Me and Descartes, sugar. I believe I exist because I can hear myself think. Outside of that, I don't believe shit. I'm not a hit man, Miss Howard. I'm not going to kill your blackmailer for you."

Outside, the rain had turned torrential. A rumble of thunder shook the ceiling and the lights in the diner winked off, so we were sitting in shadow. She shook her head. "That isn't what I'm looking for."

"If everything you say is true, he can keep the squeeze on you for years. Why should he want you dead?"

She stubbed out her cigarette, smoke trailing from her nose. She sipped and licked her lips with a very pink tongue.

"It's a little more complex than that."

"So tell me the complex bit. I can recognize an amoeba's ass."

"How colorful..." She watched me a while in the half light. Then the lights came on and somewhere a fridge began to hum. "During the time the Don managed me, I accumulated a lot of information about him, his operations and his clients. I told you some of them were important men — and women. People in the public eye. If I should ever decide to write my memoirs, Mr. Murdoch, it would cause a lot of people a great deal of embarrassment. More than that, it could bring down important political careers and, with them, the Don's power. I don't think I need to paint you a picture. It's in the Don's best interest — and his clients' — to make me very dead."

I nodded. "Have you anything more concrete than a general theory of his motives?"

"Yes, the way he's set up the drop. He's done it before to other people. I'll be extremely vulnerable." Her cheeks flushed incongruously and she smiled. "I'm between a rock and a hard place, Mr. Murdoch. I daren't risk not going — not making the drop. But I know if I do, he'll kill me. He has to."

What she said made sense. A man like she described could not afford a loose cannon, especially one as smart as Catherine Howard. But even so, I knew she was lying. For one thing, if she were for real, she'd work for Russian Pete, not some anonymous Don. And Russian Pete would have introduced her to me by now. My gut told me that every word out of her mouth was a lie that concealed layers of deeper lies. But I also knew, as I sat looking into her level, green eyes, that I didn't give a damn. I crushed out my cigarette and said, "So what do you want me to do?" And just so she didn't think I was as soft as Noddy, "And how much does this caper pay?"

She took a swig of her Martini and said, "I just want you to go in my place."

"What makes you think he won't kill me?"

"Does that worry you?"

"Yeah. I don't like getting killed. It gives me a headache."

She didn't smile. She shrugged. "Why should he? He has no interest in your death. In any case, he is expecting a weak woman, not" — she paused and gestured at me with a look that was both insulting and flattering — "someone like you. And even if he should try, you are forewarned and I'm sure you can take care of yourself. I'd advise you to be armed." Now she smiled. "Have you got a weapon, Mr. Murdoch?"

The innuendo was obvious and vulgar and made me unreasonably mad. I grunted. "Yeah, I have a weapon. What if he won't give me the material?"

"Again, you're a big boy. I'm sure you can persuade him. In any case, I think he will. The money he's asking for is considerable."

"Okay. What makes you think I won't take the money for myself and leave you in the lurch?"

She turned to Noddy. She went a little pale and her eyes were beseeching. She should have been in Hollywood. She deserved an Oscar. He looked deep into her oceanic green eyes, read a thousand impossible promises there, swallowed hard and turned to me, stabbing a big, ugly finger in my face. "'Cos if you do, Liam, I'll kick you dahn the fahkin stairs, tear yer fahkin 'ed off and stuff it up yer fahkin backside, so you'll be watchin telly fru yer fahkin arse for the rest of yer miserable fahkin life! Don't mistreat the lady, awright?"

Noddy was from the East End of London, where they

speak a language all their own. She smiled at me, telling me silently that she could make him do it. I gave Noddy a look that told him what I thought of him and his 'fahkin telly' then sighed. "Okay, how much does it pay?"

Something strange happened to her face then. I want to say that it went hard, but that doesn't even begin to describe it. I had the feeling I was looking, not at a woman, but at an animal. If you've seen the dispassionate expression on a cat's face when it goes for the kill or a lizard swallowing a live insect, you'll know what I mean. She had the alien eyes of a goat in that moment and the stillness of a snake. She spoke with no feeling at all.

"If you fail — or are only partially successful — the job pays nothing. Partial success is of no use to me. You bring me all the material — original and any copies — and it pays twenty thousand pounds, sterling."

I raised an eyebrow at her. "Twenty grand?" That was thirty-five thousand bucks.

"Naturally, I will cover all your expenses."

Outside, the rain had slowed to a wet tapping. "Expenses?" I frowned. "What expenses?"

She reached into her snakeskin handbag and pulled out a surprisingly large manila envelope. From that she extracted a Virgin Atlantic ticket and a smaller, white envelope that smelled like cash and was reassuringly fat. She handed me the ticket.

"That is a flight to New York. It departs tonight. I'd like you to be on it. You will be there for twelve hours and return with the material. I suggest you do your sleeping on the plane. All the instructions are here." She pulled an A4 sheet of paper from the manila envelope and handed me that too, along with a locker key. I put the key in my pocket and slipped the A4 in with the ticket to look at later. She said, "Go to Left Luggage at Heathrow Airport. The key fits a locker. Collect the attaché case from there. It contains fifty thousand dollars. That's the payoff." She held up the white packet. "This is two-and-a-half thousand dollars in small and medium bills. It should more than cover your needs. If there is any over, consider it a tip."

She knew — and so did I — that I was going to New York. I took the reassuringly fat envelope and peered in. By the rack of the eye it was two-and-a-half grand. I slipped it into my pocket.

"How can I contact you when I'm done?"

"You can't. Noddy will arrange it."

I raised an eyebrow at him. That was my line and he knew it, but he looked away, keeping busy washing glasses that were already clean. "All right, Catherine," I said, "you have a deal."

I left Noddy's Diner with a sour feeling in my belly that my brain couldn't identify. I was mad at Noddy for being stupid, but I couldn't place my finger on exactly what he'd done that was stupid. I drove back slow through Notting Hill to Church Street, enjoying the drizzle and the squeak of the wipers on the windshield, watching hunched people under windswept umbrellas dodge each other blindly through wet crowds. I let my thoughts range free among them. They covered just about everything you could imagine except why I had a sour feeling in my belly and exactly how Noddy had been stupid. In the end I decided Catherine Howard was as fascinating as hell and twice as hot, but she was also twice as much trouble, and it made me mad that Noddy couldn't see that. I could, but he couldn't.

That was what I told myself.

I parked and went up to my apartment. I had a duplex on the fifth and sixth floors. Most people didn't know about the fifth, which I used as a den for work and storage. I used the sixth to live in, and that was where people usually found me — if I wanted to be found. I went up there now to prepare an overnight bag. There was a light winking on my phone, telling me there was a message. I listened to it while I cracked a beer and scrambled some eggs. The message was from Russell.

Me and Russell went back a long way. I left LA when I was

still in my teens because a film producer, his Italian wife and her Italian family were looking for me, and I wasn't too keen they should find me. In fact, I decided I should move to the farthest place I could find on the planet where they spoke a language similar to my own. I couldn't handle the eternal barbecues in Australia, so I wound up in London and badly in need of bread, as my last job had paid less than I'd hoped. So I'd done some work for some 'gentlemen south of the river' — a cute English term for gangsters. What I didn't realize at the time was that the job included taking the fall for one of those gentlemen. I did six months inside and six months' community service.

That was how I met Russell. He was a mathematician by trade, but he was one of the good guys and did voluntary work on the Community Service Program. I could never understand it, but I guess he thought he saw potential in me, because he took me on as a special project and promised me he would get me on to the straight and narrow path.

I haven't got to the straight and narrow path yet. There always seems to be too much interesting stuff happening on the wide and wending one. But we'd become friends, and I figured I owed him, if only for everything he'd taught me about correctly calculating the odds. His message said, "Liam, it's Russell. I need your help. Well, not me really... It's the nephew of a friend of mine. His uncle's rather unexpectedly dead and...well, it's all a little complicated. I told him you might be able to help him out. Perhaps you could give me a call."

Everybody wanted Liam today. That's the trouble with being useful. I made a mental note to call him when I got back. I ate my eggs, drank my beer, then packed a bag and headed out for Heathrow.

More books from
Totally Bound Publishing

Allegra always knew that nothing good could come of waking up in police custody.

Curtis has found a soulmate in Julia, but happily-ever-after endings don't happen in Tombs without a fight — and this time it's to the death.

Book one in the Crossing Forces series

A bad boy FBI agent and a feisty widowed police detective collide pursuing a human trafficker in small-town Texas on their way to true love.

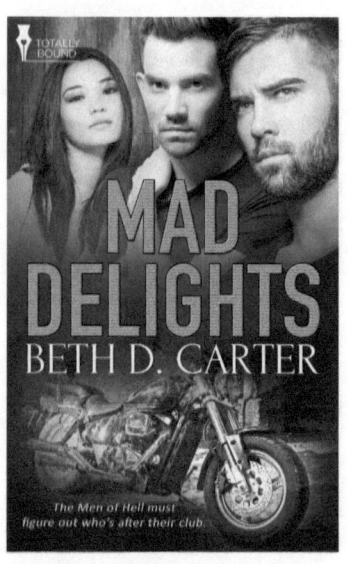

*When violence sweeps through their town, the Men of Hell
must figure out who's after their club.*

About the Author

Conor Corderoy

Conor Corderoy was born in England in 1957. He spent his childhood on Formentera, the smallest of the Balearic Islands among intellectuals, artists and writers. He had no formal schooling, though he had a governess for four years who became an alcoholic and disappeared when he was twelve. He spent his teens in Cordoba, southern Spain, where he got his first job aged sixteen, breaking in wild horses. He has since done more jobs than he can remember, including free-lance writing, law, hypnotherapy and psychotherapy. He now divides his time between England and Spain. He is an Incorporated Linguists, a barrister, a psychologist and a Master Practitioner of NLP.

Conor Corderoy loves to hear from readers. You can find contact information, website details and an author profile page at https://www.totallybound.com/

Home of Erotic Romance